No
Love Lost

By Helen Van Slyke

No Love Lost

HELEN VAN SLYKE

Lippincott & Crowell, Publishers
New York

All characters in this book are fictitious, and any resemblance to actual persons, living or dead, is purely coincidental.

Published by arrangement with Bantam Books, Inc.

FIRST EDITION
Designed by C. Linda Dingler

U.S. Library of Congress Cataloging in Publication Data
Van Slyke, Helen, birth date
    No love lost.
    I. Title.
PZ4.V2777No   1980   [PS3572.A54]   813'.5'4   79-26056
ISBN-0-690-01897-5

80 81 82 83 84 10 9 8 7 6 5 4 3 2 1

For Larry Ashmead,
with joy that we've come full circle.

And for Jay Acton,
who made it happen.

EDITOR'S NOTE

On June 28, 1979, Helen Van Slyke underwent an operation to remove a growth on her liver. She died without regaining consciousness on July 3, a few days before her sixtieth birthday. Her death was the final extraordinary event of an extraordinary life. What was not extraordinary was the fact that just before she entered the hospital she delivered the revised manuscript of this book. Helen was always the complete professional, and she didn't want any temporary "diminished performance" holding up the publication of her ninth novel. If she had any idea she was going to die, she didn't say so.

No Love Lost is as she wrote it: the last testimony to the unique talent that had endeared her to millions of readers. I'm pleased her writing has outlived her. Would that we had her *and* her books and more of both to come.

Lawrence P. Ashmead
August, 1979

The Growing-up Years

PART ONE

1

"*T*hat woman called today."

Ten-year-old Lindsay stopped short outside the living room door, sensing from the tone of her mother's voice that this was not the time to enter. There was a small silence, broken only by the rattle of ice cubes in the cocktail shaker. Papa always served drinks before dinner. Even though this was 1930 and there was something called Prohibition, Howard Thresher had no intention of giving up his martinis or his dinner wine or any other amenities of a civilized life. He'd been born a gentleman, he was fond of announcing, and by God he intended to live like one, Herbert Hoover or any other damned fool President to the contrary.

Guilty about eavesdropping, but mystified and intrigued, Lindsay stayed quiet, listening for his reply.

"What woman is that, dear?"

Pauline Thresher sounded contemptuous. "For God's sake, don't pretend, Howard. Not at this stage. You've made no secret of this one as usual. Isn't it a little ridiculous to act as though you don't know whom I mean?" Her voice rose just a shade. "Your current mistress telephoned, of course. Just as they all do eventually."

"I see. Sorry, my dear. I'll make sure it doesn't happen again. She knows better than to call here."

Pauline laughed. It was not a pretty laugh, and Lindsay shivered in the darkness of the hallway.

"You are incredible!" The laughter turned to accusation. "It's the same with every one of these poor, stupid women. They actually believe you want to divorce me. And that I won't permit it. They really think

1

I'm the villain, ruining your life by refusing to set you free. Dear Lord, I almost feel sorry for them, taken in by your lies! How convincing you must be, playing the unhappy, misunderstood husband and knowing all the while you have no intention of changing the way you live."

Howard seemed perfectly calm. "Why should I change it, Pauline? My life is exactly the way I like it. I have a delightful wife and well-brought-up children. A gracious home. These others are a totally separate part of my life. They have nothing to do with you and Lindsay and James. Nothing to do with the love I feel for all of you. I do love you dearly, you know. You and the children. I wouldn't exchange my family for anything in the world. I can't help it if some silly woman misinterprets my intentions. I'm only sorry she troubled you."

Even from a distance, Lindsay heard her mother sigh. "Why do you do it, Howard? Why must there always be another woman?" She didn't wait for an answer. "And why have I always accepted it? Twenty years of it. Right from the start. I'd be so ashamed if the world knew. More ashamed of myself than of you." Pauline sounded more resigned than angry. "Not that half the world doesn't know, in any case. You make no secret of your affairs. I don't understand you. And God knows I don't understand why I stay with you."

Lindsay could imagine her tall, handsome father smiling in that special way he had, the appealing way that made everyone love him so much. The smile was in his voice, coaxing Mama out of her bad mood.

"Darling, you *do* understand. This woman means nothing to me. None of them ever has. It's simply a gentleman's pastime, like bridge or polo. My father did the same thing. So did *his* father. So does every sophisticated man. It makes us better husbands, this kind of harmless diversion. More appreciative of women of our own class. European wives understand that perfectly. I don't know why Americans find it so hard to accept."

"Not hard, Howard, nearly impossible."

He sounded genuinely amazed. "But why, Pauline? It's so unimportant. I'm your husband. I adore you. I give you everything. You're much too worldly to be troubled by a few amusing hours I spend elsewhere. If I drank heavily or gambled away our money or abused you in any way, you'd have reason to be unhappy, but—"

"You do abuse me. You diminish me. You destroy my ego."

He began to sound angry. "What Freudian nonsense is that? You have a beautiful Fifth Avenue apartment, expensive clothes and jewels, trips to Europe and Palm Beach. You have security and social position and a husband who's proud of you. What more could any woman want?"

"Fidelity, perhaps."

"Fidelity? I think you choose the wrong word. You *have* fidelity. I am faithful to you and our life in all the ways that count. No, my dear, you mean middle-class monogamy. That's what you think you want. One woman for one man for all time. In all ways. You'd regret that, you know, if you had it. My visits to some featherbrained creature are no more significant to me than an evening at the theater, but they keep me from becoming dull and stodgy. Is that what you'd like me to be, my love? A pure but boring man? I really doubt it."

Lindsay could hear choked-back tears in her mother's voice. "Am I dull and stodgy because I'm faithful to you, Howard? Is it different for women? How would you feel if you knew I were with another man, even if he meant nothing to me? Wouldn't you feel that you weren't enough? That somehow you were inadequate?"

The ice cubes rattled again, and then Howard said gently, "Dearest, you're being ridiculous. You're a lady. There's no comparison in the physical urges of the sexes. We've been over this a hundred times. In all the years I've been totally honest with you. I haven't given you any the less of me. Why start this again just because of that ill-advised call? I told you I'm sorry about that, but it isn't as though you didn't know she existed. You've known about every one. Because they're no threat to you, darling, and I wouldn't insult you by sneaking around corners. I respect you. You're my wife. The mother of my children."

There was a long silence before Pauline said, "It's useless to talk about this any more. Just remember one thing, Howard, I know these women are in your life. I'm even spineless enough to accept that because I love you. But never, never allow one of them to approach me again, in person or by phone! I swear to you, if they do I won't be responsible for my actions!"

Lindsay waited a few more minutes, but no further words were spoken. When she entered the living room, her parents were sitting in their usual chairs, sipping their cocktails. If she hadn't overheard their quarrel she'd have thought it an evening like any other. But it wasn't. Papa and Mama were angry with each other over something she wasn't supposed to know about. She couldn't ask them about it, of course, but she'd be sure to remember every word and report to James when he

3

came home from Harvard next week for his Christmas holidays. Her big brother would explain it to her. He was eighteen. Grown up but reachable in the way most adults were not. He was her dearest friend. Closer even than Adele Frampton, who'd been Lindsay's best "outside friend" since they were babies. James was even more special than Papa's mother, who lived with them in the big apartment. "Gandy," the name Lindsay had given her when she wasn't able to pronounce "grandmother," was an unfailing source of wisdom and comfort. But the little girl sensed that this puzzling exchange was something she could talk about only to James. It was the first time in her life she'd ever heard Mama so upset and Papa so angry, and the awareness that they could argue made her wonderful, sheltered world seem suddenly less secure. She loved them so much. Along with James and Gandy, they were the most important things in her world.

As though even her surroundings had changed in the past few minutes, Lindsay looked around the big living room, her big brown eyes taking in all the familiar furnishings. It was a wonderful room with twelve-foot-high ceilings and at one end windows that gave onto a breathtaking view of Central Park. This evening the view was obscured by heavy velvet curtains in the mauve shade that was Mama's favorite, a color repeated on the big sofa and the high-backed wing chairs. A fire burned brightly on the hearth, above which hung an oil painting of Papa's father, Mortimer Thresher, who died in the great influenza epidemic of 1918, two years before Lindsay was born. That was when Gandy came to live with her only son and his wife and their six-year-old boy, James. She'd been there all Lindsay's life, a warm, devoted woman with a sense of humor her son did not share and a tolerance for human weakness her daughter-in-law tried hard to emulate. Though a plain woman, she loved beautiful things and was grateful to be rich enough to afford them. Over the years of her marriage to Mortimer, Sara Thresher had acquired the treasures she brought with her to her son's home. Hers were the delicate Fabergé boxes carefully locked in lighted cabinets that flanked the fireplace. Hers, too, the exquisite and valuable Renoir and Manet paintings on the walls of the living room, the big Georgian silver tea service in the dining room, the elegant Oriental rugs scattered through the apartment, the biggest of which nearly covered the floor of the room Lindsay was now so carefully examining.

4

"Some day," Gandy had once said, "all these things will be yours, Lindsay darling. Yours and James's. Cherish them, sweetheart, not for the money they represent—their monetary value is of no importance—but for their unique qualities. These are works of art. They represent love, the love of the artist who spent years creating them, the love of your old Gandy, who's found happiness every day of her life just looking at such an outpouring of genius. When I die, I'll be happy knowing that those who mean most to me have years to feast their eyes on all this beauty."

Lindsay had not understood all this, but the mention of her grandmother's death had a terrible, ominous sound. "You're not going to die, Gandy. Not ever!"

Sara laughed and hugged her reassuringly. "Well, not for a long, long time, I promise you. I'm not sixty yet. I know that sounds a hundred to you, but, the good Lord willing, I still have a lot of years." She turned serious. "I want to see you grow up, you know. You're going to be a beautiful woman. And a smart one. Smarter than I. Maybe even smarter than your mother. At least I hope so." Sara seemed lost in thought for a moment. Then she said, "Don't ever be foolish about men, little Lindsay. They're like children. They need a loving hand but a firm one."

The child stared at her, uncomprehending.

Sara smiled. "Such nonsense I'm talking! See what you do to me with all that silly worrying about my leaving you? I never will, you know. I'm like a penny. Not a bad one, a bright one. Remember, darling, I'll always turn up. Whenever you find a shiny penny anywhere in all the years to come, you pick it up and say, 'There's Gandy!' Will you remember that?"

Lindsay nodded solemnly. "Yes, ma'am."

"Good." Sara fished in the pocket of her dress. "Why, my goodness! Here's a shiny penny now! Here, take it. It's the first of many. Keep it for luck, dear heart. In time you'll have a thousand 'Gandys,' all telling you how much you're loved."

Sitting quietly now, listening to her parents chat easily as though no hateful words had been spoken moments before, Lindsay remembered her grandmother's strange words. I am loved, she thought. Gandy's still here, loving me just as Mama and Papa do and as James does. I mustn't worry about anything. It's all the same as it's always been. But she sat frowning, deep in thought, unaware until Gandy spoke that the older woman had joined them.

"Well, the young lady of the house must have something very serious on her mind tonight."

The three grown-ups were looking at her curiously.

"What's the matter, kitten? Something go wrong at school today?"

"No, Papa, everything's fine."

"You certainly don't look it. You look as though you'd lost your best friend."

Pauline picked up the thread of her husband's thought. "You and Adele haven't quarreled, have you?"

"No, Mama. *We* haven't quarreled."

Pauline and Howard exchanged glances and a shared question. Years of living together caused their reactions to be alike. The accent on "we" was intentional. Could Lindsay have heard the ugly argument just minutes ago?

"Well," Howard said, "*something* certainly is bothering you. Don't you think you'd better tell us what it is?"

Trapped, Lindsay said the first thing that came to mind. "Could I please have a sweetheart haircut?"

Pauline stared at her. "A *what?* What on earth is a sweetheart haircut?"

"A lot of the girls at school are getting them. It's short and straight, with bangs. Only—well, the bangs are cut in a curve, like a heart, with the point in the middle of your forehead."

"Good God!" Howard exploded. "What a hideous idea!"

Pauline was more gentle. "Lindsay, dear, I can't believe you want to cut your beautiful hair. Why, it's nearly to your waist and as pretty as spun gold!"

Lindsay didn't really want the silly haircut. She didn't know why she'd even mentioned it, just because Polly Roberts and some of those dumb girls at school had gone and done it. But she was unreasonably angry with her parents, and their horrified reaction made her stubborn. "You never let me do anything the others do! I can't go anywhere by myself. I can't pick out my own clothes. You treat me like a baby!"

"Lindsay!" Papa spoke in his no-nonsense voice. "We'll hear no more of this absurd idea. Foolish, tasteless fad! 'Sweetheart haircut,' indeed! As for your other complaints, since you persist in acting like a baby, I don't think you should be too surprised that you're treated like one. When you're old enough to make sensible decisions, your mother and I will be only too happy to permit you to do so. Until then, I suggest you remember your manners. We don't tolerate surly children in this house."

Lindsay looked at the carpet, not answering.

"Don't be too hard on her, Howard," Gandy said. "Children have the herd instinct. It's not so terrible that Lindsay wants to do what the other girls are doing. Not that I'd like to see her cut her hair. She'd soon tire of it," Gandy added, more for Lindsay's benefit than for her son's. "And I don't think she realizes how long it takes for hair to grow back."

"Mother, I'd prefer you didn't interfere." Howard spoke firmly. "We don't have to give Lindsay an explanation for our refusal. The answer is, very simply, no."

The child looked so pathetic that Pauline's heart went out to her. Howard was right, of course, but he was so tactless. He really cared nothing about anyone else's feelings. His word was law and he brooked no argument. No one knew that better than she. Now Lindsay was crushed and Gandy made to feel meddlesome. And there was nothing she could do about either. Such a stupid little thing, she thought, to make everyone so miserable. Howard was strong. Howard was generous. But Howard was also opinionated, dictatorial, and often cruel.

She looked again at Lindsay's woebegone expression. It had nothing to do with that foolish haircut, Pauline was suddenly convinced. It was a silly white lie made up on the spur of the moment to hide what was really bothering the little girl. Our first instinct was right, Pauline thought: She did overhear Howard and me quarreling over his current affair. How much of it did she understand? Enough, obviously, to trouble her deeply. Pauline recognized that unhappy look. She'd seen one very like it three years before on the face of her son.

With something momentarily approaching hatred she looked at her husband, who, believing he'd solved a minor matter of discipline, was relaxing over his second drink. Damn him! Damn him for his selfishness, his indecent lack of guilt! Not enough that he makes his wife miserable and humiliates his mother. Now he's also succeeded in bringing unhappiness to both his children. James has known about him for three years. I'd hoped Lindsay would be able to retain her illusions longer. I should have known better. Howard flaunts his indiscretions outside his home as well as in it. It's almost as though he's proud of being unfaithful. As though it makes him more of a man.

She wondered whether she should discuss it with Lindsay, as she finally had with James. Impossible. How did one explain this to a ten-year-old? Perhaps, Pauline thought, once again grasping at a dim hope, I'm only imagining she knows something. I can't be sure she was outside the door while we were fighting. Or that if she was she had any idea of what it meant. Maybe I'm so absorbed with my problem I attribute everyone else's difficulties to it.

Let it go for now, she told herself. There'll be plenty of time for explanations later. If, indeed, one could ever explain such a complex relationship as hers and Howard's.

2

$\mathcal{L}$indsay thought the time would never come when James would be home from school. Her normal eagerness to see her adored brother was heightened by the desire to ask him about the ominous conversation. The days seem to creep by so slowly. For the first time in her life, even the tantalizing preparations for Christmas did not totally occupy her attention. School closed for the holidays, and she and Gandy went shopping at Saks for the gifts they'd give the family and the special present she liked to choose for Adele. The big tree was delivered and set up in a corner of the living room, waiting to be trimmed on Christmas Eve. For the past three years Lindsay had been allowed to participate. Before that, she'd been sent to bed early to "wait for Santa Claus," but now that she no longer believed in him, she was part of the fun. She loved it: seeing the old-fashioned ornaments taken from their tissue wrappings, watching the glorious symbol come alive with lights and tinsel and silver-paper icicles, like a great sparkling giant standing guard over the dozens of packages at his feet.

But this year, anticipation was clouded by uneasiness. She was so halfhearted about everything that Gandy became concerned. Watching Lindsay toy with her chocolate sundae at Schrafft's, her grandmother wondered what was wrong. The child had been so quiet these past two weeks, ever since the night Howard had refused to let her have that ridiculous haircut. She seemed withdrawn, thoughtful, almost painfully puzzled. Very unlike her normally vivacious, almost boisterous self. Sara had thought of speaking to Pauline about it, but hesitated. She took care not to interfere in the way her son and daughter-in-law brought up their children, and she still remembered Howard's sharp rebuke when she'd put her two cents' worth into the discussion about the haircut. Sometimes she felt like a guest in the house, even after twelve years.

It would have been better if I'd taken my own apartment when Mortimer died, she thought for the hundredth time. I should have done that while I was still brave enough to live alone. Brave enough? What kind of bravery did it take? The kind I didn't have, Sara thought. I'd never lived alone. I can't imagine it, even now.

It was hard to have no real role in running a house or speaking one's mind about the little day-to-day problems that arose. But she was intensely aware of how generations could clash. She'd never be the nagging mother or the nosy mother-in-law or even the aggressively all-knowing grandmother. Still, when something was so obviously wrong, as it was with Lindsay, she wondered how Pauline and Howard could ignore it.

"Anything wrong with the sundae?"

"No, Gandy. It's good. I'm just not very hungry."

"Now *that's* a surprise! First time I ever saw you play with your ice cream. Are you sure you feel all right?"

"Yes, ma'am."

They lapsed into silence again.

"If something's bothering you, Lindsay dear, you can tell me. I mean, sometimes it's good to talk about a problem."

The little face remained closed. "Nothing's bothering me, Gandy. I just wish James would come home."

So. Whatever was on her mind was reserved for a discussion with her brother. Fair enough, Sara thought. She feels closer to him than she does to any of us. Whatever the difficulty is, James will straighten her out. He's such a good boy. So unlike his father. She blushed, guiltily, realizing what she'd just thought. But, sadly, it was true. Howard was like *his* father. Mortimer had been the same kind of strong, determined, and, yes, unfaithful man. His son came naturally by those traits. But James, she somehow knew, would be different. He was more sensitive, more considerate. Already a very gentle man.

She felt better. At least Lindsay would confide her troubles to one she trusted. And James, in turn, would be certain to give her the help and reassurance she seemed to need.

Regrettably for Lindsay, when James finally returned, looking even more beautiful and grown-up than he had at Thanksgiving, he did nothing to truly dispel the mystery. Instead, when she repeated all she'd heard, being careful to report it exactly as it was said, her brother turned on her angrily.

"You're a rotten little snoop! What's the matter with you, hanging around outside doors listening to other people's private conversations?"

She was startled and hurt. "I didn't mean to. I was just going in—"

"Then why the hell didn't you *go* in, instead of hiding in the hall?"

Why was he so furious? Lindsay watched him unpack, opening bureau drawers and slamming them. Sitting on his bed, she said nothing, but her eyes filled with tears. If James wouldn't talk to her, who would?

As he went back and forth, hanging up his clothes, James watched her out of the corner of his eye. Damn! Why did she have to be exposed to this so soon? He'd been fifteen before he discovered what was going on. He remembered how he'd felt: disbelieving at first and then outraged by his father's behavior. He'd never recovered from that anger. Probably never would. But at least I was old enough to understand what the kids at school told me, he thought. Gossip they'd picked up from their parents. Poor little Lindsay. She's too young to grasp this. I'm sure she doesn't even know about sex between married people, much less this kind of thing. All she knows is that something's not right, something that threatens her.

He went over, finally, and sat beside her, taking one of her small, sturdy hands in both of his.

"Listen, kiddo, it's nothing to worry about. You see, married people sometimes argue about things that aren't nearly as serious as they sound. Forget it. Mama and Papa probably disagree like that all the time. It's just that you haven't happened to hear them before. I'm sure they've had lots of fights in twenty years." He shook his finger at her playfully. "And you're a naughty girl to have listened in on this one, you know. That's called eavesdropping, and nice people don't do it. It's like picking up the extension phone when someone else is talking. Or opening another person's mail."

The explanation about married people fighting didn't satisfy her. Nor was she diverted by James's tactic of trying to turn the subject from their argument to her own breach of etiquette. She was sure it was all a plot to keep something from her, something the family didn't want her

11

to find out. She wondered whether her parents were going to get a divorce. The girls at school talked about divorces. Some of their parents had gotten them, and now they had two mothers and two fathers. She'd hate that.

"Are Mama and Papa going to get a divorce, James?"

"Of course not, silly! Where did you ever get such a dumb idea?"

"Well, why was Mama so upset because some woman called? She sounded like she hated Papa. And he wasn't nice to her, either."

James sighed. This wasn't going to be easy. "Honey, Mama was just annoyed that some friend of Papa's made a pest of herself, that's all. Or maybe it wasn't even a friend. Could have been some woman in his office. You know how Mama hates it when he gets business calls at home." He gave Lindsay a big hug. "Honest to Pete! Such a worrywart! The folks seemed like themselves at dinner, didn't they? And you haven't heard any cross words since, have you?"

The child shook her head.

"Well, then. See? It was just a spat and it's over. You and Adele get mad at each other once in a while. Even you and I have been known to argue. Everybody gets annoyed now and then, no matter how fond they are of each other. Husbands and wives. Best friends." He tickled her ribs. "Even brothers and sisters. But they always make up."

Lindsay giggled and then sobered when he stopped. The big eyes looked appealingly into his. "You're sure, James? Mama and Papa still love each other?"

He could answer that honestly. "You bet they do. And they love us. You can count on that. Nothing's going to disrupt your home, kitten. Not ever. I give you my word on it." He picked her up and set her on her feet, giving her an affectionate little slap on the rear end. "Now scoot! I've got to wash off this New Haven Railroad dirt. Oh, and Lindsay, I'm sorry I seemed cross with you a while ago, but you really mustn't listen behind doors. That made me angry. Promise you won't do it again."

"I won't. Hurry up and come downstairs."

"Right. Be with you shortly."

When she left he stripped off his clothes and stepped into the shower. Soaping himself vigorously under the hot water, he felt the old anger return. He remembered the day he learned about his father. At first he hadn't known what the guys at school were talking about. He'd thought it was just more of their dirty talk, all those cracks about his father being hot stuff in the hay. But when he realized they were repeating what they'd heard at home, he felt sick.

"My Dad says your old man's got it made. Sleeping with some tootsie over on the West Side."

"Yeah, Jim. Hear he goes there every afternoon."

"Jeez! My old lady would go through the roof! How come yours doesn't?"

James looked at them coldly. "I don't know what the hell you're talking about."

"Aw, come on. Sure you do. Everybody does. Your father has a mistress. Don't act like you don't know, for Gawd's sake! I heard my mother say he's a two-timer and always has been."

He'd swung on his tormentors, and the next thing he knew, Mr. Danillio, the Phys Ed teacher, was breaking up a brawl in the locker room. That afternoon James went home with a black eye and a written reprimand which required an answer from one of his parents. With instinctive gallantry, he kept the truth from his mother. He told her he got the black eye in a basketball game. Then he waited until his father was alone in the library after dinner, working at his desk. Without even knocking, as was the custom, he'd barged in and confronted Howard, who looked up in mild astonishment from his work.

"Something you want, James?"

In silent answer the boy thrust the note under his father's nose.

"Fighting, eh? I thought you got that shiner playing ball."

"That's what I told Mama."

His father smiled indulgently. "I see. Of course. She'd be upset if she thought you were brawling. Well, a man must learn to defend himself. I assume you *were* defending yourself?"

James felt his confidence begin to waver. Papa was always so in charge. It was hard to imagine him sneaking into some sleazy apartment to go to bed with a woman. Maybe they were wrong. Maybe those kids . . .

"Well, James? I asked you a question."

"I was defending *you*." It came out bluntly, accusingly. "The guys were saying—that is, they'd heard from their parents . . ." James stopped.

"Yes? Go on. Heard what?"

All right, damn you. "That you have a woman you see every afternoon. That you . . . go to bed with her."

13

There. It was out. He waited for his father's denial. Hoped for it. He was eager for the indignant response. But Howard simply leaned back in his big leather chair, perfectly relaxed, his hands clasped in front of him, his handsome face as calm and controlled as ever.

"They're quite right, son. I do."

James's jaw sagged.

"Don't look so shocked, for heaven's sake! At your age you must know the facts of life. I'm only sorry I didn't have a chance to tell you before you heard it from strangers. I should have realized you were old enough to understand. You're really a man already, aren't you? One tends to forget that children grow up overnight."

James groped for words. "It's true? You . . . you cheat on Mama? You're in love with somebody else?"

"No. That is, I love only your mother and always will. Cheat? I find that an ugly expression, vulgar in the extreme. There is no 'cheating,' as you call it. Your mother knows what I do. She's always been aware of my little arrangements and accepts them for what they are. I never allow one to go on long enough to become a serious problem to her or to me."

"But you're unfaithful! You break your marriage vows. You admit it!"

"Oh, come, James, let's not be melodramatic about this! It's not so terrible, you know. I haven't embezzled funds or murdered anyone. I simply do what most gentlemen of our class do: engage in a little dalliance. You'll undoubtedly do the same thing one day when you're married. No one in our circle thinks anything of it. If anything, it adds to a man's urbane image. Your mother accepts that. She's an intelligent woman who knows that monogamy is not a natural state for the male. I'm only sorry," Howard said again, "that this news came to you in such a sordid way. But I hope you understand it now and realize that it has nothing whatsoever to do with my family life. There's no threat to your mother or your sister or you. Does that clear it up, James?"

"Clear it up?" James was aghast. "No, it doesn't clear it up, Papa. It's dirty and disgusting and impossible to understand. I can't believe you'd do this to Mama. Or that she doesn't mind."

Howard's tone remained cool and sensible. "I wonder whether you're as upset about your mother as you are about your friends. Believe me, James, I'd make a bet that your schoolmates from the better homes have the same situation, though they may not know it. And those

14

whose fathers have no orderly, dignified liaisons are even worse. Those are the men who pay prostitutes or pick up diseased women when they're out of town. Believe me, my way—our way—is civilized and sensible. You'll realize that one day. Meanwhile, I hardly think it's worth fighting about. If the subject comes up again, just ignore it. Obviously those moronic adolescents wouldn't understand even if you tried to explain it to them. Which I suggest you do not." Howard picked up his fountain pen. "I'll dash off a note to your headmaster saying you've been punished, and there'll be no recurrence of this unfortunate event."

Wordlessly, James left the study, note in hand. I hate him, the boy thought. I'll never be like him. My wife won't endure that kind of humiliation, nor my children either. He thought again of his mother. How did she really feel about the things her husband did? She must despise him too. But she continued to live with him. Even to sleep with him, James supposed. Why doesn't she leave this terrible man? I'll never be able to ask her, of course. I wouldn't be able to discuss anything so embarrassing with her.

But he didn't have to ask. A few days later Pauline came to his room and said, "James, dear, I think we'd better have a little talk."

He knew, before she continued, what the subject was, but he simply waited.

"Your father told me about his conversation with you." She stopped, uncertain how to go on. Then, involuntarily, she raised her chin and straightened her back. "I'm sure it's difficult for you to understand. You're idealistic, as I once was. We've raised you, your father and I, in what we hoped was a normal, happy, well-adjusted environment."

Despite himself, James snorted.

"I know," Pauline said. "You think it's all a farce. Nothing but the mere facade of a home and family. But that isn't true, James. Your father is a good man, loving toward you and Lindsay and devoted to me. He's brilliant, you know, highly thought of in the banking world. He works very hard to see that we have a good life now and no worries about the future, any of us, even if, God forbid, something happened to him. Not every man is so concerned for his wife and children. He's made sure you and Lindsay will have fine educations and money of your own so you can choose what you wish to do with your lives. He's made life safe for me, and I'm grateful. I think you should be too."

James seemed unmoved. "Is that all that matters, Mama? Being

15

safe and rich? Doesn't it hurt you that he sees other women? Wouldn't you rather have a faithful husband than a big bank account?"

Pauline winced. How surely he'd struck at the core of her unhappiness, this man-child. Of course she'd have traded anything for Howard's undivided loyalty. Money was lovely. It made life easier for her and protected her children. But it was no substitute for the kind of single-minded devotion of which Howard was incapable, the kind of serene acceptance of one partner she thought she saw in other marriages. And yet she did not stay with Howard for the material comforts. She stayed because despite everything she was as much in love with him as the day they met. Emotional warts and all, he was her husband and lover. And she accepted his flaws with resignation, rebelling sometimes, but knowing, in a strange way, that his vices were as much a part of him as his virtues and that they contributed to her fascination with the whole person.

"I wish I could explain it to you, darling," she said at last. "It's not simply security that holds me to your father. It's that I love him enough to forgive this weakness within him. It hasn't been easy. I won't pretend it has. There've been many tears, many hours of soul-searching, and a great deal of open resentment on my part. Sometimes I've told myself I'm a fool to go on with it. But," she hastily added, "I don't want you to ever think I do it for you and Lindsay. I'm not 'holding a home together for the sake of the children.' I don't believe that's a kindness to anyone involved. No, I'm here because I'd rather live with a flawed Howard Thresher than with a perfect Anyone Else." She paused, searching his face for a trace of understanding. "Can you comprehend that, James dear? Can you believe I'd be totally miserable without him?"

The boy shook his head. "No, Mama, I can't. I still don't see why he does this if he loves you. And I don't see how you can love him, knowing what he does." His face darkened. "All that crap about men of our class! All that talk about how I'll do the same thing! It's not true. He's just making excuses for doing something that makes him feel like a big man."

Pauline sighed. He was right, of course. This belief of Howard's that he was following tradition was so ingrained in his own mind that he'd come to think it true. It was a convenient way to salve his conscience—if, indeed, he had one. It eliminated any guilt he might feel about how unhappy he made her. "Out of the mouths of babes," she thought. How clearly James saw what Pauline herself did not even wish to admit: Howard was a totally selfish man. What James did not see was that his father was also a dreadfully insecure one. He needed other women, not for sexual gratification but to bolster his ego. To prove, over and over again, how attractive and male he was. He needed women more stupid than his wife, more impressed with him and less prone to criticism than she. She didn't understand this need. It would take a psychiatrist to uncover the cause of Howard's well-disguised lack of confidence. Certainly there was no overt explanation. But somewhere, deep inside, he was uncertain of his manhood, dubious of his superiority, perhaps even of his intelligence. The world had no idea of this. Howard himself, she felt sure, never guessed the real reasons for his waywardness. But Pauline believed it was true. And believing that, she continued to love him, forgive him, and even reluctantly pity him.

But none of this could she say to a fifteen-year-old boy. It was far beyond even his unusual grasp of things. It might hurt him even more to know his father was weak and frightened. Sad. If she could explain what she believed, James might feel less bitter about his father, more understanding of his human frailty. Instead, Howard's son was scornful and disgusted, seeing his father only as arrogant and godless.

"James, dear, don't judge him too harshly. Or me either. There are many things you'll understand as this complex life each of us leads becomes more clear to you. Don't hate your father or feel sorry for me. We're both doing what we must do. What we want to do. You needn't follow his example, any more than I'd want Lindsay to follow mine. But I beg you to be tolerant and remember that we love you above all things, in the only way we know how."

He hadn't understood it then and he didn't understand it now. For three years he'd been scrupulously polite to his father, hiding his true feelings. After his talk with his mother, he'd felt more compassion than scorn for her. At least she loved her husband, blindly perhaps, foolishly probably, but with all the honesty in her soul. He had to respect that. But he could never feel the same about the man for whom she had such an all-consuming passion. Even though, now and then, that passion was threatened by some unbearable humiliation, as it obviously had been on the evening Lindsay heard them quarrel.

Damn this "sensible arrangement" our parents have! James dried himself and threw the towel furiously across the bathroom. Who's going to tell Lindsay the truth? Will she hear it, as I did, from her peers? God

17

knows I'm not the one to try to explain it. She's still a baby. She'd have no idea what it's all about.

And yet he knew his sister was not satisfied with the pat, evasive answers he'd given her. She was much too bright to forget the overheard words, even if she let the subject drop. He wondered whether he should tell his mother. Maybe it was wise to let Pauline make the decision to talk or not, as she had with him.

No. Ridiculous. Lindsay was much too young to be dealt the kind of blow that had affected his life. All he could do was hope she'd gradually let the questions go out of her mind, at least until she was old enough to accept the answers, even if, like James, she could never swallow the rationale.

Blast our "civilized" station in life, he told himself. It's made me cynical about marriage, distrustful of my father, patronizingly tolerant of my mother. It's shaped the whole course of my thinking, and maybe it will alter my whole future.

And when Lindsay finds out, as one day she will, God knows what it will do to her.

3

$\mathcal{U}$nsatisfied as she was with James's explanation, Lindsay was still child enough to finally put the troubling thoughts out of her mind. In the days that followed, Christmas caught her up in that wave of delight reserved only for the very young and the unwaveringly sentimental. At ten, Lindsay was the perfect age for this holiday: young enough to be greedily thrilled about her gifts without deploring the commerciality of the season, old enough to enjoy giving and to derive pleasure from the appreciation of others. It was a magic time for her, dashing to the service entrance ahead of the housekeeper to receive the endless boxes of flowers and store-delivered parcels brought up by the "back elevator man," rushing to the front door to greet the stream of family friends who arrived to exchange gifts with the Threshers. It was a nonstop period of excitement, for the little girl and for all of them. Even Howard seemed to mellow under the warmth and friendliness of the holiday. He came home early every evening between Christmas and New Year's, a fact noted with satisfaction by the adult members of his family, used to late arrivals with an unexplained gap of two or three hours after his departure from the office.

If anything marred Lindsay's pleasure in the season it was the awareness that this was far from a happy time for her friend Adele. When they compared Christmas gifts, it was all too apparent that the Framptons' celebration was far from lavish. In contrast to the expensive clothes and toys Lindsay received from her parents, Adele got only one navy jumper and white blouse and a small golden locket on a chain from her mother and father. Lindsay admired the necklace extravagantly, though she recognized from her exposure to good things that the little trinket was only costume jewelry.

19

"It's so pretty, Adele!" she said. "I wish I'd gotten one!"

Adele smiled. "It's not very much, but my folks can't afford much this year. Daddy was ruined by the stock market crash, you know. Last year my presents were already bought, so it didn't make much difference. But Mother explained that this Christmas we just don't have money to waste." She looked troubled. "I don't understand it, really. I think maybe we're even going to have to move away. Mother and Daddy were talking about it the other night. Daddy says there's nobody to buy our apartment and he can't afford to keep it, so he might have to find somebody to take it off his hands for a dollar."

"A dollar!" Lindsay was aghast. "But it's the same as ours, just one floor above! Who'd sell an apartment for a dollar? You must be wrong, Del. You didn't hear right." She thought of her conversation with James. "Were you listening when you weren't supposed to? That's not a good thing to do."

"No. They were talking about it right at the dinner table." Without warning, Adele began to cry. "I'm so scared, Lind. Daddy looks like an old man. And Mother can't keep her mind on anything. She let the maid go and she's doing all the cooking and cleaning herself. Daddy doesn't even go to the office any more. Not for months." She wiped her eyes. "I shouldn't be telling you this, even if you're my best friend. They don't want anybody to know. But it's awful. I guess we're poor now, and I hate it!"

Lindsay put her arms around her friend. She didn't understand it either. She'd heard about something called a "depression," and she'd even seen shabby men on the street trying to sell apples. But that had nothing to do with people like her and Adele. It was poor people who didn't have any money. Not the Framptons, who were the same kind of family as her own.

"It'll be okay," Lindsay said. "Don't worry, Del. I'll talk to Papa. He'll fix it."

"I'm not sure he can. Anyway, you're not even supposed to know."

"Pooh! We're all friends, your family and mine. I'm sure your father didn't mean you shouldn't tell us." Lindsay smiled. "Don't you worry. Papa won't let you move away. I'll tell him I couldn't stand it!"

Adele looked less mournful. "Do you really think so, Lindsay? Are you sure he can make it all right?"

"Of course. Papa can take care of anything." She was relieved to see her friend cheer up. "Come on. We haven't even opened our presents from each other. I'm dying to see what's in mine."

"It isn't much." Adele looked depressed again.

Lindsay tore at the wrappings on the small box which had been purchased at Woolworth's five-and-ten. Inside was a cheap diary in simulated leather. It was a sad little present, but Lindsay exclaimed over it. "My very first diary! I've been wanting one! How did you know, Del?"

The other child looked pleased. "Do you really like it? You always say you're going to be a writer some day. I thought maybe this would be a good way to start."

"I love it! I'll start tonight. And nobody will be allowed to look, except you. You're the only one who knows all my secrets."

For a moment, Lindsay frowned. There was one secret Adele did not know: that funny business between Mama and Papa before Christmas. She'd nearly forgotten it. It was so scary she couldn't even tell her friend. Resolutely, she put it from her mind.

"Come on, Del. Open your package."

Not until Adele was almost into the contents did Lindsay realize how uneven their gifts were. She'd given Adele a real gold bracelet with a little picture-book charm attached. Lindsay had put her own photograph in it as a sign of their friendship. Now she worried because her gift was so much more expensive than the one she'd received. Even at the time, Gandy had thought it too much for one little girl to give another, but Lindsay had stubbornly insisted.

"Adele and I always give each other super presents, Gandy. We're best friends."

Her grandmother had been unusually reluctant, Lindsay now realized. Probably she knew Adele couldn't buy anything nearly so expensive. Lindsay watched nervously as the bracelet came out of the Saks box. Would it upset Adele and make her start to cry again? Lindsay hoped not. It didn't matter what their presents cost. The only thing important was that they were close as sisters, for neither had one of her own. She waited, holding her breath, for Adele's reaction, letting out a sigh of relief when the little girl's eyes sparkled with delight.

"Oh, Lind, it's terrific! I'll wear it forever. I'll never take it off! It's the best present I ever had!"

"So's mine. Merry Christmas, Del. I love you."

"I love you too." The small face grew dark again. "Oh, Lind, I'll just die if I have to move away from you!"

"Don't worry," Lindsay said again. "You won't."

But Howard Thresher did not solve the problem when Lindsay spoke to him about it that evening. In fact, he did not even give her hope that the Framptons would be in the apartment above much longer.

"It's a damned shame, sweetheart," he said, "but Carl Frampton's one of the unlucky ones. I don't know how he's hung on for the past year. Lost everything in the market, along with a million other men. It's rough on his family, all right. He'll have a problem with that apartment, just as Adele told you. He won't be able to afford the maintenance, and there aren't many men around these days who're interested in buying a ten-room, twelfth-floor apartment on Fifth Avenue."

"You mean Adele really will move away?" Lindsay's lip quivered. "You can't let her, Papa!"

"I don't know what I can do about it, Lindsay. Carl had the bad luck, or the stupidity, to invest every nickel in the stock market. His greed was greater than his judgment. He'll have to start over. And he's past forty. It won't be easy, especially these days."

Lindsay understood only a little of what her father said. She didn't know about things like the stock market or the maintenance on a cooperative apartment. All she heard was that Mr. Frampton didn't have the money to live upstairs. And that meant Adele wouldn't either. On the verge of tears, she made one more try.

"Couldn't you give Mr. Frampton some money, Papa? We have a lot, haven't we?"

Howard looked at her compassionately. Poor little thing. She was heartbroken at the thought of losing her playmate. But of course there was no way he could help. He couldn't subsidize Carl Frampton. Even a loan, if he was foolish enough to give one to a man with no collateral, wouldn't take Carl very far. For that matter, Carl probably wouldn't accept charity. He was a fine fellow, well-mannered and pleasant, though his background was less impressive than Howard's own. He wished he could help, if only to erase the desperately unhappy look on Lindsay's face. But he couldn't solve Frampton's problems. He'd brought them on himself. It was his own mess and he'd have to get out of it somehow. Lindsay wouldn't understand, but that couldn't be helped.

"I'm sorry, dear," he said gently. "It's too complicated to explain. You'll just have to take my word that if I had a solution I'd offer it.

Don't worry. Adele won't move far. You'll see her almost as often as you do now. I'm sure of that."

He wasn't sure at all. God knows where poor old Carl will have to go, Howard thought. Maybe even out of New York. He seemed to recall that the Framptons came from some godforsaken town down south. Maryland or Virginia. He couldn't remember which. Perhaps he had relatives who could take him in, poor bastard. Despite his scorn for the man's stupidity, Howard felt a twinge of pity. It wouldn't be easy to swallow your pride and live off your relatives, or take any rotten little job you could get to support your wife and child. It was so easy to succeed and so humiliating to fail. Or so he supposed. Failure was an unknown condition to Howard, and a repugnant one. He worshiped success as much as he despised the lack of it.

Still, he did feel sorry for Carl. And for his wife, Louise. Damned pretty woman, Mrs. Frampton. More than pretty. Beautiful and sensuous. Adele was her image and some day would grow up to be as alluring as her mother, if she had the proper education in the social graces. But that was moot, now that Carl had doomed his wife and child to some mediocre existence.

Lost in his thoughts, he'd almost forgotten Lindsay, who stood forlornly in front of him, still hoping her wonderful father had some magic answer. I've never failed her before, Howard thought with regret. She must be disappointed in me now. Then he came to his senses. What nonsense! Lindsay would forget Adele in three months and become just as attached to some new "best friend." Good God, it wasn't the end of the world!

"Cheer up, little one," he said. "Adele's father will take good care of her. Things aren't as black as they may look right now. You'll find a new playmate, even if you don't see as much of Adele."

The child shook her head. "I don't want a new playmate, Papa. I want Adele to stay here."

He was becoming impatient. This was all a waste of time.

"Well, I'm sorry about that, Lindsay, but you must realize it probably won't happen, so you may as well accept it. It's time you learned you can't have everything just the way you want it. None of us can."

"You do, Papa. You get everything you want. Why can't I?"

Howard stared at her sharply. What the hell did that mean? What did a baby like Lindsay know? That the house revolved around him? That there was a seemingly endless supply of money and a small army of people at home and at the office just waiting to jump when he snapped his fingers? Perhaps she realized these things and felt entitled to the same privileges her father enjoyed. Well, he'd nip that idea in the bud.

"You're far too young and ignorant to make such statements, little girl. I don't care for your attitude. In fact, I won't tolerate it. You have no idea whether I get everything I want. Nor is it your business." Howard's tone was heavy with irritation. "I've heard enough of this whining about Adele. I don't wish to discuss it again. You may run along now."

"Papa, couldn't you—"

"Dammit, Lindsay, no! You're excused. Now please *leave!*"

Disconsolate, Lindsay wandered in search of her grandmother. James was out at one of the perennial debutante balls people persisted in giving, despite the unfavorable publicity such lavish spending created in a time when people were literally starving. Pauline was busy with arrangements for her annual New Year's Day open house, another un- shakable social institution. Only Sara Thresher sat quietly in her room, writing thank-you notes and personal messages to dear friends around the world who remembered her at Christmas. When Lindsay knocked and came into the room, Sara immediately put down her pen and gave the child her full attention.

"Are you busy, Gandy?"

"Never too busy for you, dear." More trouble, Sara thought, look- ing at the sad face. Or maybe more of the same, whatever that is. "Any- thing wrong?"

This time Lindsay nodded. The words came out in a rush.

"It's Adele, Gandy. Her daddy's lost all his money and they're go- ing to have to move away and I asked Papa to help them and he said he couldn't and then he got very mad at me and—"

"Whoa!" Sara covered her ears in mock confusion. "One step at a time, please!" She smiled reassuringly. "Don't be so upset, Lindsay dar- ling. Maybe it isn't as bad as it seems. Adele might not know all the facts. After all, she's only nine, even younger than you. Perhaps she just heard her parents discussing the worst that *could* happen. Grown-ups do that, you know. It's called making 'emergency plans.' I'll bet Mr. and Mrs. Frampton aren't really going to move. They're probably only talking about something that's *possible* but not *probable.* You see, sweetheart, most of us spend our lives worrying about things that never

24

happen. The Framptons could be doing just that, but Adele wouldn't realize it. So there's no point in your fretting over something that may never come to pass and that worrying won't change anyhow. What's the good in making yourself miserable? Time enough for that if your fears are realized, though I feel quite sure they won't be."

Lindsay brightened. "You really think it won't happen, Gandy? You think Adele will be able to stay?"

"I can't be sure, honey. I don't know what the situation really is. But smart men like your father and Mr. Frampton usually work through their problems. I have a hunch Adele's father will solve this one without the drastic measures she thinks he'll take. Why don't we just wait and see?"

Lindsay threw her arms around her grandmother. "Oh, Gandy, you make me feel so much better! I love you."

"And I love you, baby. Too much to see you fretting about these complicated matters." She kissed the top of Lindsay's head. "Now tell me. Did Adele like her bracelet?"

Her fears dispelled, Lindsay smiled happily. "She loved it. She said she'd never take it off. And she gave me a real, secret diary with a lock and key. I'm going to write in it every night. That's what I want to be, you know," she said solemnly, "a writer. I'm going to write lots of books and make heaps of money and buy you everything you want. And James too. And Mama and Papa, of course."

"Well, that's a lovely ambition and I just bet you'll do it, too. How proud I'll be of my granddaughter, the famous lady novelist."

"I'm going to go start right now," Lindsay said. "I'll write down what you told me about not worrying over things that probably won't happen. That's a good thing to remember, isn't it?"

"Yes, love. It's one of the most important."

If only we *could* control our fears as easily as that, Sara thought when the child left. So easy to hand out advice and so difficult to take it yourself. I worry all the time and hate myself for it. Fearful of Howard's flagrant infidelity and what it will do to his wife and children. Terrified that Pauline will leave him one day and destroy her marriage. Anxious, selfishly, about what that would do to me. What a pompous fraud I am, telling Lindsay not to be unhappy until there's a real crisis to be unhappy about. I live with imagined fear, seeing disaster around every corner. And I dare tell that child not to be concerned.

But she is only a child. She should be carefree. This is the only

25

time in her life she will be. Lord knows when she's a woman she'll have enough genuine grief.

At six o'clock the next morning Pauline Thresher was awakened by the sound of screaming sirens and excited voices yelling in the street below. She sat up in bed and listened for a moment before she glanced at Howard lying next to her. He seemed to be asleep, but as she slipped from bed and pulled on a heavy robe, he opened his eyes.

"Where the hell are you going at this hour?"

"Just wanted to see what was happening. Sounds as though there are a million police cars or fire engines or something, right below us. I thought maybe I could see from our window."

"For God's sake, Pauline, what are you going to do? Lean out from the eleventh floor to see what the racket is all about? It's ten degrees out there and pitch black, besides. It's probably only a bunch of holiday drunks being hauled off by the police. Come back to bed. It's the damned middle of the night!"

Pauline hesitated. "I think I'll go see if the noise disturbed Gandy and Lindsay."

"Are you crazy? You've lived all your life in Manhattan. What's the big deal about a few sirens?"

"I don't know, Howard. I just have a feeling that something's terribly wrong."

He burrowed back under the covers. "Women! If there isn't a crisis they'll create one."

Pauline walked softly down the hall. Light showed under only one door: her mother-in-law's. She tapped softly and Sara opened it immediately, as though she'd been standing just behind it.

"I was wondering whether to come out. Such a racket! What on earth do you suppose is going on?"

"I don't know," Pauline said. "Howard says it's probably only the police picking up a bunch of rowdies, but it sounds like more to me." She shivered. The apartment was cold—the heat didn't come up until nearly seven o'clock—but it wasn't only the temperature that chilled her. She had this weird feeling that a tragedy had taken place. One that would affect them all. Not knowing what possessed her, Pauline heard herself saying, "I'm going to slip on a coat and go down to the lobby. I don't know why I have this premonition, Gandy, but I can't shake the feeling that something awful has happened."

26

The older woman nodded. "Do you want me to go with you?"

"No, no. I'll be back in a few minutes." Pauline managed to laugh. "I'm probably going to look like the world's biggest jackass, traipsing downstairs half dressed. But I just have to know."

Howard was asleep again when she went back to their room. The noises on the street continued, and looking out the window she could see the flashing lights of official cars. Noiselessly, she put on shoes and threw her mink coat over her nightgown, all the while thinking how unlike her this impulsive act was. Howard was right. She'd lived in the city all her life. She should be used to—impervious to—twenty-four-hour activity in the streets. Why do I know this is different? Pauline wondered. Why am I so sure it's important to find out?

The big lobby when she reached it was a mass of activity. Few tenants had come down, but police were everywhere. At first she thought there must have been a robbery, but then she saw an ambulance outside and in another few seconds a doctor, distinguishable by his black bag, rushed by her and took the elevator. She watched the indicator rise and stop at the twelfth floor. Baffled, she approached Mike, the night doorman.

"What's going on, Mike? What's all the commotion about?"

The man was deathly pale. "God save us, Mrs. Thresher, it's Mr. Frampton."

"What's happened to him? Has he had a heart attack?"

Mike seemed almost unable to speak. "No, ma'am. He . . . that is, about half an hour ago . . ."

She wanted to shake him. "What? Half an hour ago, what?"

"He . . . he fell out of his bedroom window, Mrs. Thresher."

Pauline thought she was going to faint. It wasn't possible. Carl Frampton dead? No. It couldn't be. Was Carl drunk? How else could he fall out a window? He wouldn't jump. Never. He was so alive, so in love with his wife and devoted to his daughter. Even in this past year, hard as it had been for him, he'd managed to stay cheerful and optimistic. She'd heard that other men, wiped out by the crash of '29, had killed themselves. But Carl had survived more than a year. Surely at this late date he wouldn't do this unthinkable thing. She was aware that Mike was still talking to her.

"The doctor just went up to Mrs. Frampton. I guess she's in pretty bad shape, Mrs. Thresher."

Louise, Oh, God, Louise! And poor little Adele! They must be

27

alone up there. The Framptons, unlike the Threshers, no longer had a live-in housekeeper. Somehow, Pauline pulled herself together.

"Thank you, Mike," she said politely. "I'll go up and see what I can do."

"Yes, ma'am." The doorman sighed heavily. "Terrible thing. Never was a nicer man than Mr. Frampton. Always a smile and a kind word for everybody. It just don't seem possible, does it? These are terrible times, Mrs. Thresher."

In spite of her distress, Pauline thought what a small world an apartment building was. The staff knew everything: the comings and goings of the tenants, the celebrations and the scandals, and probably even the financial difficulties of the residents.

Afraid of what she'd find, Pauline took the elevator to the twelfth floor. The door of the Frampton apartment was slightly ajar, and she knocked lightly before letting herself in. Lights were on everywhere, but there was no one in sight. Hesitantly, she walked down the corridor toward the master bedroom. As she neared it, she could hear a man's voice. The doctor was speaking to Louise and as Pauline came closer she heard his words.

"But you must let me give you a sedative, Mrs. Frampton. It's imperative. You're in no condition—"

Louise interrupted. She sounded almost hysterical, yet she was making sense. "I can't take anything to put me to sleep, doctor. I have a little girl to look after. There's no one to take care of her."

"No relatives I can call for you, Mrs. Frampton? A close friend, perhaps? Or one of your neighbors?"

Pauline called softly from the hall. "Louise? It's Pauline Thresher. May I come in?"

The doctor answered. "Yes, indeed, Mrs. Thresher, do come in! You're the answer to a prayer. I was just asking—"

"I know," Pauline said. "Forgive me, but I overheard." She turned to the grief-stricken woman on the bed. They'd never been truly close friends, but they liked each other, met frequently at social gatherings, and felt close because of the devotion of their daughters. Pauline's heart ached now at the sight of her neighbor. Louise's beautiful eyes were wide with horror, pain, and disbelief. The full, sensuous mouth trembled as though it were repressing an animal scream of anguish. Yet a flood of relief came over Louise's face when she realized someone had come to help, and she began to weep.

28

The doctor lost no time in giving the sedative. He packed his bag quickly and let himself out, after promising he'd look in later that day. Only then did Louise let go.

"Oh, Pauline, thank God you're here! It was so fast. So terribly, terribly fast. I woke up and Carl was standing at the window, looking out. I didn't know what was happening. Before I could move, he came to the bed and kissed me and said, 'You'll be all right now, darling. You and Adele won't have to worry. But it has to look like an accident. Remember. An accident!' " Louise was almost screaming. "And then before I could do anything he went back to the window and he—oh, Jesus, he just stepped out of it. He didn't even hesitate!" She sobbed harder and then the sobs turned to low, despairing moans as she sank back on the pillow, her head turning from side to side as though she were being physically tortured.

Pauline felt ill, but she controlled the urge to run into the bathroom and throw up. She swallowed hard as she reached for Louise's hand, which twitched nervously outside the covers.

"You must get some rest, dear. Don't worry about Adele. I'll take her down to our apartment. Gandy will look after her, and Lindsay will be with her. Then I'll come right back and stay with you. You mustn't be alone now. I'll be here as long as you need me." She wanted to ask whom to call. There must be relatives or closer friends to help Louise through this, but the woman seemed semiconscious already. In a few minutes she'd be fast asleep. There was nothing for it but to take over for the time being. She looked at the stricken, contorted face on the pillow and thought, Damn you, Carl Frampton, you unspeakable coward! How could you do this to her and that poor child? How dare you run out on them? You're dead and safe. But what will they do now, with no money and no way to survive? It was a selfish act, this suicide. Carl couldn't face the consequences of his own failure. He left that to Louise and Adele.

Adele. Pauline realized she hadn't seen the child since she entered the apartment a few minutes before. Louise was already in a drugged sleep. But where was Adele?

She found her in her room, cowering in a corner like a frightened rabbit. Pauline went to her and took her in her arms.

"It's all right, sweetheart. Don't be afraid. Your mother is resting, and I'm going to take you downstairs to Lindsay and Gandy."

The little girl was not crying, but she was shaking as though she had a violent chill. She clung to Pauline and then she said, "I heard the noise and people coming in. And Mother was yelling. I was afraid to go out. I'm scared, Mrs. Thresher. What is it? Is something wrong with my mother? Where's my daddy? Why aren't they here?"

Pauline could scarcely contain her tears. The bewildered child was enough to break her heart.

"There's been an . . . accident, Adele dear. But your mother is all right." She tried to gently disengage the small arms. "Come on. Let's get you into something warm and then we'll go downstairs."

Adele wouldn't let go. She began to sob. "I want my daddy. Where's my daddy? Why doesn't he come and take care of me?"

Dear God, Pauline thought, what can I say to her? The truth. She'll have to know soon. Firmly, but gently, she separated herself from Adele, holding the child's shoulders and looking into her eyes. "Your daddy is the one who had the accident, darling. He's not . . . not with us any longer. That's why your mother was making that noise and why she has to have some sleep now. The people came because your daddy hurt himself."

Adele stopped crying. A terrible look of comprehension came over her face. "No longer with us?" she repeated. "Does that mean . . . ?"

Pauline tightened her grip as though she could will strength and understanding into the little body. "Your daddy died this morning, dear heart. He must have been trying to open a window when he slipped." Adele's expression was almost more than she could bear. "He didn't suffer," Pauline said lamely. "He never felt a thing." Oh, God, such cruel and inadequate words! But how else could it be told? She had to lie to Adele about its being an accident. Or maybe it really was. No one knew for sure. In any case, Pauline couldn't bring herself to tell this baby that her father had killed himself.

The child stood frozen, a petite, perfect statue. "My daddy's dead?" Her tone was incredulous. "No. You're wrong. My daddy isn't dead. No. Not dead. Not dead. Not dead." Her voice began to climb to hysteria. "I won't let my daddy die!" She broke away and ran toward the door. "Daddy!" she screamed. "Daddy, where are you?"

Pauline caught her and held her close. "Hush, baby. Hush. You don't want to wake your mother." Tears were streaming down her face as she hugged the hysterical child. Adele struggled to free herself but Pauline kept a tight hold on her until she felt her go limp in her arms.

"I know," Pauline crooned. "I know, Adele. I know how you feel."

Lies. She couldn't begin to imagine the agony in this little soul. She could only guess how Lindsay would feel if Howard deserted her. Girls always worshiped their fathers, their heroes, the first loves of their lives. To have that love and security torn away from them in such heartless fashion was monstrous. Carl Frampton was a monster to have done this to his daughter.

If only Adele were a little younger, Pauline thought, she'd not realize the awful meaning of death. Or a little older, so that she could better cope with the loss of her idol. But she was the wrong age for this tragedy. Holding Adele's soft little form, Pauline smiled bitterly. Wrong age? How absurd. There was no right age to accept the loss of one you loved. No time at which women did not grieve and bemoan the unjust fate that took their men from them. If, God forbid, Howard were to die, she'd be as prostrate as Louise, and Lindsay would be as stricken and disbelieving as Adele. We love them, Pauline thought. Wretched, selfish, egomaniacs though they often are, we still find the thought of life without them unbearable.

4

*T*hree days later, the nightmare quality of that morning had lessened, though the heavy burden of sorrow remained. Carl's sister and brother-in-law came from Wheeling, West Virginia, to claim his body and return it for burial in the family plot next to his parents. Louise's widowed mother arrived from Chicago to take over the household, including the care of Adele, who was left at home while her mother went back with her in-laws for her husband's last rites.

Pauline was against the decision not to allow Adele to go to her father's funeral. She mentioned this, tentatively, to Louise.

"She knows her father is dead, Louise, but she may find that harder to accept if he simply disappears. I can appreciate how you feel about putting so young a child through the experience of a funeral, but it may help her face the finality of it."

"No." Louise was determined. "She's too young to suffer that morbid scene. It's macabre. It could scar her for life."

"So could the lack of acceptance," Pauline said quietly. "There's a strange comfort in knowing that it's really the end. That she cannot hope to ever see him again."

Louise shook her head. "Would you put Lindsay through that?"

"Yes. Yes, I would. It would be terrible for her, but she'd be more at peace. Or so I believe. She'd finally have to believe it was true, sad as it would make her. She wouldn't go through life searching for her father. I don't mean literally, of course, but perhaps emotionally."

"I'm sure you mean well," Louise said. "You've been so wonderful through all this, I don't know how to ever thank you. But I can't agree,

32

Pauline. Adele is young. She'll get over this. Why add to her awful memories? God knows we all have enough."

"Of course," Pauline said. "She's your child. You know what's best for her."

A stricken and unhappy Adele was left in her maternal grandmother's care while her last remaining hold on security went away for a few days. Since the morning of the "accident," she'd been almost silent. After the one outburst in Pauline's arms, she'd said little. Docilely, she'd gone to the Thresher apartment and been held and comforted by Gandy, fussed over by James, and accompanied in her every waking hour by a half-understanding Lindsay. Howard, always uncomfortable among the reminders of mortality, had quickly patted her head and told her she was always welcome in his house. Adele had nodded and said, in her best private-school manner, "Thank you, Mr. Thresher. Mother and I appreciate your kindness."

Only Pauline saw the quiet despair in those young eyes. Strangely enough, she thought, I believe Louise will survive this better than Adele. Louise mourns, of course. She's lost her beloved. But she can better comprehend because she knows why Carl did it. Adele does not. God knows I didn't understand at first. I damned the man for his gutlessness and I was wrong. It never occurred to me until Howard explained it that all Carl had was his life insurance. A hundred thousand dollars worth. Enough to ensure the immediate survival of his family which, alive, he saw no way of doing. It was, in the truest sense of the word, a supreme sacrifice. And yet I can't help feeling his family would rather be poor with him than comfortable without him.

She thought back to her conversation three years before with James. Money was good to have, but it didn't replace companionship and love and the sense of sharing. Louise would never have traded Carl's life for security, but he didn't give her that option. And for that, Pauline thought, I will never forgive him. It should have been a joint decision. Since that was impossible, Carl decided he knew what was best. It was a sacrifice. Of course it was. To give up the most precious thing of all, your life, was the final gallant gesture. I'm sure he saw it that way. But you were wrong, Carl, she said silently. You underestimated your own worth. You were a husband and father, not merely a meal ticket. And it was selfish of you not to give of yourself rather than your money.

Well, it was done and over. Ridiculous how she dwelt on it. Though she sincerely mourned her loss, Louise seemed to have no such feelings. She said, over and over again, what a brave and wonderful man her husband was to die for his family. Never once had she said she wished he'd lived for it. She'd be able to stay on in the apartment and keep Adele in her same school. In time, Pauline felt sure, Louise would find another man and probably marry well. She was a beautiful woman and only thirty-three. I'll be forty-one this coming year, Pauline thought. And I feel a hundred. Funny. Howard will be forty-three, but he's changed very little in twenty years. He has one of those faces that are perennially youthful, and in some ways he seems less mature than his own son. At seventy, Howard probably will still be fit and trim, alert and vital. And, she thought ruefully, probably still chasing other women.

Though she did not show it, the death of Carl Frampton also had a profound effect on Lindsay. It had changed Adele from a laughing companion to a sober shadow, not really very much fun to be with these days. She wondered whether she'd act the same way if something happened to Papa, and she felt apprehensive that something might. In the past few days, she'd hung around him constantly, climbing into his lap whenever she could, demanding his attention until Howard became thoroughly aggravated.

"For heaven's sake, Lindsay, have you nothing to do? Go play in the park. It's a beautiful afternoon. You should get some fresh air."

"It's too cold, Papa. And Adele won't go."

"Then find something to occupy you in your room. You're driving me mad! I can't turn around these days without finding you under my feet!"

"Why don't you run in the kitchen and see how the preparations for the party are getting on?" Pauline suggested. "Gandy's out there helping Gertrude get things ready. Maybe you can help too."

When Lindsay reluctantly left, Pauline turned to Howard.

"Can't you see what's happening, Howard? Carl's death has disturbed her terribly."

"Why should it? She's a baby. What can it mean to her?"

"She's old enough to know he's gone. And she's afraid that what happened to Adele could happen to her."

For a moment he didn't understand, and then he was amazed.

"You mean she's hanging around me because she thinks I might die?"

"Exactly."

"But that's absurd! I'm not about to dive out a window!"

"Of course not. But Lindsay doesn't know that. All she sees is her best friend grieving for her father. She's realizing for the first time what it means to lose someone you love, and it scares her. Don't be abrupt with her, Howard. She wants to feel you're safe, and that you'll always be here."

"I never heard such nonsense! Is that child going to hang onto my coattails for the rest of her life?"

"I hope not," Pauline said. "I most sincerely hope not."

Even before she suggested it, she knew it was silly, but two days after Carl's death, Pauline had asked her husband whether he didn't think it would be a respectful gesture for them to cancel their New Year's Day open house. Howard looked at her as though she'd lost her mind.

"Respectful? To whom? For God's sake, Pauline, there hasn't been a death in *our* family. The way everybody around here is carrying on, you'd think the Framptons were blood relatives, or at least our dearest friends. They were neither. We weren't even close to them. Whatever gave you such an idea?"

"I don't know. I just don't feel much like celebrating. I can't get the memory of those first few minutes out of my head: Louise's terrible description of how it happened, and the terrified look on Adele's face when I found her. It was one of the worst things I've ever lived through."

There was a note of exasperation in Howard's voice, though he made, for him, an unusual effort to be sympathetic. "I'm sure it was ghastly for you, my dear, though I don't know why you felt you had to be the one to go rushing up there."

The words angered her. "*Someone* had to. God knows *you* wouldn't trouble yourself! You slept through the whole thing."

"And it would have been all the better if you'd done the same! I don't want to hear any more about this, Pauline. I'm sorry Frampton's dead, but he's just one of thousands. Men have been going out of windows since a year ago last October, but I don't imagine their neighbors have changed their habits because of it. You're being utterly ridiculous, suggesting we call off our annual party. Our friends would think we were crazy. And they'd be right."

35

She gave up. "I suppose so. I suppose it is ridiculous of me. Changing our plans won't help Louise or bring Carl back."

Howard rolled his eyes heavenward. "My God! What's happened to everybody around here? You're acting like the ghost at the feast. Lindsay is behaving like a scared mouse. Even Mother has a face long enough to reach down to the front door. It seems only the men in this family have any sense. I don't notice James sitting home, and I haven't let this disrupt my normal routine."

"No, you certainly haven't. You're still making your daily visits to your paramour, I notice. Would you care to invite her to the party too?"

"Don't talk like a fool, Pauline! You've blown this whole tragedy way out of proportion. Now get yourself together. Since you wish to speak in clichés, I'll trade you one: Count your blessings. Just be damned glad you're married to a man smart enough not to gamble away his whole future."

He was right, Pauline had to admit. She was letting this tragedy become an obsession. It was enough to feel sorry, to help in any way she could. But as Howard said, it did not involve people really close to them. She regretted bringing up that other woman. One thing had nothing to do with the other. Or did it? Had Carl's sacrifice pointed up once again Howard's selfishness? She shook her head, as though to clear it. What kind of nonsense was this? Carl's gift was the kind no woman wanted. Howard was right. She should count her blessings.

"I'm sorry, dear," she said. "I've been edgy these past couple of days. Your attitude is the sensible one. Of course we'll go right on with the open house as usual. I don't know what I could have been thinking of when I suggested we shouldn't."

Howard grunted. Women! Every crisis became a soap opera. Everything that happened to others they somehow managed to relate to themselves. No wonder he always had to have a "friend." It was a relief to spend a few hours each day with some featherbrained female who thought of nothing except how to please him. Not that Pauline was a cold woman. Anything but. She was as passionate as any he'd known, but even during their lovemaking he was aware of her thought processes. He really couldn't stand smart women. Wives should be well-bred and well-spoken, perfect hostesses, faithful and devoted. They should be sexually interested in their husbands, but they should never make a man feel uncomfortable. That was what was wrong with Pauline. She was too intelligent. Sometimes he could feel her judging him and finding him wanting. He wasn't sure what qualities she wished he had, over and above the obvious one of fidelity. It was simply that sometimes he caught her looking at him with resentment, as though she believed he felt her to be inferior. Well, that's what he wanted to feel, by God! Women should know that catering to a man was the greatest thing they could do. Pauline tried, he supposed. Just now, apologizing for her nerves, agreeing with him about the party was her way of deferring to his superior judgment. But it never rang true. She really didn't think he was smarter than she, or wiser. Or, perhaps, even stronger. The women he kept did feel those things and he liked that about them. Needed it, he had to admit.

I should never have married a college graduate, Howard thought ruefully. Shouldn't have picked out Pauline Tillford, the child prodigy with a degree at the age of twenty. I suppose I considered it an accomplishment, capturing this super-intelligent girl who was willing to give up some brilliant future for her role as Mrs. Howard Thresher. It was a coup. I was never more than an average student. I liked the idea that her love for me was stronger than any ambitions she might have had. I didn't know I'd spend twenty years wondering whether that love didn't also include her quiet condescension.

Not that she hasn't been the kind of wife I wanted in all other ways. She gives me everything. Except the one thing I need: blind adoration. And what's wrong with that? Howard asked himself. Every red-blooded male looks for that quality above all else in his woman. Take Carl Frampton and Louise: she thought the sun rose and set on him. At least he had that, poor devil.

It never occurred to him that this blind adoration he envied was the very thing that cost Carl his life. Knowing how Louise trusted him, even worshiped him, Carl couldn't bear to become a failure in her eyes. Rather than lose that adoration in life, he preferred to make it a memory that lingered after death. But Howard did not see that. He certainly didn't suspect that Pauline did.

The first day of 1931, bleak, snowy, and bitter cold with huge wind gusts, brought women shivering in their minks and sables and men freezing in their thin, elegant Chesterfields to the Threshers' annual party. Delighted to be welcomed into the cheerful warmth of the big apartment, they stood for a moment warming themselves in front of the great crackling fire in the living room, wishing each other health and happiness.

The huge Christmas tree stood in the corner, a splendid last vestige of the holiday season. Tomorrow it would be gone, put out on the sidewalk with hundreds like it, making the side streets look like some sad, abandoned forest of brittle greenery, touched here and there with a forlorn icicle still clinging to a dried-out limb.

Lindsay hated to think about the proud tree stripped and discarded, waiting for a garbage truck to haul it away. And yet she was not sorry this holiday was over. At least now Mrs. Frampton would come home, and that would make Adele happier. And school would start and things would get back to normal. She wasn't even sorry, as she usually was, that James soon would be returning to Harvard. He'd been different this year. He'd hugged her and teased her, as he always did, but since the day of his return, when she told him about the argument, he hadn't been the same. He'd spent very little time with her. Very little time at home, for that matter. And when he was in the house, she felt he was avoiding her, as though he was afraid she'd start asking more questions about their parents.

It was all very confusing, and there was no one to tell. Only James knew what she'd overheard, but Mama realized something continued to make her unhappy. The afternoon before, coming on Lindsay reading a book in her room, Pauline had tried to have a talk with her.

"Problems, kitten? You're awfully quiet these days."

Lindsay looked up into the anxious face. Mama was so beautiful and so good. It was hard to lie to her. She settled for a half-truth.

"James acts funny. He doesn't play with me or take me out. All he does is go to parties every night and sleep all morning before he rushes out to lunch. What's the matter with him, Mama?"

Pauline gave a little smile. "It's just part of growing up, darling. James is eighteen, and for the first time you're feeling the difference in your ages. He's a young man now, Lindsay dear, with interests you won't share for a few years. Try to be patient. When you're eighteen and James is twenty-six, you won't feel so far away from him."

"Eighteen! That's eight years away!"

Her mother laughed. "Well, maybe it will happen sooner. All I mean is, James is a young adult and you're still a little girl. As one grows older, the age gap doesn't seem so big. Your brother loves you very much. You know that. But he's interested in other things. Debut parties and tea dances, for instance."

"And girls," Lindsay said scornfully. "All he does is hang on the phone with that silly Candice Simms. Is he bringing her to our party?"

"Afraid he is, Lindsay. Not that I don't like Candice. She's a lovely girl. Her family and ours have been friends for years."

"Is he going to marry her, Mama?"

"Marry her?" Pauline seemed surprised. "Heavens, no! Not now, at any rate. My goodness, James is only a boy!"

"You just said he was a young man."

"I meant only in terms of his social life. Men don't marry at eighteen, dear. Not sensible ones, like James. He'll have to finish school and get a job before he thinks about that."

"Maybe he won't wait. He's awful lovey-dovey with her on the phone."

Pauline stared at her daughter and then she smiled gently. "Why, Lindsay Thresher, I do believe you're jealous!" Then she sobered. "I know. It must be hard for you. You and James have always been so close. Yet in some ways, it's as though you're an only child." She seemed almost to be thinking aloud. "It's a pity we didn't have you sooner, I suppose. Then you and James would have grown up together. It would have been more fun for you." Pauline rose from her chair. "Well, we can't worry about that, can we? Tomorrow is a new year and you'll be approaching eleven. Soon you'll catch up with your brother, in a manner of speaking."

I'll never catch up with him, Lindsay thought sadly, watching the guests mingling and chatting on New Year's Day. James kept Candice's arm tucked into his as he took her around and introduced her to his parents' friends. He was glowing with possessiveness, obviously proud of the gorgeous eighteen-year-old debutante who looked up at him with such open admiration. The parents of the two smiled in obvious approval. It was decidedly an appropriate match. Not yet, of course. They were far too young. But some day. When Candy had finished her deb and postdeb period and done the Grand Tour of Europe, there'd be time enough to announce an engagement. And after a suitable period, when James had graduated and joined his father in the bank, there'd be a large wedding, linking the Simms and Thresher families and producing, in due course, grandchildren to take their positions in New York society as generations before them had done.

Lindsay listened to her parents discussing this probability when James was out of the house. She didn't particularly fancy Candice as a sister-in-law. The girl treated James's little sister with the kind of phony tolerance adopted by people who don't really like children. She was always pretending they were equals. That was silly and annoying. Lindsay wished she'd stop trying to be friends. She was James's girl, a grown-up. Why did she try to impress everybody with how close she was to the sister her prospective fiancé adored? Heck, Lindsay thought, she expects me to act like I do with Adele! She's *dumb*. Why can't James see what a stupid thing she is? She hoped he wouldn't marry Candice. In her fantasies, she imagined he'd wait until Adele was eighteen and marry *her*. That would be lovely for everybody. Adele would be a real sister then.

Adele and her grandmother had not come to the New Year's Day party, though Pauline had asked them. Louise's mother, a dreadful woman given to high-necked black dresses and deep sighs, had thanked Mrs. Thresher but replied that she thought it "unsuitable for anyone close to Carl to accept a social invitation at this time." Pauline had refused to accept this as the reprimand it was intended to be.

"I wish you'd reconsider, Mrs. Darby," she'd said. "It's only a little at-home affair, nothing public, and I think you might enjoy meeting some of Louise's friends. Besides, it must be very lonely for you here in the apartment with only Adele for company."

"I'm quite used to being alone in Chicago," the woman said with not a little self-pity. "It's kind of you, Mrs. Thresher, but I think not."

Adele had been disappointed. She was still unlike herself these days, obviously devastated by her father's death, but, as she told Lindsay, she wished her grandmother had decided they could come to the party.

"It's awfully gloomy up there, Lind," she said. "Grandmama cries all the time. Which is kind of funny, because I know she didn't like Daddy all that much."

Lindsay's curiosity was piqued. "How do you know?"

"I heard her and Mother talking when Grandmama was here for a visit last year. Right after Daddy lost his money. She told Mother he never was good enough for her, and that she knew he'd come to a bad end. She tried to make Mother come back to Chicago and bring me, but of course she wouldn't. She told Grandmama she loved Daddy and she'd be with him the rest of her life." Adele choked, and her eyes filled with tears. "Why did he have to die, Lind? I miss him so much."

Lindsay didn't know what to do. She was a child herself, with a child's inability to find words of comfort. Instead, she sought to distract her friend. "Hey, let's practice our bridge, Adele. Come on. Maybe James and Gandy will play with us later."

The girls were just beginning to learn auction bridge, and before the tragedy they'd been caught up in it. But now Adele shook her head.

"I don't want to, Lind."

"Well, then, we could walk up to the museum."

"Uh-uh. I guess I'll just go back upstairs. Grandmama doesn't like me to be away from her for very long."

"Oh, pooh! You're behaving like a stick-in-the-mud! I wish your mother would come home and you'd start acting like yourself again! Honest, Adele, I'm sorry about what happened, but you're being a terrible pain in the neck!"

The minute she said it, she was sorry. Adele looked like a whipped puppy. She got up slowly and started for the door. As she reached it she turned and said, with dignity, "I hope your father never dies, Lindsay."

The memory of that conversation the day before brought a troubled frown to Lindsay's face. She'd been horrible to her best friend and too ashamed even to call and apologize. It was a terrible way to start a new year.

Gandy came and sat beside her.

"Having a good time, dear?"

Lindsay shook her head. "No. Awful. Everybody here is so old."

Sara Thresher smiled. "Well, that's true," she said seriously. "I'm sorry Adele couldn't come. She'd have been company for you."

"I don't think she's ever going to speak to me again, Gandy. I was so mean to her yesterday. I told her she was acting like a big pain."

"Ah, Lindsay, you didn't! She's been through so much."

"I know. I didn't mean to. I just couldn't help it." The child seemed about to cry. "Why do things have to change, Gandy? Why do terrible things happen to nice people?"

The older woman sighed. "There's no answer to that, sweetheart. Some things can't be explained. That's why we have to have faith. To believe what we've been taught about God's will. We have to trust Him and accept things for which we can find no sense or meaning. It's not easy, Lindsay. I'm not deeply religious enough to find comfort in blind belief. I don't see why Mr. Frampton had to die so young. I don't know why his wife has had this grief thrust upon her, or why his child is left fatherless when she needs him most. I wish I could tell you why such things happen. I can't. All I *can* tell you is that sometimes we strike out at the victims, as you did at Adele. It's not anger at *them,* but at the things that have happened to them. I know you hate yourself for being nasty to your friend, but you mustn't. It was a natural reflex. You weren't furious at her behavior; you were angry at the thing that caused it. In a way, you were really being protective of her, trying to help her over her hurt. Can you understand that, Lindsay?"

"I'm not sure, Gandy. Not all of it."

"You will, my love. Give yourself time. Time is a remarkable thing. It not only heals, it also teaches." She paused, watching the child try to absorb these new ideas. How wonderful a young mind was! Especially one as receptive as this. Lindsay had her mother's intelligence and her father's irresistible charm. From me, Sara thought, I hope she inherits some small degree of sensitivity, for that's all I have to offer her. The older woman looked wistful. Three valuable assets. Pray God she uses them well in the years to come.

5

*W*hen, in later years, she tried to remember the first part of the nineteen thirties, Lindsay found much of it a blur. She recalled certain things, like Mr. Frampton's suicide just after Christmas, and how it had taken Adele nearly a year to begin acting like her old self. She remembered talk of the stock market crash and the big depression that followed. But when her peers talked of being "depression babies" and spoke of how hard life was at that time, she was almost ashamed to realize that these bad years rolled by without drastically disturbing her adolescence or her happy teens.

Certain things stuck in her mind, of course. Trivial ones, mostly. In 1931 there was the first talk of the Nazi party, but it hadn't registered with Lindsay. In fairness, it did not register with most of America. Her memories were of being taken to see *Flowers and Trees,* Walt Disney's first color film. She recalled her father's pleasure when Al Capone, the gangster, went to jail for income tax evasion. And her mother's delight when someone called Hattie Caraway became the first woman elected to the U.S. Senate.

The year 1932 was more vivid. Papa was enraged when FDR was elected President. And she could still see Gandy's heartbroken face when the newspapers announced the kidnapping of the Lindbergh baby. James, by now a junior at Harvard, was engrossed in a book about bullfighting: *Death in the Afternoon* by Ernest Hemingway. Lindsay tried to read it, but it didn't mean much to her. Many years later, when she went to her first bullfight in Spain, she remembered her brother's excitement and understood it. Animal lover that she was, unable to bear the sight of a hurt puppy, she saw in bullfighting the dan-

43

ger and bravery and sexual excitement that James must have visualized. For her part, at twelve she was more interested in the fact that her idol, Greta Garbo, won kudos for her appearance in *Grand Hotel*. She was downright scornful of Adele's devotion to the new child star, Shirley Temple. A disgusting four-year-old show-off, Lindsay thought, as she impatiently sat through *Red-Haired Alibi*, the first picture ever made by the curly-haired moppet.

The biggest event in 1933 was James's graduation. She was so proud of him. The family all went, of course, and so did Candice and her parents. Candy and James had been seeing each other almost exclusively for more than two years; Walter Winchell even wrote them up once in a column about the Stork Club. But there'd been no mention of an engagement, and Lindsay prayed nightly that there wouldn't be. Earlier that year, there'd been Roosevelt's first inauguration, to which her parents were invited but declined. Papa, a rock-ribbed Republican, predicted dire things for big business and, difficult as it was for him, was almost pleased when "that man" closed the banks for a three-day period in March. Mama, perhaps spitefully, kept talking about the appointment of Frances Perkins as Secretary of Labor. "Think of it!" she said at dinner. "At last, a woman in the President's Cabinet. We're finally beginning to make progress!" Papa had simply snorted. "Just another of his damn-fool moves," he said. "The man is an anarchist. And that wife of his!" Lindsay entered her teens that year, but despite how grown-up she felt, Mama vetoed her going to see Mae West in *She Done Him Wrong*. Instead, she was dragged to *Little Women* starring Katharine Hepburn and pretended to be bored to death by it.

Funny how little things came back. In 1934 there was the birth of the Dionne quintuplets, and the F.B.I. shot John Dillinger. She was promised a trip to Europe on the new S.S. *Queen Mary* but not, of course, until she was ready for her own Grand Tour. Hitler's bloodbath in Germany and the Nazi assassination of Austrian Chancellor Dollfuss meant nothing to a fourteen-year-old girl beginning to take her first real interest in boys. Her big hearthrob was Geoffrey Murray, who was fifteen and went to Andover. She wasn't allowed to date at her age, of course, but they met at carefully arranged and highly chaperoned parties. Lindsay decided he was the most beautiful thing she'd ever seen.

"I think I'll marry Geoff Murray," she confided airily to Adele.

Her friend, intent on secretly experimenting with mascara, squinted into the bathroom mirror and said, "You're daffy. You can't get married for years and years. Besides, he hardly notices you. Every girl in school is nuts about him."

Lindsay was unperturbed. "So what? I'm still going to marry him. You wait and see. Who are you going to marry, Del?"

"Nobody. I'm not going to ever get married. Marriage stinks."

Lindsay could have bitten her tongue. Everybody said that Louise Frampton's second marriage was a disaster. Her husband had been dead scarcely a year when she married the family lawyer. Lucius Tamlin was an unpleasant man, surly and antisocial. Most people wondered why anyone as attractive as Louise had chosen him. Only Gandy seemed to have an explanation, when Lindsay questioned her about it.

"Loneliness, I suppose, Lindsay dear. Loneliness makes women do strange things. And I imagine Mrs. Frampton was frightened, as well. She had a child to support and educate. Perhaps Mr. Tamlin offered the security that had been so suddenly snatched from her."

"But why *him*, Gandy? He's awful! He's so strict with Adele. And she says he and her mother have terrible fights all the time."

"People make mistakes when they panic. I suppose Mrs. Frampton thought there might not be too many men interested in a poor widow with a dependent." Sara Thresher shook her head. "On the other hand, I might be completely wrong. Perhaps she fell in love with him."

"Love *him?*" Lindsay shuddered. "Ugh! He's so mean! How could a nice lady like Mrs. Frampton possibly love such a mean man?"

"There's no explaining people's attractions. The most unlikely people marry and seem quite happy."

"But they're not happy, Gandy. Adele says she thinks they hate each other."

"Lindsay, what a dreadful thing to say! Adele is just a child and so are you. You're in no position to know how Mr. and Mrs. Tamlin really feel about one another. No one is, except them. People have strange ways of finding fulfillment. Perhaps Lucius Tamlin gives Mrs. Frampton something she needs and wants, in a way none of us can understand. Be tolerant, Lindsay. Don't judge others by your standards. You may make mistakes yourself one day and wish for the same kind of understanding Adele's mother probably needs."

Now Lindsay watched her friend at the mirror. Adele didn't mean that about never getting married. She was sure of that. She was simply disenchanted with the atmosphere at home. When she met someone and

45

fell in love, she'd change her tune in a hurry. Lindsay, feeling very sophisticated at fourteen, wasn't sure Adele knew much about sex. Pauline had told Lindsay all about it a year ago, but who knew whether Louise Frampton had ever had such a heart-to-heart with her daughter? And close as the two girls were, it just wasn't something Lindsay could bring up. Maybe that's what held Adele's mother and stepfather together, she suddenly thought. It was impossible to imagine one's parents doing the things Pauline told her about, but they must. Maybe Mr. Tamlin was sexy and that's why Mrs. Frampton married him. Yes, it had to be that. What else could it be? Still, her mother had said that physical love between married people was a beautiful thing. Lindsay seriously doubted that Lucius Tamlin could be beautiful in any way. Now, Papa was something else. He was so handsome and suave. She idolized him even more than she did Leslie Howard, whom she'd sneaked off to see in *Of Human Bondage*.

Almost forgotten was the angry conversation of four years ago. There'd never been another of that kind in her hearing, and Mama and Papa seemed perfectly happy. I was a kid, Lindsay thought scornfully. Imagining all that stuff about divorce. James was right. They were just having a little argument. But I understand how Adele feels. If people were yelling at each other all the time in my house, I'd be as unhappy as she.

She thought again of how wonderful it would be if Adele could marry James. Her brother was still not engaged, so Lindsay was keeping her fingers crossed. Adele was becoming beautiful. She didn't have the bad skin or the stringy hair of some of their schoolmates. Neither, thank heavens, have I, Lindsay said silently. She hoped James would start noticing Adele one of these days. He hadn't so far, but if he just didn't do anything stupid in the next couple of years, then maybe . . .

James, indeed, seemed inclined to do nothing except work hard at being a playboy, out every night with a different girl. In 1935, Candice suddenly announced her engagement to someone else, an event that upset Pauline but did not seem to visibly affect James.

"I simply don't understand you, James," his mother said on one of the rare evenings he was home for dinner. "I thought you were in love with Candice. You went together for such a long time. Everybody considered you unofficially engaged. Why, the Simmses and your father and I simply took it for granted."

"Leave me out of this, Pauline." Howard Thresher sounded an-

46

noyed. "I never took anything for granted. James is old enough to make his own decisions."

"He's also old enough to get married," Pauline snapped. "Twenty-three. The same age you were."

Howard looked as though he was about to say something cutting in return, but glancing at Gandy and Lindsay, who sat quietly listening, he simply closed his mouth in a thin, disapproving line.

"Mama, I'm not ready to get married yet," James said. "I like Candy. She's a terrific girl, but she's ready to settle down and I'm not."

"You mean she isn't willing to wait while you chase around every night doing the rhumba, or whatever that silly new dance is. We've never interfered in your life, James, but when are you going to start behaving like a responsible man?"

Her son flushed angrily. "What's a responsible man, Mama? Does marriage automatically make you responsible?" Did he glance briefly, almost scornfully, at his father? "Until I find the woman who suits me entirely and totally, I'm not going to get married just because I'm 'old enough.' "

Howard was growing impatient with this conversation. "For God's sake, Pauline, leave the boy alone! He's doing well at the job. Let him sow his wild oats while he can. You women! Always pushing marriage, as though you can't bear to see anyone enjoying freedom."

It was Pauline's turn to redden. "It doesn't seem to have hampered *you* very much." She stopped, regretting what she'd said in front of the others. "Very well," she continued more calmly. "I shall not say another word on this subject. I just thought James should know how disappointed we are."

"How disappointed *you* are," Howard corrected. "You and the Simmses. They must be feeling that Candice let a good catch get away."

They continued the meal in silence. After it, unusual for him, Howard announced he was going out for a while. Lindsay saw her mother and Gandy exchange looks, and James smiled, a secret, cynical kind of smile. When James went to his room to tidy up for his own evening out, Lindsay followed him. She sat on his bed, watching him brush his hair and put on some kind of sweet-smelling lotion.

"James?"

"Hmmm?"

"What's wrong with Mama and Papa?"

"What do you mean?"

"They acted so funny at dinner."

"Hell, Lindsay, you heard it. Mama's sore at me because I'm not married, and Papa thinks I ought to take my time."

She shook her head. "That's not what I mean." She looked and sounded very mature for her fifteen years. "Remember what we talked about a long time ago? About the argument and how I thought maybe they'd get a divorce?"

James looked at her warily. "Yes, I remember. Vaguely. What about it?"

"I don't think you told me the truth."

He didn't answer, but his silence was affirmation.

"I'm fifteen, James. I understand a lot more than I did then. Mama and Papa aren't happy together, are they? You can feel it. I guess they weren't happy five years ago when I first realized something was wrong."

James drew a deep breath. Lindsay was again picking up the discord between their parents. Except this time she'd not be satisfied with some pat little explanation about how all married people quarreled from time to time. All right. Maybe it's time she knew. Fifteen seems to be the magic number in this house. I was fifteen when I found out what a peculiar arrangement Mama and Papa have.

"Lindsay," he said finally, "I don't quite know how to explain it to you. I'm not even sure I'm the one who should be trying to. It's really their job." A note of bitterness crept into his voice. "But of course they won't. They'll just let you find out from some big-mouthed kid at school, the way I did."

She tried to be patient. "Find out what?"

He sat beside her as he had that day long ago and, as he had then, took her hands in his, as though to comfort her.

"It's like this. In a funny way, Mama and Papa are happy together. Well, not exactly happy, but content. That is, Papa's content with the way his house runs and that he has a beautiful and intelligent wife and decent kids. It's just that . . . he wants other things as well. That's what causes the tension between him and Mama."

"Other things like what?"

"Like more freedom than most married men have. Papa's a good husband but he resents the restrictions marriage imposes. I mean, he's old-fashioned about some things. About the rights of men and women, for instance. The way he sees it, it's okay for men to do some things but not for women to do the same. They call that a 'double standard.' " James was doing a terrible job, as the confused look on Lindsay's face told him. Dammit, the kid wanted the truth and he'd give it to her. "The fact is, Lind, Papa thinks there's nothing wrong with a married man seeing other women, as long as he doesn't get serious about it or let it interfere with his home life. He grew up being taught that by *his* father. A kind of gentleman's agreement among the so-called upper classes."

She looked confused. "What do you mean, 'seeing other women'? You mean going to bed with them?"

"Yes. Primarily. These are not women to be seen with socially or to introduce to one's friends. They're just for amusement."

"And Papa does that?"

"Always has, honey. He's been unfaithful almost since the day he and Mama were married, I guess." Her stricken face was almost too much for him. "I know how you're feeling, kiddo, but don't let it get to you. I remember how I felt when I found out. I wanted to kill him for what he was doing to Mama. But when I talked with her, I realized it wasn't the worst thing in the world for her. She loves him so much she's willing to put up with it. And he loves her too, in his crazy way. We can't judge them. We just have to accept that this is the way it is, and the way both of them are going to continue living."

Lindsay was having trouble absorbing this incredible revelation. Papa was unfaithful. There was someone else he loved, someone they didn't know. Her mother had said that physical love between married people was a beautiful thing, but what about love between unmarried people? Surely that was a sin. The Bible called it adultery. And Papa was guilty of it. Thinking of her adored father as a sinner made Lindsay start to cry. James put his arms around her.

"Hey, don't. Don't cry, babe. Papa doesn't love you any the less. Or Mama either, though that's pretty hard to understand."

"But he . . . loves some other woman. You just said so!" Lindsay's sobs increased.

"No. No, I didn't. I never mentioned love. This thing he does, this weakness of his, has nothing to do with love. He doesn't love these women, Lindsay, he just believes they're another part of his life. Mama understands that. I don't say she likes it. That's why they quarrel some-

49

times. But she's known for a long time that it's part of Papa, and if she wants him she has to take this with him. If she can accept it, Lind, we can too."

Lindsay dried her eyes. "I'll never accept it! I hate him! How can men do such terrible things? I thought when you got married you were with one person forever unless one of you died or you got a divorce. I never heard of people pretending to be happy together when one of them was—" She stopped, at a loss for words to describe this monstrous state of affairs. "I hate him," she said again.

James shook his head. "No. You mustn't. I understand why you think you do. I did too, for a long while, after I found out. I thought he was beneath contempt. But you can't hate a man for a sickness, Lind. And the way Papa feels is sick. He doesn't know that, of course. He doesn't see that his selfishness humiliates Mama and makes her miserable. He wouldn't willingly hurt her. He just can't understand why she objects to something he finds so meaningless."

Lindsay sat quietly for a long while, trying to grasp the meaning of all this, but it was too deep for her. She trusted James. If he said Papa didn't realize how shameful his behavior was, she'd have to believe him. But in that instant, her childish adoration disappeared forever. Never again would she worship her father. She'd try not to hate him, but things between them would never be the same.

Finally she said, "Do all men feel this way, James? Do you?"

"No to both questions. Why do you think I'm not anxious to marry Candice or anyone else? Because I won't consider marriage until I'm as sure as anyone can be that this is the one and only woman in the world for me. Maybe I'll never find her. But until I think I have, I'll stay unattached. I'd hate to think of doing to any nice woman what Papa does to Mama. I couldn't live with myself. And," James added slowly, "I'm not sure I could respect any woman who'd put up with it."

"That's what you meant at dinner tonight, wasn't it?"

"Afraid it was."

"And that's what Mama meant when she said marriage hadn't hampered Papa's freedom?"

James nodded.

"But if she knows that's what marriage can be like, why does she want you to get married?"

"She still believes in it, Lindsay. So do I, under the right circumstances. Mama knows it can be a lovely way to live. When your time

50

comes, she'll want you to be married too. She doesn't believe all men are like Papa or that all women have to put up with what she's chosen to endure." He paused for a long moment. "I don't expect you to grasp all this right now. You couldn't possibly, at your age. But it's time you knew the facts and learned to live with them. We can't go on treating you like a baby. You're a young woman, old enough to look at family skeletons. One day you'll see beyond the bones and, I hope, have pity. Or at least learn from this experience not to make a mess of your own life."

Lindsay rose gracefully to her feet. She felt as though a lifetime had passed since she came into this room. All kinds of thoughts whirled through her mind, but she seemed poised and in control as she faced her brother.

"Thank you for being honest with me, James. I'll think about all this."

"Remember, think but don't judge, Lindsay."

She gave him only a sad, grown-up little smile for his answer.

For the next few weeks, she thought of little else. Sometimes Howard found her staring at him as though she'd never seen him before. This intense, analytical gaze was unsettling.

"Lindsay, what in blazes are you looking at? You make me feel as though I've suddenly grown two heads."

"I'm sorry, Papa. I was thinking about something else."

"Well, for heaven's sake concentrate on some other point in the room. I can feel your eyes boring through me!"

I wish they could, Lindsay thought. I wish I could read what goes on in your mind. So many things, unnoticed before, came back to her now. James had said their father's father had taught him this unfair attitude. That meant that Gandy must have gone through the same situation Mama did, and yet both women seemed outwardly serene and satisfied with their lives. How could they be? she wondered. How could they bear knowing that their husbands had broken their marriage vows? God would certainly punish Papa. She supposed that even now He was punishing the grandfather she'd never seen. She shuddered at the idea of Mortimer Thresher burning in eternal hell. In the past year Lindsay had become intensely interested in religion, a fact which amused her agnostic father.

"What's all this holier-than-thou attitude that's come over Lindsay?" he asked his wife. "You used to have to drag her to church, kicking and screaming. Now she goes twice on Sunday and teaches Sunday school besides."

"It's just a phase," Pauline said. "Most girls go through it. She could be doing worse things."

"Granted. But it's a little wearing to share an apartment with an adolescent saint."

Pauline laughed. "I have to agree, but I'm sure it's only temporary. I think Adele's responsible for all this zeal. She's become the big churchgoer ever since Louise remarried, and Lindsay goes along with anything Adele does. And vice versa."

"Well, it's a bloody bore. Any minute I expect her to tell me she forgives me my sins."

"I don't think she knows about your sins, Howard. At least I hope not."

He simply shrugged and went back to reading his paper, but Pauline's quiet comment got under his skin. She'd never stop trying to make him feel guilty. But she'd never succeed. Howard Thresher did not know the meaning of guilt or suffer the pangs of a bad conscience. Didn't he provide well for his family? Didn't he keep up appearances? Pauline's endless accusations, sometimes subtle, sometimes not, were a constant irritation. You'd think, he told himself angrily, that after almost twenty-five years she'd give up nagging him. It was the only thing she had to complain of. She didn't realize how lucky she was. Look at Louise Frampton, Louise Tamlin now. What a waste, that stunning woman married to that clod, all because she was so desperate for security. Pauline would never have such worries. If I died tomorrow, Howard thought, which I have no intention of doing, Pauline would be set for life. So would the children. My father left Mother and me financially safe and I'm doing the same for my family. Sins! These little adventures, sins? No way. The biggest sin was to be less than a man, unable to fight the battles. Carl Frampton committed a bigger sin with his suicide than I ever could with my affairs.

There was no one to whom Lindsay could talk about the sickening disclosures her brother had made. As James had long ago, she instinctively dismissed the idea of telling her mother what she knew, and this time Pauline was not aware of the necessity to explain. Lindsay thought of talking to Gandy about it but was uncertain of her reception. Papa, after all, was Gandy's son, her only child, and she might not want to hear such things about him. Maybe she doesn't even know, Lindsay thought naïvely. I wouldn't want to be the one to tell her. Even though her own husband did the same thing, maybe she doesn't know what Papa does. It would hurt her, and I'd never do that. I love her too much.

It was certainly not something to discuss with Adele. It was too shameful to share even with her closest friend. And Adele might tell her own mother, and then people would know how wicked Howard Thresher was, which would be too awful for Mama. No, this disillusioning discovery was something she could not mention to a living soul. Her only release was in writing pages of her thoughts about it in her diary. She'd kept a diary every year since Adele had given her the first one. There were five now, crammed with every kind of thought and wonder and all hidden away in the very back of her closet where no one could find them. It gave her some comfort to commit her young feelings to the page. The diary was the repository of her fears. It was also the treasure chest of her hopes—the place where she dared wish, seriously, for among other things, the love of Geoffrey Murray.

In 1936, she began to have reason to think that wish might be granted. When she turned sixteen she was allowed to go out with boys, provided she was home by ten o'clock and Mama knew exactly where she was going and with whom. To her delight, Geoff was one of the first who asked her out. He was very proper about it, telephoning on one of his trips home from school, asking Lindsay whether she'd care to go to Radio City Music Hall with him. She was almost speechless with delight.

"Oh, yes!" she said. "I'd love to!" There was a moment's hesitation. "I'll have to get permission, of course, but I'm sure it'll be okay."

"There's an eight-o'clock show," Geoff said. "I'll pick you up about seven thirty unless you call back to tell me differently."

An eight-o'clock show! Lindsay felt her heart sink. She'd never make the ten-o'clock curfew. Mama would just have to make an exception. She'd just *have* to!

And Pauline, seeing the eagerness in the girl's face, couldn't say no. "But I don't want you to make a habit of this, Lindsay. You're still too young for late evenings."

"Mama, I'm sixteen! Other girls—"

"I'm not the mother of other girls. In this house we have rules. Occasionally, like all rules, they can be broken. But only occasionally. Okay, love?"

"Yes, ma'am." She'd have agreed to anything at that point. A date with Geoff Murray! It was by far the most important moment of her life.

It was after midnight when she got home, and Mama was waiting up, a strange look on her face. Before Pauline could say anything Lindsay began to bubble.

"Oh, Mama, I had the most wonderful time! The show was so good, and then we went to Rumpelmayer's and had a soda and talked and talked. Geoff has some friends in England who say Edward is going to abdicate the throne to marry Wallis Simpson. Can you imagine giving up being King of England because you can't marry the woman you want to? I think it's the most romantic thing I ever heard! And Geoff's so interesting, Mama. We're both reading *Gone With the Wind*. Isn't that a coincidence? And Geoff says he's sure President Roosevelt will be reelected and—"

"And do you realize it's past midnight, young lady? When I gave you permission to stay out later than usual, I didn't think you'd take such advantage. I was worried to death about you."

"I'm sorry, Mama. I didn't mean to worry you. I thought you knew I was safe with Geoff."

"Lindsay, it isn't as though I don't trust you, but you're still young and naïve. I don't know that much about Geoffrey Murray, but men aren't to be trusted, even seventeen-year-old ones. You're not safe with any of them. It's high time you learned that. There isn't one who won't take advantage of a woman if he can, not just physically but emotionally as well. It seems to give them some kind of pleasure to lead us on and then make us miserable. I don't want that to happen to you."

Lindsay stared at her during this long, impassioned speech. Why was Mama taking on so? It had been nothing but a harmless date. True, it had been exciting. When Geoff kissed her good night in the taxi she'd felt a kind of stirring. But Geoff wasn't leading her on. And he'd never make her miserable. Mama was always so calm, so in control of her feelings. It wasn't like her to carry on this way simply because Lindsay was perhaps an hour later than she expected. It was something else, the girl realized. Something really awful had provoked this outburst of bitterness about men. Pauline even looked different, Lindsay saw now. Her face, usually so unlined and composed, seemed haggard and gray, and the slim fingers, always so graceful, locked and unlocked themselves as she spoke. "Mama, what is it? You can't be this upset just because I'm a little late getting home. Has something happened? Are you sick? What's wrong?"

Unexpectedly, Pauline buried her face in her hands and began to sob. Lindsay stood by helplessly, unsure of what to do. She couldn't remember ever seeing her mother cry, never had known her to go to pieces.

"Mama, don't!" she said finally. "Whatever's wrong can't be that bad. What can I do? Tell me what to do for you."

Slowly, Pauline raised her face and looked at her daughter. "There's nothing you can do, darling. I'm so ashamed of breaking down this way in front of you, but I just . . . I just . . . " Helplessly, she began to weep again. And then through her tears she said, "Lindsay, try to understand. I've asked your father for a divorce."

6

$\mathcal{I}$t was a ghastly business, this prelude to divorce. For once, Pauline and Howard Thresher threw discretion to the winds when it came to airing their differences in front of the family. There were no secrets from the children now, as they argued and accused and threatened. All the bitterness of nearly twenty-five years poured forth on both sides, as though their anger, so long disguised under a civilized veneer, could not be loudly or vehemently enough expressed. Lindsay, Gandy, and James were helpless to stop them and unable to escape the ugliness that pervaded the once seemingly serene household.

Howard, who did not want the divorce, refused to leave. "Not on your life!" he said. "If it's a question of desertion, I won't be the one who deserts."

"It won't be a question of desertion," Pauline shouted. "The grounds for divorce in this state are adultery, as you damned well know! And I'll have no trouble proving that!"

"Won't you now? You don't know very much about the law. The accused must be caught in the act, and you can't think I'd be stupid enough to allow that to happen to me!"

"Damn you, Howard Thresher! If I hadn't been such a fool I'd have had you followed! I could have caught you a thousand times in one of your little love nests!"

"But you didn't, did you?" For a moment his anger vanished and he became conciliatory, reasonable. "Pauline, I beg you not to do this. I've never deceived you. You've always known about that part of my life. It hasn't affected my feelings about my family for over twenty-five years. Why uproot us all now, just because—"

Pauline's fury was monumental. "Just because you finally went too far? Isn't that what you're saying?"

His rage returned to match her own. "Yes, that's what I'm saying! All right, I admit Joanne shouldn't have come here the other night. It wasn't my doing but it was an ugly scene and I've apologized for it a hundred times since. She was drunk and half-crazy because I'd broken off with her. Yes, it was disgusting! But God damn it, Pauline, it wasn't the first time some stupid woman has contacted you! Just because it was in person, rather than on the phone . . ."

It was Pauline's turn to calm down. "No, it certainly wasn't the first time one of those women has come to me. But there comes a point, Howard, where even someone as spineless as I must make a stand. I can't take any more of it. I can't take the humiliation and the frustration any longer. I couldn't divorce you before; for one thing, the children were too young. I swore to your son that I didn't stay with you because of them, but it wasn't true. I didn't want them growing up torn between their parents, so I stayed and took your insults. And I did believe I loved you more than I could ever love any other man. Enough to swallow my pride when you went elsewhere looking for satisfaction. But I was kidding myself. Your lack of consideration ate at me like some malignant growth, gnawing at my insides, making me sick with bitterness. When that woman . . . that Joanne . . . came here the other night, I was revolted. Not only by her but by you. It's absurd. I love you, Howard, but I can't respect you or myself. I'm forty-six years old. If there's ever a chance for me to make a new life, it's now."

"And what kind of new life do you think you'll make?" he asked. "You're not trained to earn a living. You've never worked a day in your life. And you won't get a penny from me if you walk out. Child support for Lindsay, okay. But nothing more, Pauline. Not one damned red cent if I have to fight you through every court in the land!"

She stared at him helplessly. "You can't mean that, Howard. You wouldn't be so cruel. What are twenty-five years of devotion worth? Am I not due some kind of severance pay for this unhappy employment?"

"You forget. I'm not firing you. You want to quit."

"Oh, my God! I can't believe this. I can't believe you want me to stay with you, knowing how I feel about this marriage."

He sensed he'd won, but he spoke unemotionally. "I've told you many times, Pauline, that I am content with my life the way it is. And that includes you and this household. I'll regret it if our relationship

57

changes, but I can't force you to feel affection for me. If you're as repelled by me as you say, I won't come near you. You needn't worry about that. We'll simply maintain the appearance of a solid family and go about our business as we have for years." He waited a moment and then said, "Shall we consider the matter closed? No more talk of divorce?"

Pauline shut her eyes to block out the sight of his superior smile. "I . . . I don't know. I'll have to think."

"Think all you like, my dear. I'll be very impressed if you come up with a way to live without me in anything remotely like the comfort you and Lindsay are used to."

When he left their bedroom, Pauline threw herself on the bed and stared hopelessly at the ceiling. He'd beaten her again. How could she support herself and Lindsay in any decent fashion? Alone, she might manage. To be at peace she could live in a furnished room, clerk in a department store, make ends meet somehow. But Lindsay was at an age that should be the most exciting time of her life. She should have pretty clothes and pocket money, should make a debut in two years and attract a solid husband of her own class. Without Howard, she'd have none of those things. She'd be "the poor one" in her crowd. If, indeed, her crowd didn't drop her entirely.

Maybe James could help, Pauline thought desperately. He had a good job. Perhaps the three of them . . .? No. Out of the question. He didn't earn enough to support his mother and sister. Nor should he be asked to. She'd never be one of those mothers who expected her children to take care of her. She'd messed up her own life. It was unfair to ask James to pay for it.

Her thoughts were interrupted by a light tap on the door and the entrance of her husband's mother.

"Pauline, can we talk or am I disturbing you?"

She sat up and tried to smile. "No, you're not disturbing me, Gandy. Come in."

The older woman lowered herself slowly onto the boudoir chair near the window. "I have something to say to you, Pauline. Something you may find very odd indeed." She was trembling slightly but her voice was firm. "I know what's going on between you and Howard."

Pauline grimaced. "I'm sure everyone in the house does. We've been behaving badly. I'm sorry. I know it's embarrassing for you and the children to hear us scream at each other." She paused. "It won't happen any more. I can't get a divorce."

"That's what I came to talk about. You see—"

"No need to worry any longer, dear. We're staying together."

Sara Thresher shook her head. "You don't understand what I'm trying to say. Hear me out, please. Howard came to me a few minutes ago and told me there'd be no divorce because he won't make any kind of settlement on you and you couldn't possibly support yourself and Lindsay."

"That's true. He holds all the cards, I'm afraid."

"That's outrageous! He doesn't own you. He's my son, my only child, but he's behaving like a tyrant. How dare he blackmail you into staying where you don't wish to be! Lord knows I don't want to see this family break up, but it would give me much greater pain to see you trapped here because of Howard's ruthlessness."

Pauline didn't answer. What was she driving at?

"I've come to make you an offer," Sara said, as though she could read her daughter-in-law's mind. "I'm a rich woman, Pauline. I can well afford to set up a household for all of us, and I'd like to. Howard's wrong about this. Dead wrong. You're entitled to a peaceful life and so is Lindsay, and if I can provide it, why shouldn't I?"

Pauline couldn't believe what she was hearing. "You'd do that? You'd take my side against Howard?"

"It isn't you against Howard; it's justice against tyranny, the way I see it. Oh, it hurts me to go against my own son, but I would any time he took unfair advantage. If you like, we'll find an apartment together, with Lindsay. James, too, if he wishes it, though I imagine at his age he'll welcome the opportunity to go out on his own. I'll even be glad to give you money to go to Reno for six weeks, since that's the only way you can get a divorce."

Pauline was stunned. "I . . . I don't know what to say. You're a re-markable woman, Gandy. An extraordinary human being."

Sara shook her head. "Not really. I love Howard; he's my flesh and blood. But I see in him all the terrible things I saw in his father. I never had your courage, my dear. I never could bring myself to leave Mortimer even though he crushed me every day of my life, the way Howard does you. My generation didn't take kindly to divorce, and I never had enough backbone to go against society. But I lived in hell for nearly forty years with Mortimer Thresher, and, son or no son, I don't wish the same for you."

Pauline was still in a state of disbelief. "But Howard will be so angry with you if you do this!"

"Let him," Sara said tartly. "As my mother used to say, 'If he gets mad he'll just have to get glad.' I'm not afraid of Howard or his temper. And I have every right to do anything I please with my money. Most of it was mine even when I was married. My family left me well off. And Howard inherited from his father, so I'm not depriving him. If I choose to spend what I have on my daughter-in-law and my grandchildren while I'm alive, that's a darned sight better than letting them be miserable while they wait for me to die."

Pauline was half laughing, half crying. "How can I thank you? How can I ever thank you for what you're doing?"

"You don't have to. In a way it's selfish. As though I'm finally paying back Mortimer for all he put me through. I like that feeling, Pauline. It makes me truly independent for the first time in my life."

On her nineteenth birthday, in 1939, Lindsay was a sophomore at Vassar and a raving beauty. Popular and sought-after, she'd made her debut the previous Christmas and been "formally introduced" to society and its most eligible young men. Not that she was interested in any of them. She'd been engaged to Geoffrey Murray for nearly a year, though Pauline refused to allow them to make it official. Privately, Pauline despaired of her chances of getting Lindsay to stay in school the full four years. Knowing her strong-willed daughter, she was sure Lindsay would eventually rebel and insist on leaving Vassar and marrying Geoff. But not quite yet. Her fiancé was completing his own education and, being a sensible boy, so far was willing to wait until he could properly support a wife.

How changed everything was, Pauline thought. It was nearly three years since she got her decree in Reno and returned to the Park Avenue apartment she shared with Lindsay and Gandy. True to that lady's predictions, James had decided not to come with them. He'd taken a small apartment of his own in the East Fifties and seemed thoroughly content with his bachelor life. Too content for my taste, Pauline mused. At twenty-seven, James showed no inclination toward marriage. Sometimes, guiltily, his mother allowed herself to wonder if he could possibly be . . . no. She quickly dismissed the thought. James was too interested in girls. It seemed as though he had a new one every week. There was nothing effeminate about her son. His reluctance to marry, she feared, stemmed from his exposure to her own unhappy experience. The thought made her sad. She was even truly sorry that her son despised his father and had left the bank almost as soon as she'd left Howard. She'd begged him not to, but he wouldn't listen.

"I don't want to be within spitting distance of him, because I just might do that. Go on working for him? Forget it. I don't want to even know he exists, much less have to see him every day."

"You're wrong, James," she'd said. "I'm touched by your loyalty, but I don't want you or Lindsay to take sides in this. It has nothing to do with you or your sister. Your father loves both of you very much. Our troubles are between the two of us. It pains me to see you bitter on my behalf."

"It isn't only your behalf. He represents everything I despise about the so-called upper class. I couldn't stand him if I met him casually. Why should I like him because we happen to be related?"

"He's your father, James. He gave you life."

"That's easy enough to do. Am I supposed to be grateful?" James smiled. "Gandy makes more sense than any of us. There's an example of judging people for what they are, not being blinded to their faults because you share the same blood."

There was no denying that, Pauline admitted. Despite Howard's initial shock and rage when his mother told him her plans, Sara had stood firm. It must grieve her that her only son does not even speak to her now, Pauline thought, but she never discusses it. What a fantastic woman: at sixty-nine, energetic, uncomplaining, endlessly generous with her understanding as well as her money. There were times when Pauline felt guilty about letting Gandy support her and Lindsay. Howard's ridiculously small contribution toward Lindsay's support didn't even pay her college tuition. He'd contested the divorce, as he said he would, and as a result she, "the deserter," had come off in bad shape financially.

"Never mind," Sara said. "There's plenty for all of us. I'll never outlive my money, nor will you and the children have to worry when I'm gone."

"It seems wrong, though," Pauline had worried. "I mean, I feel closer to you than I ever did to my own mother, but still—"

"Pauline, you are the daughter I always wanted. I couldn't feel

61

more for you if I'd given birth to you." Her eyes misted. "I never loved Howard as I love you. I suppose that's wrong of me. Unnatural. But it's the truth. You can bear a child and really never know him. Thank the Lord you never had that experience."

Pauline smiled at her affectionately. "I wonder what idiot started all those terrible jokes about mothers-in-law. He should have known you. The only people more devoted than I am to you are your grandchildren. They worship you. If I were the envious type, I'd be jealous."

"They're nice young people. And they have more than enough love for both of us."

Yes, they are nice people, Pauline thought. Totally different in personality, though: Lindsay so outgoing, so bubbly, eager for life, love, and marriage; James so deep and thoughtful despite his man-about-town ways.

With mixed emotions, Pauline accepted Lindsay's decision to continue seeing Howard. Though she knew the facts, including how shockingly little he contributed to her well-being, his daughter did not bear the outward malice toward him that James did. When it comes to their fathers, girls are different, Pauline supposed. I never knew mine. Never knew either of my parents; they died together in a railroad accident when I was five. But I suppose if they'd lived, I'd have had the same pull toward my father that Lindsay has toward hers.

She remembered when Carl Frampton died and Lindsay had clung to Howard for weeks thereafter, as though she feared something would take him from her. Even when the divorce happened, though Lindsay supported her mother's decision, there seemed to be a lingering sadness in her, a wish, reluctant but real, that she didn't have to lose her father. When she was home from school, she saw Howard once or twice a week, for lunch or dinner, and reported on him when she returned. Pauline did not discourage these bulletins. She was glad Lindsay didn't hate her father. And, she admitted to herself, she was curious to know how he was. After over twenty-five years of living with a man, you didn't suddenly lose all interest in him, even if you were happy to be free.

Howard lived in their same Fifth Avenue apartment, with a housekeeper to see to his needs. In the beginning, Pauline had been sure Howard would remarry quickly and she'd been amazed that he still had not. He was the kind of man who needed a wife for the amenities a housekeeper could not provide. To him, "wife" was synonymous with "hostess." She'd felt sure that Howard would quickly find someone to preside at his dinner parties, be gracious to his business contacts, make the proper social engagements, and keep track of invitations and Christmas card lists. Her own analysis made her smile. What a poor opinion she had of her own role. But it was accurate. The only other thing she'd done that was important to Howard was to give him children.

Ashamed of her curiosity, she actually encouraged Lindsay to talk about Howard after her visits.

"How is your father? Is he well?"

"He seems fine, Mama. He went to San Francisco last month, to a banker's convention, and said he had a very good time. He's finally having the apartment redecorated, by the way. It's going to be ultra-modern, he says. Very chrome and leather."

"Oh?"

"I teased him about turning it into a typical bachelor's place, but he said no, he just wanted a change from what he'd lived with all his life. I must say, it's about time he did something with it. When Gandy took out all her things the place became a barn. I don't know how he's lived in it for three years."

"I'm sure he doesn't spend very much time at home." There was an implied nastiness in Pauline's comment and Lindsay caught it.

"No, he doesn't. He has a cook, of course, but he says he takes most of his meals out. And, of course, he gets a lot of invitations. Any unmarried man does, I suppose. Especially one who's rich and attractive." Lindsay hesitated. "Sometimes I think he'd like to be back with you, Mama. I mean, he talks a lot about the way it used to be, the entertaining and the dinner parties you gave and what a marvelous homemaker you were. He seems to have—well, mellowed, I guess. He doesn't seem so bitter about the divorce any more."

"Very big of him, I'm sure."

Lindsay frowned. "Don't you miss him, Mama? Not even a little bit?"

Pauline considered her answer. "Miss him? Yes, Lindsay, I guess I do, in some ways. I miss having an escort. Unmarried middle-aged women are not beset with invitations, as you may have noticed. I miss being married in all the surface ways. The social acceptability of it is infinitely easier than being an extra woman. But I don't miss the unhappiness of wondering where your father is so many evenings. Or, worse still, why he felt it necessary to seek the company of other . . .

people. Peace of mind is a precious thing, my darling. And I do have that. It more than makes up for the things I don't have."

"He never meant to hurt you, Mama. Even James admits that. It's just the way he was. Maybe now . . . "

"No, dear. Men like your father don't change. I'm not nearly as sure as you are that he'd like his old life back. But even if he did, it wouldn't be any different. And I couldn't go through that again, not even for all those things I miss."

"But what about—well, sex? You're still a young woman. You haven't even been out on a date in three years."

How to answer that? Of course she missed sex. Howard was the only man she'd ever known. A virgin when they married, she'd remained faithful through all the years. Sometimes, in desperation, she'd thought of taking a lover, if only to spite Howard, to give him a taste of his own medicine. But she never could. Her standards wouldn't permit it. Her husband had been a good lover, though she ruefully admitted she had no basis of comparison. Miss his lovemaking? Yes, she missed it. It was lonely in the big double bed. Sometimes she had to force herself to remember how often, in the middle of his lovemaking, she had felt anger, knowing he enjoyed the same passions with other women. At those times, she hated him. But she never denied him, because she would also have been denying herself.

She realized Lindsay was waiting for an answer.

"I have normal desires," Pauline said simply. "Most women do. But that's not enough reason to consider a reconciliation with your father. Not," she repeated, "that I have the remotest idea he'd be interested."

"Do you think you'll get married again?"

Pauline smiled. "Nothing's impossible, my love. So far, I haven't seen a candidate, but I promise if I do, I'll give the matter very serious thought. Would you like me to remarry?"

"Yes. James once told me you still believe in it when it's right. I do too, Mama. I think it's the way people were intended to live."

Pauline glanced at her suspiciously. "But only when they're ready for it. I hope James added that. Marriage isn't for children. Look at me. I was not quite twenty-one when I married your father. Not nearly old enough to know what I was doing. And too young to have experienced the fun I should have had before I settled down."

"But everybody isn't the same," Lindsay said. "You regret marrying Papa, but that doesn't mean—"

"Wait. I didn't mean I regretted marrying your father. We had some wonderful times. My regret is that he is the way he is, and that I couldn't handle it. But marriage brought me a lot of good things too, Lindsay. A mother-in-law who's the most intelligent woman I've ever known. And two bright, loving, superior children. I want an even better marriage for you. One with more equality, perhaps. At least one based on mature judgment and respect for each other."

"Geoff and I have those things, Mama."

"Yes, I'm sure you do. All I ask is that you give them a chance to ripen, so that when you do marry it will be a well-considered act, as well as one of love."

Knowing what she was planning, Lindsay felt a terrible sense of guilt as she listened to her mother's reasonable request. It hadn't been easy to talk Geoff into the idea of eloping. It had required all the seductiveness of which she was capable. She had even played on his gentlemanly instincts.

"If you won't marry me," she said the night before, "then for God's sake take me to bed! I don't think you're human. Three years we've gone together and nothing more than some heavy smooching. I don't know about you, Geoff, but I want to make love. Real love. We're not children. Okay. You don't want to get married, but you must want me."

"Of course I want you, Lindsay! My God, I'm crazy with wanting you! But you're not some little tramp I can sleep with. You're the woman who's going to be my wife."

"Darling, it's 1939, not 1839. You won't hate yourself in the morning." She moved closer to him. "Geoffie. Sweetheart. Don't make us wait any longer."

"Dammit, Lindsay, no!" He moved away from her. "Maybe I've been brought up under some stupid, old-fashioned code of ethics, but I can't do that with you. We have to wait, honey. It won't be long. A couple more years, that's all, and then we'll have forever."

She lashed out at him. "A couple more years! That's fine for you, isn't it? You can have sex with some girl you don't care about. You can go to one of those houses. But what about me?" Before he could answer, she went on. "Women feel the same urges. All right. If you won't have me, I'll damned well find somebody who will!"

"Lindsay, you wouldn't!"

"Oh, wouldn't I? If you can do it, why can't I? Why are only men allowed to be experienced before marriage? And be unfaithful afterward, for that matter. I saw my own mother be patient and loyal while Papa went tomcatting all over town. Well, not for me. I have as much right as any man to sex, and if I can't have it with the man I love, I'll find it somewhere else. And I damned well won't wait two years!"

"You don't mean that. I know you don't. You love me."

"Of course I love you. I've loved you since I was a kid. And I'll marry you when you're ready. But meantime, I'm not going to go around being frustrated and nervous. And I'll tell you something else, Geoff Murray. Don't you ever dare, now or in the future, reproach me for it. Just remember you had the chance to be first, and you turned it down."

"Lindsay, don't. Don't say such things. I'd die thinking of you with someone else."

"Well then?"

He sighed. "I won't let you do something you'll regret. Something we'll both regret." There was a long pause. "We're being foolish, Lindsay, but if this is what you want, we'll do it. We'll get married."

"You don't have to. Marry me, I mean. We could—"

"No. You're crazy and impossible, but I love you. If you won't wait two years, if this is so important to you—"

"It is, darling. Because I love you so much. Because I can't stand not being close to you."

"Your mother . . ."

" . . . will have a fit," Lindsay finished for him. "I know. She plans a big wedding with all the trimmings. And like you, she plans it in the future. I'm sorry about that. I hate to make her unhappy. But she'd be unhappier if I started sleeping around."

He made one last effort to dissuade her. "Lindsay, there's more to life than sex. It's not something to base a marriage on."

"But we're not really basing it on that. We plan to marry. We're in love. All we're doing is pushing the date up a little."

Listening now to her mother's gentle, loving voice, Lindsay felt a moment of remorse. Pauline would be hurt. By this time tomorrow night she'd have a telegram from Elkton, Maryland, saying Lindsay

66

and Geoff were married. I have to, Mama, she said silently. He's the only man I want, and I can't wait forever.

"For God's sake!" James said over the phone. "You're kidding! She's crazy, that kid. They're both in school. How the hell do they expect to live?"

"I don't know." Pauline looked again at the telegram. "They just couldn't wait. I'm not all that surprised, James, though I hoped against hope Geoff would be the levelheaded one. I know Lindsay's much more impetuous, but I was counting on Geoff not to be foolish."

"Well," her son said lamely, "at least she picked a nice guy."

"Yes. There's that to be thankful for. I suppose I have to call your father. Somebody should tell him."

"If you want me to do it, I will."

"No. I think he should hear it from me. She's his daughter too."

"What did Gandy say?"

"She's disappointed, as I am. Marriage is hard enough, without starting out with so many problems. But what can we do, James?"

"Nothing. Make the best of it. I hope they'll both finish school."

"I hope so too. But I don't quite see how they can."

"Other kids do. They stand being separated during the school year."

Pauline smiled without happiness. "You don't know your sister."

Her hands were clammy as she dialed her old phone number. Except for a civil exchange at Lindsay's debut, it had been three years since she'd spoken to Howard. She hadn't even passed him on the street or run into him in a restaurant. Not that she often dined out, but she was glad she hadn't seen him at table with some other woman. Absurd of her, but she'd hate having to literally face what she already knew: that her husband thrived on the admiration of a pretty girl. Correction: ex-husband. Strange, she still couldn't think of him that way. She still felt married. Worse, she still loved him. Their situation had finally become unbearable, but there were many times, many lonely hours, when she regretted the divorce. Principles! she thought bitterly at those moments. Principles seemed less important from this distance. She'd acted in anger, in outrage, the culmination of years of hurt pride. And what was her return? A triumph of virtue and an abyss of loneliness. She'd gladly go back to her old life, she admitted to herself, if there were any way to do so with dignity. But she couldn't humble herself to this man. Not, she thought realistically, that Howard might even be inclined toward a reconciliation. He probably was enjoying his freedom. And why not?

A strange voice answered the phone.

"Mr. Thresher's residence."

"Is he there, please?"

"Who's calling?"

Pauline almost whispered, Mrs. Thresher. And then, realizing he might think it was Gandy, she added, "Mrs. Howard Thresher."

"One moment, please."

There was a long pause before Howard said, "Pauline?"

"Yes. How are you?"

"Very well. And you?"

"Fine. That is, personally fine. I'm calling about Lindsay."

She heard the instant note of alarm. "Lindsay? What's happened to Lindsay? Is she sick? Hurt?"

"No, no. She's all right. I just received a telegram from her. She and Geoffrey Murray were married in Elkton last night."

There was a moment of silence. "Eloped? Those kids ran off and got married without telling us?"

Strange how, even though it meant nothing, Pauline warmed to the use of the plural pronoun: "us." As though they were still a family. Stop it! she admonished herself. Stop being a damned sentimental fool.

"Yes," she said. "I'm afraid they did."

Howard exploded. "My God, how could you let this happen? Have you no control over that child? Do you give her no supervision? What the hell kind of mother are you?"

All the romantic daydreams disappeared. He was what he always was: arrogant and accusatory. Impossible. How dare he accuse her of being a negligent mother? She didn't attempt to hide her anger.

"You seem to forget she's nineteen years old! She's not a baby who can be watched day and night, she's a young woman with a mind of her own. Very much your daughter, I'd say, hell-bent on having her own way no matter whom she may hurt in the process!"

"Don't give me that! It was your duty to look after her. If nothing else, I'd have thought you'd make sure she didn't make the same mistake you think you did!"

"I don't think she did," Pauline said furiously. "Geoffrey is a thoughtful, loyal young man who'll care about her feelings. He won't humiliate her or concentrate only on his own pleasure!"

"Goddammit, Pauline, don't start that again! Don't drag all your grievances into this. Our marriage has nothing to do with this one!"

"Hasn't it? Do you think if Lindsay still had her own father at home she would have been in such a hurry to replace him with another man she could cling to?"

"Oh, for Christ's sake! Don't talk such rot! You've always blamed me for everything. You're such a saint you even managed to get my own mother on your side."

It's all so pointless, so fruitless, Pauline thought. Accusations and counter-accusations and what difference does it make now? She managed to answer him calmly.

"You're right about one thing: our differences don't matter any more. That's ancient history. I simply thought you should know about Lindsay. There really isn't anything more to say."

"Wait! How will they manage? Where are they going to live?"

"I'm sure I don't know, Howard. And I don't really consider it my responsibility. Perhaps you'd like to take it on."

He wanted to throttle her. Dammit, she must have seen this coming. Why did she wait to warn him until it was too late? I could have talked to Lindsay, he thought, if I'd had any idea what was in her mind. I'd have told her how precious these years are, how foolish to tie herself down before she'd had time to enjoy. As for that young fool Geoffrey Murray, I'd have pounded some sense into his head. College boy! What does he know about taking care of a wife? Probably so sex-crazy he talked Lindsay into marrying him, knowing he couldn't have her any other way.

"Have Lindsay call me when she returns," he said gruffly.

"Of course. She won't have to be told to do that. She still adores you, Howard. I'm sure you must find great satisfaction in that."

Pauline gently hung up.

For a moment she sat staring at the phone. She'd lied when she said she felt no responsibility. Of course she did. She would, the longest day she lived. For if she blamed this marriage on Lindsay's losing her father, she also had to face the fact that she was the one who took her away from him.

7

*S*nuggled against her new husband in the big double bed, Lindsay
had never been so happy. Geoff was wonderful. Sex was fabulous. Even
more so than she'd imagined. She remembered last night, her wedding
night. On the way to Elkton, she'd begun to have doubts. Geoff looked
so serious, almost unhappy, as though he resented the choice she'd
dared give him. Maybe I'm wrong, Lindsay had thought as they drove
through the gathering darkness. Maybe he'll regret this, even come to
resent me.

And the little ceremony had been so tawdry. The Justice of the
Peace had bad breath and a two-day stubble of beard, and his yawning
wife, their witness, seemed half asleep during the quick ritual that united the young people.

But later, when they arrived in Washington and checked into the
Shoreham, everything was perfect. Geoff held her close and told her
how much he loved her, swearing he'd try never to give her a moment's
unhappiness. And she'd promised the same to him, secure once more in
the knowledge of belonging to a strong, handsome man. This was better
than being Papa's little girl. There was the same sense of well-being,
with the delicious addition of physical gratification beyond her wildest
dreams. I was made for this, Lindsay thought. Made to be loved passionately and respond with such intensity that for moments I don't
know who or where I am. The memory of those hours stirred her, and
she leaned over and kissed Geoff awake. He reached for her, and again
Lindsay knew the joy of being a seductive woman.

Only much later, over their room-service breakfast, did Geoff re-
vert to his serious, troubled self.

"We have to make some plans," he said.

"Yes, darling. Anything you say."

He grinned at her. "What a nice, obedient wife! Where is that demented, headstrong creature who shanghaied me?"

"Enjoying her captive, what else?" Lindsay smiled contentedly. "Note those feathers around my mouth, please. I am the cat who ate the canary. Oh, Geoff, I'm so happy! Isn't marriage the greatest?"

"Speaking as the voice of experience, I'd say you're right. Twelve hours and I'm not tired of you yet."

"You'll never be tired of me. I won't give you a chance to be."

"How are you going to manage that, my love? You know what the next two years will be. Both of us in school, seeing each other on weekends and holidays. It won't be easy, Lind. I'm not sorry we did it. Don't misunderstand me. But we have to be realistic about the way we're going to live. My family won't support us, and neither will yours. It'll be like having a long engagement, except that when we're together we'll really be together. Like last night." A dreamy look came over his face. "You were wonderful, sweetheart. Virgins aren't expected to be so adaptable. I think you must have been a courtesan in a previous life. Were you? Were you Madame Pompadour, maybe? Or Scarlett O'Hara? Yes, you were always Scarlett; even at sixteen."

She scarcely heard the last part of what he was saying.

"Not live together? What are you talking about?"

"Honey, we can't set up housekeeping at this point. I assumed you knew that. I have to finish school, and so do you."

"*You* have to, but I certainly don't. What am I going to do with a college education? I'm a married woman. That's the only career I want."

"Wrong, babe. That might be all very well for a while, but what about later? What happens when our children are grown and you have nothing but time on your hands? You might want to work one day, and you'll have no qualifications, no experience, and no formal education."

Lindsay looked at him in astonishment. "That could be twenty years from now! Who can plan what they'll do when they're forty?"

"If your mother had, she might be a happier woman today."

"That's not fair! That's rotten of you, Geoffrey Murray! What are you trying to tell me: that we'll get a divorce some day?"

He put his arms around her. "Of course not, sweetheart. I plan to be with you the rest of my life. But anything can happen. I might die—"

71

"Stop that! I don't want to hear such talk!"

"All right," Geoff said. "Forget the future. We have to be practical now, Lind. If you quit school and we take an apartment off campus, how are we going to pay for it? As I said, I don't think we can count on our families, and frankly I really wouldn't want to."

"I can get a job."

"Doing what?"

"How do I know? Working in a shop, maybe. Or on a newspaper. You know I always wanted to be a writer. I can write in the evenings while you're studying. It'll be wonderful, both of us at our desks at night, doing something useful. Maybe I'll turn out a best-seller and make us rich right away." She was all smiles and confidence again. "You'll see, darling. It will be fun."

Geoffrey shook his head. She was such a child. A woman in body but so young emotionally. He was only twenty, just a year older than his bride, but in terms of maturity she could have been his adored, unrealistic daughter. It was a mistake, he thought sadly. Much as I love her, much as I want her, I should never have agreed to this marriage. We're not ready, either of us.

"Lindsay, love, we have to be practical. You don't know the first thing about housework or cooking, and I think you'd hate it if you did. But even if you had those skills, how could you possibly work, write at night, and keep a house clean, shop for food, and prepare it?"

"Wouldn't you help?"

"Of course I'd help. As much as I could. But Harvard is tough. With classes all day and assignments at night, where would I find time to be useful around the house? No, we just can't do that now," he said again. "We can stay with your folks or mine when we're not in school. We can even have weekends in Boston. But we can't afford to take an apartment, and we couldn't maintain it even if we found the rent money somewhere."

Lindsay's eyes filled with tears. "You're being beastly. You're sorry you married me, aren't you? Why did you, if you didn't intend us to live together?"

He bit his tongue. He wanted to remind her that she hadn't given him much choice. It was marriage or a sneaky coupling with him. Or, worse still, with someone else. He'd thought he was doing the right thing for her. Perhaps he'd been wrong. Perhaps it would have been better for them to have slept together. At least Lindsay wouldn't have

72

expected to live with him. It was 1939. Nice people didn't share the same roof unless they were married. But, Geoff thought, nice guys also didn't seduce the girl they planned to marry. Or allow her to do the seducing. But he said none of this. Instead, he held her even closer and said, "Baby, I love you. I wanted to marry you. You don't really doubt that, do you?"

The muffled voice against his shoulder said softly, "No. I don't doubt it. But I can't be separated from you now. Please, please let's try it my way. I'm sure Gandy will help us if we can't make it on our own."

He sighed. "Hasn't Gandy done enough for you already, sweetheart?"

"She doesn't mind. She told Mama she'd rather spend her money on us now than leave it to us. And Papa will help too." Again she brightened, looking up at him with a smile. "It's just temporary, anyway. Until you finish school and get a job. Then we'll pay them back. Oh, please say yes, darling." She began to caress him lovingly. "You don't want to be without me, do you?"

Geoff felt excitement return. Dammit, he was incapable of refusing her anything when their bodies were pressed together. It was crazy. However they tried to solve it, it was crazy. But how could he say no?

"All right," he said. "We'll work something out. God knows what, but we'll find that out when we get back to New York."

Adele and Lindsay faced each other over a small luncheon table in the Palm Court of the Plaza Hotel.

"All right," Adele said, "now tell me everything."

Lindsay grinned wickedly. "Everything?"

Her friend made a face. "You know what I mean. Tell me about your wedding. I'm still mad at you, you know. You always promised I could be maid of honor."

"I know, Del. You would have been if things had worked out differently. But we just couldn't wait. Mama and Papa and Geoff's parents would never have agreed to our getting married while we were still in school, so we had to do it this way." Lindsay laughed. "It wasn't very glamorous, I can tell you that. The ceremony, I mean." She described the dreary little house in Elkton and the participants. "It was exactly like the movies. Dreadful! But after that—well, it was wonderful. Geoff is more romantic than Clark Gable."

"A regular Rhett Butler," Adele said teasingly. "Honestly, Lind, you're something. How old were you when you told me you were going to marry Geoff? Thirteen? Fourteen?"

"Fourteen. I knew it then and I've never doubted it for five years. And I was right. That's the way you have to look at things. Make up your mind what you want and stick with it until you get it." She looked searchingly at her companion. "What do you want, Del? What have you made up your mind to do?"

"I don't know. Nothing special. Teach, maybe. I love children."

"So get married and have a flock of your own."

Adele smiled. "You make it all sound so simple. But there's nobody I want to marry now. Probably not ever."

"That's what you said when I first told you about Geoff. You mean you still feel that way?"

The other girl nodded. "More so."

"Things still bad at home?"

"Bad? No, not really. Mother and Lucius still fight like cats and dogs, but I'm not around that much. Thank God for school. And, as you well know, when I'm home I keep busy with other things: the nurse's aide stuff at Lenox Hill and the special summer courses at Columbia. I'm too busy to think much about guys."

Lindsay did know all that. She and Adele remained as close as ever, confidantes and secret-keepers as they'd been all their lives. Adele was the only one Lindsay told before she and Geoff eloped. Her friend had not tried to dissuade her. She knew better. All she'd said was "You're sure this is the right thing, Lind? It's an awfully big step. Marriage is a terrible responsibility." Lindsay had assured her that she knew exactly what she was doing, and Adele had said nothing more than "You know I wish you all the happiness in the world. Both of you."

I wish Adele could find happiness, Lindsay thought now. She's such a terrific girl. It's not natural that she doesn't want to fall in love. Her mother's life has soured her. Maybe she blames Mrs. Tamlin for Mr. Frampton's death somehow. Certainly she blames her for marrying that awful Lucius. But it's pointless to be so against marriage for yourself because of your parents' failures. It would have been easier for me to feel that way. Mama's divorcing Papa because of his unfaithfulness should have left a worse taste in my mouth than anything that hap-

pened to Adele. Thank God it didn't. I'm me. I'm different. I won't repeat the mistakes I saw around me when I was growing up.

"You'll start thinking about men the minute you find the right
one," Lindsay said. "It's just taken longer for you. Hell, like we said,
I've had my mind made up for years."

"Sure. You're probably right. Don't worry about it. I don't. Now
tell me, are you honestly going to have an apartment in Boston? I can't
believe your folks let you quit school."

"They weren't thrilled, but what could they do? I told them I
wouldn't be separated from Geoff. I'd rather scrub floors for the next
two years than be away from him. I'm going to get some kind of job,
and with Geoff's allowance and mine, we'll make it. It won't be Mil-
lionaire's Row, but we'll find a decent place, and at least we'll be together."

"It's going to be quite a change."

"Don't I know it! And haven't Mama and Papa and Gandy reminded me of it every hour on the hour for the past two days! But it's
what I want, Del."

And you always get what you want, Adele thought. What a fortunate, uncomplicated creature you are, Lindsay Thresher Murray. So
certain life will be good to you. So free of questions about your worthiness. Not that you're unworthy. But what will you do if one day things
don't fall into place exactly as you expect them to?

"What did James say about you and Geoff?"

Lindsay shrugged. "I don't understand James these days. I adore
him, but I don't know what he cares about. He said I was a bloody
spoiled brat, of course, just what I'd expect him to say. And I said he
was the same. Twenty-seven and not even thinking of settling down.
Whoever heard of such a thing? If he thinks I've made Mama unhappy,
he should look at what his own peculiar life-style does to her."

"Peculiar life-style? In what way?"

"Oh, I don't know. He just doesn't seem to give much of a damn
about anything. Mama doesn't know it, but he's living with some girl.
The only reason I know is that I dropped by his apartment one day a
couple of months ago and there she was. I asked James later whether he
was going to marry her and he just laughed and said not a chance. He
said if he had Papa's genes he sure wasn't going to make some woman
suffer for them." Lindsay looked sad. "He's still so bitter about Papa.

75

It's made him kind of—I don't know, reckless. You know, Del, I used to hope you and James would fall in love, but now I'm glad you didn't." She hesitated. "I know it sounds nutty, but I have a terrible feeling about him. Like—like he doesn't care whether he lives or dies."

Adele looked at her curiously. "What an odd thing to say, Lindsay. Just because he doesn't want to get married?"

"It isn't only that. It's like an undercurrent in him, a kind of to-hell-with-it attitude. Oh, he's sweet and darling to Mama and Gandy and me, but underneath it's as though he has no purpose and no hope." Lindsay laughed. "I do sound certifiable, don't I? It's only that I really love him very much. We've always been so close. And in the last few years I've felt I couldn't reach him at all."

If Lindsay had had any idea of the real state of James's mind, she'd have been more than vaguely troubled. The sensitive boy had grown into a thoughtful and deeply concerned man, convinced that the world was heading toward a catastrophe greater than any it had ever known. With growing alarm he had read everything he could find about the now-certain menace of Nazi Germany, convinced it was only a matter of time before America found itself involved. He was amazed that people took so lightly the recall of the U.S. and German ambassadors in 1938. And when the real war in Europe began the following year, he couldn't believe most people seemed to think it was "their business over there."

He tried to discuss it with his mother, whom he considered a highly aware woman. But even Pauline would not entertain the idea of her country's involvement.

"We did that before, James," she said. "We sent our boys overseas to fight in 1917. It was a terrible time. We'll never do it again. Let England and France fight their own battles. There's an ocean between us."

He was amazed. "Mama, you're much too intelligent to believe that! My God, Pan Am is flying a regular schedule to Europe these days. And you've read what's going on. Barrage balloons over London. Their women and children evacuated. Hitler sweeping everything in front of him. We can't let that go on, not if we're a civilized nation!"

"We also can't fight the world's battles, James. I remember the last war. You don't. It was heartbreaking. So many killed. So many hideously wounded, disabled for life. No. The American people won't let that happen again."

"It didn't really come close to you, Mama. Papa didn't have to go because he was a married man with a child—me." James stopped suddenly. "I see," he said gently. "You're afraid for Geoff and me, aren't you?"

Pauline's lips trembled. "Yes. I'm afraid for you. And for all the young men. And for their wives and mothers and sweethearts. Oh, I'm not a fool, James. I know it's probably going to happen. And if it does, God help us all. I only pray it will be over before this family gets involved. To see them take you and Geoffrey . . ." Her voice trailed off.

"Geoff's married and still in school. He'd be deferred. Lindsay may even be pregnant by then."

His mother didn't answer. It was the one thing she'd prayed would not happen. Lindsay and Geoff had a hard enough time as it was, with his being in school and her working in a dress shop in Cambridge and trying to keep their minuscule apartment in order. Yet they seemed happy enough. And proud, too. Gandy wanted to do more, to send money for a daily maid, even to subsidize them so Lindsay wouldn't have to work. But they'd refused. Lindsay agreed to take the same allowance she'd had in school, but nothing more. Pauline guessed her daughter might well have accepted her grandmother's generosity, but Geoffrey was adamant.

"We made our decision, Gandy, and we'll live with it. Thank you. You're more than generous. But Lindsay knew we'd have to struggle. She's doing okay. We both are."

Pauline worried about them, wished they'd waited, but resigned herself to the fact that her daughter had chosen a strong and reliable man. Pregnancy was the only thing she dreaded. Young and resilient as they were, they couldn't handle their new life and a baby as well. But after this chilling talk with James, she'd welcome even that news if it kept Geoffrey from being drafted.

"Maybe the worst won't happen," Pauline said. "President Roosevelt says—"

"Mama." James's voice was reproachful. "You don't believe that. You know it's only a question of time. A year, two years, maybe sooner if it looks as though England can't hold out." He hesitated. "I . . . I hate to do this to you, but I've made a decision. I'm single and eligible and I don't want to be a draftee. I'm going to Canada and enlist in the Royal Air Force. They're taking volunteers."

"James, no! You can't! You mustn't! Please, I beg you. Why must

77

you be so foolish? The war may not come to us. Or if it does, perhaps you won't be called. You're twenty-eight already. When and if it happens, they may take only younger men." Pauline rushed on, pleading. "At the worst, if we get into it, you can go to Officers' Training School and get a commission. Maybe you'd be assigned to Washington—"

"Mama, I can't wait. I can't keep on at my stupid, unimportant job and do nothing about the world's coming to an end. I'm the kind of person who *should* go, Mama. I have no wife, not even a serious sweetheart. No one to leave behind and worry about. Or have them worry about me."

Pauline looked stricken. "You have me, James. You're my only son."

"I know. I know how this must seem to you. I'd give anything not to worry you, Mama, but I think you'd want me to do what's right. It's not a hasty decision. I've been thinking about it for a long time. And I'm going to be okay. I'll come home with a chestful of ribbons and a British accent. That should wow the girls, don't you think?"

"Don't. Don't try to make jokes." Pauline took a deep breath. "When do you plan to go?"

"In about two weeks. I've told them at the office. I just have to clear up a few things, sublet my apartment, stuff like that. And I thought I'd run up and see Lindsay and Geoff. You and Gandy and I will have some fun before I go. Maybe I can get tickets to *The Man Who Came to Dinner*. And I'll buy you some of those new nylon stockings as a going-away present. How about that?"

She tried to hold back the tears. "Fine. Just fine. James, are you planning to see your father?"

"No, Mama. What's the point? I haven't spoken to him in nearly four years."

"He is your father, nonetheless. Don't you think you owe him the chance to say good-bye?"

"I think I owe him nothing. I can't be such a hypocrite as to stage a big tearful farewell, for God's sake." He looked at her and smiled. "Oh, darling mother-of-mine, are you secretly hoping that the influential Howard Thresher will convince me to wait for a nice juicy job in Washington later?"

Pauline blushed. It had crossed her mind that Howard might talk some sense into James, man to man. She should have known better.

The last person in the world to influence her son in any way was his father.

If only he'd married when I wanted him to, Pauline thought, he'd have children by now. Dependents to keep him safe at home where he belongs. Why was he being so headstrong about this? Idealism was strong motivation, she supposed. Certainly her James wasn't a violent man. She couldn't remember his ever even being in a fight. Only that once, years ago, when the boys at school had told him about his father. That awful day when his respect for Howard was destroyed forever.

When James left the apartment, Pauline sat for a long time staring sightlessly out the window at the rooftops of New York. Gradually I'm losing everything, she thought. First Howard. Now the children. Soon it will be just Gandy and me, and how long can I hope to have her? She's seventy. One never knew from day to day. . . .

At last, impatiently, she pulled herself together. She would not indulge in this disgusting self-pity. She'd made a choice about her marriage. As for James and Lindsay, they were adults and free to choose their own lives without the burden of responsibility toward her. Gandy will live a long time, Pauline told herself. Seventy was no age these days, especially when one had good health and an alert, interested mind. Like a dog shaking drops of water off its coat, Pauline tried to brush off her depression. She had to believe everything would be all right. And though she was not a religious woman, she'd pray every day for the happiness of her daughter and the safety of her son.

8

*S*he'd have bitten off her tongue rather than confess it, but there were times in the first year when Lindsay wished she hadn't been so hell-bent on getting married. Not that Geoff wasn't wonderful. The physical side of their marriage was perfect. Well, nearly perfect. Often Lindsay was so tired after a day in the shop, a rush to the grocery store, and then home to the little apartment to tidy up and cook dinner that all she wanted was to sink into bed with a book, read for a few minutes, and drop into an exhausted sleep while Geoff sat in the living room poring over his school assignments.

Sometimes Lindsay resented his "easy life." Very little had changed for him. Oh, he tried to help her with the housework, drying the dishes, doing some of the heavy chores on Sunday, the one day they were both home. But he knew less about cooking or keeping house than she did, so these dreary duties were mostly left to her.

She wished he weren't so damned proud, at her expense. She'd gladly have taken the extra money Gandy offered for a daily cleaning woman or even used it to make going out to dinner possible on a regular basis. But her husband would have none of it.

"I know it's hard on you, Lind, but we're not children. We can't keep depending on others. It's enough that we continue to take our allowances."

"A good thing we do!" she said. "If we had to live on what I earn, we'd starve. It's easy enough for you to be so high and mighty. You're not doing two jobs. You're not even doing *one.*"

He didn't answer, but his level look spoke volumes and Lindsay was ashamed.

"I know," she said. "I shouldn't kick. It was all my idea, but I honestly did think—"

He finished the sentence for her. "That your life would be exactly the same, only better. You'd be married to me, you wouldn't have to go to school any more, and people would still be waiting on you hand and foot."

"That's not fair! Nobody waited on me hand and foot."

"Come on, sweetheart. Did you ever cook a meal or dust a tabletop before? Did you have to watch every penny or, for that matter, have to earn it? Wasn't it great to buy whatever took your eye at Bergdorf Goodman? Hell, Lindsay, I could name a dozen things you're deprived of now. Don't think I don't feel terrible about them. And don't think I'm unaware of what a good sport you've been. But you should have thought of all that before. You knew me well enough to know I would never take charity."

"Charity? From a person's own family?"

"The source doesn't matter. It's still a handout. And the less obligated I feel, the happier I am."

He was right, of course. There was still time to have backed out even after they were married. She could have done what he wanted: stayed in school, been with him on holidays and weekends, had the luxuries she was used to without the work she despised. But that would have been being only half married. And Lindsay was never one for halfway measures. With all she missed, the fun, the freedom, the comforts, she was determined never to admit it. She loved Geoffrey and she loved being Mrs. Murray. Besides, it wasn't forever. One more year and he'd be out of school. When he got a good job everything would change. They'd get out of this dreary place and begin to live like civilized people.

"Darling, I'm sorry to be so rotten," she said. "I don't regret what we did. Not a minute of it. Besides, it's only another year and then everything will change. You'll be successful and we'll look back at all this and laugh."

"Don't count on everything's changing overnight, honey. I'll be a twenty-two-year-old college graduate with no business experience. I doubt anybody's going to give me a fifty-thousand-dollar-a-year job."

"Papa will help if we ask him."

"But we're not going to ask him. I don't want your father's help. I won't be hired because I'm somebody's son-in-law."

She lost her patience. "Why are you being so beastly? It's as though you want to suffer. And make me suffer along with you. I don't understand you! I can understand James refusing to have anything to do with Papa, though I find even that a little juvenile; he's angry on Mama's behalf. But what possible harm would it do if Papa made some contacts for you? Everybody uses contacts to get good jobs!"

"Not everybody. Some of us would like to get them on merit." His voice softened. "I know I sound like a stuffed shirt. Maybe I'm bending over backwards not to take advantage of your family: your father, your grandmother. But Lind, darling, I feel strongly about a man's responsibilities. It hurts me to see you working and partially supporting us, but I'd rather see us struggle for a while than expect other people to bail us out of a situation we walked into with our eyes wide open." He paused. "The only way I'd let you lean on your family is if I had to go away somewhere. Then I'd want you to go home and be safe."

"Go away? Where would you go?"

"Nowhere, probably. Not for a while, anyhow. Maybe never. But you remember what James said when he came to see us. He's convinced it's only a matter of time before we're at war. I'd have to go. They'd let me finish school, maybe. And I might not be called up immediately because I'm married. But at my age, and with a wife who wouldn't be without funds, I'd eventually be drafted."

She was stunned and then angry. "James is crazy! A damned, crazy romantic who thinks it's exciting to wear aviator wings and swagger around London! I keep up with things. It's America First. I've read those speeches Charles Lindbergh and other smart people are making. This country isn't going to war. It's ridiculous."

"I hope you're right, but I'm afraid I agree with James. Isolationism simply isn't possible in this day and age. Americans are funny people. As long as a war doesn't touch their own soil they think they can stay out of it. But let something happen to any part of this country and we'll be in it up to our eyeballs."

Lindsay set her chin stubbornly. "I don't want to talk about it. You and James. Men! I think they love playing soldier!"

Geoffrey shook his head. "No. I'd hate it. But if it was my duty—"

"Oh, damn your duty!" Suddenly she laughed. "Do you realize we're fighting, darling? And over something that will never happen? We must be nutty. How did we get so far from my once-pampered life to this absurd discussion of war? Hey, cheer up! I've made the best beef stew in the world and I have the blisters to prove it. I'm going to feed my wonderful, high-principled, stubborn husband, and then"—Lindsay looked at him invitingly—"then I'm going to make him forget there's any kind of imaginary dark cloud floating somewhere out there thousands of miles away."

Geoff smiled at her. She was still a girl. Still pretty little Lindsay Thresher who refused to face ugly things. He loved her intensely and prayed she was right about everything. But in his soul, he knew she wasn't.

Sara Thresher eyed her daughter-in-law speculatively across the breakfast table. Pauline looked terrible. She seemed to have aged ten years since James went away. His letters told them little, subject as they were to censorship, but the radio and newspapers told enough. Too much, the older woman thought. Like millions of others, she wept through the broadcast of Winston Churchill's "blood, toil, tears, and sweat" speech and sat frozen with terror as Ed Murrow described the London blitz, the nights of constant air raids and fire and death. She mourned the surrender of France and the occupation of her beloved Paris, that city of beauty and culture. Worst of all, because humanly and selfishly it came nearer home, she shivered at the news of the R.A.F. night bombing runs over Germany, knowing her grandson must be part of them, waiting every day, as Pauline did, for the letter that would say he was still unharmed. Chilling, too, was Congress's passing of the Selective Service Act to mobilize the U.S. military. It was coming close, terribly close. Geoffrey would graduate next June. Every night Sara sank to her knees beside her bed and prayed for the end of this madness, before this senseless war, started by a madman, could engulf them all.

The only bright spot—and a dubious one at that, Sara thought ruefully—was that even Howard seemed to mellow under the pall of anxiety that covered them all. James had not gone to see him before he left for Canada, but Pauline had called her ex-husband and told him. This time, as opposed to his brusqueness at the time of Lindsay's marriage, Howard had seemed genuinely moved, almost repentant. He'd asked if he could visit Pauline and his mother.

"I've been stubborn," he said on the phone. "I don't expect you to forgive me, Pauline, but perhaps we can be friends. It's been four years. Mother is getting on. I'd like to see her, if she'd let me."

Pauline had agreed to consult Gandy and get back to him, and the two women talked at length when Pauline reported Howard's surprising request.

"I didn't know what to say, Gandy. I wasn't sure how you felt."

Sara sighed. "I'm not sure myself. If it were any other man, knowing how he behaved toward you, I'd say without hesitation that I never wanted to set eyes on him again. He's been a terrible human being. Selfish. Vindictive. Arrogant. Those are not qualities I can tolerate in anyone, especially in my son." She looked at Pauline with a little twinkle. "I'll be truthful with you. I don't really like Howard. I know that's a terrible thing to say, but he was a self-centered child and a vain young man who was a carbon copy of his father. When I can be dispassionate about it, I admit that I never found him lovable in the least." Then she became serious. "But he's my son, for all that. It hurts me, this estrangement, in an emotional way, having nothing to do with logic. Flesh and blood. One can't escape their hold, I suppose, no matter how rational one tries to be. Yes, I guess I'd like to see him, Pauline. But more importantly, would *you?*"

Pauline smiled gently. "I don't mind, dear. It's been long enough not to hurt any more. It's odd how remote I can feel about the man with whom I lived for a quarter of a century. He's become almost a stranger to me. Some old acquaintance I haven't seen for a while. I don't mind if he visits, as long as you want it. I'd always want to see James, no matter what he did. It's the kind of thing mothers can't help."

So Howard had come for tea and had made a point thereafter of dropping in once a week to ask for news of James. He was in touch with Lindsay and troubled, as the women were, about her future.

"This damned war!" he fumed. "FDR is campaigning on promises to keep us out, but how can anybody in his right mind believe that? The country is booming with European orders for arms and war equipment, and Roosevelt still says we're neutral. Neutral! We're selling destroyers to Britain and God knows what else we're doing that nobody knows about. And what's more, he'll be elected again, mark my words. Wendell Willkie doesn't stand a chance. A third-term President for God's sake! What are we coming to?"

"You think they'll take Geoffrey into the army?" Pauline's question was rhetorical. Of course they'd take him. Poor Lindsay. She'd suffer the same anxiety about her husband that I feel for my son.

"Afraid they will," Howard said in answer to her question,

"though for the moment we're not sending young men into combat."

The three of them fell silent.

"I had a letter from James yesterday," Pauline finally said. "He's fine. He's been made a captain. Of course he doesn't say exactly where he is, but it must be quite near London. He seems to get there quite often and says it's incredible how calmly the English behave under this nightly hell."

"Damned fool. Why doesn't he stay out of there? As if it's not bad enough to be flying combat, he has to go where they're bombing the city. All very well for the British and their 'stiff upper lip' nonsense, but why does James have to behave like one of them?"

His mother managed to smile. "I do love the British. So civilized. So understated. I remember once, years ago, talking to an English friend of mine and saying that his people never seemed to get excited. Do you know what he said to me? He said, 'My dear Sara, the control you talk about, we've only had that since Cromwell. Before that we behaved like a nation of Italian tenors!' "

The others laughed. Trust Gandy to turn the conversation to a sane and comforting angle. For the thousandth time, Pauline thought how extraordinary she was. If only Howard had inherited some of her warmth and humor. He seemed more reasonable these days, but he was still Howard, always would be, she supposed. Last week as she walked to the door with him he'd asked her if she'd like to go out to dinner one night. Pauline had shaken her head.

"Thank you, but I think not. I'm not quite that sophisticated. Dining with one's ex-husband is a bit too Noel Coward for me."

He'd seemed surprised by her refusal. Typical, Pauline thought. I'm sure he thought I'd jump at the chance to be with him again.

"I hardly see anything improper about it," Howard said.

"Not improper. Possibly awkward. We wouldn't want to start tongues wagging after all this time, would we?"

Howard stared at her. She was positively enjoying this. I don't matter to her at all, he thought. Here I am, offering to take her out to dinner, and she's practically laughing at me. He felt unreasonably annoyed. Why should it bother him? God knows there were plenty of younger, prettier, more agreeable women. He'd only been making a gesture of kindness. She must be bored out of her mind living alone with an old lady.

"I doubt we'd start any gossip, Pauline," he said huffily. "People are well aware that I intend to remain happily unattached."

"I'm sure *many* people are aware of that." She seemed amused. "Particularly a great many women who must have expected you to re-marry long ago." She seemed unemotionally curious. "Frankly, I'm one of them. Why haven't you married again, Howard? Not that it's any of my business."

"You're right, Pauline. It is none of your business."

He departed hastily and walked for blocks, thinking about the first truly personal conversation they'd had in years, wondering why he had asked her out. For the same reason, you damned fool, that you go there every week, he answered himself. Of course you're concerned about James. Naturally, you like to see your mother. But it's Pauline who draws you there. You still haven't gotten over her. Maybe you'd like to marry her again. She was the perfect wife all those years: everything a man could want. If only she hadn't been so ridiculously middle-class about his habits. She'd spoiled one of the best marriages any two people ever had. And all because he occasionally saw some silly little fluff of a thing. Stupid. That's what she was: stupid. What in God's name would ever make him think he'd want back into *that* again?

Pauline, a half smile on her face, wandered into the living room when he left.

"Guess what, Gandy. Howard invited me out to dinner."

"Oh?"

"I thanked him politely and declined. Seeing him to talk about our children is one thing. Having dates with him is something else."

Sara nodded. "Except that he's still in love with you, Pauline."

"In love with me? No. I think not. Howard liked me as a wife. Perhaps he was even in love with me once, in his own peculiar way. But no more. I think his ego simply cannot handle the fact that I or anyone would leave him. I suspect he'd like to get me interested in him again only to prove that he could. Perhaps even to be the one who walks away this time. I may be doing him an injustice, but I can't help but feel he'd consider himself vindicated."

Sara looked at her affectionately. "I don't think you do him an in-justice. I think you're much smarter than I. You see through Howard much more clearly than his mother can. As you say it, I know you're right. Howard never could bear a loser, particularly if he was it. I'm truly glad you feel the way you do, Pauline. I know my attitude is shamefully unmaternal, but I'm glad you don't care about Howard any more."

Pauline nodded, but deep inside a nagging voice said, Don't you? Aren't you still in love with him? Didn't it take all the willpower you have to refuse his invitation, hoping, perhaps, it was the prelude to something more? Don't you wish, in fact, you still had a husband?

And the reluctant, silent, hopeless answer was yes. Dammit, yes.

Lindsay's twenty-first birthday and Geoffrey's graduation came within a week of each other in June 1941, and for everyone it was a time to rejoice, to put aside differences and feel happiness for the young couple.

Lindsay was ecstatic. Everyone she loved was coming to Boston: Mama, Papa, Gandy, and Adele. Geoff's parents too, of course. If only James were here, she thought sadly, it would be the happiest day of my life. She pretended to Pauline that there was no need to fret about him, but despite her simulated confidence, Lindsay worried every day about her brother, just as she secretly was frightened for her husband's future, though outwardly she continued to maintain that America would never go to war. Sometimes she even managed to believe it herself. She visualized, finally, the kind of married life she hoped for. She and Geoff would get a smart little apartment in New York. They'd finally be able to afford part-time household help and she could go back to doing the things she loved. She might even have time now to try her hand at some writing. She'd always wanted to, but there'd been no time or energy for that in the past two years.

Only one other thing marred her feeling of contentment: Geoff had accepted a job in a New York advertising agency, and a low-paying one at that. She'd been surprised and angry when he told her.

"An advertising agency! You must be kidding! I don't get it. You've been trained in business administration."

"Advertising *is* business, honey, big business. Sure, I have to start modestly. I'll only be a junior account executive, but there's a big future. I'll only make six thousand dollars a year to start, but—"

"Six thousand dollars!" Lindsay was horrified. "We can't live on that kind of money! It's not fair, Geoffrey. I want to live like civilized people. God knows we've had enough scrimping these past two years. I'd think you'd have a little consideration for me. You didn't even consult me before you took the damned job! That's unforgivable! It's my life too, you know. My future. The least you could have done would have been to discuss it with me!"

He nodded. "I know. That was wrong of me, but—well, hell, I knew you'd be against it, and it's something that really interests me. I know I can be a big success at it in time. It's a fascinating world, much more exciting than some stupid corporation where I'd just be one of a hundred faceless young guys going over profit-and-loss statements." He looked at her appealingly. "Please don't be mad, Lind. I know I should have consulted you. You're dead right about that. But I know you want me to be happy in my work. If I wasn't, you wouldn't be happy either."

She tried to calm down. "How on earth did you ever get such a job?"

"A guy in my class, his father owns Ford, Wheeler & Koch, one of the big agencies. They're looking for ambitious young college graduates. Even sent a guy up here to recruit."

"I see," Lindsay said coldly. "What was all that talk about not taking favors? Apparently it's all right to take them from anybody except my father."

"Dammit, Lindsay, it's not the same and you know it! These people were interviewing. I had no more advantage than a dozen other guys. Nobody pushed me or asked for special favors for me. I got the job because I had the right qualifications, not because I was somebody's relative!"

"And because you're a friend and classmate of the owner's son. I don't think there's much difference, Geoff."

He looked defeated. "Okay. If you hate the idea that much I won't take the damned job. I'll look for something else."

"And have you hate me because I kept you from doing what you want? I couldn't do that." Lindsay relented. "Oh, hell, honey, if this is what you have your heart set on, it isn't the end of the world. I guess a lot of young couples live on less."

His smile was her reward. "You're wonderful, darling! It's going to be great. You'll see. We'll meet a lot of bright, interesting people in that business. Real go-getters. And we'll be able to afford a nice apartment. Not grand, but a hell of a lot better than this. And Lind, I want you to have a good cleaning woman. And of course you won't have to work. Six thousand goes further than you think."

"Sure. I know. I was just sore that you didn't at least ask my opinion before you decided. I'm still sore. But it's probably going to be pretty glamorous rubbing elbows with all those Madison Avenue types. And I do want you to be happy, Geoff. I love you so much."

"And I you, baby. More than I can say." He grinned. "Bet our families will be surprised. Your father with his stuffy banking business and mine in real estate. They'll probably think we've lost our minds."

They probably will, Lindsay thought. Papa will never understand, and Mama will worry about us. Mama. I'm behaving just like her. Going along with whatever my husband wants, even if it disappoints me. What was it Gandy said so long ago? Something about not being foolish where men are concerned. Something about their being like children who need a firm but loving hand. Well, I'm loving but not very firm. I should have stood up for my right to be part of this decision. I watched Mama being the weak one in her marriage and look how that turned out. Damn. I've let Geoff call all the shots for two years and I'm still doing it. But when we get to New York, things will be different. I'll make him see that it's far more sensible to go into a real business than play with this kindergarten stuff. Papa and I will work something out together. I hate to think what he's going to say when he hears what Geoff's decided to do. He'll be livid.

Howard Thresher was more than livid. He was nearly apoplectic. They were all gathered at a big table in the dining room of the Ritz-Carlton in Boston when Geoff made his announcement. Both his father and Lindsay's stared at him as though he'd gone mad.

Before the senior Mr. Murray could speak, Howard jumped in. "What the hell kind of craziness is that, Geoff? Advertising? Most fly-by-night business in the world! Good God, is that what your parents put you through Harvard for? To dream up brassiere ads for *Vogue?*"

"That's not exactly what I'm going to do, Mr. Thresher. I won't be a creative person. I won't make ads. My responsibility will be helping to manage various big accounts, some of them spending millions of dollars in magazines and radio."

"Spending millions they may be," Howard said, "but I know how these people work. One day they take their account from your agency to some other and that's the end of everybody working on it. Don't you know how notorious advertising agencies are for firing people? You're a married man. I'm amazed you feel so little responsibility to provide a safe, sane future for your wife, even if you care so little for your own!"

"I care a great deal for Lindsay's future, sir," Geoff said stiffly. "If I didn't believe this was a great opportunity, I wouldn't have decided to be part of it. We're coming into something new, you know. Television. Three years ago there were twenty thousand television sets in New York City alone. The number must be triple or quadruple that by now. It's going to be the biggest advertising medium the world has ever seen. It's going to revolutionize the industry, and agencies will make fortunes from it."

"Television." Howard almost spat out the word. "Pictures in the air. I certainly thought you'd consider something substantial and proven."

"Like banking?"

"Why not? Or real estate with your father. Some business a man can be proud to be part of. Advertising is a whore's business, son, the province of ne'er-do-wells and dreamers."

Geoffrey turned to his father. "Do you agree, Dad?"

Mr. Murray looked disturbed. "To some extent, yes. People will always need homes and offices and money. Bankers and realtors have a substantial place in any community. But Geoff, there's something else I've been thinking of. Another area I wish you'd consider."

The group looked at him curiously. Stuart Murray cleared his throat nervously. "I dislike being an alarmist," he said, "but I'm one who thinks we'll soon be in the war. I'd like to see you in some industry supplying ships or munitions. Or even in some government service. Anything, in fact, where you'd automatically be deferred from military service because you were in an essential job." He looked faintly embarrassed. "Perhaps that sounds less than patriotic, Geoffrey, but your mother and I have talked about it. We know it's selfish, but you are our only son, our only child. We don't want you drafted and killed for some senseless cause. If you won't think about that for our sake, then at least consider it for Lindsay's. You have a young wife. One day, we hope, you'll have children to carry on the Murray name. It would seem only prudent, indications being what they are—"

"Damned sound thinking, Stuart!" Howard boomed approval. "You're one hundred percent correct. I happen to be very friendly with Henry Kaiser, who's making ships out on the West Coast. I'm sure a phone call to him—"

It was Geoffrey's turn to interrupt. "Sorry. I can understand your thinking. I haven't disregarded the possibility that the army will call me. But Dad, Mr. Thresher, all of you, I have to take that chance. We don't know there'll be war and I'm not going to predicate my life on that possibility. But if America does have to fight, I'm not going to weasel my way out by planting my behind firmly in some job where I'm untouchable because I'm in charge of making up time sheets for shipbuilders. I'd loathe myself. I'd be a fake and a coward."

"And alive," Howard said cynically. "If you don't care about your own skin, then you might consider the possibility of my daughter's becoming a widow before she's twenty-five."

There was a moment of strained silence. The women at the table had taken no part in this discussion, but now Pauline spoke quietly.

"You're wrong, Howard. You and Stuart are both wrong. Geoffrey isn't a child to be instructed in his duty. He's a man and a strong one." She glanced affectionately at Lindsay. "And he has a strong and sensible wife who'll be behind him in whatever he decides to do. It's not easy for any of us to contemplate someone we love going to war. God knows I know that all too well. There's not a day when I don't worry about James, not a moment I'm not praying for his safety. But I know he did what he had to do, and I'd have been wrong to try to stop him. It's the same for Geoffrey. He must plan his life as he thinks best, with conviction and with courage. To live every day in fear of dying is to die a thousand times. Geoffrey's right. As long as we can, we must live normally, trusting that all the terrible things will never happen, taking one day at a time and being happy with it. It's the only way we can keep from going mad with fear."

Howard looked at her with disgust. "My God! Of all the impractical, sentimental drivel! You can bet if I'd known what James was up to I'd have found a way to stop him, just as I'd have found a way to stop Lin—" He halted abruptly, embarrassed by what he'd half blurted out. "I'm sorry," he said, "I didn't mean that. I thought Lindsay and Geoffrey were too young to marry. I would have tried to prevent it. But I'm glad I didn't. I'm proud of the way they've handled it, both of them. They've been very sensible. Which is all the more reason why I hope they'll be sensible now."

Sara Thresher had listened attentively without saying a word. She looked at Lindsay and Adele, so young, both of them, so much to live for at their age. What are they thinking, the young women of this generation? she wondered. What must they think of these men who advocate the evasion of duty and the disregard of pride and dignity? It affects

Adele only indirectly, because of her affection for Lindsay. But what of Lindsay? No one has even consulted her.

"Lindsay, darling, how do you feel about all this?"

"I feel the way Geoff does, Gandy. The way Mama does." Lindsay lifted her chin. "Whatever my husband does is going to have my blessing, just as Mama said. We're not afraid."

Sara nodded. "You're right, child. Fear is for the old. Lack of it is one of the joys of youth."

9

*A*dele was in her room in the dormitory that Sunday afternoon in December when the news came. Like Americans everywhere, at first she couldn't believe what the radio was saying. The Japanese had attacked Pearl Harbor. Ships sunk. Lives lost. The President going before Congress tomorrow to ask for a declaration of war. She tried to absorb what it meant. James had been right. He knew it was coming. They all knew, but only James was so certain. And now they were in it with him.

Involuntarily, she glanced at the dresser where she kept his letters. She'd begun writing to him when he went away, not telling anyone, not even Lindsay. He'd replied with casual, friendly letters at first, written to a friend of his little sister's. But in time the letters had taken on a new warmth in response to her own. Shy in person, Adele had dared express herself in writing. She'd loved James forever, and though at first she could not come straight out and tell him so, her devotion was unmistakable, between every line. James, sensitive and perceptive, came to realize her feelings and, to her amazement and joy, appeared to reciprocate. The romance, unthought of by him when he left, flourished with the lack of inhibition the written word provides. Scarcely able to believe it, Adele now knew that James saw her in a new light and, miraculously, loved what he saw.

She longed to tell Lindsay, who'd once hoped for just this very thing, but something held her back. Her discovery was very private, very precious, too precious to share even with her dearest friend, the sister of the man she loved.

She thought of his latest letter, received only a week ago. For the first time he had spoken of a life together.

How strange, darling Adele, that it took a separation to bring us together. How extraordinary that the little girl I left behind has become the dearest woman on earth. You cannot imagine how I yearn to see you, to really look at you for the first time, as I never have before.

Sometimes I think it must be a fantasy that you have become so real to me in a way that matters so much. And then I begin to worry. Will I be the same James she says she's always cared for? Am I too old for her, perhaps? Nine years is a vast difference. Well, perhaps not vast, but frightening in terms of the way our lives have been shaped these past two years. Sometimes I feel like an old man. I've seen so much, my dearest, while you've been growing up.

But then I know, as only a man in love can know, that this was always there, if I hadn't been too blind to see it. And now I have something to come home to and someone wonderful and gentle and sweetly strange and yet familiar waiting for me. Will you wait, love? Can it be true you've waited all this time and I was too self-absorbed to know? The answer must be yes. I live for a lifetime of yeses between us.

Momentarily, Adele forgot the danger he was in, the danger so many of her friends would now share. She thought only of this new happiness she felt and of the life that lay ahead when all this was over and James came home. But the euphoria was short-lived as the radio continued to send out its terrible messages, delivered in the matter-of-fact tones of announcers and commentators who could hide their emotions in dispassionate reportage. Her thoughts went to Lindsay, and she remembered the table conversation at the Ritz. Her friend had been wonderful, quietly stating her loyalty to her husband, but Adele didn't believe a bit of it. Lindsay was a practical person and would agree with her father and her father-in-law, undoubtedly wishing Geoff would heed their advice. But I give her full marks for standing by, Adele thought. I hope she'll stick to her guns now that the older men could, and probably would, say "I told you so."

On impulse, she picked up the phone and called the Murrays' apartment in New York. After the third ring, Lindsay answered. Adele knew she'd been crying.

"Lind? Are you okay?"

There was a split second of silence. Adele could imagine her swallowing hard, trying to compose herself. Finally, in a near-normal voice,

Lindsay said, "Sure. As well as anybody could be today. I guess you heard the news?"

"Yes. But I still can't believe it. What does Geoff say?"

"He . . . he's not here. He went out for a walk." Lindsay began to cry. "Oh, hell, why I should I lie to you? He stormed out. We had a terrible fight. He says he's going to volunteer, Del. That way he can apply for Officers' Candidate School and get a commission. He says it's better than being a G.I." Lindsay's weeping increased. "Damn him! Why didn't he listen to Papa? He could be in some draft-exempt job right now. But no. He had to do what *he* wanted. So bloody righteous about his duty 'if the time came.' Well, the time came, didn't it? Just the way our parents said it would. He doesn't care what happens to me. He never has. Those awful years in Cambridge. And now—"

"Lindsay, stop it! Stop feeling sorry for yourself! I only hope you didn't say those things to Geoff."

"Of course I said them!" Lindsay suddenly stopped crying. "You bet your damned boots I said them! Why shouldn't I? They're true. Men! What do they care about us? Did Papa care what his running around did to Mama? Did James care that he broke her heart going off to war? And now Geoff. He could have spared me this if he hadn't been so bloody pigheaded." Lindsay took a deep breath. "Okay. Let him go. Let him have his damned freedom. That's what he really wants. That's what they all want. But I'm not going to sit home and wring my hands and weep. I'll have my freedom too. And by God I'll enjoy it!"

Adele tried to be reasonable. "Lind, honey, you don't mean a word you're saying. You're just unhappy and frightened. I don't blame you. I know how you feel about Geoff. You'd give your life for him. Don't pretend to be so hardhearted. There's nothing wrong with admitting you're scared for the person you love. We're all scared." She stopped. She'd been on the verge of telling Lindsay about herself and James, but this was not the time. Lindsay was too deep in her own emotions to want to hear about someone else. "Listen, I'll be home next week for the holidays. Hang on. We'll have a good long talk."

"You're so lucky, Adele." Lindsay suddenly sounded wistful. "You're right never to fall in love. Never to get married. It's no good putting yourself at someone else's mercy."

Despite herself, Adele smiled. If you only knew, she thought. You will know soon. I wonder how you'll react.

*   *   *

95

"I can't believe it!" Pauline said. "James and Adele? I'm delighted, of course. Adele is like a daughter to me. But I had no idea."

"Nobody did." Lindsay nervously lit a cigarette. "She didn't even confide in me until she came home last week. Romance by correspondence. I wonder how that will work out. He didn't know she was alive when he left."

"You don't sound particularly pleased, dear. I'd have thought you'd be happy. Seemed to me you were always trying to matchmake between those two."

"That was when I was a kid, Mama. When I thought everybody I loved should love each other." Lindsay gave a little laugh. "When I thought marriage was the niftiest thing since Benny Goodman and banana splits. Boy! Little did I know!"

"Lindsay, you mustn't. You mustn't feel so bitter about Geoffrey's decision. It's the wisest one."

"Really? You could have fooled me. I'd have thought the wisest one would have been to take Papa's advice and his own father's."

"You didn't say that in Boston."

"How could I? Give me credit for a little taste, Mama. I'm Geoff's wife, and wives are supposed to stand up in public for what their husbands believe, aren't they? God knows you made an impassioned enough speech that day! And Gandy was pretty sentimental too. What was I supposed to do? Say the men were right? I thought it, but what good would it have done to say it? Geoff wasn't about to budge from his position, and things would have been even worse for us. I'll say one thing: he was right about the job. He loved it. We had a good six months. But we sure as hell are going to pay for it now."

"There'll be many women paying, darling. Suffering and worrying as you'll be."

"Frankly, Mama, I find that small comfort. Misery loves company? Baloney! I can't care very much about what other women are feeling. I just know what I'm going to go through. And it didn't have to be this way. That's what's so damned frustrating."

"Think how Adele must have been feeling all these months. And she didn't complain. Didn't even tell us."

Lindsay stood up and began to pace the room. "I love Adele, but she's a total ninny. Always has been. All that mooning forever over her father. The withdrawal when her mother married Lucius Tamlin. I admit he's a boor, but so what? Adele didn't have to carry on like it was *her* husband! And the garbage she spouted about never wanting to marry. I think she still feels that way, if you want the truth. I think it's very convenient to carry on a love affair by long distance. It's just the dreamy, moody kind of thing she'd do. As for James, I don't understand him for a minute. The war sure must have changed him if he can work himself up into being in love with a girl he remembers only as a spooky little kid! I think they're both fantasizing: James being romantic about 'the girl back home,' and Adele feeling very safe because she has all the hearts and flowers without the demands of a real man. I wouldn't be surprised if she's frigid, Mama. It wouldn't surprise me a bit if she ran like hell if James suddenly materialized."

Pauline was shocked. "Lindsay, how can you say such things? Adele is your oldest and dearest friend!"

"It's possible to be objective about the people you love, Mama. I can be objective about Geoff. I can see how willful he is, even though I love him. Didn't you feel the same about Papa? You loved him while you recognized his shortcomings, though in the end you couldn't put up with them. Love isn't blind, Mama. It may be temporarily myopic, but unless you're a moron there comes a time when you can still love a person but can't delude yourself that he or she is perfect."

"How reasonable you are, Lindsay." There was a faint note of sarcasm in her mother's voice. "How very black and white things must seem to you."

The irony did not escape Lindsay. "You think I'm being a smart-ass twenty-one-year-old. All right. Maybe I am. I'm hurt. Very hurt by the decisions Geoff takes without caring if I approve or not. I love him, but I know he's not perfect. Is that so terrible? Is it so shameful to be analytical instead of fatuous? Can't I love people—Geoff, Adele, you, Papa, even Gandy—without pretending they're saints? I'll stick by them, I'll defend them. But that doesn't mean I'm stupid about them. If you want to come down to cases, Mama, when I got to be old enough to understand your situation with Papa, I thought you were not too bright to walk out on him. Sure, he hurt you. Your ego must have taken a helluva beating, knowing he was seeing other women. I don't say that's right. In fact, I think it's crummy. But you had other things. A good life. Social standing. Every overt appearance of a happy marriage. And you chucked it because you couldn't stand knowing Papa was sleeping

97

around. And I think you're sorry. I think you still love him. But you couldn't accept him as he is. You couldn't love anything except perfection."

Pauline shook her head wearily. "I can't argue with you, Lindsay. But each of us is different. There's a breaking point that comes at different times to everyone. I don't have your strength, my dear. You must get that from your father. I envy you your dispassionate mind, but I also deplore it. It takes away some of the humility, even some of the vulnerability that's appealing in women. You post-World War One babies are a different breed. I suppose that's lucky. It may help you survive World War Two with less pain. I pray to God it will. You're going to need all the strength you have in the days ahead when Geoffrey's gone."

Suddenly, without warning, Lindsay began to cry. "Oh, Mama, I'm so damned scared! I try to put up a big front, try to be angry with Geoff, but I can't. I love him so much I don't know how I'll live without him."

Pauline went to her and took her in her arms, comforting her as though she were a child. "Hush, baby. I know. I understand. You did your little act for yourself, not for me. And you don't believe it any more than I do. But you'll be all right, Lindsay. And so will Geoff. We'll all be all right. It will be hard, but we'll survive. We're made of sturdy stuff, this family, and thank God we're not ashamed to be human."

When Geoffrey, handsome in his new lieutenant's uniform, finally left for Officers' Training School in Fort Leavenworth, Kansas, it was a loving and cheerful Lindsay who bid him good-bye.

"You could come with me, you know. We could get a little place nearby and be together whenever I could get away."

She shook her head. "No, darling, not now. You'll be too busy. And I don't fancy myself a hooker."

He looked puzzled. "What are you talking about? A hooker? A hooker's a prostitute."

"Gotcha, college boy. There was a General Hooker in the Civil War, and the women who followed the army were called hookers. Well, I'm not following an army, not even for you. I've heard about those poor wives who tag along, living in God knows what kind of accommodations, wangling seats on trains, hanging diapers to dry in the lavatories of railway coaches. Not for me."

"You don't have any diapers to hang, babe."

Lindsay looked serious. "No. Are you sorry, Geoff? Do you wish we'd had a baby?"

"Not as it's turned out. But we will, sweetheart. As many as you want when I get home. You'll be a terrific mother."

"Come on. I'd be lousy at it. No patience."

"Maybe not. But enough common sense for two people, and enough love for any army."

She blinked back the tears. "Speaking of armies, you're going to miss your train if you don't get out of here."

Geoff held her close and kissed her. "I love you, Lindsay. When this is over, we'll have a wonderful life."

"You betcha, lieutenant." She took his face between her hands and cradled it tenderly. "Take care of yourself, darling."

"I'll call as soon as I can. You take care of *yourself*. Are you sure you want to stay in this apartment? You could go to your mother's. I worry about your living alone, Lind. You never have, and—"

"And I'm too old and married and too damned set in my ways to go back to living with my mother. I'll be fine, Geoff. Really I will. I'll keep busy, and I'll write every day."

That had been six months ago, and for a while she *had* been fine. She kept busy, working at the Stage Door Canteen, serving coffee and doughnuts, dancing with soldiers in New York on leave, telling them proudly that her husband, too, was in the army. After a few months, Geoff got leave and they had a glorious three-day reunion, with only a token visit with their families, spending most of the time alone in the apartment, making love and simply being lazy as though it were a holiday weekend in peacetime. She did not tell Geoff that her father was working on getting him a post in Washington when his training was complete. Let him never find out, she prayed. Let him think it was just good luck. But when his orders came through they were not for Washington at all. He was assigned to the European Theater of Operations as an aide to a general stationed near London. Geoff was delighted and Lindsay hard put to hide her dismay.

"Overseas!" she said. "Oh, God, no!"

"Honey, I couldn't be luckier. Staff work at E.T.O. headquarters. No front-line stuff. I admit I'm relieved. I'm not as brave as I pretend to be. I'd just as soon ride out the war from some nice desk job, hanging around people like Eisenhower." He grinned. "I'll probably see old James. The long-distance romance still flourishing?"

"As far as I know. Adele's finished school, but I don't know what she's going to do. She's considering joining the WAACs."

"The Women's Auxiliary Army Corps? You're kidding! I can no more imagine Adele in uniform than I could you!"

Lindsay bristled. "I don't know why that's so hard to imagine. I'd be damned good at it. Probably a lot better than Adele. I think she has some goofy idea she might get sent to England and be near James. It's crazy, of course. She's written to him and I'll bet money he scotches that idea."

"Of course he will. In the first place, she couldn't know where she'd be sent, even if she requested overseas duty. And in the second"—he began to laugh—"I swear, darling, the very idea of Adele strutting around saluting is enough to boggle the mind."

Lindsay looked thoughtful. "I don't think she'll do it, but I must admit Adele seems very different these days. I always thought of her as so—well, passive. She seems strong, somehow. Very confident. More at peace with herself, I guess, than ever before. Strange, isn't it? The world's falling apart and Adele is flourishing."

Geoffrey raised an eyebrow. "Love is a wonderful thing."

"I guess so. I guess I was wrong thinking she only wanted to play at it. James sent her a ring, you know. They're officially engaged now. Doesn't it beat all?"

"These are strange and unexpected times, my love. War makes odd bedfellows."

She looked at him lovingly. "Just be sure you don't try out that theory when you're thousands of miles away."

"Why the hell should I when I have the best waiting for me at home?"

Almost as soon as Geoff was on his way, Lindsay called her father.

"Papa, what happened? I thought you had it all set for Geoff to be in Washington! He's going to Europe, for God's sake!"

"Honey, I'm sorry. That's what comes of having overzealous connections. The man in Washington who was going to do me a favor thought he'd improve on my request. Instead of Geoffrey's being assigned to a menial job in Washington, this stupid ass wangled him the post of aide to the big brass at European headquarters. A promotion

100

comes with it, by the way. Geoff doesn't know yet, but he'll be Captain Murray when he arrives."

"I can't stand it! How dare that idiot friend of yours do this? What kind of moron—"

"Calm down, Lindsay. The martial mind is beyond our comprehension. This fool thought he was doing us a service. In his eyes, it's the chance every young officer hopes for. Listen, my dear, it could be worse. Be thankful I have influence, or your husband might have ended up fighting on some godforsaken, malaria-ridden island in the Pacific."

"I know, Papa. Thank you." Lindsay sounded defeated. She hesitated. "Geoff says he might see James."

There was a pause, "I suppose he might," Howard said. "I understand from your mother that he sent Adele a ring."

"Yes, Papa, they plan to be married."

"She's too good for him, you know."

Lindsay didn't answer.

"Adele's a lovely, unselfish girl. And your brother will take advantage of that. He has charm, no denying that. But he's always used it promiscuously, whether it was to influence your mother and your grandmother or to attract girls like Candice Simms and God knows how many others. I doubt he could sincerely care about any one woman, and I hate to see Adele hurt."

Lindsay, for all her troubled state of mind, nearly laughed. Listen who's talking about using charm promiscuously! My God, it's the *pot de chambre* calling the bidet white! Of all people to talk about not hurting, my father is the last one who should utter a word. But of course he doesn't see himself as he is. We never see ourselves.

"I don't think it's that way, Papa. I think James has waited until he was absolutely sure he'd found the one woman he could be faithful to." Lindsay couldn't resist a sly dig. "He feels very strongly about that, you know. Faithfulness is terribly important to him."

"That's not what I've heard. However, I can't concern myself with those two. They're adults. James is what? Thirty? And Adele?"

"A year younger than me. Twenty-one."

"Old enough to know her own mind, I should think." Howard dismissed the subject. "Don't worry about Geoffrey, my dear. He'll be perfectly safe. In fact, he'll probably have a marvelous time."

"In a war?"

"War has many aspects, Lindsay. I daresay it can be quite agree-

101

able if you're billeted in a smart hotel in London with nothing more arduous to do than see that the proper champagne is served at your commanding officer's dinner parties."

"You think that's what Geoff will be doing?"

"I shouldn't wonder. My friend in Washington is very influential. You're managing all right alone?"

"Yes. Except I'm bored. Working for the U.S.O. is okay, but it doesn't give me the feeling of contributing very much."

"You're boosting morale. Very important, morale."

"I suppose so, but it seems sort of nebulous."

"Lindsay, that's ridiculous. What would you rather be doing? Working in a factory? I can hardly picture you as Rosie the Riveter."

She could sense his impatience to be through with this conversation. Trivial family matters always bored Howard, and to him her sense of uselessness was not worth his valuable time. She could imagine what he was thinking: Let her air her little grievances with her mother. That's what women are for. To listen. To be patient. To cluck over such nonsense as their married daughters' boredom. Okay, Papa, I won't trouble your great big masculine spirit further with my unimportant state of mind.

"It's none of my affair, Pauline, but Lindsay worries me lately."

Pauline looked up from the letter she was writing to James. "How so, Gandy? You think something's wrong? Has she said something to you?"

"It's what she hasn't said that bothers me. I'm probably being a silly old woman, but I get the impression that Lindsay feels put upon. When I ask about Geoffrey, she says, 'Oh, don't worry about him, Gandy. He's having a big old time in London.' She seems not to even want to talk about him, as though he's deliberately deserted her. I don't understand it. You'd think she'd be happy that he has a reasonably safe post. When I read what's going on these days, I wonder she's not giving thanks that her husband wasn't part of the landing in Sicily, or that he's not in the air corps with that round-the-clock bombing of Germany." She stopped, distressed by the look on Pauline's face. "Oh, my dear, I'm sorry. I shouldn't have mentioned that."

"It's all right. I know James is part of that operation. He hints at it in his letters to Adele and me. There's nothing to do but pray."

Sara sat quietly for a moment, trying to concentrate on the socks she was knitting for the Red Cross packages that went overseas. There was so little any of them could do these days except pray, especially women her age. Lindsay could entertain those poor lonely boys who came to the U.S.O., and Adele could immerse herself in her work for the American Women's Volunteer Service, driving army and navy cars at all hours of the day and night, picking up and delivering military personnel. Even Pauline made her contribution as a nurse's aide in the veterans' hospital. But I sit and knit and fret, Sara thought with distaste. And much good I'm doing anybody.

"It's Howard's fault that Lindsay's bitter," she said finally. "He never should have told Lindsay that Geoffrey had such a glamorous assignment."

Pauline smiled at her affectionately. "I think he meant well, Gandy. At least he did get Geoff in a reasonably safe spot. Don't be too hard on him. It's not his fault if Lindsay doesn't appreciate that. For that matter, in her heart I think she does. It's just that she's lonely and bored and a little sorry for herself. That child has never been exactly ecstatic when things didn't go her way. I'm sure she thinks the war is a great personal inconvenience started only to disrupt her life."

"Now who's being hard on someone?" Sara was indignant. "Lindsay is very unhappy, Pauline. And I don't know what we should do to help."

"Gandy, darling, there's nothing we *can* do. She's a married woman. It's time she learned that her days of being a spoiled child are over. The minute she gets Geoffrey back, she'll be fine." Pauline looked wistful. "We'll all be fine when our boys return. Until then, we have to make the best of it. Lindsay and Adele and you and I."

"Somebody should tell Lindsay that her husband isn't having such a wonderful life."

"I'm sure she knows that, dear. Lindsay likes to put on an act sometimes. Anything for attention. But underneath she's a very sensible young woman."

"I hope so," Gandy said dubiously. "I certainly hope so."

Her grandmother's analysis was closer to the truth than her mother's confident appraisal. Though it was true she was glad Geoff was in no terrible danger, Lindsay was more than a little resentful of his exciting life and, regrettably, began to say so in her letters to him.

"It must be wonderful to lead such a star-studded existence," she wrote, after he'd told her of actually being introduced to Winston Churchill. "You're certainly proving Sherman wrong. War isn't hell. Apparently it's a hell of a lot of fun if you're in the right place."

His return letter sounded annoyed and disappointed in her. "I can't believe the querulous tone you've adopted lately, sweetheart. It's not like you. Certainly you wouldn't be happier if I were diving into ditches to avoid strafing enemy planes or going on nightly bombing runs as James is! What's wrong, Lindsay darling? I'm sure it must be hard for you, with everyone away, with rationing and all that, but you do sound as though you're furious that I'm not having a harder time of it here."

"What kind of monster do you think I am?" she snapped back in the next V-mail letter. "Of course I'm glad you're not in danger. But how would you like to be a woman stuck at home with no company but your own sex or a bunch of unwashed hillbilly G.I.s stepping all over your feet at the Stage Door Canteen? Adele decided not to join the WAACs (or, rather, James decided for her), but right now it doesn't seem such a bad idea to me. Maybe I could get sent to London. At least we'd be together. I'm thinking of asking Papa to arrange it, the way he maneuvered your cushy tour of duty."

She knew she shouldn't have written that last part, but she didn't care. Let Geoff be annoyed to learn that his father-in-law had pulled strings. He certainly didn't mind having the benefit of them now that he was there!

There was such a long silence from him after that that she began to be frightened. He must be furious. Well, let him, she thought defensively. Why shouldn't he know that it was thanks to her he was enjoying the war? But when at last a letter from him did arrive, all her righteousness melted in a puddle of regret.

I am shocked and disappointed in you, Lindsay. You know how strongly I feel about anyone seeking favoritism for me, and your deliberate revelation of something you've known so long can only mean that you wish to punish me for being away. You have succeeded in making me aware that I was handed my captain's bars and my assignment not through worthiness but through the influence of your father. You've made me feel ashamed, thinking of all my friends who had to take their chances in Europe and Africa and the hellholes of Guadalcanal. Friends who died or were hideously wounded because they didn't have

fathers-in-law with friends in high places, or wives who couldn't resist med-
dling for their own selfish interests.

Her regret had quickly turned to anger. The nerve of him! Lectur-
ing her because she was concerned for his safety. Incensed because she'd
asked her father for one simple little favor. Who the hell did he think he
was? He should be damned glad she had connections. If he'd used them
earlier he'd never even *be* in the bloody army!

Furiously, she replied, saying just that and more. Reminding him
how stiff-necked he'd been while he was in school and she was working
her fingers to the bone. Saying again that if he hadn't stubbornly insisted on taking the advertising job, he'd be in an essential industry instead
of strutting around in his silly uniform. Pointing out that she did not
appreciate being called meddlesome or selfish, particularly when all her
efforts had been for him.

Weeks went by with no word of reply. And stubbornly she did not
write either. But secretly she worried that she'd driven him away with
her hurt pride and her anger, justified though she believed them to be.
More than one night she cried herself to sleep, still feeling injured but
wishing she had exercised more restraint. If he were here she could set
it right with gentle teasing and fierce lovemaking. She'd have been glad
to do that. But she couldn't unbend in a letter. He owed her an apology.
And miserable as she was, she'd wait for one before she wrote another
word.

When she finally heard, his tone was cool. He did not refer to her
outburst, but simply made innocuous comments about his daily life,
asked dutifully for her mother and Gandy and Adele, and said to tell
the last-named he'd seen James, who was fine and eager to get home to
her.

The almost impersonal letter was worse than another blast of anger. It was as though he'd withdrawn from her, that he didn't feel
enough emotion to even rage at her. This deliberate disregard of their
heated exchange was more revealing than his furious accusations. It was
devastating. For the first time, Lindsay truly feared the result of her
willful behavior.

10

*I*n May of 1944, Geoffrey and James met as they frequently did for a drink at the Savoy in London. Geoff seemed unusually preoccupied, and his brother-in-law looked at him quizzically over his whisky and water.

"Something on your mind, buddy? Heavy goings-on at H.Q.?"

Geoff nodded. Very heavy indeed. D-Day, as the army called it, was being planned, probably for June if the weather held out. The Allies would land in Normandy. It was the biggest military secret of all time, and Geoff could not reveal it even to James. "Pretty heavy," he said. "Sorry I can't talk about it."

"You shouldn't. Let's talk about something else. How's Lindsay?"

Geoff looked unhappier than ever. Things were not going well between him and his wife. Her letters were bitter and accusatory for no reason, and he was both baffled and irritated by them. He tried to tell himself that she was simply lonely and frustrated. Lindsay was a highly physical woman. She'd proved that years before when she made it impossible for him not to marry her. She was not the kind of woman who could survive without a man, and yet Geoff felt sure that she was being faithful and feeling deprived because of it. Still, that was no reason to take it out on him. He couldn't help this separation. Millions of other women were enduring the same hardship. And a great many men too. It had become a joke around H.Q. that Lieutenant Colonel Murray was a monk. He probably was one of the few officers who had not formed some kind of liaison in England. For all that he felt desire, he couldn't bring himself to be with any woman except his wife.

"Hello, there," James said. "Remember me? We're supposed to be having a drink, not taking a vow of silence."

106

"Sorry," Geoff said again. "I was thinking about Lindsay."

"Miss her a lot, don't you? I can understand that. Hell, I miss Adele, and I don't even have the kind of memories you have. Crazy, isn't it, this thing with Adele and me? God, I hope it's going to work out when I get home."

"It will. She's always been in love with you. Lindsay used to tell me how she dreamed you and Adele would fall in love."

"She never mentioned it to me. I never thought of Adele except as that pretty little kid who was Lindsay's playmate. Maybe just as well. I might have married her before I left."

"Maybe you wouldn't have left if you'd been married."

"You did."

"Yes. Except when Lindsay and I got married I didn't know there was going to be a war. You always felt certain of it, didn't you, James? Long before the rest of us." Geoff stirred his drink absently. "Do you mind if I confide in you? I mean, would it embarrass you if I really spilled my guts about the way things are going with Lindsay and me?"

James settled back in his chair. "Nothing embarrasses me, pal. Go ahead and talk. Get it off your chest. I have a feeling you need to."

Slowly at first, and then with greater passion, Geoff began to talk about his marriage, the way it happened, the problems while he was in school, and the ultimate discovery that Howard Thresher had maneuvered his military career. "I was in a rage when I found out," he said, "and it started something terrible between Lindsay and me, something that seems to be snowballing. Hell, I got over being angry at your father a long time ago. That was just wounded pride. I know it's childish to resent being helped when the motivations are good. But this . . . this rift between Lindsay and me seems to grow deeper and wider. She's lonely and unhappy and unreasonable. And, frankly, I resent her nagging and taking out her frustration on me, so I react badly to her sniping and that makes her more indignant and—well, it's gotten so that we're behaving like a couple of edgy old fogies tossing barbs at one another across the Atlantic. What the hell's the matter with us? I love Lindsay and I'm sure she loves me, but this separation is destroying us and there's not a damned thing I can do about it. You know us both, James. What can I do to set things right?"

James took a deep breath. "This is going to sound like a rotten thing to say, particularly coming from Lindsay's brother, but I think you'd better find yourself a woman."

"What?"

"I told you it would sound lousy—even ludicrous, when you remember that I despised my father because he was unfaithful. But these are different times. I'd kill you for cheating on Lindsay if you were together, but you've been away from her for two years. And for two years you've been celibate. No good, man. You're tight as a drum. Tied up in knots. Everything gets magnified out of proportion when you have no physical release. Everything you've told me is garbage about the differences between you and Lindsay. Doesn't amount to a hill of beans. But it seems to because you're under terrible tension in your job and you compound that tension by refusing to give way to what nature intended. For God's sake, Geoff, you're twenty-five years old! At the peak of your virility and sublimating all your urges. No wonder you're a wreck. Get in the hay with something soft and pretty. You'll get your perspective back. And Lindsay need never know you did her a favor."

"Some favor." Geoff frowned. "I don't know. I've thought about it. I can't sit here and tell you I haven't wanted a woman. But I don't know if I could do that to Lindsay. I . . . didn't have much experience before we were married. Sure, a girl or two, but nothing much. I was practically a virgin. And Lindsay was literally one. She'd never known any man but me and I'm sure she still hasn't. It seems a hell of an unfair thing to do to her. I'd probably feel such guilt I'd want to kill myself."

James shrugged. "Have it your way."

"I know I sound like a stupid kid, but—"

"Oh, for Christ's sake, Geoff, cut it out! You damned well do sound like a stupid kid. And a scared one. I wouldn't be surprised if you're *afraid* to approach a woman, since you've practically slept with only one. You give me a swift pain. What are you? Some kind of Victorian throwback? We're in a war, man, We're away from the women we love. But that doesn't stop us from being human!"

Geoff began to get angry. "And what about Lindsay? Would you expect me to okay it if she slept with somebody while I was away?"

"I wouldn't expect you to know. Any more than she will. But I hope she has sense enough to recognize what's biting her too. And enough guts to do something about it."

"You're unbelievable!"

"No," James said quietly, "I'm a realist. Look. I don't really owe anything to Adele. I mean, we're not married. But even if we were, I'd still have sex over here, and I wouldn't worry about her doing the same back home. For God's sake, Geoff, we're not talking about romance; we're talking about biology. You could sleep with twenty girls and still be in love with your wife. And still want to go home and be faithful to her from there on in. This is a different time and place. I'm not advising you to fall in love with some pretty little lieutenant in skirts or some available young nurse. God forbid! I'm telling you to relax so you can handle yourself and save your goddamn marriage!"

Geoff thought for a moment. "And you'd give the same advice to Lindsay?"

"Damn right I would. She probably needs the same thing you do. And if she got it, she wouldn't be such a shrew."

Geoff began to laugh. "Nobody would believe this conversation. You sound like Dorothy Dix. Advice to the lovelorn. I wish I could be sure that's the answer," he said, serious again. "I really wish I could convince myself that's all that's wrong."

"What else?" James asked. "You made it okay when you were together, didn't you? Put the pieces together, pal. It isn't such a puzzle after all."

On a hot July afternoon, Lindsay mixed a martini and handed it to her friend, curled comfortably in the corner of the couch. Adele looked wonderful these days. The smart uniform suited her, her eyes sparkled with excitement, and her whole body exuded energy and health.

"I must say the A.W.V.S. seems to agree with you."

Adele smiled. "It's so interesting, Lind! I wish you'd join up. We work out of a private house on East Sixty-Sixth Street between Fifth and Madison. I sleep there one night a week. I love the work, I really do. And now that we're driving regular army and navy cars, it's even better than in the beginning when we had to use our own."

"But it's six days a week! And sometimes you're driving in the middle of the night! Doesn't it make you nervous?"

"Not a bit. It's fascinating." Adele bit her lip. "I guess I shouldn't tell you this. It's supposed to be top secret. But they're flying in all kinds of important people from Europe. Scientists, especially. Sometimes I'm at LaGuardia at three or four in the morning, picking up V.I.P.s from all over. It makes me feel—well, worthwhile. As though I'm helping in my way, as James is in his."

"Sounds too tough for me," Lindsay said. "Bored as I am with lonely servicemen, I think I'm better suited for the canteen. Just as Geoff is better suited for headquarters, though he pretends he wishes he were in the trenches."

Adele pretended not to notice the bitterness. "How is Geoff?"

"Oh, he's just terrific. He had a wonderful time playing soldier before D-Day. It must have been fun, moving all those little pins around on the map."

"Don't talk like that, Lind. He's just doing his job." Adele was almost pleading. "I know he misses you terribly. This separation is as hard on him as it is on you." But maybe not as hard, at that, Adele thought. She'd heard about James's conversation with Geoffrey. Her fiancé had written her a very serious and thoughtful letter. At first she'd been shocked that he would give such advice to his sister's husband. But as she read on, she began to understand and to accept the fact that all those men, even James, needed a few moments of forgetfulness. She could handle what she recognized as James's tacit admission of his own "sins." They took nothing away from his love for her. As Geoff's, were he to have them, would not diminish his devotion to Lindsay. But she couldn't, as James gently suggested, recommend that Lindsay also have an affair. That sophisticated she wasn't. She was still a virgin, and she thought perhaps that handicapped her in understanding the needs of one who wasn't. She would not condemn Lindsay if she had an affair. She simply didn't feel right about mentioning such an idea to her. Even if Adele overcame her moral reservations, Lindsay would be smart enough to know that such an idea would never originate with her "straitlaced" friend. She might put two and two together and arrive at a conclusion too close to the truth.

As though she were a mind reader, Lindsay suddenly said, "This separation, as you call it, is more than hard, Del. It's damned near unbearable. You wouldn't know. You're still innocent. But once you're loved by a man, you miss it terribly. I know women aren't supposed to feel that way, but they do. I know Mama did when she left Papa. And I do. God, how I want to be loved! It's been so long. And it could go on for years until I'm a withered-up old lady with no sex drive left!"

Adele tried to laugh. "Don't be crazy. James thinks the war will be over next year, with France and Belgium already liberated, Guam recaptured, Churchill in Moscow. A dozen other encouraging things. Everything is moving fast. Geoff will be home long before you're an old crone, though you might be as ancient as twenty-five by the time he makes it."

Lindsay had to laugh too. "I'm sorry, Del. I get goofy ideas sometimes. And I must say, Geoff's letters have been much more tender lately. We're almost back to our old, loving exchanges. There was a long period there when we couldn't seem to communicate. But it seems okay again. He's stopped being mad at Papa. Apologized for being so beastly. Even wired roses to me on my birthday. He's dead set on making up with me, and of course I'm more than willing."

Adele felt a twinge of anxiety. It sounded as though Geoff was overdoing it. She did not doubt his love for Lindsay, but knowing what she did, Adele wondered if this sudden change of attitude was as much guilt as devotion. Well, so be it. As long as they're reconciled. She changed the subject. "How's your family?"

"Mama's okay. And Papa's incredible. I swear he hasn't changed in twenty years. He'll be fifty-six in August and he could pass for forty. The man is maddening. Not a line or a wrinkle. I wish I could say the same for Mama. She's two years younger and looks twenty years older. She worries so much about James and Geoff. We all do, of course, but Mama shows it. So does Gandy. Of course, she's really old, bless her heart. Past seventy-four."

"That's not so old these days, Lind. And Gandy has always been so full of life."

"I know. But she suddenly *seems* old. I can't bear to see it. Dammit, this war does terrible things to women!"

"And to men too, dear girl."

"I know. We have it easy by comparison. At least I guess we do. I'm not sure it isn't harder to be the one left behind than the one who's involved. There's less danger, of course, but you can die from boredom almost as easily as you can from bullets."

Adele smiled. "You won't die from it. None of us will. Try to be patient, Lind. It won't be long now. But I still wish you'd join up with me. You'd get such satisfaction out of it."

Lindsay shook her head. "Sorry. No can do. I was born a queen bee. No good trying to make me into a worker at this stage of the game."

When he parted from his brother-in-law that evening in May,

111

Geoff was almost more troubled than he'd been before they met. James had meant well, and his advice was matter-of-fact and, as he said, realistic. But it was so damned cold-blooded to think of making love to a woman he didn't care about. It would be using her. Unfair to her, even as, in his heart, he felt it would be unfair to Lindsay. And he wasn't sure he was capable of it. Not physically, but emotionally. He was afraid. James was right about that. But not afraid he couldn't perform; frightened that despite any resolution he might make, he'd get too deeply involved. He'd seen it happen before. Guys starting out for fun and ending up falling in love, writing those letters home to their wives, saying they'd met someone else and wanted a divorce. What if that happened to me? Geoff thought. I'd despise myself. I'd break Lindsay's heart. She doesn't deserve that.

And in the next breath he told himself he was being ridiculous. There were far more men having affairs that would end when they went home than there were those forming permanent, disruptive attachments. They were the sensible ones, like James, who didn't pretend to be honorable. They made it clear from the outset that it was just fun and games, that there was someone back in the States who meant everything. If the girl didn't understand that, all bets were off. He heard the other officers talking. There was even gossip about the top brass. None of these high-ranking officers would divorce their wives. They were simply living through their life-or-death assignments with whatever comfort they could find.

It was in this frame of mind, several weeks later, that Geoff had his first real conversation with a young English officer named Pamela Schramm, "Leftenant" Schramm, unmarried, twenty-two, with creamy, flawless English skin and a figure that even a military uniform couldn't disguise. Several times since her assignment to H.Q. a few months earlier, she'd tried to be friendly with Geoff, but he'd turned her off abruptly, perhaps sensing, even then, that she was the first serious threat to his self-imposed code.

It began innocently enough. Everyone was jubilant over the way things were going. Despite the casualties, the Allies had taken Orvieto and Cherbourg. The Russians had captured a hundred thousand Germans at Minsk, and some German officers had tried to assassinate Hitler. In the Pacific, Premier Tojo resigned and the Japanese suffered heavy losses in the battle of Leyte Gulf. It was winding down. There was a long way to go, but it surely was coming to an end and the Brit-

112

ish and Americans were openly optimistic about peace in the foreseeable future, Geoffrey and Pamela among them.

"Isn't it smashing, Colonel Murray? It will be over soon. I know it will."

"God, yes! Can't be soon enough for me. For any of us." He was fascinated by the girl's excitement. "I'm sure you'll be happy. Probably get married and settle down, right?"

"Oh, I don't know about that, sir." A shadow crossed her face. "I was engaged, but he was killed last year. He was R.A.F. Bought it over Germany in one of the raids on the Ruhr dams."

Geoff felt awkward. "I'm so sorry."

"So am I. But life goes on, doesn't it? No good pining. It won't bring Charles back. And I don't think he'd want it that way. He was a very lusty man, colonel. He loved life. We all do, don't we?"

"Yes, of course. It's very precious."

"Not all that precious, sir. You and I have seen a lot of it wasted. A lot of life and a lot of time."

He glanced at her sharply.

"Forgive me if I'm out of line, colonel, but one can't help hearing talk. I admire you very much. Your wife is a fortunate woman. Still, I wonder what makes you so much stronger than the rest. Sorry to speak so bluntly, but you're a very attractive man and they say—" Pamela blushed. "Oh, dear, I can't think what got into me, colonel. I do beg your pardon. I've been terribly out of order. Apologies, sir."

She looked so distressed that Geoffrey laughed. "I should have you court-martialed, lieutenant, for such a breach of etiquette! But instead, I'll inflict an even more severe punishment. Will you have dinner with me tonight? We could perhaps find some quiet little restaurant and try to ignore the glassware rattling on the tables while those bloody Nazis keep sending over their disgusting little V-two rockets."

Her laughter matched his. "I think it's super punishment, colonel. I'll be delighted."

She was utterly enchanting. Gay, relaxed, amusing, and not a little flirtatious. It was quite clear from the outset that Pamela was attracted to him and undoubtedly willing. Not that she was a tramp. On the contrary, she was a young woman of breeding and grace. But the war did something to these English girls. All around them they saw so much death and destruction, so much bleeding and dying and suffering, that the moral code of their mothers and grandmothers seemed foolish and wasteful. Every day was a gift, every moment a bonus. One could die in the next second from a German rocket. What did an ecstatic hour or two mean except forgetfulness and pleasure for oneself and the man who shared it?

Geoffrey, quite aware of her unspoken feelings, nonetheless felt uncomfortable. He knew he could go to bed with her that night and they'd both enjoy it. But she mustn't think for one moment . . .

They talked and laughed and had a wonderful dinner. And as they left the restaurant, Pamela, with her disarming honesty, looked up at him with a smile.

"Where now, colonel?"

He began to stammer like a schoolboy. "I—I don't know. That is—"

"Don't you want to make love to me? I'd like that."

Her frankness was disconcerting. For a moment he thought of a younger Lindsay: Marry me or sleep with me or I'll find someone who will. This girl wasn't proposing marriage, but it was the same kind of honesty.

"Pamela, you know I want to make love to you. I've wanted to all night. But you must understand—"

"Geoffrey, I already know you're married. Remember me? I'm the one who marveled at your faithfulness. If that still holds true, it's okay. No hard feelings. But if it doesn't—well, I have this flat. Belongs to a friend who's gone to Canada with her children. I use it whenever I like. Charles and I used it. It's jolly comfortable."

"You and Charles? Won't that be painful for you? I wouldn't want to remind you of happier times."

"There are no memories there except loving ones. If you want to come there with me, my friend, I'll be delighted. And you needn't worry that you're making some kind of commitment. I accept this for what it is, no strings attached."

"It doesn't seem fair to you. You know I'll have to go home one of these days. I wouldn't want you to be hurt."

"Oh, rot, colonel! I'm a big girl. I haven't been around all that much, but I've been around enough. I know your kind. You're good and generous and loyal, but I don't want you as a husband, and I shan't weep when you leave. I'll only remember how sweet you are."

114

"Pamela you're very understanding. Very special."

"Not at all. I'm very selfish. I need to hold someone too."

It was the first of many joyful nights. Pam was a passionate, giving girl, as much concerned for his pleasure as her own. She told him about her family and encouraged him to talk about his own and Lindsay's.

"Your father-in-law sounds a bit of a rotter."

"I suppose he is. Or was. I used to find his attitude unbelievable."

"And now?" Pam looked at him mischievously.

"I still do. That is, he had no reason to be . . . unfaithful. He had a beautiful and companionable wife. He didn't need other women. He wasn't sexually deprived, from what I understand. He was simply feeding his ego."

"Right. Silly ass. But it must have been hard on Mrs. Thresher. And on Lindsay."

Hearing Pam speak his wife's name so casually gave Geoffrey a twinge of guilt. He had them often, these days, not only because of the affair but because what he had feared did, indeed, seem to be on the verge of happening. I'm falling in love with this girl, he thought despairingly. She's becoming more to me than simply a woman I go to bed with. She understands me as Lindsay never has, accepts me without demands or criticism. We share something that will always be there: this bloody war. We've lived through it so far, and we'll never really be able to forget. The word love had never been spoken by either of them, but Geoff knew. They were falling in love, and it was hopeless, impossible.

Sometimes he thought of telling her that it must end before it went further. Before either of them was trapped by tenderness. But he couldn't bring himself to do it. Out of remorse, he wrote more often to Lindsay, loving letters, despising himself for his hypocrisy, telling himself over and over that he was only following James's advice and that Lindsay would never know. I'm taking nothing away from my wife, he told himself. I'm only trying to survive. But he knew it was a lie. He'd found in Pam the kind of mature relationship he'd never had with Lindsay. Pam was two years younger, but she was eons older in terms of wisdom and serenity and unselfishness.

There were moments, in the midst of their lovemaking, when he thought wildly of asking Pam to marry him. He knew now he didn't want to leave her. The thought of never seeing her again, never hearing her laugh, never feeling those soft arms around him plunged him into total despair. But that's what would happen. He knew it and so did Pamela. And their passion was all the more intense because of it.

With her acute sensitivity to his moods, Pam was aware of his torment. "You mustn't worry, luv," she said one night. "What we're doing isn't wrong. It's beautiful."

"I know that. God help me, it isn't because I think it's wrong. It's because I can't bear the thought of its being over."

"Not to worry about tomorrow."

"How can I not?" Geoff forgot all his resolutions. "I love you. You know that."

"Yes. Of course. And I love you."

"Then how can we let it end? How can I go home and pretend to be happy when I'll be thinking of you every minute? How can I be the kind of husband Lindsay deserves when my mind and my heart are here with you?"

She cradled him in her arms. "You'll forget, my darling. In time this will seem like a dim but very nice memory."

"Never. I can never forget. And what about you? Can you let me go so easily?"

"Not easily. Never think that. But sensibly. We knew from the beginning what this was and how it would end. Nothing has changed."

Geoff's face was contorted with misery. "Yes it has. Everything has changed. We've fallen in love."

Pam pulled away from him. "And we'll fall out," she said briskly. "I'll marry someone and have kids and think of my lovely American now and then. But I won't die of a broken heart. Nor will you. People don't do that, Geoffrey. They live through interludes and put them aside and go on doing what they're meant to do."

"My God, how can you be so clinical about this?"

She laughed and crept back into his arms. "Isn't it lovely for you that I am?"

11

The holidays were the worst of all for Lindsay. Not only did she miss Geoff, remembering other Christmases and New Year's Eves, but it made her sad to see the lonely G.I.s at the canteen. Poor devils. So far away from home and everyone they cared for. So frightened for the impending moment when they'd be shipped overseas to be targets for the killing that went on and on. She read about the German Ardennes offensive in December of 1944, the terrible Battle of the Bulge, and felt genuine relief that her husband was not at the front. Gone now was her resentment of his "comfortable" job. She'd never be sorry her father had maneuvered it. She'd thought several times of asking Howard to use his influence to get leave for Geoffrey, but she dared not. If Geoff found out that once again he was receiving favored treatment, he'd never forgive her. Still, she was terribly lonely and almost constantly depressed these days. She thought sometimes of forgetting her troubles for a few hours, taking some nice soldier home with her for the night. There were plenty of opportunities, God knows. Never an evening went by that some young man didn't make a pass at her. But she laughed them off, pointed at her wedding ring, and said, "Hey, soldier, would you want your girl to do that to *you?*"

Everything seemed bleak and dismal. Even Adele's cheerfulness was wearing thin. To Lindsay's surprise, she told her she was thinking of leaving the A.W.V.S.

"Why, for heaven's sake? I thought you loved it!"

"I did. But now we're only transporting wounded. I feel so ashamed, Lindsay, but I can't take it. Every time I see one of those young men in pain, it tears my heart out. And I think of James and I'm

117

afraid for him. Between the two things, I don't see how I can go on. I know it's awful of me, but I dread every day now."

"You shouldn't feel guilty, Del. God knows you've done your duty. James would be the first to understand if you quit, but he'd hate your worrying about him. He's going to come through okay. Look what he's survived. Almost three years with the U.S. Ninth Air Force, ever since they transferred him from the R.A.F. He leads a charmed life."

"I hope so."

"I guarantee it."

Only a few days later she remembered those words and almost superstitiously regretted having said them.

The telephone call came at eight o'clock on a gray bitter-cold morning in January. For a moment, Lindsay didn't recognize her mother's voice. Pauline was barely able to speak.

"Lindsay, come quickly."

Her first thought was of her grandmother. "What's wrong, Mama? Is it Gandy?"

Pauline began to sob. "No . . . it's James. I've just had a telegram. He's been—been—"

Lindsay grasped at a slim hope. "Wounded, Mama? James is wounded?"

The answer was a wail of anguish. "He's dead. James is dead."

She went cold. No. It couldn't be. Not James. Other people's sons and brothers were killed, but not theirs. Not James. She tried to compose herself. "I'll be there in ten minutes, Mama. Hang on. I'm coming."

In a daze she threw on some clothes and rushed out to find a cab. Thank God it's early, she thought trivially. Another hour and there wouldn't be an empty cab in New York. Everybody would be taking them to go to work. Her mind seemed to blur, and she tried to focus on what must be done. I have to call Papa, she thought. I'm sure he doesn't know. And Adele. Oh, God, Adele. What will this do to her? All her hopes of happiness erased by the terrible words on a little yellow piece of paper. I told her James led a charmed life. That he'd survive. It's as though I put a jinx on him. For the first time the realization that this was not a nightmare came over her and she wanted to cry. Determinedly she held back the tears. I have to be strong for Mama and Gandy and Del. I can't go to pieces.

She found her mother pacing the floor in the apartment, the message clutched tightly in her hand. Gandy sat in an armchair beside the unlit fireplace, staring straight ahead, dry-eyed but gray as death itself. Lindsay ran to Pauline and put her arms around her. The woman's body shook as though she had a chill. For a long moment they stood holding each other wordlessly, until finally Lindsay gently moved away.

"Come and sit down, Mama. Have you had anything to eat or drink?"

Pauline shook her head. "I don't want anything."

"You must take something. I'll make a pot of coffee, at least." She remembered the cook-housekeeper didn't come in until ten. "Let's get some food, Mama. Something warm will make us feel better." How ridiculously one behaved at times like this! Babbling about hot food when the woman in front of her was dying of sorrow. And Gandy. She hadn't even spoken to her grandmother. Lindsay went over to her now and knelt beside the chair. "Are you all right, darling?"

Sara nodded. "Take care of your mother, Lindsay. Make her go to bed. Call the doctor. She needs a sedative."

"Yes, of course. I should have thought of that."

How contained Gandy was. How strong and sensible, Lindsay thought. Her grief must be as terrible as ours, but she's determined not to cause trouble. Her first thought now, as always, is of others.

But Pauline refused to go to bed. She also refused to allow Lindsay to call the doctor. She didn't say so, but she was remembering that time, years ago, when Carl Frampton died and Louise abandoned her responsibilities, allowing her child to be taken care of by the Threshers. Somehow, in her shocked state, she associated this death with that one. She had to stay on her feet. She had to take care of Lindsay, the way she'd taken care of Adele. She forgot they were not children, that James was not their father. Totally disoriented, she began to talk as though James had killed himself.

"He didn't mean to do it, you know," Pauline said in an odd, strained voice. "It was an accident. He wouldn't deliberately desert his wife and child."

Lindsay and her grandmother looked at each other in alarm. What was Pauline talking about? She was not crying now. Her eyes were glazed and she seemed in a trance. Lindsay was frightened. My God, Mama's losing her mind, she thought. Accident? Wife and child? What

119

was she saying? They stared helplessly at this remote woman who carefully enunciated every strange word.

It was Gandy who acted. She rose from her chair and said quietly to Lindsay, "Call the doctor. Now." Then she went to Pauline and took her gently by the arm. "It's all right, dear. It was an accident. He didn't mean it."

"He fell, you know. He didn't jump. He was only trying to close the window."

Sara understood. Pauline was back in 1930. It was Carl Frampton she was talking about, not James. Her mind had blocked out the idea of her son's death.

"We have to take care of Adele, Gandy. She's up there all alone. Will you look after her, please?"

"Yes, dear, I'll see to it. Don't you worry."

"I have to be with Louise, you know. Howard won't even get out of bed to help."

"That's all right. We'll manage."

Lindsay came back into the room and mouthed the news that the doctor was on his way. Thank God he lives in the next block, Sara thought. We can keep humoring her until he arrives.

"Lindsay will help me take care of Adele, Pauline dear. Now sit down here for a minute before you go back upstairs."

Lindsay stared at her grandmother. Had they both gone crazy? But at least Pauline allowed herself to be led to a chair. She sat back wearily and closed her eyes. "Why are they so selfish?" She seemed to be speaking to no one in particular. "Why do they desert us?"

"Mama, what—"

Gandy cut Lindsay off with a warning shake of her head. "That's better," she said to her daughter-in-law. "You take it easy for a few minutes. Lindsay and I know what to do."

"He shouldn't have done it, you know. It was a dangerous, foolish thing to do up there in the dark. He should have called someone."

Gandy moved quietly to her granddaughter's side and spoke in a voice too low for Pauline to hear. "She's hallucinating. The shock. She's confused this with Adele's father's death."

"What?"

"It's all right. I'm sure it's a temporary thing." Gandy looked sad. "There are some things too hideous for the mind to accept at first. Dear

Lord. Why this? Why James?" The old lady wiped her eyes. "He was such a good boy. He loved his mother so much, and she thought the sun rose and set on him. On both of you. Oh, Lindsay, my heart is breaking for her."

Lindsay reached for her grandmother's hand and held it tightly. There were no words.

An hour later Pauline was put to bed and sedated, after an almost physical struggle between her and the doctor. Howard Thresher stood in the living room reading the words aloud over and over as though he couldn't believe them.

"REGRET TO INFORM YOU YOUR SON, MAJOR JAMES THRESHER, UNITED STATES AIR FORCE, KILLED IN ACTION JANUARY 1, 1945, IN THE BRAVE PERFORMANCE OF HIS DUTY." Howard crushed the telegram in his fist savagely. "Words! Goddamned empty words! They're *sorry!* The government is very *sorry!* But that won't bring back my son, will it? It won't restore his mother's sanity."

"Papa, she's not insane. The doctor assured us that after a good rest, she'll be herself again."

"Be herself? She'll never be herself. Not after this. She might be reasonable. At least I hope so. But this kind of shock is something you never get over. Dammit, why didn't she stop him? Why did she let him go?"

Lindsay was horrified. "Papa, don't say things like that! You know she'd have stopped him if she could. And what difference would it have made? He'd have gone sooner or later. Like Geoff."

"At least you had the good sense to warn me about that. I could make it fairly easy for Geoffrey. I'd have done the same for James if anyone had had the decency to consult me!"

"That will be quite enough, Howard." His mother spoke firmly, as though he were a child. "This is no time for recriminations. We have to get through this together. Lindsay, what about Adele? You called her, of course."

"Yes, Gandy. I thought I'd go over there as soon as I was sure Mama was all right."

"Poor child." Sara sighed. "She loved him too."

"He's the only man she ever loved," Lindsay said. "God, I don't know how I can face her."

"You must," Gandy said. "She needs you, Lindsay. You're not only her dearest friend, you're James's sister. I'm sure she wants to see you more than anyone else."

Walking over to the Frampton apartment (she could never think of it as the Tamlin apartment even after all these years), Lindsay hoped Adele's mother was being some help to her. She doubted it. Louise Tamlin was a silly woman, and that husband of hers was an insensitive clod. Why on earth had Adele continued to live there? Lindsay wondered. She should have her own place. In this case, it probably would have been all right with the Tamlins if she had moved out, but for some reason Adele clung to the nest. Wrong. She should have been on her own long ago, but she never seemed to want to leave, in spite of the lack of affection she felt for her stepfather. She'll probably never leave now, Lindsay thought. I have a terrible feeling she'll never marry. She'll be the typical spinster daughter living at home, eventually taking care of ailing, aging parents, giving up her life for two people who couldn't care less. She'll be pathetic and foolish, living on the memory of a lost love that was hardly even a love at all.

I won't let her do that, Lindsay decided suddenly. I won't let her die with James. I'll nag her until she starts moving again. I don't expect her not to grieve. We'll all grieve: Mama and Gandy and Adele and I. Even Papa. He was so hard on James. But he loved him. It was there in his anger this morning.

The minute she let herself into the little borrowed apartment and saw Geoffrey sitting there, his face in his hands, Pamela knew something terrible had happened.

"Geoffrey? What is it? Bad news?"

He looked up and she saw he'd been crying. "It's James. My brother-in-law. Shot down over a goddamn German airfield in eastern France. They were following the Luftwaffe's retreat." He got up and went to the little bar in the corner to make himself a stiff drink. "Jesus! What's it all about? He was the best guy who ever lived. Decent. Civilized. The first one to do his duty. And now, so near the end . . ."

There was nothing to say. Wearily, Pam pulled off her cap and sank onto the convertible couch that also served as their bed.

"I've asked for emergency leave, Pam. Don't know whether I'll get it, but I should be there, at least for a little while. Lindsay must be out of her mind. And her mother. And poor Adele. They were engaged.

122

Goddammit!" he said. "He was the most alive person I ever knew. The best." Geoff stopped suddenly. "If it hadn't been for him, I wouldn't have you. He was the one who told me—"

"To find yourself a woman." There was no reproach in her voice. "Very sensible of him, darling. He understood human nature."

"I didn't mean that the way it sounded. You're not just any woman to me, and you know it. I love you, Pam. I hate to leave you even for a few days, but I'm needed back there."

"Of course you are, luv. I'm sure they'll let you go. You should go. I'll be waiting here for you. Not to worry."

He managed to smile. "Your favorite phrase. 'Not to worry.' Do you really feel that way?"

She smiled back at him. "I have to, colonel darling. And so do you. We really have no choice, now, have we?"

Lindsay could hardly believe it when Geoff got a message through to her saying he was coming home on leave. He couldn't say exactly when. That would depend on when he could hitch a ride on a plane. But she counted the hours. The prospect of his return was the only bright spot in her dark world.

Mama was lucid again and that was almost worse. Knowing what had happened, she moved around the apartment like a ghost, scarcely speaking, never smiling. In time they would send James's body home with full military honors. Pauline was expressionless when Howard told her.

"It doesn't really matter," she said. "He's gone. What's left isn't James."

"I know, my dear, but it will be some comfort to us to know his final resting place."

Pauline didn't appear to hear him, but Lindsay did and was surprised and touched by her father's patience in these past few days. After his initial angry outburst, he'd been a Howard Thresher she hardly recognized: gentle, tolerant, infinitely sympathetic toward his ex-wife. I think he still loves her, Lindsay mused. How strange it would be if this tragedy brought them together again. She'd always hoped for that and suspected her mother had too. Perhaps now, linked in this bond of sorrow, they'd find comfort together. It would please James if only he could know. For all his bitterness toward Papa, he'd have liked to see them peacefully reunited. Maybe now it was possible. His son's death had had a sobering effect on Howard. It might make him see a great many things in a new light.

If only Mama would respond even a little, Lindsay thought. She hardly seems to notice him. She hardly notices any of us. And Adele is almost in the same state. A zombie. A member of the walking dead. Nothing Lindsay had been able to say or do could shake her friend out of this stunned listlessness, so like Pauline's. It had been sad and frustrating since that first morning, a week ago now, when Lindsay had gone to see her. Adele had been in her room, in bed. Her mother had been fluttering around, just as Lindsay expected, crying and wringing her hands, bemoaning the terrible injustice of it all. Lindsay had wanted to slap her. This was doing Adele no good. She needed comfort less than she did some kind of shock treatment and, hard as it was to do, that's what, at last, Lindsay tried to administer.

Adele refused to get up, and Lindsay sat on the edge of her bed and scolded her lovingly, day after day.

"Del, I know how you feel. It's almost too much to bear. But you must bear it. You can't change it. James wouldn't want you to act this way. He loved his life, and you're being unfair to him, refusing to pick up your own again. I thought you cared too much about him to dishonor his memory this way."

"He doesn't know, Lindsay."

"How can you be so damned sure? Have you solved the mystery of life after death?"

Adele turned away wearily, not answering.

"Well?" Lindsay demanded. "Have you?"

"Oh, Lindsay, stop, please. I know you're trying to help, but you can't. Nobody can. Everything's over for me. There's no future. There'll never be anyone like James. Please, Lind, go away. I don't care what happens to me. I just want to be left alone."

"For what? So you can drown in your self-pity and pull the rest of us along with you?"

"I won't pull you along. You're strong, Lindsay. I wish I had one tenth of your strength."

"Do you, now? What do you know about my strength? What does everybody think I am, some kind of iron butterfly? My God, Adele, there's a limit! I can't prop up you and Mama and worry about Gandy and try to hide my own grief. That's my brother who died, remember? I loved him too. He was my idol, my best friend, one of the dearest people in the world to me. I'd like to take to my bed, too, and cry and carry on, but I haven't had time because the rest of you are draining me of every ounce of stamina I have!"

For the first time, Adele looked almost angry. "You have Geoffrey. You've always had everything you wanted. I know you've lost your brother. But you haven't lost your lover."

"And neither have you." Lindsay made her voice deliberately hard. "A schoolgirl romance on paper, that's all you had, Del. Face it. You and James were never lovers. You never even kissed him in your whole life, except for maybe a peck on the cheek! You loved him, I know that. And in the end he loved you. But it was a game of let's-pretend. Sure, maybe it would have come to something if he'd come back. Or maybe it wouldn't. Who knows how James would have felt when he saw you again? For that matter, who knows how *you* would have felt? There are so many things we'll never know, Del. Fantasies we have to forget. No good pining for what might have been. You're young. Your whole life's ahead. Damn you! Get out of that bed and start living again!"

It was like talking to a stone wall. Adele closed her eyes and kept them closed until Lindsay, in desperation, gave up and left. It was hard to say such awful things to her friend. Terrible to hurt her that way. But somebody has got to make her see things as they are, Lindsay thought. Somebody has to save her from herself.

Encouraged by her father's patient new attitude, Lindsay finally dared approach him with the problem. "I just don't know what to do," she said. "God knows I can imagine her suffering. But she can't just lie there forever, Papa, like some swooning heroine in a Victorian novel. What should I do? I want to help her. I feel sorrier for her than I can say. But I can't reach her. She doesn't want to be helped and that's the truth of it."

Howard looked troubled. "It's terrible," he agreed. "I've always been fond of Adele. She's like a second daughter to me. Do you want me to go and see her, Lindsay? Do you think I could possibly help?"

"I'd be grateful if you would. Go to see her, I mean. As for help, I'm not sure anybody can. But she's always been fond of you too. And you are James's father. Would you mind, Papa? I hate to put you to the trouble, but I'm at the end of my rope."

"I'll be glad to talk with her, Lindsay. It's no trouble. I still live on the floor below, so it's hardly out of my way." He frowned. "That poor child. Her father a suicide and now her fiancé gone. I don't suppose

Mrs. Frampton—that is, Mrs. Tamlin—is much use. Pretty woman, but not too brainy as I recall. Haven't seen much of her in the past few years."

"She hasn't changed, unfortunately. Still helpless and stupid. She's doing Adele more harm than good."

"Well, I'll run up there tonight and see what happens. From what you tell me, I'm sure I can't do any harm." He looked at her affectionately. "You're a good girl, Lindsay. Sometimes you've been a peck of trouble, but you're basically fine. Good, sturdy stuff. I'm proud of you."

She was overcome. It was the first real compliment she could ever remember her father paying her. "I guess I'm like you, Papa," she said, almost shyly.

Howard gave a little laugh. "There are those who would say perish the thought! Your mother among them, I'm afraid. Anyway, we understand each other, kitten, don't we? We do the best we can."

Kitten. How many years since he'd called her that? He has changed, Lindsay thought again. He really has mellowed. She wanted to say she wished he and Mama would get back together, but she dared not. It wasn't her business. She wasn't a child who needed both parents under one roof. But I'd be so happy if they were, she thought. We're such a funny half-family these days.

"Have you heard any more from Geoffrey?" Howard asked.

"No. I expect the doorbell will just ring and there he'll be."

"What's the matter, did you take away his latch key?"

Lindsay looked startled before she realized he was teasing her. Papa making jokes? Good grief, this was another world! She smiled. "I only hope he remembers how to use it. It's been so long. I can't believe he's coming home. I wish it were for good, that's all."

Howard looked pensive. "Well, let's see about that. No promises, but let me see what I can do."

"Oh, Papa, would you? Could you?"

"I haven't the faintest idea, but I can give it a try. Just one thing, Lindsay. In the name of heaven, don't mention such a thing to anybody. Particularly not to Geoffrey."

She raised her right hand. "I solemnly swear. That's one thing you don't have to worry about. I've learned my lesson."

12

It was ten days after James's death before Geoffrey managed to hitch a ride on a plane going to New York. Flying westward, his thoughts were of two women: the wife who waited for him and the lover he'd left behind. It had been so hard to leave Pamela. In only a few months he felt closer to her, in many ways, than he did to Lindsay, whom he'd known almost all his life. Sharing danger brought people together, formed between them a unique bond of understanding that was as strong as a marriage vow. He was glad the separation was a temporary one. What was going to happen when he was sent home to stay, he had no idea. He avoided thinking about the moment when he'd have to make that final choice. Not that Pam expected him to divorce Lindsay and marry her. Not one such word had ever been spoken between them. But it must be in her mind, Geoff thought, as it is in mine. I know it's what I want, he admitted to himself, but I don't know whether I'll have the strength to do that to Lindsay.

He fretted, too, about what he'd feel when he saw his wife. He still loved her. It was possible, he realized, to love two women in quite different ways. Lindsay had put up with a great deal during her marriage to him: two hard years while he was in school, three lonely ones while he was in the army. Her physical allure never failed to excite him, but it was responsible for their too-early marriage, a marriage that, he now knew, should not have happened. They were kids wanting to mate. In terms of companionship and understanding, they were never really on the same wavelength. Their ideas of life and happiness were quite different.

And yet she was loyal and loving and, above all, innocent of any suspicion that he might have found someone else. He knew she waited eagerly, believing he was the same Geoff she married. He was not. He was no longer the college boy playing house, or the advertising hopeful content to woo clients and carve out a career for himself in the agency. He wasn't certain now what kind of career he wanted, or what kind of life. He was much more mature, much less idealistic. Even the "easy duty" had toughened him and made him jealous of every precious minute of his life. He couldn't imagine drifting back into his old world of cocktail parties and lunches at "21" and Brooks Brothers suits and advertising presentations to overstuffed clients.

No, he hadn't figured out what he did want, and yet he felt, somewhat uneasily, that after this trip home he might know what he *didn't*.

He got a lift into town and then, with some difficulty, managed to get a taxi to take him to his apartment. Their apartment, his and Lindsay's. He had to share the cab with two other people, a practice which surprised him. He'd forgotten that a scarcity of taxis had made doubling up permissible, but he didn't mind. He realized he almost welcomed the delay as they dropped off the other passengers, as though he wanted to postpone as long as possible the reunion with his wife.

The driver, true to form, was garrulous and complaining when Geoffrey idly asked him how things were in New York.

"Ain't been around for a while, huh?"

"No, I'm stationed overseas. Just home on leave. It's been almost three years."

The older man behind the wheel snorted. "You'll see some changes. This damned sharing thing, for instance. You'd think I'd like it, right? Three fares instead of one. Well, let me tell you, buddy, it's a pain. Nothing but arguments. People trying to jump in both sides of the cab. Like animals. Hell, I've seen many a fist fight between guys. Even women, slamming each other to get in and bawling hell out of me for not taking sides. But I don't get involved. I just sit back and let 'em fight it out. Makes no matter to me."

Geoff smiled. "You must be making a good living, though."

"Sure, but what good is it? What can you buy? Food's rationed and so's gas. You gotta have damned coupons. Cigarettes are tough to get unless you're willing to stand in line for an hour, and then they'll only give you two packs. Dimouts. Blackouts. Air-raid drills. Everybody at you to buy those damned war bonds. All kinds of hicks in town.

Nickel tippers, fa gawd's sake! I tell you it's tough, this war. Tough as hell."

Geoff began to get annoyed. "If you want tough," he said, "how about the guys who are getting killed and wounded? How about the civilians in every other country who barely have enough to eat and who live every moment of their lives wondering whether a bomb will destroy their homes and their families? We're mighty lucky in this country. We don't know what hardship is all about."

"Listen, pal, I'm as patriotic as the next one, but I ain't blind. Maybe we ain't got it as bad as the Limeys or the Frogs or the Wops or even the stinkin' little Chinks, but we didn't start it, did we? They brought it on themselves, dumb bastards, and we're Uncle Stupid, havin' to save 'em again. I did my time in the last war. The big one. The war to end all wars, they told us. Some joke! I blame it all on that nut in the White House. That crazy Rosenfeld. That's his real name, you know. He don't admit being a Jew, but—"

"Stop the cab," Geoffrey said grimly.

"Huh? What's up? We're still six blocks from—"

"I know where we are. I'll walk the rest of the way. I don't want to be in the same car with anyone as bigoted and ignorant as you."

The cabbie pulled over. "Okay, big shot. You sure can get out. You owe me two fifty on the meter."

"And that's exactly what you're going to get," Geoff said.

"What the hell do I care?" The man turned around and stared at him. "I don't need your damned tips, colonel. That's what you are, aren't you? A chicken colonel? Probably been sitting out the war in some nice, safe, fancy spot. Bet you've had all the steaks you want. And the gas and tires to go gallivanting around. And plenty dames to go to bed with. I don't need your insults, pal. You army guys don't spend much time worrying about what's happening back home. You think we ought to kiss your rear ends because you're in uniform. Well, let me tell you—"

"Shut up! Shut your moronic face!" Geoff threw the fare at him, opened the cab door, and got out, slamming it behind him.

Welcome home, he thought grimly as he walked up 52nd Street. And then, suddenly, he stopped and laughed. What was the matter with him, letting one soured-on-the-world idiot throw him this way? That's not the way people at home feel. Not the sane ones. They appreciate what we're doing.

He sobered. And what have you been doing, Colonel Murray? Damned little. Not working as hard as you did on Madison Avenue. Having plenty of time off to spend with your mistress. Eating and drinking well, just as the man said. If you were James, you'd have a right to resent that fool cabdriver. But the truth is, you've probably had it easier than that surly slob of a hackie. Feeling depressed, he slowly made his way to where Lindsay awaited him.

When he opened the door, she flew into his arms, half laughing, half crying, covering his face with kisses, calling him darling and sweetheart and lover and saying over and over how happy she was to have him home, how proud she was of him, how wonderful that he could be with her when she needed him most.

He looked into the eager face and felt ashamed. She loved him so deeply, so unquestioningly, so wholeheartedly. Thank God she can't read my mind, Geoff thought. I'm glad to see her. Truly glad. I do love her, he told himself again. She's my wife. But even as I return her kisses, I'm thinking of someone else. I mustn't. I must give this a chance. This is reality: Lindsay and our apartment and all the familiar things. I'd almost forgotten them in that other world.

"You must be exhausted," she said finally. "Here. Let me take your coat. Sit there in your favorite chair and put your feet up. Can I make you a drink?"

"Love one."

"Martini, I assume?"

"Whisky and water, if you don't mind."

Lindsay looked at him with amusement. "My goodness, how British we've gotten! I assume whisky means Scotch. Have you given up ice, too?"

He grinned. "Sure have. Funny how quickly you can pick up new habits."

"There's nothing quick about three years." She brought him his drink and climbed into his lap. "Oh, Geoff, it's been so damned long! It's been hell without you. Have you missed me too?"

"What a totally unnecessary question!" It's beginning, he thought desperately. The evasions, the sidestepping answers. But Lindsay didn't seem to notice. She put her cheek next to his and sighed with contentment, running her hands lovingly through his hair.

"How long can you stay?"

"Lindsay, honey, I just got here!"

"I know, but I don't want to waste a minute. Speaking of which . . ." Pointedly, she raised her head and looked toward the bedroom.

Oh, God, Geoff thought. Of course she'd want to make love right away. It's been such a long time for her. Not that he didn't want to. The feel of her body, the soft touch of her hands, the quickened breathing all brought back the old desires. Her body could do that to him, no matter what guilt he felt or what a cheat he knew himself to be. He responded as he always had, and Lindsay laughed with joy. For a moment, Geoff hesitated.

"Honey, it's two o'clock in the afternoon."

"So?"

"All I mean is, shouldn't we make a few phone calls first? I should let my folks know I'm back. And yours too. And there's Adele. . . ."

"To hell with them. Geoff, you're home. We're together. It's miraculous. I can't believe it! Let the others wait. What does it matter? I want you to myself, to be close to you again." She suddenly sounded uncertain. "Isn't that what you want too?" She searched his face. "There's nothing wrong, is there? I mean, I was sure you'd be as anxious as I."

"Of course it's what I want, baby. I just thought . . ."

She was smiling again. "Don't *think,* my love. *Act.*"

To his shame, he realized he did want her very much. Maybe that desire was good. Maybe it was the beginning of the answers he needed. Or maybe, he thought, I'm just like every other man, always willing to have or be had by a passionate woman.

But this isn't just any passionate woman, he reminded himself. This is my wife. This is Lindsay, who's been waiting for me and wanting me.

He stood up, scooping her up in his arms, carrying her toward their bed. For a fleeting second he thought of Pamela and could almost hear her say, "I understand, Geoffrey. I truly understand." Do you, Pam? he wondered. I'm not sure I do. I wish to God I did.

Every evening for the past ten days, without fail, Howard had gone up to see Adele. At first he found her as unresponsive to his visits as she was to Lindsay's. She simply sat propped up in bed, listlessly making polite responses to his conversation. He'd felt awkward and clumsy. He wasn't good at this kind of thing, and if he hadn't felt such pity for her, he wouldn't have gone on with it. Certainly nothing seemed to help.

He also saw why his daughter had such scorn for Louise Tamlin, who hovered around looking tragic. It was Louise who vetoed his suggestion that Adele might feel stronger if she got up and moved around a little, even if she didn't feel like leaving the apartment. He suggested this to her mother on the third evening when she walked with him to the door and thanked him for coming to see them.

"You really should try to get her going, Louise. It's no good for her to lie there day after day. My God, she'll be weak as a kitten."

Louise's mouth turned down at the corners. "She's suffered a great loss, Howard. I can only sympathize with that. I remember when Carl—"

"I know she's suffered a loss. We all have. And I remember yours, too. But this certainly isn't the same. Carl was your husband, the father of your child. And he did it deliberately."

She winced, and Howard felt ashamed.

"I'm sorry," he said, "I didn't mean to be cruel. But the circumstances really are quite different. Besides," Howard gently pointed out, "as I recall, you didn't lie around like this. You went on and did what you had to do. Adele acts as though she'd like to die too."

Louise was indignant. "Are you implying I wasn't crushed by Carl's death? You saw me, Howard. I was nearly out of my mind!"

Women, he thought. Why do they deliberately take everything the wrong way? Besides, as I recall it didn't take Louise long to recover. She married that idiot Tamlin in less than a year. The way Adele's going, she might not live a year. I never believed people could grieve themselves to death, but that child's giving it a damned good try.

"Of course I'm not implying that," he said in reply. "I know you were devastated by Carl's death. I simply hoped that having lived through such an awful experience yourself, you might be able to give Adele the benefit of what you learned about life's having to go on."

Louise looked sad again. "She's always been a strange child. Withdrawn. Quiet. I don't think she was ever interested in a boy before James. Sometimes I don't think she ever will be again."

"That's absurd!" Howard was really annoyed now. "She's a beautiful young woman. Intelligent. Charming. Very appealing to men. Of course she'll meet someone else. But not while she languishes in that bed!" He shook his head. "Dammit, Lindsay's right. We've all got to help. You. Me. Lindsay. Everybody. We've got to snap her out of it!"

"Well, I'm sure we're all trying, Howard."

He gave up. "Yes. Of course. Well, I'll be up tomorrow night."

Geoff's return was a source of joy to his parents and to Gandy, too. Pauline tried to be happy, but in spite of herself she would look at her son-in-law and wonder why he was alive and well while James was dead. What awful thoughts! She couldn't believe she felt that way. God in heaven knew she didn't want anything to happen to Geoffrey. She loved him dearly. But I loved my own son more, she thought sadly. I can't help feeling this unreasonable resentment. It's frightful and frightening.

She tried to return his hug with enthusiasm but succeeded only in limply putting her arms around him and accepting his kiss on her cheek. Geoff sensed what she was feeling. It must be hell for her, he thought, seeing me and wishing, despite herself, that it was James. He didn't resent it. He felt the depth of her grief and wished there was something, anything, he could do. At that moment, he knew he couldn't hurt her more by hurting her daughter. I can't be so selfish, he told himself. This poor woman. First an unfaithful husband and then the loss of a son. It would be inhuman to make her watch Lindsay's unhappiness if I asked for a divorce.

But in the next breath, he knew he could not shape his life to suit Pauline. It is only Lindsay I have to think about. Lindsay and Pamela. And, God help me, myself.

He still didn't know how he felt. Since his return he'd made passionate love to his wife and enjoyed it, the joy diminished only by the guilt he felt at the sight of her serene, untroubled face. I'm acting all the time, he thought. Not when we're making love. I still feel rapture with Lindsay. But I'm acting as though everything's the same. As though we'll pick up where we were as soon as the war ends. And I'm not sure. I'm still not sure.

He would have been even more troubled had he recognized that Lindsay found him enormously changed. She told no one, but she was disturbed. This was not the same Geoffrey. Something had happened to him. Something more than the army. Oh, his lovemaking was as wonderful as ever. Almost more wonderful than she remembered. But some-

133

times when he didn't know she was watching, he seemed very far away, as though his thoughts were on something or someone else. She couldn't put her finger on it. On the surface, he was the same sweet, loving, gentle boy she married. But more often, when he was off guard, he seemed troubled and restless, as though he was brooding deeply about something. For the first time she felt a constraint, a sense of being unable to reach him. She thought of talking to her mother about it, but that was impossible. Pauline herself was in another, unreachable world. And Gandy should not be disturbed with these perhaps imaginary fears. The elderly lady was strong, but she was worried about her daughter-in-law. Papa wouldn't understand either. This was a feminine, intuitive kind of thing. He'd either get angry and come right out and ask Geoff what the hell was the matter with him, or he'd dismiss it as one of Lindsay's crazy ideas. Neither would serve her purpose.

At last, desperate to talk to someone, she decided to confide in Adele. Lord knows, Del's in no shape to take on my troubles, Lindsay thought, but on the other hand, she's finally gotten up after a week. Maybe Papa's visits have helped, after all. And maybe having somebody else's worries to concentrate on might help her out of her own introspection. It can't do her any harm. And I've just got to get these nebulous doubts off my chest, if only to have someone tell me I'm just nervous and apprehensive because Geoff has to leave again. And he will leave soon. Papa's efforts to have him transferred back, to Washington or New York, don't seem to have come to much. He admitted that things seem so hot in Europe now there's small chance of bringing anyone back soon.

Late one afternoon, unannounced, she dropped in to see her friend. Adele was in her room, but she was dressed and sitting in a chair.

"Well, you're looking better!" Lindsay grinned at her. "Get you! I hardly recognized you with your clothes on!"

Adele gave a little smile. "How are you, Lind? How's Geoff? It was so good to see him for a few minutes last week. He looks wonderful." She hesitated. "I want you to know I'm sorry. About all those things I said to you. I didn't mean them, you know. I was half crazy."

"Forget it." Lindsay dismissed her words with a little wave of her hand. "I'd have behaved much worse in your place. I said some rotten things to you too. But I thought maybe I could shock you into some kind

134

of emotion, even if it was anger. Anyway, I'm glad you're better. I hear Papa's been a regular gentleman caller."

"He's been marvelous. He's quite a man, your father. I never really knew him until now. We've had some good talks, Lind. He's a kind person."

"I know. I find him changed too, since James . . . that is, I think he's much more tolerant and understanding."

"Or perhaps *we've* changed, Lind. We never were able to see any sensitivity in him when we were young. Now that we have troubles of our own—well, maybe we're more responsive. Or at least more grown up."

"Could be. I'm not sure I like being grown up, though."

Something in her friend's voice alerted Adele. Lindsay looked tense and edgy. Strange. She'd seemed so happy a week ago.

"Lindsay? Are you all right?"

"Sure. Having Geoff back is . . . oh, hell, I'm not going to lie to you, Del. There's something wrong. I don't know what it is. I couldn't tell you a single incident. But I just feel something's happened to him. He's different."

"It's been nearly three years, Lindsay. He's seen a lot of terrible things. You can't really expect him to be the same."

"I know. I keep telling myself that. But it's something more. He's trying to be himself. Our sex life is great. We have fun and laugh just as we used to. But sometimes I catch him looking at me as though I were a stranger he was meeting for the first time. Or as though he's comparing me with somebody else. Isn't that nuts? I know I'm imagining it, but I can't shake this anxiety. It's right there, always under the surface."

Adele didn't answer, but, as on the morning of Pearl Harbor, her gaze involuntarily went to the dresser where she kept all her letters from James. The slight glance didn't escape Lindsay.

"Something I can get you?"

Adele flushed. "No. Why do you ask?"

"I saw you look toward the dresser and I thought maybe there was something over there you wanted me to hand you." Lindsay waited. There was something wrong, something revealing in the way Adele's eyes had been drawn to the other side of the room while her friend spoke of her worries. Why did Adele seem so flustered? Lindsay had no idea. She simply sensed from Adele's self-conscious attitude that it had to do with her. Or with Geoffrey. Or both of them. She took a wild stab.

"Del, do you know something you're not telling me? About Geoff, I mean?"

The reply was too vehement. "Of course not! What could I know?"

"I haven't a clue. But when I was talking, your eyes went right to the drawer I know you keep James's letters in." A suspicion suddenly dawned. "Did he write something about Geoff? Is that what it is? Did he tell you something? Del, if you know anything that explains what I'm feeling, for God's sake tell me! You're my best friend. You owe me that much."

Adele's hands began to tremble, and she clenched them tightly to keep Lindsay from noticing. Of course she knew what it was. James had written to her about Geoff's affair with the English girl. She could remember the words in his letter, the one that had followed the earlier one:

My darling, I suppose I shouldn't tell even you this, but your marvelous understanding of my advice to Geoff emboldens me to do so. He's found himself a nice girl over here, and it's made the difference I predicted. He's more re-laxed, better able to cope with his own stresses and Lindsay's. It's a momentary thing, no threat to his marriage, but of course Lindsay must never know. I hope you don't think me a complete bastard for pushing my own sister's husband into this. Strange as it seems, it is as much for Lindsay's sake as for his. He was go-ing to explode with tension and react to Lindsay's whining (yes, I'm afraid that's what it's been) in a way that might have destroyed them both. I've not met the girl, but Geoff tells me she's a good sort, very relaxed and undemand-ing. Not a "home wrecker" in any sense of the word. She simply needs someone too. I gather she's been as unhappy as he. Her fiancé was killed recently and I suppose she's as lost and lonely as Geoff. I wanted you to know, not to burden you with this secret, but to tell you that in an odd way this is the best thing that could have happened to Geoff and Lindsay. He'll come home a better, wiser, and more loving man because of it. If I didn't believe that, you know I'd never have encouraged this "betrayal" of my sister.

When the letter arrived, Adele had been appalled. How could James sanction his brother-in-law's infidelity? I'd have understood it better, she thought then, if Geoff had casually picked up a woman for the night. But to attach himself to one, and a lonely one at that, seemed the ultimate folly. He's bound to get involved, she thought. That's how these things start. Oh, James, why did you give him such advice? Don't you know how vulnerable men are, especially when they're thousands of miles from home? What will you do if this destroys Lindsay's marriage, rather than saving it? But she hadn't written that to him. Instead, she replied that she was sure he was right about Geoffrey, and she only prayed that the girl was, indeed, as sensible as she sounded and that Geoff was level-headed enough to keep the affair in perspective.

I'm far too naïve about these things to have an opinion. I trust your judgment totally, my love, and I defer to your knowledge about men, since I have so little. But do keep an eye on him, James. Don't let him do anything foolish. It would kill Lindsay, and you'd never forgive yourself.

He'd answered reassuringly and spoken no more of it in the letters that followed. She'd tried to put it out of her mind, instinctively knowing it was potentially explosive and, yes, morally wrong, for all that James tried to justify it.

And now here it was, she thought, listening to Lindsay's fears. It's that woman. That's what's wrong with Geoffrey. He's fallen in love with her. Lindsay senses something. She's probing the edges of this bombshell that could blow up in her face, shattering her marriage and tearing her to pieces with it.

Lindsay was looking at her suspiciously. "You *do* know something, Del. I can see it in your face. You've never been a good liar. What do you know that I don't?"

"Nothing! I told you before. How could I know anything about Geoff?" She hoped she sounded convincing. "Lindsay, dear, I think you're just a bundle of nerves, worrying about Geoff's leaving again. I'm sure you're imagining all these things. He seems quite the same to me. If I knew anything that would help you, wouldn't I tell you? You've been so good to me. All of you have. I'd never hold out on you if I thought I could help with your problems."

That was true enough, Adele thought. If I thought telling her would help, I would. But it would only make things worse. It's not my place to reveal Geoff's secret. It's his. If, indeed, his involvement with the English girl has become more than an outlet for his loneliness and fears.

For the first time since she heard of James's death, she realized she'd put aside her own misery to concentrate on someone else's. I'm going to survive, Adele thought with amazement. Poor Lindsay. So troubled. And rightly. But I owe her a debt of gratitude. She's made me think of something besides myself for the first time in weeks. And yet the burden of knowledge lay heavily on Adele. She wondered if it was right not to tell Lindsay what she knew. I can't do otherwise, she told herself. I could never be the one to tell her. Never. Not even if she finds out later and hates me for not being honest with her. With an effort, Adele attempted to turn Lindsay's mind to other things.

"How are your mother and Gandy?" she asked.

Lindsay looked startled. She was not ready to abandon the subject of her own fears, and Adele's sudden switch of topic surprised her and convinced her beyond anything else that her friend really did know something she was not going to tell. So be it, Lindsay thought. Whatever it is, I can't drag it out of her. I'll just have to muddle through this alone.

"They're just the same," she said. "Mama's functioning. That's about the best I can say. Gandy's not well, I'm afraid. She'd never admit it, but I know she's sick. She won't go to the doctor, damn her stubborn little old heart. I think she's afraid that would only add to Mama's terrible state of mind." Lindsay shook her head. "They're not good, Del. But at least Papa's helpful. He comes by the apartment to see them most every day. I wouldn't have believed he'd show such concern. He was always so impatient with sickness or nerves. Didn't believe people should have either. Now he seems actually sympathetic."

"I know. As I said before, he's been kindness itself to me. Along with you, Lind, he's the best medicine I could have. I think I finally got up because I was ashamed to have him see me lying there in bed every evening. He was delighted that I finally moved. In fact, he's said he'll take me out to dinner whenever I'm ready to go."

"I hope to God you're going to do it! You must get out of this house, and that's certainly an easy way. Papa will be a good escort. No problems, no need to put on an act as you would with someone your own age. It will be like going out with your own . . ." Lindsay's voice trailed off.

Adele smiled sadly. "Yes, like going out with my own father," she finished. "I wonder what that would have been like. You're lucky to have yours. Even divorced, he's around when you need him." Adele thought for a moment. "Have you told him anything about Geoff? About your feelings, I mean?"

Lindsay laughed. "God, no! That's not the kind of thing you can discuss with Papa. He's strictly a black-and-white man. No gray areas for him. He'd think I was crazy if I told him I was worried and didn't know what I was worried about. He may have changed, but not all that much! At best, he'd think I was just a hysterical female. Or he'd grab Geoff by the scruff of the neck and try to shake some answers out of him, which would be not only futile but probably dangerous. Geoff's had quite enough of Papa's meddling in his affairs." Lindsay glanced at her watch. "Good grief, it's late! I've got to run. Geoff's taking me to the Stork Club tonight."

"Wonderful! Celebration?"

Lindsay shook her head sadly. "Sorry to say, it's a premature 'bon voyage.' His leave is up day after tomorrow. I suggested we have a night on the town tonight and spend tomorrow evening at home alone. Candlelight, Glenn Miller recordings, and me in my sexiest sheer black negligee. That seems the appropriate memory for him to take back, don't you think?"

"I'm sorry, Lind. But at least he's alive. Try not to worry. Everything's going to be okay for you two."

Lindsay's heart softened. "I know. I'm sure it will. Del, I'm sorry I came over here and made such a fuss. You have so much more to be sad about. You must think me the world's most selfish, spoiled brat."

"No. I love you very much. I want you to be happy."

"And you too. We just have to give it time, all of us. Promise me you'll try to do a little more to get your mind off things. Let Papa take you to a swell dinner. At least that's a start."

Adele smiled. "We'll see. Maybe later, if the offer still holds."

His last night of leave was both agony and ecstasy for Geoff. Lindsay was never sweeter, looking at him adoringly across the candle-lit dinner table, making wild, almost desperate love to him later, and then lying close, her head on his shoulder, her hand trustingly in his.

"It won't be much longer, will it, darling? The war, I mean. Papa says the talk is that the Germans will give up by spring. And once they're finished, the Japanese will have to surrender too."

He couldn't suppress a touch of irony. "Papa knows best. I'm sure he's better informed than I am, what with all his top-level connections."

Lindsay didn't answer.

What a bastard you are, Geoff Murray, he told himself. She loves

139

her father. Why do you have to go on making nasty cracks about him all the time? Hell, the man is well-intentioned, I suppose. I have to give him credit for the way he's behaved since James was killed. "I'm sorry, Lind," he said. "That was uncalled-for. I don't know why I'm so rotten about him. He's only tried to help us, I know. And he's been very decent these past weeks, to your mother and Adele especially. I'm being unfair. Forgive me, honey."

"It's all right. I understand better than you do. You and Papa constantly clash because you're so much alike. You're strong, independent people. That's why I love you both so much."

Alike? Maybe we are at that, Geoff thought bitterly. We've both cheated on our wives. We have that in common. But with Howard it never became serious. That's the difference. Several times he'd come close to telling Lindsay about Pam. But to what purpose? He still wasn't sure he wanted a divorce, and unless he did there was no point in telling Lindsay anything about the other woman. "Other woman." Such a sordid phrase to describe her, as though she were some cheap little thing he kept hidden away. As Howard Thresher always did. Geoff hated this secret, but to reveal it to his wife, unless he wanted to marry Pamela, was selfish and cruel. His confession wouldn't make him feel better, and it would only bring Lindsay pain. And yet he felt dishonest, both to his wife and his mistress. Making love to either was cheating both. My God, what a mess! What was he waiting for? Some revelation from on high? Some sign to tell him what to do? You want both of them, he thought with disgust. You stupid, selfish sonofabitch, you really wish you could manage both without losing either.

"Geoff?" Lindsay was looking into his troubled face, barely discernible in the dim light they'd left on in the bathroom. "What is it? I know something's wrong. Can't you tell me?"

This was his chance. She'd opened the door but he couldn't step through, fearful of what he'd come to on the other side. No. Not yet. Not until I see Pam again, now that I've been with Lindsay after so long.

"There's nothing wrong, darling. Nothing except the fact that we're going to be separated again. It's hard being without you, Lind. Everything gets mixed up. For you too, I know. It hasn't been easy for you, has it?"

What was he hoping? That she'd confess she too had been unfaithful? Is that what I want to hear? Geoff wondered. He thought of

James. How would I react if Lindsay told me she'd slept with someone else? Could I possibly be as understanding as I may expect her, one day, to be of me? Would it ease my conscience to know I wasn't the only one who'd strayed? Maybe. More likely I'd want to kill her and the man she'd been with. My God, I'm going crazy! I don't know what I want.

"Yes, it's been hard," Lindsay was saying. "I've missed you terribly. Missed this. I confess to you, darling, that sometimes I was tempted. But I couldn't do that to you, Geoff. I care for you too much."

"I'd . . . I'd have forgiven you, Lind."

"Would you? I suppose you would have, dearest. You're so wonderful. But I'd never have forgiven myself. I may seem very casual, but I feel strongly about promises. I promised myself to you, and I wouldn't break that vow." She hesitated. "Besides, I'm a burnt child, remember? I saw what infidelity did to my mother and father. It killed their marriage. Even if Clark Gable came along," Lindsay said teasingly, "I'd have to tell him: no, I love my husband."

Could *you* forgive *me?* he wanted to ask. In light of that, I suppose not. He groaned inwardly, involuntarily holding her closer. Lindsay misunderstood the gesture.

"Yes. Make love to me again, Geoff," she whispered. "We're going to be very lonely people once more. These memories are all we have to live on."

13

$\mathcal{G}$eoffrey went back to Europe at the end of January, and by the end of March the doctor confirmed what Lindsay already knew.

"You're pregnant, all right, Mrs. Murray. About two months along. We should have a nice baby the latter part of October."

Should "we," indeed? Lindsay silently mocked. Too bad "we" won't have a husband by then. Or a child either, if I can help it.

The news was the very last thing she wanted to hear. Pregnant! Under other circumstances she'd have been joyful, but not now. Not since two weeks ago, when she found out about Geoffrey and the woman he'd been sleeping with since last summer.

The revelation had come about in an unexpected way, all the more terrible because it disclosed not only the faithlessness of her husband but the deception of her best friend and the destruction of the ideals she'd cherished about her dead brother. Everybody in the world was rotten, she thought. She wouldn't bring a child into a world so filled with lies and pretense and cynicism. She felt sick with humiliation. James advising his brother-in-law to have a cheap affair. Adele knowing it and disloyally keeping the secret from her. And Geoffrey. Geoffrey coming home on leave, pretending devotion, making love to her when he'd barely left that other woman's bed. What a fool she'd been! She'd known something was wrong, but she'd put it out of her mind, convincing herself she was only imagining a change in her husband. And then, blind idiot that she was, deliberately trying to get pregnant while he was home, discarding her customary precautions, eager to have his child. The joke's on me, Lindsay thought. The only thing I have to be grateful for is that I found out about him in time to stop a pregnancy by this coward, this hypocrite I thought I loved. Thank God Papa told me what a fool Geoffrey was making of me. Though I doubt he'd have done so if he'd had any idea I was carrying a child. He'd have bullied Geoffrey into "doing his duty" if he'd known I was pregnant. That's the last thing I want: to have a man forced to stay with me for such a reason.

The revelation had happened so strangely, that evening two weeks before. Her father had called and invited her to dinner. Lindsay had accepted, saying in a half-joking way, "I'm surprised you have a free evening, Papa. Adele tells me she's been dining with you almost every night."

He'd sounded strange on the telephone. "She's part of what I want to talk to you about, Lindsay. I mean, indirectly, Adele's involved."

Even then she hadn't been alarmed. "Involved? You make it all sound very cloak-and-dagger, I must say! What's going on?"

"We'll discuss it later. Want to meet me at the Union League about seven thirty?"

"Sure. I look forward to it. You're my second-favorite man."

Howard was waiting for her at the entrance, and they went directly to the table.

"Would you like a drink, Lindsay?"

"I don't think so, thanks."

"Maybe you'd better have one. I don't have very good news."

For the first time she felt frightened. It couldn't be that something had happened to Geoff. Papa wouldn't ask her to dinner to tell her news like that. Mama? Gandy? Adele? No. Again, he wouldn't pick this way to report an emergency. Puzzled, she ordered a martini. Howard indicated he'd have the same.

When the waiter left, her father looked at her gravely and said, "I don't quite know where to begin, Lindsay."

She tried to be flippant. "How about with the bald, ugly truth? Whatever it is."

"All right. Geoffrey's having an affair with an English girl. It's been going on since last summer. I don't know how serious it is, but I thought you should know."

She felt as though every bone in her body had turned to water. As though everything was draining out of her, leaving her without strength enough to pick up the glass the waiter set in front of her. She stared uncomprehendingly at her father.

"What are you talking about, Papa?" Her voice was barely a

whisper. "That can't be true. He would have told me. He never mentioned a word when he was here."

"I know. Perhaps he never means to mention it, Lindsay. I debated a long time whether or not I should tell you, and I'm not sure even now that I made the right decision. But dammit, I can't abide that kind of cowardly behavior!" Howard pounded his fist on the table. "I won't have him making a fool of you! You know about me, Lindsay. You know I saw other women when your mother and I were married. But I never hid it from her. I never pretended. I don't condone infidelity, not my own or anyone else's. But at least I had enough respect for my wife not to go sneaking behind her back, making a laughingstock of her."

Lindsay was in shock. "A laughingstock," she repeated. "Is that what Geoffrey's done to me?"

"In a way, yes. It's bound to be the talk of his base. You can't hide things like that. And that woman. She must enjoy thinking how they're putting something over on you. Geoffrey too, for all I know." Howard was angry for her. "A hundred people in Europe must know. How long do you think it will be before the news gets back here?"

She was trembling. "How . . . how did you find out?"

He looked unhappier than ever. "Adele told me. I'm betraying a confidence by letting you know. She tried to make me promise I wouldn't. I suppose she just couldn't keep it to herself any more, but it was my decision to tell you, Lindsay. I believe it's your right to know. From here on in, any move you choose to make will be with full knowledge, at least. You may choose to forgive and forget. Or not. But at least, like your mother, you'll have that option."

Lindsay barely heard the last part. "Adele knew? And didn't tell me?"

"She didn't want to hurt you, my dear. She felt, still feels, that it's one of those fleeting, wartime things, necessary for a man separated so long from his wife. At least, that's what James convinced her of."

"James? James knew?"

Howard sighed. "James more than knew," he said gently. "He encouraged Geoffrey to do what he did. He wrote it all to Adele, how Geoffrey was tense, and troubled by your attitude. How it meant nothing for your husband to have a little 'temporary diversion' that would only strengthen his love for you and help hold your marriage together. Yes, James influenced him to find himself a woman for 'therapy.' That was his theory. And Geoff bought it. So did Adele, since she thought

144

James was the nearest thing to God. It wasn't until she saw you when Geoffrey was home that she began to have serious misgivings. She wanted to tell you then. You were so confused and troubled, guessing at something and not knowing what. But she was afraid you'd be devastated. And she decided it was Geoff's place, not hers, to bring this out in the open."

Lindsay gripped the edge of the table. For the first time in her life she thought she was going to faint. The room blurred and swam around her, but she held on until the feeling passed and she could speak again.

"I'll never forgive them," she said. "Not any of them. It was a conspiracy. All of them laughing behind my back, just as you said."

"Wait, darling. Not Adele. She was frantic with worry for you. And, God rest his soul, not James. Perhaps his advice was misguided but I have to believe, as Adele does, that he really thought you'd never know, and that Geoffrey would be all the better husband for it. As for Geoff, what can I tell you? I'm the last man to criticize, as I said. We're all subject to temptations of the flesh, Lindsay dear. I'm only angry that he wasn't man enough to tell you. That he didn't pay you the compliment of feeling you'd understand."

"Why should he have thought I'd understand? Mama didn't understand."

Howard looked as though she'd struck him. "That's true enough, I suppose. Although for a long time I thought she did know the difference in the way a man feels about his wife and his mistress. I was guilty of many transgressions, and no need for them. At least Geoffrey had a real need. You were thousands of miles away."

Lindsay looked grim. "That was hardly my fault, was it? If he hadn't been so pigheaded about going overseas, he wouldn't have had those 'needs,' as you call them. And what about *my* needs, Papa? I nearly died of longings too, but I didn't sleep with somebody to satisfy them." She laughed and it was a chilling sound. "My God. The old double standard. It still goes on, doesn't it? According to you, it's okay for men to cheat as long as it never gets serious and they're manly enough to tell their wives. What a crock, Papa! Their confessions are only a way of unloading their guilt, as yours were. What would you have done if Mama had been sleeping around? I'll tell you what: you'd have killed her. Oh, it's just fine for men to be tomcats, but God forbid a woman is anything but the faithful kitten. That's what you always called me, remember? Kitten. A nice, faithful, untroublesome little cat

145

on the hearth. That's how you think of women, Papa. That's how all men think of them, including James and Geoffrey!"

"Don't, my dear," Howard said. "Don't be so bitter."

"What the hell do you expect me to be? Am I supposed to thank Geoffrey for deceiving me? Or Adele for not being enough of a friend to tell me? Or forgive James, my wonderful, perfect brother, for advising my husband to go out and get himself a woman? I suppose the only one I can thank is you, Papa. At least you had guts enough to tell me what the others were too sneaky to admit."

Howard was silent for a long moment. Then he said, "And now, Lindsay? What will you do now?"

"I don't know. My impulse is to file for divorce. But maybe not. Maybe I'll just live life my way for a while. Maybe I'll give Geoffrey a dose of his own medicine. See how he likes it when he finally finds out his wife is doing anything she damned well pleases with *her* body, too!"

"Lindsay, stop! Don't say things like that. You don't mean them."

"Don't I, Papa? You just watch me. And remember to tell Adele to write all the news to Geoffrey, since she's the respository of all confidences!"

Howard was alarmed. "You mustn't tell her I told you, Lindsay. She'd be terribly upset. She's such a sweet, gentle girl."

"Of course she is." Lindsay was scornful. "My best friend. Darling, pathetic, loyal Adele. Like a sister to me. She was quick enough to side with my brother in this whole thing, wasn't she? And underhanded enough not to warn me what was happening. Upset? Who cares if she's upset?"

Howard looked down at his drink. "I care. I care very much. You see, I've asked Adele to marry me."

For a moment Lindsay forgot her own problems. "What? What did you say?"

"I've asked Adele to be my wife. I didn't mean to tell you tonight. It just came out. We've told no one yet, not even her parents."

"We? You mean she's accepted?"

Howard nodded. "Yes, she has." He held up his hand to silence her. "I know what you're going to say: I'm much too old for her. Chronologically, that's true. But sometimes years don't count. As with all things, each case must be judged on its own merits. Adele is extremely mature for her age. We are companionable, content together. We

146

both want serenity and a good life. I'll do my best to make her happy. I think I can."

Lindsay was aghast. "Papa you'll soon be fifty-seven years old. And she's only twenty-four. It's ridiculous! More than thirty years' difference! My God, don't you care what people will say?"

"Not particularly. Do you?"

"I care what Mama will say. Hasn't she been through enough? Must you humiliate her this way, having people snicker and say you must be going through change of life? That you're a cradle snatcher?"

"You seem to forget that your mother and I have been divorced for a long time. I fail to see how anything I do could embarrass her any longer."

"You're being a fool, Papa. You can't possibly believe a girl Adele's age could really be in love with you. Don't you see? She's always wanted a father figure. Always. And she's finally found it."

Howard was calm. "Was James a father figure? She wanted to marry him."

"Right. And when she couldn't she decided to marry *his* father!" Lindsay began to plead. "Don't do this, Papa. Please don't do this. You'll regret it. You'll both be miserable."

"I see no reason why we should be, Lindsay. You may consider me senile, but I assure you I'm not. I can well fulfill my husbandly duties."

"I'm sure of that," Lindsay said sarcastically. "And probably still offer aid and comfort to any number of other ladies on the side, as you did when you were married to Mama."

"That's a low blow."

"Is it? Not low enough, I think, for this debased idea. Marry Adele? It's practically incestuous! You always said she was like another daughter to you. Why, she's younger than I am. It's unthinkable!"

Howard looked pained, but he was unshakable. "I'm sorry you feel that way, my dear, but it doesn't change my intentions. Adele has taste and intelligence. She'll be a gracious hostess and a good wife."

Lindsay looked scornful. "Has it occurred to you that you could be describing Mama? It must be true that men marry the same woman the second time around. Adele is what Mama was at twenty-four, I suppose. Except you're not twenty-six." She was distraught. "And as for *her* I have nothing but contempt for that dreary, frightened, fading little mouse! She's not even capable of being a friend, much less a wife!"

147

Lindsay's voice grew heated. "And you! Have you changed so completely, Papa? Are you going to be a faithful husband this time around? Or
will Adele not be exciting enough for you either, once you've gotten
used to being able to marry a girl less than half your age?"

Without warning, Lindsay burst into tears. It was all too much.
She was betrayed by her husband, deceived by those she trusted. Her
marriage was over, whether or not she divorced Geoff. And now this.
This revolting business of her father and Adele. He's a dirty old man,
she thought. And she's sick in her head. Why should I care what happens to them? I don't, except for how Mama's going to feel and how
hurt Gandy will be. They're going to suffer enough when they find out
about Geoff and me. And now this. She tried to control her tears, and
the efforts brought on hiccups. Howard pushed a glass of water toward
her.

"Hold your breath and take deep swallows, honey." He spoke as
though she were a child.

"Leave me alone!" Lindsay threw her napkin on the table and rose
from her chair. "I want out of here!"

"Sit down, Lindsay. You haven't even had your dinner."

She was still standing, trying to be dignified, an impossible accomplishment when every few seconds a hiccup jarred her. People at nearby
tables were looking at them curiously. "I'm going home," she said. "I
don't care if I ever see you again."

"Lindsay, you're making a scene. Sit down and behave yourself!"

"Go to hell, Papa!"

Every detail of that evening flashed across her mind in an instant
as she sat across from the unctuous obstetrician who'd just told her the
"good news." Calmly, Lindsay crossed her legs and lit a cigarette.

"I don't want a baby, doctor."

His cheerful smile faded. "I don't think I understand, Mrs. Murray."

"What's to understand? I want to terminate the pregnancy."

He shook his head. "I'm afraid that's impossible. You're physically
healthy and mentally sound. There's no way I could recommend an
abortion for you."

"I understand it's not that difficult." Lindsay said. "A psychiatrist
could testify that giving birth would endanger my mental state. And he
wouldn't be lying. It would. My husband has been guilty of adultery

and I'm going to divorce him. Having a baby now, on top of all this stress, would certainly throw me into a nervous breakdown."

The doctor shook his head. "I'm sorry about your domestic problems, Mrs. Murray, but I see no signs of emotional instability in you and I doubt any reputable psychiatrist would find them either. There is no reason why you can't have a normal, healthy child and come through the birth process with no serious side effects. It's unfortunate, of course, about your husband. But perhaps now, when you consider the child, you'll change your mind about the divorce. More than one couple has. Many women find it in their hearts to forgive a momentary lapse, in view of such wonderful news."

You make me want to throw up, Lindsay thought. You and your bloody platitudes. You probably cheat on your wife too. But she kept her face impassive. Indeed, she looked up at him helplessly.

"You're so good, doctor. So understanding. But it's impossible. My husband doesn't love me. He wouldn't want a child."

"How do you know that, my dear? Did you tell him you suspected you're pregnant?

"No. He's been overseas for nearly three years." The expression on the man's face made her laugh. "I know what you're thinking," Lindsay said, "but you're wrong. He was home on leave in January. It's his child, all right. That's not why I don't want it. It's not I who've been unfaithful." She looked pathetic again. "Please help me. I can't have this baby."

"I'm sorry," he said again. "There's nothing I can do. Without certification by three doctors, the law does not permit abortion."

Lindsay's face hardened. "Then I'll just have to go outside the law, won't I? There are medical men less righteous than you. They're expensive, but they exist. Perhaps you could find it in your heart to recommend one? You have my word that I'll never tell how I heard of him."

"You know I can't do that, Mrs. Murray. I wouldn't dream of it. Not under any circumstances. You're a married woman, young and healthy. It may not be convenient for you to have a child, but there's no way around it."

"Of course there is. Don't tell me you don't know the names of any abortionists."

The doctor looked grim. "No, I don't. But even if I did, I wouldn't send *any* woman to such a person."

She stood up. "All right, then I'll find one on my own. It can't be that difficult in a city as big as New York."

"Please, Mrs. Murray, I beg you—"

She turned and left the office without another word.

It was one of those rare March days, soft and sunny, with the promise of spring. As she strolled down upper Park Avenue, Lindsay felt the sun warm on her face, but inside she was cold with fear. Despite her defiant words, she had no idea of where to find an abortionist. How did one start? Through friends? If any of her friends had had this illegal operation, she didn't know it. Whom could she talk to? Not Mama, obviously. Not to Adele. She hadn't spoken to her former friend since the day after her dinner with Papa. Adele had called, and it had been a dreadful exchange.

"Lindsay? I just spoke with your . . . with Howard. Are you all right?"

"Oh, I'm terrific, as you might well imagine."

"I'm so sorry. About Geoff, I mean. I suppose I should have told you when I first knew, but I just couldn't bear to. I kept hoping it would end and you'd never know. James thought it would."

"So I understand." Lindsay's voice was frigid. "Nice of you all to protect Geoffrey that way."

"It wasn't like that, Lind. Truly it wasn't. Those things happen in wartime. You know they do. Can't you forgive him? I'm sure he loves you. I just know this girl doesn't mean anything to him. Please try to be sensible about it, dear. Don't wreck your marriage because of one mistake. Remember the circumstances under which it happened."

"How lovely of you to be so concerned for me. Are you speaking as my friend or my future stepmother?"

There was a little pause. "I'd like to talk to you about that too."

"What's to talk about? I don't need a degree in psychology to figure you out. Or Papa either. It's a very common thing. Very common and very vulgar."

"Lindsay, you don't understand. I love him. He's kind and gentle, and he makes me feel safe."

"Really? How amazing. Two months ago you were dying with grief over my brother. What marvelous recuperative powers you must have, to fall madly in love again so quickly."

Adele's voice was choked, but she managed to say, "It was you who kept saying I had to go on, Lindsay. That I was dishonoring James's

150

memory by not picking up the pieces of my life."

"Yes, dammit, I did say those things. But I never dreamed you were going to choose my father as your healer!"

"Is it so terrible, Lind? We're both lonely and alone. It's not as though I were breaking up a marriage or doing anyone harm."

"I don't think we have anything more to say, Adele. I really don't want to talk to you. Not now or ever again."

Without waiting for a reply, she'd hung up. Adele did not call back. Neither did she hear from her father. But that evening Pauline telephoned.

"I gather you know," she said without preamble. "About your father and Adele. I've just spoken to him."

Lindsay felt her pain. "Yes, Mama. He told me last night. It's outrageous! How could he do such a thing? How could she? They're mad, both of them. I hate them. I'll never speak to either of them again!"

"I was afraid you'd feel that way. You mustn't, Lindsay. I know you always hoped your father and I would get together again. You didn't have to say so. I could see it in your face, especially after James. . . . But it could never have happened. We'd grown too far apart. You must believe that. I never wanted him back. And he never wanted to come."

You lie, Mama, Lindsay thought. Gracefully and beautifully, with dignity as always, but it's still a lie. You still love him. What must you be feeling in your heart?

"I'm sorry, Mama. I wish I were more tolerant, but I'm not. I wouldn't have been surprised by Papa's remarriage. *That* I admit. But to someone suitable, at least! To someone near his own age. Adele! It's incredible!"

"If it makes them happy, you should be happy for them, Lindsay. Be glad other people are as fortunate as you. You have Geoffrey. You can't begrudge others a chance at the same kind of good marriage."

So he didn't tell her that part, Lindsay realized. I'm glad. One blow is enough on top of her bereavement. I won't tell her either. At least not until I'm sure what I'm going to do.

Now, crossing 79th Street, she still didn't know what she was going to do. It had been hard to see her mother and grandmother and not tell them about Geoff, but she hadn't the heart. Not just yet. She hadn't even written to her husband. She'd started a dozen letters and torn up every one. Soon he'd wonder why there was no word from her. Or may-

151

be Adele will tell him why, Lindsay thought bitterly. She seems very good at meddling in my marriage.

Frantically, she turned back to the problem at hand. What *was* she going to do about this unwanted baby?

Pamela watched him carefully. Ever since his return from home two months ago, there'd been a change in Geoff. He seemed more thoughtful, more troubled. She'd hoped, honestly, that being with his wife would bring him to a decision one way or another. Of course she hoped that it would be a decision in her favor, that he'd realize he wanted her and not Lindsay. She loved him deeply. But she would have accepted the other choice if she'd had to. Anything was better than this indecision. It had worsened since his leave, and it was tearing him to pieces. Her, too. She couldn't bear to see him suffer. She'd rather give him up, terrible as the thought was.

What has happened to us? she wondered. We thought we could take this kind of thing or leave it. Love has happened to us, you fool, she answered herself. What started as a casual let's-forget-our-troubles fling has grown into something terribly important, something we don't know how to handle.

When he'd come to the apartment for the first time in weeks, she'd been there ahead of him, looking her prettiest, smiling her welcome. Geoff had held her and kissed her.

"I missed you."

"I'm glad," Pam said. "Me too. How did it go?"

Geoff shrugged. "James's mother is in terrible shape. His girl too. Adele. Even his father is more subdued than I've ever seen him."

Pamela waited and then she said quietly, "And Lindsay?"

For a moment he avoided her eyes. "She's heartbroken about her brother, of course. But . . . but she had me. She was happy about that." He turned to face Pamela. "We made love, Pam. It's only fair to tell you that."

She smiled. "Darling, do you really think me so unworldly? Of course you did. I expected you to."

"And you're not jealous?"

What a child he was! "Jealous? Yes, I'm jealous, but it's a little ridiculous of me, isn't it? She *is* your wife. After almost three years, she'd certainly expect that."

He shook his head. "I can't tell you how I felt. Ashamed, actually.

152

As though I were being unfaithful to you. But I wanted to, Pam. That's the hell of it. I wanted her too. My God, what kind of animal am I? I'm not in control of myself any more!"

She tried to make light of it. "You're human. And kind. What's so frightful about that?"

"No, I'm not. I'm a damned coward. On the way over, I made up my mind I'd tell her about us. And I couldn't. I let her think everything was fine. That I was her faithful, loving husband, in every way. I just couldn't bring myself to talk about you."

She was silent. Finally she said, "And what would you have told her, Geoff? That we're in love? That you want a divorce? Or would it have simply been an honorable confession?" There was no reproach in her voice, no ring of sarcasm. She honestly wanted answers, but she suspected he had none. His reply confirmed that.

"I don't know," Geoffrey said. "I don't know what I would have said. I do know I love you. I'd like to get a divorce and marry you. But the same old devils plague me. How can I hurt Lindsay? How selfish and uncaring can I be? And it wasn't the moment to be cruel. It really wasn't, not after they'd just heard about James."

Hurt Lindsay? Pam wanted to ask. What about *my* hurt? What about what you're doing to me? Stop that! she ordered herself. He's told you he loves you and wants to marry you. That's enough for now.

"Darling, you're back. That's all I care about. Let's don't worry about the future. Let it take care of itself. It will, in any case."

He held her close. "Oh, Pam, I do love you. You know that, don't you?"

She hugged him tightly to her. "Of course I know that, you silly ass!" She laughed. "You Americans, bless you! I've heard about your— what do they call it?—your 'New England consciences.' Your left-over 'Pilgrim guilts.' It makes you quite endearing, you know. Very honorable, as opposed to our jaded, old-world outlook. Very refreshing indeed."

He looked at her searchingly. "Don't try to kid about it. It's very serious."

She was sober. "I know that, luv. I know it very well. You'll do the right thing, Geoffrey. Whatever you decide in the end will be the right thing."

14

*A*s the days went by, Lindsay became more distraught. She'd found no doctor, and three months, she knew, was the very latest at which she could abort with any degree of safety. It would be risky at any time but perilous after that. Besides, she admitted to herself, at this stage she felt that the child still wasn't sufficiently developed to be a person. Later, it would be like taking a life. As though some unseen hand guided her, she wandered into the Stage Door Canteen one evening. She hadn't been in for some time, and one of the girls she'd met there greeted her with surprise.

"Well, will you look who's here? Welcome back, Lindsay. The boys missed you."

Lindsay didn't particularly like Marge Baldwin. In spite of their surface friendship at the canteen, Lindsay'd never sought her out socially. It was snobbish of her, she supposed. Marge was a pleasant enough girl but rather crude. She was a waitress, given to swapping off-color stories with the soldiers and sailors, a tough, overdressed girl who, Gandy might have said, seemed "free with her favors." The good-hearted whore, Lindsay thought. Yet she had to admire Marge. After a tough day on her feet, she still had enough heart to come to this place and dance with the boys, kid with them, make them feel welcome and wanted. She does much more for them in every way, Lindsay thought, than I do. And God bless her for it.

She smiled at Marge and said, "I haven't been very conscientious lately, I know. It's disgraceful of me, but my husband was home on leave."

"What the hell. You were still doing your bit for a man in uniform. It must have been nice, having him back even for a little while." Marge looked wistful. "My guy's over there too. Of course, he's only an N.C.O."

"I didn't know you were married!"

"I'm not. Sam and I've been together five years, but I guess we'll never get married."

Lindsay was curious. "Why not?"

"His family's very religious. Orthodox. It would kill his mother if he married a girl who isn't Jewish. While she's alive, Sam wouldn't do that to her."

"I see. I'm sorry."

"It's okay," Marge said. "I kind of respect him for it. There was only one time, I really got sore, but I got over it." She smiled openly at Lindsay. "I was pregnant, and in the beginning I thought he ought to marry me. He would have, I suppose, but I knew he'd have his mother on his conscience." She looked thoughtful. "I always have the feeling you think I'm a pushover, Lindsay. You're wrong, in case you care. I horse around with the guys, pretend to be sexy, but I'm faithful to that jerk over in Europe. I love him and I'd like to have had his kid. Maybe one day I will. I don't wish hard luck on anybody, but his mother can't live forever, can she?"

Lindsay was only half listening. "No," she said absently, "she can't." There was an awkward pause before Lindsay said, "Marge, may I ask you something very personal?"

"Sure. Shoot."

"You obviously had an abortion if you didn't have Sam's baby. Where did you . . . I mean, how did you find a doctor?"

The older girl looked at her suspiciously. "There are ways," she said noncommittally. "Why do you want to know? Do you need one?"

Lindsay nodded mutely.

"And you want to get rid of it? Why, for God's sake? Isn't it your husband's?"

Lindsay wasn't offended. "It's his, all right. But he doesn't know, and I don't want him to. We . . . we're not getting along, Marge. Things aren't good between us. This is no time to add a child to the marriage." She wasn't going to tell the full story. She couldn't admit to this near stranger that Geoff had found someone else. "I wonder if you can help me? Just give me the name of a doctor, that's all. I won't say where I got it. I'd be very grateful to you."

155

Marge looked troubled. "I don't know, Lindsay. It's no picnic. In fact, it's rough. Maybe too rough for a girl like you. You don't go to a hospital, you know. It's done in somebody's house or apartment, with only a local. And if there are complications later, there's hell to pay. Hospitals want to know where you had it done, who the doctor is, all that mess. I was lucky. I didn't start bleeding, but women do sometimes. Jeez, I don't know," she said again. "I hate to recommend that. Especially to you. You're married. You can afford to have a baby. Maybe it would bring you and your husband together again."

"No. I can't have this child. I won't have it. Please. You're my only hope. I don't know where to turn."

"Let me make a phone call," Marge said reluctantly.

She came back a few minutes later and reported it was okay. A doctor in New Jersey would do the operation for seven hundred dollars, cash in advance.

Lindsay felt mixed emotions: relief that she'd miraculously found a source just when she'd almost given up, fright at the thought of the dangerous illegal procedure, and a small stab of regret that she couldn't have Geoff's baby. If only things were different. If only he loved her and wanted their marriage and their child. She still loved him, she realized. Angry, hurt, offended as she was, he was the only man she'd ever loved.

"Thank you, Marge," she said. "What do I do?"

"Your appointment's day after tomorrow. We'll take a bus to Newark. The whole thing will be over in less than an hour, and then I'll bring you back to your apartment and spend the night. You'll need somebody to watch you the first twenty-four hours, just in case."

Lindsay was amazed. "You'd do all that for me? Marge, I can't impose—"

"Don't be such a damned martyr. You can't go alone, for chrissakes. You'll be weak as dishwater afterwards. And if there should be an emergency later, God forbid, who's going to be around? Are you going to tell your family what you're going to do?"

"No, but—"

"No buts about it, kiddo. You're a nice dame, Lindsay, even if you're not too bright. Meet me at Penn Station, nine o'clock Wednesday morning. We'll take it from there."

"But why a train? Can't we take a cab? I don't mind the expense."

Marge looked at her. "Honey, I'm sure you could afford a limou-

156

sine, but it doesn't work that way. The doc won't let a taxi pull up anywhere near his house. We take a train, then a bus, get off two blocks
away, and walk. That's okay *going*. It's a little tougher coming back,
but it can't be helped."

Lindsay looked frightened. "We have to take a bus back, too?"

"Well, maybe if we're lucky we'll find a cab near the bus stop, but
I can't promise. Listen, Lindsay, are you really sure you want to do
this? I told you it was pretty bad from all angles. The doctor is a real
M.D., of course, but he's no Park Avenue specialist. It'll be crude and
quick and it's gotta be secret. The guy could go to jail, you know."
Marge looked angry. "Damned laws! What makes people think they
can stop gambling and prostitution and abortion just by making them illegal? God, when I think how many women die on those makeshift operating tables, I could—" She stopped abruptly. What a dope she was!
Lindsay was already scared out of her wits, and she was making it
worse. "Not that you're going to die," she said. "You're in good hands.
This guy knows his business. Not like some of those butchers who
aren't even doctors. They're the ones to steer clear of—the women who
do it on their kitchen tables for poor slobs who don't have seven hundred dollars. Or dames with no money at all who try coat hangers and
knitting needles on themselves." She shuddered. "At least you're getting
the best that can be had. And you're going to be okay."

Lindsay spent two terrible days before she appeared at the train
station on Wednesday morning. She'd hardly slept. It was not only the
idea of the operation that frightened her. Despite herself, she had
qualms about terminating the life inside her. Would she always feel a
terrible guilt for this selfishness? She believed it was her right to make
this decision without consulting Geoff. She felt she owed him nothing in
the light of his conduct. Yet she wondered how he'd feel if he knew she
was destroying his child. I don't care, she thought stubbornly. This . . .
this thing I'm carrying should never have been conceived. It was done
with such joy on my part. But what of its father? How did he feel, making love to me and knowing there was another woman waiting for his
return? He's too callous to care about something as trivial as an unborn
baby; he doesn't even care about me. She squared her shoulders and
tried to smile at the waiting Marge, but on the long ride she spoke
hardly a word, and walking to the doctor's house she felt as though she
were walking to her own execution. She had no idea where she was.
She was alone with this woman she knew only slightly, going to see a

157

doctor whose name she would never know and whose address was a secret from her.

All she managed to get out on the way over were a few words of thanks to Marge. Lindsay couldn't get over her kindness, and she tried to express her gratitude. Marge brushed it off.

"Hell, you're such a baby yourself it would be crazy to let you do this alone."

"But to come with me . . . to be good enough to stay with me later . . . I don't know how I can ever repay you."

"Maybe I'm only repaying what somebody did for me," Marge said. She was inscrutable. "Or, how do you know, Lindsay? Maybe the doctor is giving me a cut of his fee. For all you know, this could be a sideline with me, hustling patients for him."

"I don't believe that. I know you're just being wonderful. Maybe you are repaying. That wouldn't surprise me. Maybe I can do the same for some other desperate woman one day."

They went the rest of the way in silence, Lindsay nauseated by fear. They climbed the steps of a small, nondescript frame house and were let into a shabby living room with frayed furniture and cheap prints on the wall. It was all anonymous and ugly and smelled musty and sour, as though it hadn't been cleaned in a long while.

The woman who admitted them wore a housedress and curlers in her hair. Lindsay supposed she was the doctor's wife.

"He'll be right out," she said curtly and vanished.

In a few minutes the doctor appeared. He was a short, stocky man with a trace of beard. He wore a white jacket over suit trousers, and he didn't smile as he looked at Marge and Lindsay.

"Which of you is the patient?"

"I am." Lindsay's voice faltered.

"You have the money?"

She opened her purse and handed it to him. It was in small bills as Marge had instructed, and the doctor counted it carefully before he spoke again.

"All right. Come with me, Mrs. Smith. You wait here," he said to Marge. "She'll be out shortly."

"Can't I go in with her? I think she'd feel more relaxed."

"No need for that. We'll take care of her. Ready, Mrs. Smith?"

Lindsay rose. She felt as though her knees would not support her. She took a deep breath and nodded.

158

"This way." The doctor led her into an adjoining room. There was an operating table and instruments laid out beside it. On the other side was a curtained alcove. The doctor handed her a worn hospital gown.

"Take off everything from the waist down," he said. "You can leave your things in there."

She nodded obediently and, holding the gown, went into the alcove. Slowly, she took off her shoes and skirt and began to loosen her stockings from the garter belt. Her hands were shaking so violently she could hardly undo the garters. It's all right, she kept telling herself. In a few minutes it will be over. She pulled off her stockings. And then she saw it. On the stool where she was meant to pile her clothing, there was an enormous cockroach. Lindsay stared at the insect in horror. What in God's name was she doing in this dirty little room, preparing to let her body be violated by some half-clean, money-crazed doctor? She put her hand over her mouth to stifle a scream. For a few moments she stood there, her eyes on the awful bug, her heart pounding furiously.

"Mrs. Smith, are you ready? I have other patients waiting."

She heard the words and knew she couldn't do it. Couldn't degrade herself this way. Couldn't let this creature take her baby. She forgot her fears for herself. Her only thought was that the child could not be obliterated in this sordid atmosphere. Or in any other, she realized. Not even in the most sterile and legitimate clinic could she deny this evidence of her love for Geoffrey. Not even if she never saw him again.

Slowly, she dressed and went back into the operating area. The doctor looked at her with annoyance.

"What's the matter with you?"

"I'm sorry. I've changed my mind."

"Nonsense. You're just frightened. It won't hurt. I'll give you a little shot and—"

"No," Lindsay said. "I want my baby."

He looked disgusted. "Well, I can't give you your money back. You've canceled the appointment."

"It doesn't matter. Good day, doctor."

Marge's eyes opened wide when she saw Lindsay. "What happened?"

She could hardly speak. It was too disgusting, too sickening. "I was wrong, Marge. I couldn't go through with it. I'm sorry you went to all this trouble for nothing. I want the baby. I realized it when I got in there. It wasn't that I was too scared. I just knew it wasn't for me.

Please forgive me for taking you on this wild-goose chase. You must think I'm crazy."

The other woman's face lit up. "Crazy? I thought you were crazy to even consider getting rid of it! Lindsay, I'm glad. Honest to God, I am. You were talking yourself into something you didn't really want to do. I *had* to do it. I had no choice. But you're different. You're lucky and so is your kid." She put her arm affectionately around Lindsay's shoulders. "Come on, let's get out of here. I'm going to make you pay off for this trip, though. You can buy me the most expensive lunch in town." Marge laughed happily. "And damned if I won't enjoy it all the more because for once in my life I won't have to serve it!"

It was quite a different trip back to town. Perhaps it's foolish, Lindsay thought, to go through with having this baby, one I might have to raise by myself, but it's already precious to me. It will be a girl, she decided. No man-child to lie and deceive women and break their hearts. No swaggering male to go strutting off to war if, God forbid, there should ever be another. And yet I love men, even though the ones nearest to me have been faithless and arrogant. I love Geoff, she thought again. I want him back in spite of what he's done. I haven't meant any of the things I've said lately. I can't be promiscuous, can't be unemotional about my body, the way I told Papa I'd be. I equate sex with love, as most women do.

And I won't divorce Geoff. Not yet, anyway. There's nothing to do but ride out this period of my life. Wait and see and hope.

She turned to Marge. "I've been thinking about what you said a couple of days ago. Maybe you're right. Maybe a baby will help Geoff and me get back on the track. I know having a baby to save a marriage is the wrong reason for getting pregnant, but I didn't do it for that. I lied to you, Marge. When my husband went back, I thought things were fine with us. I only found out recently that he has someone else over there." Lindsay wondered why it suddenly seemed so important to make this confession. Maybe it's because I really have no close friends, she thought. Not since Adele. Lindsay frowned. Even her attitude toward Adele was now to be questioned. What, after all, had she done? Only tried to protect me from the knowledge of Geoff's affair, Lindsay thought. As for marrying Papa, is that really any of my business? What Freudian thing has made me so angry about her and Papa? I've been wrong about her. I'm going to see her and apologize. She'll be so happy, especially about the baby.

"Mama, I'm going to have a baby."

"Oh, Lindsay, what wonderful news!" Pauline was radiant. "Does Geoffrey know? When will it be?"

"October. And, yes, by now he knows. I wrote to him last week."

"He must be ecstatic!"

Lindsay suppressed a rueful smile. She'd told her mother nothing of her troubles, and Papa had had the good taste to keep his mouth shut too. Thank God for that. Especially now, when she meant to patch things up with Geoff. She'd written him a long letter, apologizing for her silence, saying she'd been so busy with her war work. It was an unlikely excuse, but she couldn't think of a better explanation. She told him all the news: Papa's marriage to Adele, Gandy's worsening health, which worried them all so dreadfully because she seemed to be simply letting go of her grip on life. The letter made no mention of the other woman. It was difficult to write cheerfully as though to a devoted husband, but since she'd decided to get him back, Lindsay knew this was the best way.

Darling, I've saved the most wonderful news for last. You're going to be a father in October! All's well. The doctor says I'm healthy as a horse and we should have a big, bouncing something-or-other. How I wish I could see your face as you read this! And, even more, how I pray this damned war will be over and you'll be home in time to pace the waiting room and hand out cigars when the doctor says, 'Colonel Murray, you have a fine daughter.' Because it is going to be a girl. I've made up my mind to that. I know men are supposed to want sons, but you will indulge me, as always, won't you?

So now you have even more reason to take care of yourself and hurry back. I haven't told Mama and Papa and Gandy yet, but I will, now that you've had the news. I know they'll be happy too. I think it may give Gandy something to live for. She just plain wouldn't allow anything to keep her from seeing her first great-grandchild!

She looked at Pauline's delighted face and was glad, once again, that she hadn't gone through with the abortion. It would give Mama something to care about too. She'd taken the news of her ex-husband's marriage very well. Though she was not "civilized enough," she confessed to Lindsay, to see them socially as a couple, she'd written a note to Adele, wishing her happiness. And Howard continued to drop by occasionally, alone, to see his mother. It was a touch awkward, she admitted in her understated way, but to deprive him of his visits to Gandy would be unkind to both mother and son.

"Have you told your father?" Pauline asked.

Lindsay shook her head. "Not yet. I wanted you and Gandy to be the first to know—after Geoff, of course." And after Marge and that terrible quack doctor, she thought silently.

"Howard will be so pleased. He's very fond of Geoffrey, even though he's been annoyed with him in the past. He's coming by this afternoon, Lindsay. Why don't you stay and tell him then?"

"All right."

"If only James could have known." Pauline looked sad. "He'd have loved being an uncle to your child. He adored you, Lindsay."

Lindsay didn't answer. If James had lived, how different things would have been in many ways. Adele would never have violated his confidence about Geoffrey's affair. James would have come home and married her and she'd have been my sister-in-law, not my stepmother. I'd never have known my husband had been unfaithful. I wish I hadn't found out. Just as I wish I could have kept that little-girl idealism about my honest, upright big brother. Spilt milk. Water over the dam. Touché cliché. No use wishing things were different. They happen, all of them. And we have to live with the results.

"I think I'll go tell Gandy the good news before Papa comes."

"Yes, darling, do. She's in her room."

Lindsay visited her grandmother every week, but it seemed to her that Sara Thresher visibly aged every seven days. It was hard to figure out why. She was seventy-five, of course, not an inconsiderable age, but in these times not so old that she should seem to be dying for no reason. The doctor had assured Pauline that there was nothing organically wrong—no fatal disease, that is.

"She's just wearing out," he said kindly. "The body is like a machine. The parts don't last forever. But I wouldn't worry yet, Mrs. Thresher. She seems frail, but she has a strong constitution. She's simply slowing down. We all do, I'm afraid."

But when Pauline and Lindsay discussed it Pauline shook her head. "I don't know," she said. "It's as though the heart has gone out of her."

"Say it, Mama. She's still grieving for James. As you are. And don't tell me she's happy about Papa and Adele. She knows how unsuitable it is, and I'm sure she frets that you're hurt by it."

Pauline didn't deny either thing. But she did say, unexpectedly, "I've always felt guilty about my divorce from your father, Lindsay, because it was harder on Gandy than anyone else. She was so marvelous about it. So strong. But in her heart I know she hated it. And then, when she had to take sides against her own son, it must have been a wrenching thing for her."

"But that was nearly ten years ago! She didn't act as though it affected her so terribly."

"She was ten years younger, Lindsay. Better able to handle her feelings, I suppose. And, as you say, in these past few months there's been James and . . . and Howard's remarriage. It piles up. I know she worries about Geoffrey too. And she's fearful for you, alone and anxious in that apartment."

That conversation had been only a week before. Maybe my news will give Gandy a new lease on life, Lindsay thought now. Like Mama, she has no idea there's anything wrong with my marriage.

Her grandmother was sitting by the window, simply staring out at nothing. She looked very old and ill, but she brightened when Lindsay came in, smiled, and stretched out her hand.

"Come in, child! How are you, Lindsay dear? How's Geoffrey?"

"Everything's fine, Gandy. Super-fine, in fact. I have a terrific bulletin for you."

Tears came to Sara's eyes when Lindsay told her about the baby, but they were tears of joy. She sat up straighter, her face flushed with happiness as she asked a dozen questions about the pregnancy and was relieved to get satisfactory answers.

"A great-grandchild!" she said. "A new life to replace the one we lost. Oh, Lindsay, I'm so happy for you!" She hesitated. "May I ask a favor? If it's a boy, will you call him James? That was my father's name, you know. And it would seem—well, a nice tribute to your brother."

Lindsay bit her lip. She'd forgiven James, or at least tried to, but she wasn't sure she wanted her baby named for him. Petty! she scolded herself. He was your brother. You adored him for years. Besides, it would make Gandy happy.

"If it's a he, James will be his name," she promised. "But I must warn you, Gandy, I intend to have a girl, and she'll be named Sara Pauline Murray, for you and Mama."

Sara brushed at her eyes. "Fair enough," she said. And then with a hint of her old impishness she added, "But Sara really is a very dull name. Now I always thought, years past, that if I had a daughter I'd call her something exotic like Salome or Mistinguette. Something dramatic." Sara's eyes twinkled. "In fact, if it hadn't been for your grandfather, I'd never have named our son 'Howard.' Much too boring. I'd have called him Lancelot, perhaps. Or Louis after Louis Pasteur, who discovered a treatment for rabies three years before your father was born."

It took Lindsay a few seconds to realize her grandmother was teasing. Then she laughed, delighted that the elderly woman still had her sense of humor. "You darling old fraud!" she said. "For a minute I thought you were serious." She hugged Sara hard. "Gandy, there's nobody like you. I could eat you with a spoon!"

"Good heavens, don't do that," Sara said in mock protest. "You'd break all your pretty teeth on these tough old bones!"

Geoffrey read the letter twice. He didn't believe for a moment that Lindsay had been "too busy to write." Her silence had troubled him, and he worried that somehow she had heard about Pam since his return to London. At least, he'd thought, she's okay. Adele wrote to him now and then, as did Pauline. From them he'd already heard of Howard's engagement, and both of them reported that Lindsay was well and keeping busy. No mention that anyone at home suspected his liaison.

And now this! Lindsay writing of her pregnancy and her happiness! For a moment he was angered. She planned it, he thought. She deliberately didn't take her usual precautions, and in his craving for her he hadn't even noticed. How could she? It was wrong. Not only because of his indecision. She didn't know about that. But to deliberately conceive a child with one's husband overseas was sheer madness! What if he never came back? It was like her: headstrong and willful as always, thinking only of what *she* wanted.

But almost instantly his resentment faded. They were going to have a child because Lindsay, in her innocence, was eager to give him one, to have, always, a part of him. It settled everything. He realized he would go home to her. What he felt for Pamela was a different kind of love. More infatuation than love, a passion made all the more exciting by its illicit nature. He would never forget her. Never. He owed her so much. She had given unselfishly, asking nothing in return; and without her, Geoff thought, he'd have lost his sanity. But he supposed he'd

164

known all along that his future was not with Pamela, no matter what wild thoughts might have crossed his mind. Since they were kids, he and Lindsay had belonged to each other. It felt right. Nothing else had the same degree of solidarity.

When Pam let herself into their borrowed flat, she knew before he spoke that the decision had come. She recognized the pale blue sheets of paper he held in his hand: Lindsay's notepaper. And he had a strange expression, oddly pained and pleased at the same time.

"You've finally heard."

Geoff looked at her squarely, an unspoken apology in his eyes. God, how handsome he is! Pamela thought. How sweet and kind, and how much he hates what he's going to tell me.

"Lindsay's pregnant."

Pam started. She hadn't been prepared for that, though she wondered in that instant why she wasn't. Of course. Lindsay Murray was no fool. She managed to smile. "Well, congratulations, old thing! So you're going to be a daddy. When's the big event?"

"October." He looked miserable. "Pam, you know what this means. I can't . . . I couldn't—"

She interrupted him. "Of course you couldn't, darling. What kind of rotter would run out on his wife when she's having his baby? Geoff, luv, it isn't a surprise to either of us, is it? Not the pregnancy, but the idea that one day you'd go back to Lindsay. We both really knew that, didn't we? No matter what fantasies we indulged in, we were deep-down certain of the outcome. Cheer up, luv. We've had a perfectly smashing time, and I wouldn't have changed a second of it. I'll remember you with a very special kind of love forever. A nice, happy, that's-my-friend kind of love."

He was filled with admiration. How many other women would be so generous, so understanding? She was letting him off scot-free, anxious that he have no feelings of guilt or remorse. When he could speak, he said, "Pam, you know what you mean to me. That will never change. And I'll care for you always. I wish things were different for us. You're the best woman who ever lived. You'll stay in touch with me, won't you?"

He was, in many ways, such a little boy and she loved him for it. She shook her head. "No, dear heart, I shall not stay in touch. When you go home, you must go with no hangovers from this time and place. We've done nothing wrong, Geoff. I'm not ashamed of what we've had, but I wouldn't want to tarnish this shiny image by exchanging secret letters or planning sneaky little trips across the ocean. Don't you understand? While you were here you were nobody's husband. You were another lovable Yank, far away from home and lonely. But back there you belong to Lindsay. And that's as it should be."

"But what about you?"

"Darling, much as I love you, my life won't end. It didn't when I lost Charles. That hurt. This will too, when the time comes. But I shan't perish of it." She smiled. "Not to worry, luv. Not to worry."

15

*I*t was not an easy thing to say even to himself, and God knows he'd never have admitted it to anyone else, but within three months of his marriage, Howard Thresher knew he'd made a terrible mistake. How could he have been such a fool? he wondered. What was he thinking of, marrying a girl thirty-three years his junior, and a virgin at that? His honeymoon had been a nightmare. Using all the influence he had, he'd been able to get a compartment on the Twentieth Century Limited, the super-deluxe train to California, because Adele had never been to the West Coast and was eager to see it. Travel of any kind during the war was difficult, nearly impossible for civilians, but Howard had managed it, thinking how romantic it would be to be locked in with his bride for three days and two nights from Chicago to Los Angeles. Romantic? It had been hell. Adele's introduction to sex was traumatic for both of them. She hated it and cried herself to sleep each night, apologizing all the while.

"It's all right, darling," Howard had said at first. "I understand. Give yourself time. We have to get used to each other. You'll see. When you relax, things will be different."

"I'm so sorry, Howard. I always imagined it would be wonderful, and it's so . . . so untidy." She looked distressed. "Oh, I know it isn't you. I mean, I'm sure you're wonderful. It's just that I thought I'd feel differently when I made love. I thought it would be beautiful, and it's like . . . animals."

He didn't know what to say. It was almost impossible to believe, in 1945, that a young woman could be so naïve. Incredible enough that she was untouched at twenty-four. Even more mind-boggling that her attitude about sex was so prudish and Victorian. He was bitterly disappointed and not a little troubled. Either Adele was frigid or he did not perform as a man her own age might have. Instantly he dismissed the latter thought. At fifty-seven he was as virile as ever and certainly more experienced than any young buck she might have gone to bed with. He understood the nuances of lovemaking, and there'd never been a woman who hadn't responded to his expertise—until now. He also rejected the idea that she was frigid. Like most enlightened people, he did not believe there was such a thing. Any woman could be aroused with the right approach by the right man.

And he stubbornly insisted he was that right man. For the month of their wedding trip, he was careful, undemanding, and especially tender, but it was no good. It was like being with a taut, frightened child, and even when he tried to relax her with liquor or surprise gifts or seductive overtures, she pulled away from him, submitting only reluctantly and with ill-concealed distaste, openly relieved when it was over.

He kept telling himself it would be better when they got back to New York and were settled in the apartment, but it wasn't. Adele insisted on having her own bedroom, saying she just didn't rest well in a room with anyone else. But when he came into her bed, though she never refused him she looked at him with such dread that Howard felt like a rapist. At last, after two months of marriage, he lost his temper.

"Goddammit, Adele, this can't go on! Sex is a big part of marriage, and it's repulsive to you. Or maybe *I'm* repulsive to you. Whatever, we can't live like this. I love you. You're my wife. What in God's name did you expect?"

"I told you," she said in a low voice. "It's not you. I'm the one. I thought it would be different."

"Different how? You knew the facts of life. Why does the reality offend you so?"

Her eyes filled with tears. "I don't know, Howard. I'm sorry."

"Sorry! What good is that? It's been two months. Two frustrating, demoralizing months of this childish nonsense! It's a wonder I'm not impotent by this time!" He was in a towering rage. "I've done all I can. Treated you like you were made of spun sugar, tried to be patient. But time's run out. Either you're a wife to me or we call it off."

She looked frightened. "Oh, no! Don't say that! I love being married to you."

"What do you love about it? Being Mrs. Somebody? Giving nice dinner parties? Having a home of your own? You certainly don't love being a wife in the normal sense of the word. What did you expect?" he asked again. "Tell me, Adele, what did you really expect marriage to be?"

She looked away. "I thought we were both alone. And lonely. I thought it would be companionable. Nice for both of us to have someone."

Howard laughed. "Nice? Companionable? You must be crazy! I'm fifty-seven, not eighty-seven. I have a housekeeper, and if I needed a companion I'd hire one. Can't you get it through your head that I fell in love with you? Is that so ridiculous? Is it farfetched that at my great age I still want sex in my marriage? For God's sake, Adele, what do you want, a husband or a father?"

She began to cry, and Howard felt ashamed of himself. She can't help it, he thought. There's something wrong with her. Something I can't fathom. He forced himself to be calm. "Sweetheart, I think you should have the doctor check you out. Maybe there's some tiny thing. . . . Women sometimes find sex painful, and minor surgery—"

Adele shook her head. "I've seen the gynecologist. There's nothing wrong."

"Then it's all in your mind. Perhaps a few sessions with an analyst would clear this whole thing up. Maybe it's a mental block, possibly even related to the loss of your father. I don't know. I don't know that much about psychiatry. Never approved of it, actually, but at this point I'll accept any help we can get from any source."

"You think I'm crazy! Maybe I am. My father killed himself, and you have to be even temporarily deranged to do that. Maybe I inherited—"

He cut her off. "Don't be absurd! Of course I don't think you're crazy! Haven't I known you since you and Lindsay were babies?"

"I wish I were like Lindsay. She's lusty, like you. A girl like Lindsay would give you what you want. Even children."

He was exasperated by her whining. "For God's sake, Adele, I don't want any more children! At my age? I'll be a grandfather in a few months. But I do want a wife. A real wife. So if I make an appointment for you, will you see someone and try to get some help?"

"All right. If it will please you. But I know it won't do any good, Howard. I just can't stand—"

169

"Don't say it! Have you no idea what that does to me? Can't you possibly imagine how a man feels when he's rejected or, even worse, grimly tolerated by a woman who thinks she must do her duty and get through with it as soon as possible? Where in God's name did you get your puritanical ideas? Certainly not from your mother!"

"My mother is no better than a tramp. My father was hardly buried before she took up with that awful man."

Howard smiled wryly. "Maybe she was lonely too, Adele. But she had sense enough to know that physical pleasure can ease a great deal of emotional pain." He patted her hand. "I'll find a doctor tomorrow, my dear. I'm not giving up on this until we've exhausted every resource."

It had been as futile as he feared, and even more disturbing. Adele spent a month with the psychiatrist and reported there was nothing anyone could do about the way she felt.

"You've had twenty sessions, Adele. You mean nothing has come out of them? Nothing that will shed a light on our problems?"

She set her lips tightly. "Nothing. It's just the way I am."

"I find that hard to believe."

"Are you accusing me of lying, Howard?"

"No. Of course not. I simply thought there might be something you're not telling me. Maybe something you haven't quite recognized yourself." She made no reply and desperately Howard went on. "Well, if the doctors can't help, maybe you need another woman to talk to."

For the first time, Adele was sarcastic. "Whom would you suggest? My mother? The first Mrs. Thresher, perhaps? Or possibly Lindsay? I'm sure you'd be absolutely delighted to have them know all about our troubles."

Howard was silent. She was right, of course. Louise Tamlin wouldn't understand. And the last thing he wanted was Pauline or Lindsay knowing what a fool he'd been. If only Adele had another friend. She'd made up with Lindsay, or, rather, Lindsay had finally apologized to her. But aside from that, the new Mrs. Thresher's social contacts were entirely among *his* friends. She gave perfect dinner parties, nearly as flawless as Pauline's had been. She entertained his business contacts and was enchanting. The men with whom he was associated looked at him enviously, comparing this slim, beautiful girl to their middle-aged wives, patting him on the back and winking suggestively as

170

they said, "You're a lucky dog, Thresher." Little did they know. And little did their wives know. These women were all thirty years older than Adele. They were polite, accepting her dinner invitations and returning them, but none had tried to be friends with her. Nor would Adele have known what to say to them if they had tried. She did not even lunch with them. The idea of her confessing her marital difficulties to such ladies was ludicrous.

He was nearly desperate. He'd stopped even trying to force himself on his wife. It's back to my old ways, he thought wearily. This time he'd really intended to be a faithful husband. He'd had enough of the other thing, the mistresses he'd had all the years he was married to Pauline. He didn't want that any more. He'd hoped his young, beautiful new wife would be more than enough for him. Instead, she was nothing. And unless they could solve their sexual problems he'd start cheating on her. Not that she'd care, Howard thought. If anything, she'd probably be relieved. Probably, hell! Certainly.

Yet he was curious. It was unnatural for a healthy twenty-four-year-old to be so cold. He couldn't believe the doctor told her nothing. One morning, on impulse, he phoned the psychiatrist's office and asked for an appointment to discuss his wife's condition. He was given a date two weeks later, and on that afternoon he showed up, feeling slightly embarrassed, at the doctor's Park Avenue address.

He was surprised to find that Dr. Seward Golden was a woman. He recalled now that his own internist, who'd recommended Dr. Golden, hadn't specified her sex, and Howard simply took it for granted that it was a man. And Adele hadn't mentioned it. Strange. Especially when they'd had that talk about Adele needing a woman to talk to. He had no idea. Seward was obviously a family name and could be either gender. Howard frowned. Somehow he wished it had been a man Adele had seen, someone who understood the nature of the masculine drive.

Dr. Golden was petite and fifty-ish with short gray hair and a cordial manner. She motioned Howard to a chair and looked at him appraisingly.

"What can I do for you, Mr. Thresher?"

He felt vaguely uneasy. "I came to talk about my wife. She's been seeing you for a month." The stupidity of that statement made him smile. "But of course you know that. She's been here five times a week."

The doctor nodded and waited for him to go on.

171

"The thing is," Howard said, "she claims there's no answer to her problem. Our problem. I find that hard to believe."

Dr. Golden smiled pleasantly. "Why so?"

"Well, because . . . well, she's young and healthy and normal in every other way. It's not natural. There must be an explanation. She's human. She has emotions. There has to be something blocking her from the full enjoyment of . . . of . . ."

"I believe the word is 'sex,' Mr. Thresher." She seemed amused. "Your wife is not responsive to your sexual advances, and you find that impossible to accept. Am I correct?"

"Yes. Exactly."

"Tell me, Mr. Thresher, does Mrs. Thresher know you've come to see me?"

"No, and I don't want her to."

"But you do understand doctor-patient confidentiality. You must know I can't discuss this matter with anyone, not even you, unless your wife wishes me to."

Howard was annoyed. "I don't see why you can't. I'm her husband. I'm equally involved in this. Dammit, I pay your bill!"

"But your wife's thoughts are her own. She's shared some of them with me, but I'm not at liberty to betray her confidences. It would be unethical."

Howard tried to calm himself. Stupid medical mumbo jumbo. A lot of high-flown talk about ethics. He became his most charming.

"I can understand that, Dr. Golden. And I respect you for it. I don't want to pry into Adele's innermost thoughts, but this is very important to me. To us. I only want to understand and try to help her. To see if there's something I'm doing wrong."

"But you don't believe you are doing anything wrong, do you?"

Howard flushed. "Frankly, no. I've always been attractive to women, always able to please them. Perhaps that sounds boastful, but this is the first time in my life I've come up against this kind of rejection. Look," Howard said earnestly, "you're a sophisticated woman. I can speak plainly to you. I'm a helluva good lover. I'm doing my part. Trying harder than I ever have. There's nothing wrong with me, Dr. Golden, but there obviously is something terribly wrong with my wife." He was actually pleading. "I love her. I know there's a big difference in our ages, but that doesn't affect me physically. And Adele has always been a

172

quiet, mature, sensible girl. I don't think she could identify with a man her own age. Even my son—" He stopped abruptly.

"Yes, Mr. Thresher? What about your son?"

"He was killed. Adele was engaged to him. I guess you know that." Howard hesitated before he said, defiantly, "Even James was somewhat older than Adele. Eight or nine years. She never ran around with young boys the way Lindsay, my daughter, did. Adele has always seemed much older. She worshiped James like an older brother. And after he died . . ."

Doctor Golden waited.

Howard looked stricken. "She married me because I'm the nearest thing to James. That's it, isn't it? She was denying James's death. But in bed I'm . . . I'm his father, not her husband." Howard put his head in his hands. "My God, why couldn't I see that? She was so grief-stricken. She clung to me. And I thought she loved me. But she loves a ghost. Every time I come near her, she wishes it were my son. God almighty, sex with me must seem like incest to her!"

The doctor felt sorry for him. He was an intelligent man, and his reasoning had brought him very close to the truth. A very painful truth. For a moment, Dr. Golden wanted to slap Adele Thresher. She'd done a terrible thing to a man whose ego was so frail it accepted any kind of devotion, believing it to be love. But one couldn't really blame Adele. She was lost and frightened, desperately alone and unhappy. The father of the man she had loved must have seemed like salvation to her. How was she to know, in her sexual innocence, that every overture he made would seem like a betrayal of his son? Adele was not frigid, nor Howard lacking. They were simply two confused, insecure people with no awareness of their motivations. Howard's need for reassurance of his masculinity had drawn him to this dependent girl. And her neurotic absorption with her loss had blinded her to the real reason she accepted him in marriage.

Adele knew this now. She'd discovered it in her sessions, but she obviously hadn't told her husband. What did she plan to do? Dr. Golden wondered. Try to maintain this hopeless relationship? And what of him? Now that the truth was out, could he go on living with his son's unavoidable reject?

"I'm sorry, Mr. Thresher," she said. "But perhaps it's better that you know. Better for both of you."

173

"Does my wife know?"

Dr. Golden hesitated. She'd told him nothing. He'd simply put the pieces together himself as he talked. She'd still maintain her silence. There was no need not to.

"Why don't you ask her yourself, Mr. Thresher?"

The evasive reply was his answer. Adele knew. She must be going through hell, Howard thought, trying to live with this thing and keep it from me, hoping to spare my feelings. Disappointed as I am, I can stand it. I can always go outside for my pleasures as I've done for years. But what of her? What kind of marriage can this be for Adele? He turned helplessly to the doctor.

"What in God's name shall I do?"

She felt genuinely sorry for him, sorry enough to violate her own code of professional behavior.

"I doubt there's much you *can* do, Mr. Thresher. Not at this time, in any case. I'd hoped your wife would continue with her therapy. We might have made a breakthrough eventually, but I gather she's decided to discontinue the sessions." Dr. Golden held up her hand to silence him as he was about to speak. "No," she said, "you can't force her to keep seeing me. It would be pointless. Therapy can only succeed when the patient wants such help. In this case, Mrs. Thresher doesn't. I'm afraid she almost enjoys her mourning, and her rejection of you feeds her sorrow and increases her self-pity. It's not that she's a bad woman. She doesn't mean to punish you for your son's death, though that's what, in effect, she's doing. In a distorted way, she's also punishing herself, illogically and pointlessly, of course, but compulsively as well." The doctor looked sad. "We can only hope that time takes over with its proverbial healing power. One day she may see how wrong she is in her feelings toward you and come to love you as you love her. That is, if you wish to go on with this marriage-in-name-only."

"I can handle it," Howard said. "But what's your honest opinion? Do you think my wife will ever see things differently?"

Seward Golden shrugged. "I wouldn't want to hold out any false hopes. But even in the medical profession we sometimes pray for miracles. If you can be patient, and if you can control your very normal resentment—well, perhaps Mrs. Thresher will heal herself, but I couldn't set a timetable for it." She looked at him compassionately. "You must love her very much. This is not an easy thing to endure. It will strain your patience at times and leave you with an emptiness no outsider can

174

fill. But in her way she loves you too, Mr. Thresher. Always remember that."

"Yes," he said, "I will. Thank you, doctor. Thank you very much indeed."

The war in Europe ended in May, and in June Geoffrey came home. Lindsay was five months pregnant, and the sight of her in a maternity dress filled him with happiness. It made everything real, seeing her beginning to bulge with his child, and any lingering doubts he'd had in the past two months disappeared in the glow of this final realization. He'd not been with Pamela since the day Lindsay's letter arrived. No credit to myself, he thought. I'd have gone on seeing her, but she'd have no part of me after the decision was made. He could still hear the lovely English voice, managing to sound so light and unreproachful.

"I think we'd better close the book on this one, dear heart. I'd feel a bit of a tramp, you know. Silly, isn't it? I'm probably an utter ass, giving up what time we have left. But now that we know the end of the story, I'd jolly well hate to mess up the last few chapters. Let's have a nice, clean, swift finale, Geoffrey darling. A happy ending."

Happy for me, he'd thought bitterly. All very well for me to go home to Lindsay and the baby. There are tender things waiting there for me. But what of Pam? I've messed up her life, no matter how she denies it.

"I'll never forget you," he'd said. "I don't know if that means very much, but I love you. Remember that, if you ever need me, ever need anything."

And now he was standing in his old apartment, looking at his wife, barely thinking of that other girl. He grinned at Lindsay and whistled.

"Well, will you look at my potbellied friend! Good Lord, I'm married to the Goodyear blimp!"

His tone was affectionate and teasing, and Lindsay knew it. The banter covered his emotions, made the reunion less maudlin. She felt a surge of joy, realizing how thrilled he was. I'll never let him know I knew about the other thing, Lindsay told herself. It's over. It doesn't matter. It was wartime. Period.

She played the game. "Potbellied, am I? Well, I didn't get that way by myself, thank you very much!"

Geoff laughed. "You look wonderful, Lind. Even in that funny dress. How long have you been wearing those things?"

175

Lindsay looked embarrassed. "Almost two months. Long before I had to. Mama thought I was crazy. She accused me of actually pushing out my stomach to look more pregnant than I was. She was right about that. I wanted the whole damned world to know. I practiced walking in a way that made me stick out more in front."

She didn't say that she'd flaunted her pregnancy for more than pride. She was so grateful she hadn't terminated it. She'd come so close that now she wanted to go in the other direction; advertising her impending motherhood because she'd so nearly lost the chance to have it.

"You are a loony." Geoff looked sober. "I'm glad to be home, Lind. Here, with you. The years we've lost." He shook his head. "God, what a waste war is."

"But how lucky we are. You're back, and in one piece. So many others weren't that fortunate."

"I know. I used to feel guilty being in a reasonably safe place. You know that. I resented your father's interference, but now I'm grateful." He smiled. "Even though I'll have a tough time explaining to my kid how I sat out the war in England."

"She won't mind. She'll know how brave you are."

"I take it we're still having a girl?"

"Of course. I told you I'd made up my mind."

"What if it's a boy?"

"No problem. I'll just send him back. I'm used to returning merchandise when my order isn't properly filled."

He took her in his arms. "All nonsense aside," he said softly, "you know I'm delighted about the baby. I admit I wasn't, at first. Just for a few seconds. I thought you were wrong to have a child when I was so far away. I was afraid for you, Lind. Nobody knew I'd be back in time for its birth."

"I know. I wasn't too thrilled about it myself, in the beginning." She spoke without thinking, but Geoff picked up her words and stepped back, looking at her curiously.

"Not thrilled? I don't understand. You must have wanted a baby. You made no effort, obviously, not to have one."

Damn. He was too sharp. How could she explain why she'd changed her mind once she'd discovered she was pregnant? He mustn't know what I nearly did, Lindsay thought. And he mustn't know the reason for it.

"I mean I had second thoughts too. You're right. I tried to get pregnant when you were home in January. But when you left, I knew I'd been foolish. I kept hoping it didn't take, and I was worried when it did." She looked at him lovingly. "But the doubts didn't last long, darling. I knew it would turn out right, and it has, hasn't it?" She stopped suddenly, and a shadow of fear crossed her face. "They're not going to ship you out again, are they? God, don't tell me they'll send you to the Pacific!"

"No. I think not. It looks like I'll be assigned Stateside. I think you can count on my pacing the waiting room and handing out those cigars, just the way you planned. Things always work out for you, darling, don't they? You must have been born under a lucky star."

Was there just a tiny trace of bitterness in his voice? Was he thinking of other things? That woman in England, perhaps? Lindsay refused to let old doubts mar her contentment. Yes, things did work out for her. Geoff was right about that. But not without pain.

Not without a fierce determination to *make* them go her way. I'm a fighter, Lindsay thought. A survivor. Like all the women in my family.

In July, Geoff was discharged, retaining his officer status in the reserve. He went back to the advertising agency, Ford, Wheeler & Koch, to his old job, saying it was a good thing the government insisted a veteran's position be held for him.

"Nonsense," Lindsay said. "I'll bet they couldn't wait to get you back. That damned place probably would have gone under if you hadn't come home!"

"I admire your blind faith, lady, but I'm sure *they'd* have survived even if *I* didn't. Still, I must admit they seemed glad to see me. And I am bloody glad to get back. Even Ralph Ford came out of his ivory tower and shook my hand."

"The great man himself?"

"None other." Geoff went into an imitation of the sixty-year-old chairman, throwing out his chest and pretending to puff on a cigar. " 'Good to have you back, my boy! We're proud of our fine young men.' And then, better still, Wheeler told me they'd been talking about me and hinted they had bigger things in mind. So we're going to be okay, I guess."

"Of course we are, darling. Better than ever. We've both grown up, Geoff. At least I have."

As he had before, he had the uneasy feeling that Lindsay knew

177

about Pam. If so, she wasn't going to mention it and apparently did not hate him for it. She *has* grown up, he thought. The Lindsay I left would not have been so tolerant, so forgiving—and, God knows, not so considerately silent.

16

On August 14, 1945, World War II ended, and exactly two months later to the day Lindsay gave birth to the daughter she'd confidently predicted. Sara Pauline Murray weighed seven pounds, two ounces, and came screaming into the world quickly and with remarkably little pain to her mother.

Standing at Lindsay's bedside, looking down at her daughter and granddaughter, Pauline shook her head in amusement. "You are something, darling," she said. "Who else would have a big beautiful baby after only three hours of labor? And a girl, of course. Just as you expected."

On the other side of the bed, Geoff grinned. He hadn't stopped grinning since the baby arrived. "She's a witch, Mrs. Thresher. Don't you know that? Your daughter casts secret spells the way other women do the laundry: as a matter of course. Did you doubt for one moment that we'd have a daughter? I didn't. I know better."

"I suppose you'd all be happier if I'd been wrong," Lindsay said, pretending indignation. "Or maybe you wish I'd been in labor for forty-eight hours like nice, refined ladies always are."

"Sure," Geoff said. "We wanted you to suffer. You can't imagine how disappointed we all were when you came through this so easily. It's embarrassing to tell people that your wife gives birth like a peasant."

The three of them laughed contentedly, and Sara Pauline gurgled in Lindsay's arms.

"Sara Pauline," her grandmother said, "I can't wait for you to meet your great-grandmother. She's so happy about you."

Lindsay looked troubled. "Gandy's worse, isn't she? I know she must be, otherwise she'd have been here. Nothing but real sickness could keep her away."

"She's not good, Lindsay," Pauline said gently. "I haven't wanted to worry you these past couple of weeks, but she's going downhill fast." The lump in her throat made it difficult for Pauline to speak. "I think she's simply holding on until she can see the baby. She's been living for that. I don't know how much longer we'll have her, but I do know she'll be serene now, and I thank the Lord for that."

Lindsay's eyes filled with tears. "I can't bear it, Mama. I can't imagine a world without Gandy."

"Hush, darling. You mustn't upset yourself. It's bad for little Sara. And big Sara wouldn't approve of it."

"I'll be home in a week. And as soon as I can, I'll take S.P. to see her great-grandmother. That's what we're going to call the baby: S.P. There's only one Sara. And one Pauline. So since she has both names, we thought it best to use her initials." Lindsay brightened. "Geoff says it's a good thing we didn't name her Pauline Sara and call her P.S. She'd have sounded like an afterthought."

Pauline smiled. "S.P.," she repeated. "Yes. I like it. Has your father seen her yet?"

"He's coming in a little while. With Adele."

"Ah. Fine." Pauline immediately prepared to leave. "Well, darling, I must run. Gandy is waiting to hear all about you both." She leaned over and kissed Lindsay. "God bless you. And you too, S.P., you funny little thing."

When she left, Lindsay sighed. Geoff took her hand.

"Don't be too sad about Gandy, sweetheart. We wouldn't want her to suffer. Let's hope the goddamned cancer takes her quickly, before she has terrible pain."

"Yes. I know that's the right way to feel, but it's so hard, Geoff. Three months ago we didn't even know she had it. And now it's a matter of weeks, probably. Maybe days. I try to tell myself that's merciful, but I can't adjust to it. I just can't accept it."

"Honey, remember what your mother said. You must try to stay calm." Geoff tried to change the subject. "She sure beat it out of here when she heard your father and Adele were coming, didn't she? It must be damned awkward for her, seeing them together."

"She never does. Papa comes alone to see Gandy."

180

"Things working out all right for them? Adele and your father, I mean."

"I don't know. I suppose so. They seem content. Not ecstatic, but then it's not exactly a Romeo and Juliet marriage."

"It was a big surprise," Geoff said. "Who'd have thought Adele would be your stepmother? I'm glad it hasn't spoiled your friendship."

"It almost did for a while." In the months since Geoff's return they hadn't seriously discussed Howard's marriage, almost as though they sensed it was a tricky subject that might endanger their own. "I thought it was disgusting," Lindsay went on. "For a while I didn't speak to them. But I grew up about that too. Mama helped. She's not bitter, so why should I be?"

"Adele's a nice girl. It was a tragedy she lost James. Everything would have been different if he'd lived."

Lindsay didn't answer, but she heard the echo of her own thoughts in his words. Yes, everything would have been different, she told herself again. In more ways, my darling Geoffrey, than you'll ever know.

S.P. was barely two weeks old when Lindsay took her to see Gandy. Sara, bedridden now, with nurses around the clock, looked heartbreakingly thin and fragile, but her smile was as warm as ever, and she still had spirit, as she proved.

"Shoo!" she said to the day nurse. "You're a darling girl, but who needs you hovering around when I'm being introduced to my namesake?"

The young woman smiled at Lindsay. "Your grandmother's quite a character. We're all crazy about her, Mrs. Murray."

Sara snorted. "Crazy about your outrageous hourly fees, that's what you are. Don't know why I keep you around." But the words were said in an affectionate tone and accompanied by the twinkle Lindsay always associated with her. "Now scat!" Sara said again.

They laughed as the nurse pretended to cower before she closed the door. "You're wicked," Lindsay said, "talking so tough to that nice young woman. Fortunately, she knows what a softy you really are."

"Of course," Sara answered. "I'm fond of all three of them. And grateful too. It's a blessing to spend your last days in your own bed. So many old people die in hospitals or nursing homes, surrounded by anonymous faces. I'm lucky." She managed to sit up straighter against her pillows. "Enough of that." She stretched out painfully thin arms.

"Let me get a good look at my great-granddaughter. Let me hold her, Lindsay. Don't worry. I'm strong enough."

Gently, Lindsay placed S.P. in Sara's arms. The baby looked up and smiled, her big round eyes attempting to focus on the face above hers. I wish I had a photograph of them, Lindsay thought. They make such a tender picture, the white-haired elderly lady in her pale pink bed jacket and the infant in a little sacque of the very same shade. Seventy-five years apart, one knowing everything and the other knowing nothing, and yet there's a kind of magic between them.

Sara couldn't take her eyes off the baby. "She's beautiful, Lindsay. She looks like you."

"Thanks, Gandy, but I don't think two-week-old babies look like anybody except Winston Churchill. Minus the cigar, of course."

The casualness did not deceive Sara. Lindsay was sorrowing already. Of them all, Sara thought, she'll take my death the hardest. Harder even than Pauline. I've been around this child all her life and I understand her better than her own mother does. I must make my leaving easier for her if I can. She must understand that it isn't so hard to go when you've seen all your wishes come true. Or most of them, at any rate. She put her finger gently under S.P.'s tiny chin and tilted the small face upward toward her own.

"Winston Churchill indeed! Don't be foolish, Lindsay. She's the spit 'n' image of you at that age. I remember as though it were yesterday. And she'll grow up like you, too: hard to handle, a peck of trouble, but worth every minute of it." She gently stroked the baby's cheek, and S.P. made little gurgling sounds. Sara smiled. "She's perfect. I thank the Lord I got to see her."

"Don't talk like that, Gandy. You'll be with her when she's growing up, just as you were with me. Shopping trips to Saks and sundaes at Schrafft's. She's not going to be deprived of those wonderful memories."

"Darling, we don't have to pretend, do we? Her grandmother Pauline will have those pleasures, not me, and I'm happy she will. It's the way things are meant to be. We're four generations, Lindsay, and that's a remarkable thing. But it can't last forever." Sara looked down once again at the baby before she said, "Give Sara Pauline to her grandmother now, will you? My arms are getting a little tired. Besides, I really want to talk with you for a few moments without this delicious distraction."

Mutely, Lindsay took her daughter out of the room and left her in

Pauline's charge. Then she returned and sat beside her grandmother, holding the slim hand with the old-fashioned wide gold wedding band. For a moment they sat in silence, each lost in her own thoughts, and then Sara began to speak softly but firmly, knowing these might be her last words to the girl she loved so much.

"Lindsay, I want you to know how proud I am of you. You've become a fine woman and, most importantly, a sensible one. The way you've handled your marriage is mature and admirable. I know it wasn't an easy thing to do, keeping still about that woman in London, not wanting to worry your mother and me and, I suspect, never letting on to Geoffrey that you knew. But it was right and strong and worthwhile. More than commendable. Almost heroic."

Lindsay's eyes widened. "You knew? You and Mama both knew?"

"Of course. You didn't really think Howard would keep quiet about such a thing, did you? He came running here the minute that silly Adele told him. We begged him, your mother and I, not to tell you. But oh, no. My righteous son thought it was his duty to break your heart."

"I had no idea," Lindsay said. "I wish I'd known. I desperately needed someone to talk to."

"Yes. Perhaps we were wrong not to tell you we knew. But since both your mother and I have had unfaithful husbands and handled them badly, we hardly felt in a position to give you advice." Sara smiled. "That's not quite true. We had such faith in you that we believed you'd work it out for yourself, in your own way. And you did, without a couple of indignant women messing up your thoughts and maybe steering you in the wrong direction. My own mother used to say, 'You never get in trouble keeping your mouth shut.' Pauline and I decided that was best in this situation. Howard had done enough talking for all of us."

"It was a terrible time," Lindsay said. "I hated Geoff. And Papa and Adele too. Even James. I felt betrayed by my own brother."

"I know. No one could blame you. But you mustn't blame him, Lindsay. James wasn't willfully setting out to destroy your marriage. He was only giving Geoffrey the kind of advice men give each other. Strange creatures. They think sex is the cure-all for everything. Let them see an unhappy man and they think finding him a woman is the answer. Let them see a lonely woman and they instantly decide that the solution to her frustration is to have a man." Sara shook her head. "If

183

only it were that simple. It might be, at that, if women didn't attach such emotional importance to sex. They'd be better off if they could view it as a dispassionate physical need, the way men do. Your mother couldn't, and she destroyed her marriage because of it. I couldn't, and I had a miserable life, full of anger and resentment. But you're different. You knew Geoffrey's infidelity was meaningless to him, and you wisely waited it out. I applaud you for that, my dear. Your generation is much more intelligent about human behavior than mine or Pauline's."

Lindsay looked troubled. "I'm not so sure about that, Gandy. Times change, but people remain the same. You're right. I've never told Geoff I knew what he was doing in London. Probably I never will. But I'm not sure I'll ever completely forgive him. I'm trying to be as sensible as you think I am, but it's a bit of an act. I still resent the fact that while I was faithful to him he didn't have the same respect for me."

"Don't dwell on it," Sara said. "It's part of the past, over and done with. A slip. An error in judgment. I doubt if it will ever happen again. Geoffrey isn't as insecure as your father or as vain as your grandfather. As long as he has you, he won't go looking for anyone else." Sara took a deep breath. She was so tired, so terribly tired. But it was important for her to finish this conversation with Lindsay. She might never have another chance.

"There are a few other things I need to say to you, Lindsay. Please listen and don't interrupt with those ridiculous cheerful lies everybody insults me with these days. I'm going to die very soon. I know that and I accept it. I'm not afraid. But I like to leave things in a tidy condition. I revised my will after James was killed. Everything I have goes to you: the bulk of my estate and all my personal possessions. I've made a few specific bequests of what Howard is to have, mostly things of his father's. He's a rich man in his own right. He doesn't need my money, and I certainly don't want that silly fool of a girl he married to have it.

"I've also left certain personal things to your mother. I love her dearly, more than I love my son, God forgive me. She'll also have this apartment and the income from a trust fund as long as she lives. She'll be independent, and that's very important. Because I know when I'm gone you'll want to take Pauline to live with you. Don't do it, Lindsay. I don't think she'll want to, but even if she does, don't let her. It's a mistake I made. My life in your home was a good one, mostly harmonious, but I was wrong to be there. A woman needs her own roof, her own

184

way of doing things. She's never happy feeling like a guest, even with her kin. Pauline will be able to afford any place she wants, this one or another. Don't worry that she'll be lonely. She may be, but she'll be self-sufficient, and that's the greatest blessing any woman can have."

Lindsay tried to be as calm as her grandmother, but all this matter-of-fact talk about arrangements after death made her want to cry out in protest. Don't die, Gandy, she wanted to say. Please don't leave us. But she simply nodded, pressing Sara's hand.

"Darling, I understand," she said. "Don't talk any more. It tires you too much. We can finish this conversation later."

Sara shook her head. "I'm all right. Just a few things more. Don't ever stop being kind to your father, Lindsay. He's a shallow, foolish man who won't admit his mistakes. Marrying Adele was one. I know that and so does he, but he'll never admit to it. He'll end up unhappily, dear, and there'll be no one to care about him in his last days. No one but you and, oddly enough, Pauline. She still loves him, heaven help her." Sara spoke with effort now, as though it was difficult for her to breathe. "I love you, Lindsay. Always remember that. And remember what I told you about finding a shiny penny. Whenever you do, pick it up and say, There's Gandy, who loves me."

Lindsay began to weep quietly.

"Hush, child. There's nothing to cry about. You'll see me a thousand times in the years ahead. And I know you'll treasure what matters to me, not just the worldly possessions but the people." She managed another smile. "Including that wonderful little person with those ridiculous initials for a name." Sara closed her eyes. "I think I'd like to rest now, if you don't mind."

"Yes of course, darling. I'll see you tomorrow."

Sara nodded. "Tomorrow and every day as long as you live."

Lindsay was never to see her again. Early the next morning, Pauline called and said in a strangled voice, "It's over, Lindsay. She's gone. Quietly, in her sleep. Without suffering."

Lindsay grieved deeply, as her grandmother had known she would. In the two days before the funeral, she refused to even go near the place where Gandy lay receiving the last respects of hundreds of people.

"I don't want to see her," she told Howard. "I want to remember her alive and talking and laughing. She made little jokes right up to the end, teasing me about the baby's name. No, Papa, I won't go and stare at something that isn't Gandy. She'd hate it. She'd hate what you're doing to her now."

Howard drew himself up haughtily. "What are you talking about? I'm seeing she gets the respect she deserves. Hundreds of people have come to the funeral home. There are so many flowers we've had to take an extra room. She was a well-known woman, Lindsay. My father was an important man in New York. People haven't forgotten that, even though he's been gone more than twenty-five years, rest his soul. They're only giving his widow the deference she should have."

"Is that all she was to you, Papa? The widow of a well-known man? Or the mother of another prominent figure? What about all the things she was on her own? What about the dignity, the kindness, the compassion that made her a great lady? She wouldn't have wanted this vulgar display. You want it. But I don't have to be part of it."

"Like hell you don't!" Howard was furious. "You're her only living grandchild. You're her principal heir as well." Lindsay heard the resentment in his voice as he spoke that last sentence. "It's only fitting that you be there and receive people's condolences with me. God knows it's awkward enough having both Adele and Pauline around to feed the gossip. Your absence causes talk, makes people think there's some kind of estrangement in this family. I won't have it, Lindsay, do you hear me? I simply will not stand for it!"

So that's it, she thought. You don't give a damn whether I'm there or not, except that my absence makes you look foolish. Well, to hell with you, Papa. You wanted to turn this into your own show, so go ahead and play bereaved son. You're not going to make me part of your act. And then she thought of her grandmother's last words, the plea to be kind to this pathetically immature man. I'll do it for you, Gandy, she decided. I'll be kind to him for your sake, just as you were generous to everyone.

"All right," she said wearily. "I'll come to the funeral home tonight. But I won't look at her."

"Do as you like," he said stiffly, "but at least be there. And for heaven's sake comport yourself decently at the services tomorrow! I won't have you making a spectacle of yourself with your tears. Try to have some of your mother's self-discipline, if that's possible. She behaves like a civilized human being and she was closer to my mother than you ever were." She heard the bitterness again. He knew Gandy loved Mama more than she loved him, Lindsay realized. That must have hurt. Hurt so much that he's putting on this show to prove his devotion to his mother and, in a way, her nearness to him.

He cares so much about public opinion, Lindsay thought. I wonder how he dared be so flagrant about his affairs when he was married to Mama. And where did he find courage to marry a woman young enough to be his daughter, knowing people would whisper and snicker behind his back? He must have been madly in love with Adele, knowing what the gossip would be. Either that, or it was to give more evidence of his great virility. He cared more about that than he did his damned image. He's always cared more about his reputation as a lady-killer than his stature as a husband or father. And yet she couldn't hate him, really. She never had. He was a shallow, foolish man, just as Gandy said. But he was Papa. And she'd stand by him always, the way she'd been asked to do.

The Grown-up Years

PART TWO

17

"S.P., for heaven's sake stand still! I can't adjust this veil when you keep turning your head every which way. What do you want to do, go down the aisle looking like a tipsy nun?"

The twenty-year-old bride-to-be laughed and turned completely around, giving Lindsay an exuberant hug. "I'm sorry, Mom. I do give you a hard time, don't I?"

"That's the understatement of the year. Never mind. I was warned. Your great-grandmother told me you'd be hard to handle."

"Gandy? Gandy told you that? How did she know? I was barely born when she died."

"She saw you only once. You were two weeks old, but she took one look at you and knew you'd be a hell-raiser." Lindsay smiled, remembering. "I'm afraid she also said you'd be just like me: a handful but worth it. And you have been, you brat, even though sometimes I thought you'd mounted an organized campaign to drive your father and me crazy."

"Come on. I haven't been that bad, have I? Out of respect for you and Dad I never joined a civil rights protest. I'm strictly anti-pot. And I haven't even gotten pregnant out of wedlock. Now that's not too bad for a liberated woman in 1965, is it?" S.P. was teasing her, the big brown eyes, so like Lindsay's own, shining with laughter.

"You're impossible," Lindsay said. "A fresh, uppity kid who hasn't got sense enough to stay single."

S.P. looked thoughtful. "You and Dad don't think I'm making a mistake, do you? I mean, you do approve."

191

"Would it make any difference if we didn't? Suppose I said, no, I don't approve. Would you call off next week's wedding?"

"Mom, you are kidding, aren't you?" S.P. actually looked anxious.

"Of course, I'm kidding! You know we love Robin. But I'd be lying to you, darling, if I didn't say I wished you could have waited a little longer. You're awfully young for marriage."

"You were a year younger. You were only nineteen."

Lindsay sighed. "I knew you were going to say that. The ultimate, irrefutable argument. And next you're going to tell me that your father was only twenty and Robin is twenty-five."

S.P. grinned. "Well it worked out jim-dandy for you, didn't it? Last year you celebrated your silver wedding anniversary."

"Don't remind me. Twenty-five years. My God, it's indecent to live with the same man that long! I've always thought marriage contracts should have renewal clauses, up for review every five years, so you could decide whether to pick up your option."

"Mo-ther!"

"Okay. I'm kidding. Well, half kidding. There were times when I might not have renewed. Or your father either, I'm sure. Marriage is no picnic, baby, don't fool yourself that it is. But it's the only way to live if it's right. Or as near right as any intimate relationship can be. We've done better than most, your dad and I, but there were rough spots in the beginning. Like during the war. Separation is hard on young married people. Harder than being together where you can yell and scream and fight things out nose to nose. I'm glad Robin won't get in this terrible thing in Vietnam. For many reasons."

"Yes. Thank God for old football injuries." S.P. frowned. "I think if he were threatened with the draft, I'd make him run away to Canada. With me, of course. It's such an obscene war, Mom. Why the hell doesn't LBJ get us out of it?"

"Baby, don't ask me questions like that. I had enough trouble trying to grasp the enormity of World War Two. Sometimes I still can't believe it. Thirty-five million killed. Ten million more in Nazi concentration camps."

"You must have been crazy with worry over Dad."

"Yes," Lindsay said briefly. "I was."

It seemed a hundred years ago, so much had happened in the past twenty. Geoffrey had moved steadily upward in the agency until now, at forty-six, he was president of it, head of a multimillion dollar business. And because of that business, S.P. had met Robin Darnevale, the same kind of bright young account executive Geoffrey had been. In two years, Rob wooed and won the boss's daughter and now with Geoff's blessing was taking her to Chicago, where Robin would head the office of Ford, Wheeler, Koch & Murray.

Lindsay hated to see her move so far away. They'd been close through her growing-up years, closer than Lindsay had been to Pauline, somehow. Not that she and S.P. were pals. Lindsay detested that idea. Mothers were mothers and daughters daughters and they weren't supposed to be girl friends. But she'd been comfortable with S.P., and she knew the girl felt the same. They'd miss each other, but S.P. was entitled to her own life, her own home and husband. Besides, Lindsay consoled herself, Robin would be coming back to the New York office often, and there was no reason S.P. couldn't come with him. There was plenty of room for them in the big Park Avenue apartment. Thank God she and Geoff had never had the least urge to move to the suburbs. They were city people, like Pauline, who still lived in the apartment she'd shared with Gandy, only five blocks away.

At seventy-five, Pauline was a handsome, composed woman, staunchly independent, with the vigor and energy of someone twenty years younger. She was endlessly busy with charities and committees and her "do-gooder projects," as she deprecatingly called them. After Gandy's death, there'd been no question that Pauline would remain in the comfortable apartment she now owned. They'd barely discussed it. Pauline had merely said, "I'd like to stay on here, Lindsay. The furnishings are yours, so take any of them you want. Gandy left them to you."

"I don't want them now, Mama," the twenty-five-year-old Lindsay had said. "Our apartment is too small. Keep them for me until I need them."

"Very well." Pauline hesitated. "I simply thought that now . . . now that you're a very rich young woman, you and Geoff might move to a bigger place. You could get a nanny for S.P. if you had room for one."

Lindsay shook her head. "Uh-uh. Geoff won't hear of my using my money for anything like that. He says I can spend what I want on clothes for myself and S.P., but he's responsible for the rent and the food and the household help. And right now we're in no position to splurge."

Pauline had looked at her quizzically. "And you don't mind?"

"Sure I mind. I think it's goofy. But he has his pride, Mama."

They hadn't moved until S.P. was five and Geoff could afford a three-bedroom apartment on East 57th Street. Even then, Lindsay didn't hire a nanny. She loved taking care of S.P., getting up early to take her to private schools, kindergarten at first and later to the primary grades until she was old enough to go alone on the school bus. They stayed in that apartment until S.P. was fifteen. Geoff was made president then, and they bought the big co-op on Park, hired a full-time, live-in housekeeper, and finally took some of Gandy's beautiful antiques. Lindsay wouldn't have taken them even then, but Pauline insisted.

"You have the proper setting for them now, Lindsay, and you should enjoy them. Gandy would want you to."

"But what about you, Mama?"

"Darling, wherever there are holes, I'll replace. Not with such priceless things. At my age, I don't need them. But don't worry, my apartment won't look as though the furniture has been repossessed. It really has far too much in it now."

Lindsay had taken her grandmother's beautiful things, the furniture and paintings and precious bibelots, and rejoiced in them. Beyond that, they became a new interest for her. She read everything she could about antiques, went to all the shops and shows, and became something of an expert. It was a hobby that fascinated her, and she knew more about it than most decorators. It had happened at a good time, as well. S.P. was a young lady by then, already busy with her own social life. At her debut she'd been introduced to Robin Darnevale, her father's employee. It had quite literally been love at first sight, culminating in the soon-to-happen marriage.

In her heart, Lindsay did wish, as she'd said, that they'd wait a little longer. Geoff agreed. But beyond a mild discussion with the young couple, S.P.'s parents had not made any attempt to dissuade them.

"They might elope, honey, the way we did," Geoff said later. "I know you have your heart set on a big wedding for S.P. Want to take the chance?"

Lindsay shook her head. "No. Robin's a fine young man and he loves her. He's not marrying her because she's your daughter. And S.P. adores him." She smiled. "She's my daughter, too. Remember how I blackmailed you into marriage?"

"Things were different in those days," Geoff said. "Twenty-year-old girls usually were virgins. I'm not sure the same tactics would work today."

"Geoff! You don't think—"

"I don't allow myself to think, Lind. She's a nice girl, but it's a different world."

Yes, it is that, Lindsay thought now as she fussed over the last-minute preparations for the wedding reception at home. God knows it's a world Papa can't begin to understand.

Papa. At seventy-seven, Howard Thresher was an old man. Testy, impatient, hypochondriacal. He was still married to Adele, and the age difference between him and his forty-four-year-old wife was now staggeringly apparent. She was still a beautiful woman, though as colorless a personality as she'd ever been. She treated Howard with the deference she'd show any man old enough to be her father, but there was no love lost between them. That was obvious. Sometimes Lindsay caught him looking at Adele as though he hated her. What had their life been like these past twenty years? Was it a wild, passionate thing in the beginning? In a way she felt sorry for Adele. There'd been such promise there once, long ago when she was so insanely in love with James. She'd quivered with life and desire then. But when he died she became the frightened, helpless thing Howard Thresher wanted, for reasons no one would ever understand.

She'd long since made her peace with Adele, but she could never feel warmly about her again, never trust her fully. Geoff, on the other hand, admired Adele hugely, thought she was bright, appealing, even sexy. And Adele was almost coy around him. Sometimes Lindsay thought her childhood friend would like to have an affair with Geoff. Why not? She was the first one to know he was vulnerable. But that was twenty years ago. In all that time, Geoffrey Murray had never given Lindsay cause to be the slightest bit suspicious of him. Time had almost erased the memory of that unknown English girl. She rarely thought of those awful days, except when she saw Adele or when, as earlier, she had obliquely referred to marital problems in her talk with S.P.

Her thoughts went back to Howard Thresher. All her life she'd had ambivalent feelings about him. As a child he'd been her hero. She literally worshiped him, her urge for his approval almost enhanced by his half-indifferent manner. Later, when her parents were divorced, she had a tug-of-war with her loyalties, half of her sympathizing with Pauline, who'd reached the breaking point; the other half still drawn to the man who hadn't wished his marriage to end. For a while, during her crisis with Geoff, she'd thought she hated her father, considered him a fool to marry Adele. Worse than a fool. She'd looked on him as a traitor, allying himself with her enemy.

Twenty years later she could look back and almost clinically analyze the raw emotions of that time. The people she blamed were not at fault, any of them. Her anger at Geoff had spilled onto anyone even remotely involved in the hurt he'd caused her. Even onto her dead brother. Poor James. She silently begged his forgiveness and knew she'd never stopped loving him, any more than she'd ever stopped adoring Howard, weaknesses and all.

In the past couple of years, she and her father had become very close. Closer than at any other time in their lives. On his part, she supposed, it was the introspection of old age, the belated realization that he'd never been the kind of father a girl hoped for. As for Lindsay, she now felt pity for this disappointed man. His code of honor, his unshakable pride had forbidden him to speak of the details of his second marriage, but a mature, more discerning Lindsay could read between the lines. When S.P.'s engagement was announced, Lindsay had one of her rare, frank talks with Howard. He'd been openly opposed to this marriage.

"She's too damned young! She's still a child!"

"Papa, she's twenty. I know that's young. Geoff and I feel the same. But she comes from a long line of women who marry early: Gandy, Mama, me. I'm hardly in a position to moralize. Anyway, I suppose we should be grateful she and Robin are all for matrimony. Millions of young people don't seem to believe in it any more. They prefer to live together, and I'm sure that would distress you even more."

"Not necessarily," Howard said testily. "At least they'd find out if they're compatible. Not too bad an idea in many ways. Probably save a lot of grief later on."

Lindsay could hardly suppress a laugh. Howard in favor of his granddaughter "living in sin"? Wonders never ceased! She'd never understand this complex man.

"Come on, Papa. You don't really mean that. You'd hit the roof." She teased him gently. "Don't tell me you've changed your mind about the old double standard. I thought your convictions about the purity of women were pretty hard and fast. Can this be enlightenment I detect?"

196

He hadn't smiled. In fact, he'd looked pained. "Morally, it's hard for me to condone, Lindsay. You're right about that. But as a practical man, I've had to face the fact that some people are not . . . not physically suited. A man takes it for granted that his wife will have the same feelings he does. It doesn't always happen that way. A girl without experience can sometimes be disappointed, even repelled by the man she marries. That's a bad thing. Bad for both of them."

Lindsay was amazed. "Are you saying you think S.P. and Robin should sleep together before they marry? *You*, Papa?"

There was no answer.

With a sense of certainty, Lindsay realized he wasn't speaking of his grandchild. He was talking about himself and Adele. My God! Has that little beast rejected him all these years? How could she? "Repelled," he'd said. What humiliation for this man. For *any* man. But once she'd gotten over her shock, she wondered why she was surprised. From the time they were children, Adele had expressed disinterest in, even distaste for, marriage. I thought she'd gotten over those silly ideas. She'd seemed so in love with James. But if sex still revolted her, why had she married Papa? She had to know he was a man of strong appetites. And why had Howard stayed married to her if they were physically unsuited? His damned pride, she thought pityingly. How unhappy he must have been all these years, yet he wouldn't admit his mistake. It was funny. Wrenching and funny. Papa the seducer marrying a virgin and finding she couldn't stand him. I could kill her, Lindsay felt fiercely. All she wanted was to be safe. She probably thought he was too old to be demanding. And she's destroyed him. She's made an old, angry man of him.

But she couldn't say any of this to her father. The wound was long-standing and too deep to heal. Could any man awaken Adele? Lindsay doubted it. She was a cold, uptight woman. Adele, the snow queen. Maybe James could have done it. No one would ever know. But if he hadn't been able to, he'd have had less false pride than Papa. He'd have kicked her out on her icy little rear end, which is what she deserved.

She looked at Howard, who seemed lost in thought.

"Well, Papa, for all we know, our precious child may already know how compatible she and Robin are. In a way, like you, Geoff and I almost hope so, in spite of our 1940s morals. But in any case, I think she and Robin will be happy. You just have to look at S.P. to know

197

what a down-to-earth young woman she is. She knows the facts of life. Girls her age are very wise these days. And she's loving, Papa. She'll know the joy of giving and the thrill of receiving. I'm absolutely sure of that. Ready for marriage? I can't say. Ready for love? Without a doubt."

He sighed. "I hope you're right, Lindsay. There's nothing sadder than a loveless marriage." For a moment he let down his guard. "I always loved your mother, you know. Really loved her. I hurt her. I was young and greedy and I demanded more understanding than any woman could give. I want you to know I regret what I did to her all those years. Regret it bitterly. I've learned my lesson too late. But I've paid for it. Indeed I have. Paid for it a thousand times over. There is a hell on earth, Lindsay. Every one of us is punished for his sins. And we get our comeuppance right here, one way or another." The old man's eyes misted. "I hope Geoff never has to pay for his sins. You've forgiven him, haven't you? I hope you have. I was wrong to tell you. So damned self-righteous I was! Damning others for the same kind of conduct I once indulged in. I thought those days were over for me, and I could preach the wrongness of them." He gave a bitter little laugh. "Nothing worse than a reformed whore, is there? And nothing phonier. Geoff made one mistake. I made dozens. You don't hold it against him, do you, Lindsay? Don't make him pay forever for that slight fall from grace."

He made her want to cry. "I've forgotten it, Papa." What harm in a little half-truth? "It was twenty years ago. He was a lonely serviceman and I was far away. To this day, I've never told him I know. He's been a good husband. A good father. If there was any atoning to be done, I'm sure Geoff has punished himself. He doesn't need me to accuse him."

"Good," Howard said. "You're a good girl. I'm proud of you."

Even now, his approval warmed her.

"Don't be too hard on yourself, Papa. Mama's never been that hard on you. She understood. She's always loved you too. She had pride, that's all. As you had. As you still have."

He looked at her discerningly. She understood, all right. But he didn't want her pity. Couldn't stand hers or anyone else's.

"Don't misinterpret anything I've said." Howard was seemingly confident again. "I'm a very happy man, in spite of whatever regrets I may have. Life's been good to me. I have no complaints. None at all. I have a devoted wife, a lovely daughter, and a beautiful grandchild."

"Of course. You're a fortunate human being. Everyone loves you."

He seemed mollified. "Yes, they do, don't they? That's a very nice thing to know."

The wedding was a dream. S.P. was radiant, walking down the aisle on the arm of her handsome father. Lindsay took her eyes away from the bride long enough to look at Robin, whose whole face seemed to be suffused with love and wonder. They'll be all right, Lindsay thought, wiping away a tear. There's more than desire between them. There's understanding and respect and a wonderful sense of completeness. Unlike the generations before them, they're marrying for all the right reasons.

She reached out and squeezed the hand of Pauline, who sat next to her. Her mother responded with a pressure that said, This is good. This is as it should be.

Pauline was, indeed, happy to see her beloved granddaughter joined to the fine young man she cared for so deeply. Her joy made even the awkwardness of the situation easier. She'd never, ever get used to seeing Howard with another woman. Not even after twenty years. He looks so old, she thought. So tired and dispirited. As though he's ready to give up. She felt a pang of sorrow. This is not my Howard, this stooped old man with the lifeless eyes, this fearful elderly gentleman who, Lindsay told her, saw his doctor nearly every day, watched his diet, went to bed at ten o'clock, and did not smoke or drink.

He's seventy-seven, Pauline thought in mild astonishment. Strange. She seldom thought of age. And never thought of herself or Howard as "senior citizens." Such a distasteful phrase. And yet a dreadful premonition ran through her. Howard was already two years older than his mother was when she died. She suddenly felt with certainty that he soon would follow Gandy. What a dreadful, morbid idea, and in the middle of a wedding! What on earth was wrong with her? Still, she knew, and she involuntarily shuddered.

Lindsay felt the motion in the hand she held. For a second she turned and looked inquiringly at her mother. Pauline smiled and made a little motion, indicating it was nothing. She only prayed it was. Whatever he'd done, she'd loved him all her life and she'd love him beyond.

*   *   *

S.P., dressed in her going-away clothes, stood at the bend of the stairs that led up to the second floor of her parents' duplex. Laughing, making feints with her bouquet toward the women below, she finally turned her back and tossed the flowers over her shoulder. She heard polite laughter and faced around to see Adele holding the little nosegay.

For a moment, S.P. stared at her. She'd never cared for Grandpa's second wife. Pauline was the only grandmother she acknowledged, now that Daddy's parents were both dead. Adele catching the bridal bouquet? It was ludicrous. What was she doing in that crowd anyhow? Only the young, unmarried girls were supposed to be standing anywhere near the spot where the flowers might fall.

"Nice pitch, honey," Robin said under his breath. "Keep working on that throwing arm and next year I'll see if I can get you a contract with the Dodgers."

S.P. smiled and joined in the laughter, but even as she did so, she said between clenched teeth, "What the hell was she doing there? Why didn't she stand back with Mother and Grandma where she belonged?"

Still grinning and waving at the guests, Robin said, "Don't blame *her,* killer. You threw that thing so hard it damned near landed on Lexington Avenue."

They ran down the steps together, hand in hand, the picture of happiness. How young they are, Geoff thought. How strong and certain. That's my little girl. Because of her, I'm here now. If it hadn't been for her, who knows? I might have stayed with Pamela. Funny. I still think of her. I've been happy with Lindsay. I don't regret my decision. Yet there are moments when I yearn for someone who needs me. Pam never said it, but she needed me. It was in her eyes, in the brave, nonchalant way she covered up her disappointment. Lindsay's so self-sufficient. She's been a wonderful wife, a sensational mother. But I never half felt for one moment that she depended on me. Not just because she has money of her own. She's been what she was when we met: positive in her belief that things always work out the way she wants them. Why should she doubt it? They always have. I love her. She's gone along with my wishes always. And yet I feel I'm the weaker. It's the one flaw in our marriage, this unwanted knowledge that I'm not the gallant protector I'd like to be.

He also had an uneasy feeling that life would change for Lindsay and him now that S.P. was leaving. She held us together more than we realized, Geoff thought. Lindsay doesn't know the baby brought me home, that her very being has made me a better, more honest man. S.P.'s been my real love, the voice of my conscience, the one woman in my life who needed me. Robin takes my place now, he thought sadly. I've lost my little girl.

She came toward him and kissed him, twining her arms around his neck. "Thank you, Daddy. It was a beautiful wedding. Thank you for everything."

"It was nothing," he said lightly. "I'd have done it for the bride of any benighted advertising man." He held her close for a moment. "Be happy, Sara Pauline," he said. "Be very happy, baby."

She looked up at him adoringly. "I will, Daddy."

There were big hugs and kisses for her mother, for Pauline and Howard and Robin's parents. There was a dutiful, but less enthusiastic, embrace for Adele, who still held the bouquet.

"Sorry about that," S.P. said, looking at the flowers. "My aim sure was wild."

Adele smiled. "Another old adage gone wrong," she said. "I'm the one who's sorry. I should have ducked."

In another hour, everyone was gone, the caterers had cleaned up the last remnants of caviar and wedding cake, whisked the champagne glasses and ashtrays out of sight, accepted the thanks of the bride's parents, and departed. In the merciful quiet, Lindsay dropped into a chair in the library and let out a sigh of relief.

"Tired?" Geoff asked. "Want me to make you a drink?"

"I'd love one. Every time I got my paws around a glass, someone pulled me away. I'm the soberest mother of the bride since Carrie Nation married off her young 'uns."

He smiled. "I didn't know she had young 'uns."

"Just a figure of speech, my love. Neither do I know. Or care." Lindsay yawned. "It really went well, didn't it? I mean, the church was beautiful, and things seemed to go without a hitch here at home." She frowned. "All except that damned Adele. The nerve of her, catching the bouquet! What in the world made her do such a stupid thing? She knows very well the one who gets it is supposed to be the next bride."

"I don't think she really meant to catch it, Lind. I think she just reacted involuntarily to that crazy wild pitch of S.P.'s."

"Well, it was embarrassing. And dumb. But *she's* dumb. Always has been."

201

"Funny. I used to think you admired Adele extravagantly. You were so impressed with the work she did after she finished school. And you couldn't praise her enough in your letters to me during the war, all that A.W.V.S. stuff and how wonderful she was. Hell, honey, you even wanted her to marry your brother."

Lindsay frowned. "Adele changed. Besides, I wanted her to marry my *brother,* not my *father.*"

"Come on, Lind. Why do you hold that against her? All these years! They fell in love. Okay. It was May and December, but you can't hate her for that."

Lindsay didn't answer. I hate her for it more than you know, she said silently. I hate her for what she's done to him. And, yes, I still hate her for what she almost did to you and me.

"Adele's always had you fooled, hasn't she, Geoff? You really think she's sweet and warm and helpless. Maybe you should have married *her.*" Lindsay knew she was being ridiculous and impossible, but she couldn't help herself. "I think she's had a yen for you for years."

Geoff flushed angrily. "If I didn't know you were dog-tired and not responsible for what you're saying, I'd feel like slapping you! I can't help it if you're jealous of anybody your father loves, Lindsay. That's *your* problem. But for God's sake don't try to involve me in it!"

He was right. She was behaving like a shrew. The strain of the wedding and the weeks of preparation for it, plus that revealing and disconcerting talk with her father, had set Lindsay's nerves on edge. And Adele standing there holding her step-granddaughter's bridal bouquet was the last straw. But that was no reason to snap at Geoff. He hadn't done anything. Lately.

She smiled apologetically. "I'm sorry, darling. I am done in. I think I'll call it a night. Coming up?"

"Think I'll work awhile. Some papers from the office I should go over. Good night, honey. See you in the morning."

"Night." She gave him a fleeting kiss. "Don't stay up too late."

Not that I'd know, Lindsay thought. For the last two years they'd had separate bedrooms. It was only civilized. Each of them slept better alone. Geoff snored lightly, which bothered her. And she had a bad habit of waking up in the night and putting on the light, which disturbed his sound sleep. She, in fact, had been the one who suggested they no longer share a bedroom. She'd even been coquettish about it.

"It probably will put new bloom on this romance," she said. "You creeping into my bed and leaving in the wee hours like an illicit lover."

He hadn't been in favor of it, but he hadn't strenuously argued. He'd merely said, "We've never needed much stimulation in twenty-four years. And I do like knowing you're there when I wake up."

"I know. But do you really like the sight of me in night cream and pin curls? I'll be much more glamorous every night waiting for you to come into my room." She flirted with him, even while she felt a twinge of uneasy remembrance. "We can pretend I'm your mistress and you're a deprived husband with a dreary wife in Westchester."

He'd laughed and said okay, if she thought that was best. And for months he had come to her nearly every night. He had to agree there was something exciting about it. People long married come to take everything for granted, most of all their lovemaking. But as S.P.'s marriage came closer and his sense of loss deepened, the strength of his desire lessened. Now, almost dutifully, he became her lover only once a week, sometimes less frequently. He was sure Lindsay noticed but did not comment. She always welcomed him with open arms and the same kind of eagerness she'd had the night they ran away together. She never tired of him, nor he of her. But it had inevitably become familiar and yes, dammit, slightly routine. For him. For both of them, he assumed.

Watching her walk up the stairs to her room, Geoff thought again what a beauty she was. At forty-five, she still had a young, unlined face and a perfect body. She'd always had a wonderful, graceful carriage. "Lindsay carries herself like an empress," her grandmother had once said. "And frequently behaves as imperiously as one," Pauline had added dryly. Geoff smiled at the memory. They loved her unqualifiedly, all of them. Including me. She's one hell of a woman.

Why, then, did he feel this vague sense of desolation and emptiness? What was it he was looking for? Not Pamela. She was only a distant, long-gone dream. He'd not heard from her since the day he left London. She must be married and with kids of her own. No, he wasn't yearning for his wartime sweetheart. He wasn't even consciously yearning for any woman.

Male menopause, he told himself ruefully. You're probably going through it. Heading toward fifty. It happens to a lot of men. Forget it. Don't get crazy discontented like a lot of middle-aged guys. Alone, he suddenly laughed aloud. Great God, maybe he was having the "empty nest syndrome," that awful feeling that comes when the children grow up and leave home! Nuts, that's what he was. Totally round the bend.

Fathers didn't have that. It was an emotional malady reserved for "deserted" mothers left with no interest in life. I'm a man with everything to keep me busy and happy, Geoff thought. Why am I pitying myself like some forlorn, bored housewife?

Abruptly, he ran up the stairs and, without knocking, entered Lindsay's room. She was just slipping into her nightgown. Geoff looked at her appreciatively and then, assuming a jaunty attitude as he leaned against the doorjamb, he raised one eyebrow and said, "Your husband out of town, lady?"

Lindsay, playing the game, let the gown fall to the floor. "Come on in, soldier," she said. "My old man won't be back till tomorrow."

18

The year that followed S.P.'s marriage crept slowly by, dragging with it subtle changes in all their lives. Geoff's restlessness grew more obvious. He began to travel more, for one thing. It seemed to Lindsay that he was forever off to one of the branch offices in Los Angeles or Dallas or, most often, Chicago. Not without jealousy, Lindsay knew he invented trips to that city for the express purpose of seeing their daughter. Occasionally, he took Lindsay along, but more often he didn't invite her, saying, when she asked, "It's such a quick trip, honey, and I'll be tied up in meetings most of the time."

"That's all right. I could visit with S.P. while you're busy."

"Lind, dear, you know she's working. What would you do with yourself all day? There's only so much poking around Marshall Field even an inveterate shopper can do."

Lindsay had no answer. S.P., who'd never shown any interest in a career, had suddenly gotten caught up in the excitement of a job. To her mother's total surprise, she'd arrived in New York alone six months earlier and announced she was going to be the Estée Lauder cosmetics saleswoman in Bonwit Teller, Chicago.

"They brought me to New York for training, Mom. May I stay with you for a week? They'd put me up in a hotel, but I'd rather be here."

"Of course. We're delighted, darling, but what's this all about? You, working? That's a bit of a jolt."

S.P. grinned. "Yep. Ain't that a kick in the head?" Then, more seriously, "I had to do something, Mother. I was bored out of my skull. I hardly know anybody in Chicago and I was just moping around, killing time all day. When it got to the point that I was getting addicted to soap operas, I said to myself, That's it, old girl. Enough already! So I goofed myself down to Bonwits, and sure enough the Lauder people were looking for a rep. I didn't think I'd get it. No experience. But they took me and here I am, all set for my schooling. Isn't it super?"

Lindsay was dismayed, though she tried not to show it. She wasn't opposed to the idea of S.P. having a job if she wanted one. It was all to the good. She was a firm believer in every young woman's knowing how to support herself if the time ever came that she needed to. Not that S.P. had such worries. Even if, God forbid, she should be widowed, there was plenty of family money. If she was left alone, she wouldn't have to fret about that, the way some women did. Fleetingly, Lindsay remembered Adele's mother, driven to a quick marriage because she didn't know how to take responsibility for herself and her child. That wouldn't happen to S.P. But she could become like me, Lindsay thought. She could find herself middle-aged and useless, her children grown and married, her husband involved in his own work. Yes, early training in some kind of career was a very sound notion. But a cosmetics salesperson? It seemed such a futureless job.

"It's super," she'd agreed, "but why this kind of work, honey? Why not something in an office where you'd have a chance to grow? Selling in a specialty shop isn't exactly what I'd picture for a girl of your background. I mean, there's nothing wrong with it, but—"

"But it seems kind of lower-class to you, right? Well, it isn't. I promise you. There are a bunch of nifty ladies in that department. And I do mean *ladies*. I was damned lucky to be chosen. As I said, no experience. You have an old-fashioned idea about selling, dear. It's no longer done by grade-school types in dingy black dresses and arch-support shoes. The girls in the cosmetics department are snappy. Some of them are just like me: working to keep their heads on straight, rather than being concerned about the salary or the chance for advancement."

"All right," Lindsay said, "I concede I'm old-fashioned. After all, I am a doddering old lady of forty-five with archaic ideas from another generation."

"Mom, you know I didn't mean that! I hate it when you're sarcastic. I just meant—"

Lindsay smiled. "I know what you meant, darling. And you're right. My damned sharp tongue always gets me in trouble. I simply thought you might really want a career. In advertising, maybe. I'm sure your father—"

"No. I don't want anybody hiring me because I'm Daddy's girl or Robin's wife. And I have no qualifications for any kind of office work. I can't type or take dictation or write copy or do artwork. And frankly, Mom, I'm not all that hell-bent on being a career woman. In a few years I'll want a baby or two or three. I'm just putting myself on the hold button for a while. And this job will be fun."

Lindsay relented. "I'm sure it will be. I didn't mean to sound snobby, S.P. And I don't really think selling in a store means measuring a yard of fabric from the end of your nose to the length of your arm." She smiled. "Truth is, I envy you. I wish there were something I could do. It gets pretty lonely around here. You're away, your father travels half the time. Even your grandmother never has a spare moment between projects. But I just sit. I've done enough needlepoint pillows to furnish a sultan's harem. Read enough books to cause premature blindness. Visited enough art galleries and antiques shops to wear the soles off my Guccis." Lindsay laughed. "And I don't even get paid for it."

Now, as Geoff reminded her that S.P. was busy all day, Lindsay sighed. To be idle was a terrible thing. It made one old and dull. Her heart constricted as she wondered whether Geoff found her as boring as she felt. He certainly spent as much time away from her as he could decently manage. And as for their sex life—well, it had become, she thought, minimal at best. That fact alone pained her. She was a passionate woman and her husband's ardor had always more than matched her own. But not in the last year. Without bitterness, she wondered whether Geoff found women while he was away on his business trips. Could well be. Twenty-seven years married. They'd even celebrated their silver anniversary. Lindsay's lip curled. Appropriate it should be silver. Silver was cold and hard and substantial. A middle-of-the-road metal. An unlikely golden anniversary at least sounded warm and sunny. And an improbable diamond jubilee had glitter, not that they were likely to see it.

"Geoff," she said suddenly, "I'd like to go to work."

He couldn't have been more astonished if she'd said she'd like to jump off the Brooklyn Bridge. "You'd *what?*"

"I have to have something to do. Something interesting. You're all wound up in the agency. S.P.'s far away and busy herself. Even Mama goes like a steam engine. I've been thinking I'd like to be more active."

He recovered quickly. "Well, fine, Lind. Any idea what you want to do?"

"Unfortunately, no. Like S.P., I have no training, and I don't think my feet would stand up under a day on the selling floor of Bendel's. But there must be something."

"Maybe you should just involve yourself more in volunteer work, the way your mother does. There's a lot of good you could do, working in a hospital or fund-raising for some charity. How about Recording for the Blind?"

She shook her head. "Those are all good things. Necessary and worthwhile. I admire the women who do them. But I want something more challenging." She smiled. "The truth is, I guess I want to earn recognition of some kind. Achieve something and get paid for it. Not that we need the money, but it's the yardstick of success. I don't want to give my time. I want to do something more . . . more professional. Something where I feel I'm earning my way."

You want to be a leader, Geoff thought cynically. As usual, you want to call the shots. In the next instant he was ashamed of himself. That was unfair. Lindsay was only feeling what a great many women felt these days: that if she put in time she should be compensated for it. But, as she said, what could she do? Except for that brief period right after their marriage when he was in school, Lindsay had never held a job. Thinking of that, he said, "You hated working when we were in Cambridge, remember? What makes you think you'd like it now?"

Lindsay smiled. "I hated that job because I *had* to do it. We needed the money because you wouldn't take Gandy's help. I hated it because I felt put upon by your independence, my love. This is different. This I *want* to do. Besides, as I said, I have no intention of going back to selling things. That's okay for S.P., but I'm too long in the tooth for such hard work."

"No work's easy, Lind."

"I know. But there must be jobs where you can sit down once in a while."

He teased her. "Why don't you become a telephone operator? Or how about cashier in a greasy spoon? They'd give you a nice high stool."

She didn't laugh. "I'm dead serious, Geoff."

208

He matched her tone. "I know. I'm sorry. I didn't mean to sound as though I was making fun of you. But damned if I know where you should start. Your interests are pretty esthetic: art, antiques—"

Lindsay interrupted him. "Hey, maybe that's it! Antiques. Why not? I know more about them than most people. Thanks to Gandy, I cut my teeth on them, you should pardon the expression. Why couldn't I open a shop, Geoff? Import antiques and sell them to decorators? Or maybe the public? At least that's an area in which I feel confident. What do you think?"

He couldn't help looking dubious. "I don't know. You certainly are knowledgeable about them, but you haven't the faintest idea of how to run a business. It isn't as simple as buying and selling. It could get pretty complicated, I'd think, with leases and inventory and overhead. To say nothing of the intricate business of importing, with shipping and customs and all those things." He shook his head. "Sounds a little ambitious for a beginner, honey. Even anybody as gung-ho as you. Maybe you ought to work in an antiques shop for a while. Learn the business before you start on your own."

"No. I can do it." Lindsay's eyes shone with excitement. "I can hire good people to help me with all that paperwork stuff. What was it Papa used to say about being a successful executive? 'Deputize, supervise, criticize.' I can do that, Geoff. I'll do the buying myself. It might mean three or four trips to Europe every year, but you wouldn't mind that, would you? You're away so much of the time yourself."

He glanced at her sharply, but there was no reproach in her voice. She was simply stating an accepted fact about his absences.

"Well," he said, "I guess there's no harm in trying. How much capital do you think you'll need for your start-up costs?"

She stared at him blankly. "Start-up costs?"

"How much will you need to open the doors and keep the place going for the first year or so? Lind, dear, you'll have to do a lot of exploratory work. Find a location that's suitable and within reason, rentwise. Figure your fixtures and inventory and fixed expenses, among other things. You'll need plenty of yellow pads and sharp pencils before you make the first step. I'll get one of the boys from accounting to lend you a hand, if you like. Then, when you know how much you need, I'll help you get financing."

"Financing? What financing?"

"Honey, nobody uses his own money to go into business. We'll borrow from the bank. Or get a few people willing to invest in a risk venture."

She shook her head. "No. I'm going to do this with my own money. I don't want partners and I don't want to owe money to the banks."

"Lind, that's crazy! I can't let you do that. It's not the way business works these days."

"It's the way *my* business will work," she said stubbornly. "Gandy left me the money, and I can't think of anything she'd rather have it used for. In fact, that's what I'm going to call the business. GANDY INC." She bubbled with enthusiasm. "There, smart one, I've already got the name. Now it's just a simple matter of putting it on the door."

"You're impossible. I can't let you risk your inheritance. It's stupid, Lindsay. All right, you don't want partners, but at least let's try to get a business loan from the bank. That's what everybody does. Owing money gives you a good credit rating. You have to understand that. It doesn't work the way it did when we were growing up. Anybody who's anybody has a bank loan. It's expected. Just like people no longer pay off the mortgage on their houses. Property's more valuable with a mortgage, to say nothing of the tax advantages. Lindsay, take your hands away from your ears! You must listen to me."

"I won't. I don't care about your damned business rules. Gandy Inc. is going to be all mine. And I'll succeed at it too. You wait and see."

Geoff sighed. "I'm only trying to help. You're so damned independent."

"And pigheaded and stubborn and non-clinging-vine." She grinned at him. "Poor Geoff," she said. "You really should have married a helpless nitwit. Not a mule, like me." She came and sat in his lap. "Never mind, darling. I know I'm a little crazy, but I love you." She began to make seductive overtures. "Let's celebrate my big idea," she whispered. "I know it's four o'clock of a Sunday afternoon, but I can make my room very dark. Don't you dig the idea of two tycoons in bed together?"

For a moment he'd responded to her caresses, but her last sentence abruptly took away all desire. "No thanks," he said rudely. "I never make love to another businessman."

Lindsay looked as though he'd struck her. "I see," she said quietly. "Sorry to offend your male ego." She rose and moved away from him.

Dammit! What made me say such an idiotic thing? Geoff fumed.

She was being sweet and happy and I spoiled it. Why do I hate it when she's strong and self-assured and independent? This is Lindsay. No different than ever. He smiled apologetically. "That was a half-ass thing to say, Lind. Forgive me." He came to where she was standing and tried to put his arms around her. "I love your ideas, all of them. Including the one about going upstairs."

Lindsay shrugged him off. "It was a dumb idea, that one. Forget it, Geoff. I think I'll go get out my pencils and paper." She paused in the doorway. "You'll hate it if I succeed, won't you? You'd like me to be a damned doormat. The little woman at home, waiting with bated breath for the master's return, incapable of having a thought or ambition of her own. Well, it's 1966 and I suppose there are women like that, ones who like being useless and brainless and pathetic, but you'll have to look elsewhere for them. Not," she added sarcastically, "that you already haven't, I'm sure."

She disappeared before he could answer. Just as well, Geoff thought. What good was a terrible fight about something he couldn't really explain? What's happened to us, Lindsay? What's pulled us so far apart? It was oversimplification to say people's needs and values changed as they matured. Other couples weathered a quarter century of marriage without this chasm growing ever wider between them. Why are we drifting apart? Is it because we were never right for each other in the beginning? A bit late for that kind of speculation, he thought ruefully. These were questions for the first years of a marriage. Small good it does us to ask them now. Us. Almost for the first time he realized Lindsay must be as troubled as he. This urge for an outside interest was an indication a blind man couldn't miss. He'd never thought whether or not she was content. He'd simply assumed it, as he assumed her love and her fidelity. My God, he thought, I'm as bad as Howard Thresher! I expect Lindsay to accept my word in all things, to turn her eyes away when I'm boorish, to suffer my neglect and the faithlessness she correctly suspects.

The latter thought made him wince. He had been with several other women this past year. Never before. Not since Pamela. Lindsay sensed it, though she'd not referred to it until this afternoon. I've hurt her badly, Geoff thought, and for what? They mean nothing to me, these easy conquests out of town. He supposed it was a sort of childish rebellion against the sameness of his life. A senseless search for something to fill the void S.P. left behind. You disgusting fool! he told him-

211

self. What do you think you're running *to?* What the hell are you running *from?*

Pauline, chic in her navy spring suit and hat, let herself in the door of Gandy Inc. and stood watching Lindsay working at her little desk in the rear of the shop. In one year, her daughter had established a business that was beginning to cause favorable talk. Mrs. Murray was sought after by the top New York decorators, who knew they could bring in even the most vulgar clients and have them fall under the spell of Lindsay's charm and taste. There was nothing in the place that was not elegant and precious and desirably expensive. She's made it work, Pauline thought happily. I'm so proud of her.

Observing Lindsay without her knowledge, Pauline wished her child were as happy in her personal life as she was in her work. Lindsay was reluctant to talk about it, but her mother knew the marriage was little more than a shell these days. She's almost worse off than I was when I was married to her father, Pauline thought. At least I had a concrete reason for my misery: his endless absorption with other women. But if Geoff was unfaithful, no one knew it for sure. He was discreet and not so self-indulgent that he felt the need to purge himself with mea culpa confessions about his sins. There was simply this unbridgeable gap between Lindsay and Geoff, according to what Pauline gathered.

"We're not interested in the same things any more, Mama. We're polite to each other. Even affectionate. But we're like strangers."

"Why, Lindsay? I'm not foolish enough to think romance lasts forever. You've been married for twenty-eight years. But for most of them you and Geoff seemed devoted. Did S.P.'s leaving make such a difference?"

"I don't know," Lindsay said wearily. "Maybe. It left a terrible hole in our lives, but that shouldn't cause such a change. If we were together only because of a child, it couldn't have been much of a marriage to begin with."

Pauline frowned. "You're not thinking of divorce, are you?"

"No. I don't think either of us really wants that. I mean, for what? There's no other man in my life. And as far as I know, there's nobody important in Geoff's."

"But you're only forty-seven, Lindsay. Still a young woman. You

212

must be lonely for . . . for love. Are you going to live this way the rest of your life?"

Lindsay smiled. "I may seem young to you, Mama, but sometimes I feel a hundred and forty-seven. Anyway, what's around for a woman my age, even if I were interested? Men of my group are either married or, as S.P. would say, 'light in the loafers.' Homosexuals, you'd call them. No, I really see no point in changing things."

"Heaven knows I'm not advocating you leave Geoffrey," Pauline said. "I just want to make sure that if you contemplate it, you do it while you still have a chance for another life."

"Forgive me for saying this, Mama, but you divorced Papa in 1936. And you were a year younger than I am now. You never found another life, dear. Why do you think I could?"

"I never wanted one, Lindsay. Maybe if I'd looked, I could have found someone else, but I never cared to try."

Lindsay regarded her with love. It was hard to believe Mama was seventy-seven. She was straight and spry and she had none of the hang-ups of her generation. The only time I've ever seen her crumble, Lindsay thought, was when James was killed. Even when Gandy died, heartbroken as Mama was, she was in control. I wonder how she'll feel when Papa goes.

They were sitting in the Palm Court of the Plaza Hotel when this conversation took place a month earlier. Lindsay had looked around and sighed nostalgically. "I love this place. It never changes for me. If they've remodeled, I don't even notice. It's like it was when Gandy used to bring me here for tea. I felt so grown-up and important."

"She'd be very proud of what you're doing, Lindsay. It's the kind of thing I imagine she'd like to have done herself, if she'd been able to. She was a wonderful lady, your grandmother. Like a mother to me. I still miss her, after all these years. I see her in you sometimes, darling. The same spunk. And of course the same sensitivity to beauty. You certainly didn't get that feeling for precious things from your father or me. It was a gift from Gandy. A very big gift."

"There's nothing wrong with your taste, Mama. It's impeccable."

"Thank you, but it's not the same. I only know what's right for me. I could never run a business. Your father used to get so annoyed with me because I had absolutely no head for figures. He never even allowed me to have a checking account of my own. Said I'd mess it up be-

213

yond repair. I expect he was right, though I've had to learn. Amazing what you can do when you must, isn't it?"

"Yes," Lindsay said. "Amazing."

Standing in the shop a month later, Pauline thought her daughter was, indeed, amazing in her own right. She'd done this all on her own, accepting help from Geoff's "figure men" only in the beginning. Now she ran the show herself, with only a part-time bookkeeper and a tax accountant to help her with the business details. She'd hired two people, a bright young girl to work in the shop and a talented young man to help her with clients. She worked twelve-hour days, six days a week. And she more than loved it. It was, truly, her salvation.

As though she finally sensed her mother's presence, Lindsay looked up from her papers and gave Pauline a big wave.

"Hi! You been there long?"

"Only a few minutes. You seem engrossed in your work."

"Not too engrossed to knock off for a swell lunch. I made a reservation at Lutèce. All right with you?"

Pauline arched her eyebrows. "Very fancy. Is this a special occasion?"

"Yes, as a matter of fact it's two special occasions."

In the small, chic restaurant they ordered and then Lindsay sat back, looking pleased. "Okay. Item number one: I'm being photographed for *Vogue*. In glorious color. They're going to do a story on me and my apartment and the shop. It'll be worth a fortune to me. Every silly woman in New York, San Francisco, and Houston will beat on her decorator to get something from Gandy Inc."

"That's wonderful, darling! I couldn't be more pleased for you! Don't tell me there's something even more exciting!"

"There is. How do you feel about being a great-grandma, Mrs. T?"

Pauline caught her breath. "S.P.'s going to have a baby?"

Lindsay smiled. "I can't think of any other way you could earn that title."

"Lindsay, how marvelous! I hope they're pleased."

"Delighted, apparently. So am I." She winked mischievously. "I'm not so sure about Geoff. I don't think the grandfather role fits his new swinging image. To tell you the truth, Mama, sometimes I think Geoff would like to believe that in spite of her marriage S.P. is still a virgin. He's obsessive about that girl. Like she's still his sole, exclusive property. Anyway, we're going to have a Christmas gift. She's expecting in December."

"I'm thrilled, Lindsay. I really am. Have you told Howard?"

A shadow crossed the younger woman's face, "Not yet. I ... I haven't told you, Mama, but he's very ill. I talked to Adele last week. I don't think he'll live to see S.P.'s baby."

Pain flicked across Pauline's features, but her hand was steady on her wine glass as she raised it to her lips. She took a little swallow before she said, "How long, do they think?"

"They can't be sure. But not long, I'm afraid. The cancer's all through him, dear. We have to hope he'll go fast, like Gandy."

"Yes." Pauline looked sad. "Poor Howard. He always said he'd live to be a hundred. Now I suppose he won't make eighty. Eighty! It seems impossible he's nearly that. How ... how's Adele holding up?"

Why do you care? Lindsay wanted to say. Why do you care what happens to that heartless bitch? But of course Mama didn't know what her husband's second wife had done to him. She took comfort in the thought that Howard was happy.

"Adele's all right." Truthful. Noncommittal.

"You must tell him right away about the baby," Pauline said. "I'm sure it will please him. Maybe if it's a boy S.P. will name him Howard. He'd like that, Lindsay. Do you think she would?"

"I don't know, Mama, but it can't hurt to promise."

"No, it can't, can it? He won't know." Pauline quickly wiped away a tear. "It will be the end of something for me. Isn't that foolish? Divorced thirty-one years and I still feel he's part of my life."

"I envy you, Mama. How wonderful it must be to love someone that much."

Pauline managed to smile. "Wonderful? I don't know. I think Freud would say it's sick. Maybe so. But it's an illness from which I never wanted to recover."

Lindsay looked pensive for a moment. Pauline truly was amazing. Imagine a woman of her generation even being aware of psychiatric theories! In recent years, Lindsay had come to appreciate qualities she'd never recognized in her mother. In my maturity, we've become friends, Lindsay mused. Probably because in so many ways we're alike. I'll always love Geoff the way she loves Papa. Even though I know our marriage has gone sour, I live in the hope we'll find each other again. A dim hope it is, but maybe our first grandchild will do it. She knew she was grasping at straws. I want my husband back, she thought fiercely. How much? a small voice inside asked. Are you willing to be the kind of woman he wants? Isn't it too late for you to change? If it brought Geoff back to you, would you give up this late-blooming career which makes you feel important? I don't know, she answered that inner self. God help me, I really don't know.

She pulled herself together, chattering easily through the rest of lunch, trying hard to divert Pauline's mind from the terrible news about Howard. As she paid the check, she said, "It's such a beautiful day, Mama, how about walking me back to the shop. Do you have time?"

"I'd love it. I have to go back up that way anyhow. There's a meeting at the Hospital for Special Surgery at four."

Lindsay suddenly had second thoughts. "Maybe it's too far." They'd taxied down to 50th Street. "It's twenty-five blocks or so."

Pauline laughed. "Afraid your decrepit old mother can't make it? You forget, dear, I'm a native New Yorker. This is the only city in the world where people walk. Everywhere else, they hop in their cars to go two blocks. I enjoy a nice stroll. Especially if we go up Madison. I never tire of window-shopping on that avenue."

They sauntered northward companionably, chatting and looking in windows. In the upper Sixties, Lindsay suddenly spotted a charming little picture frame in petit point.

"Look at that, Mama. Isn't it sweet? Do you mind waiting a minute while I go in?"

"Go ahead. I'll stand here and enjoy the sunshine."

Lindsay dashed into the shop and asked the price of the frame.

"Fifteen dollars," the clerk said pleasantly. "All handmade." She looked at Lindsay appraisingly. "It would be perfect for a picture of a grandchild."

The unknowing, offhand remark suddenly depressed Lindsay. My God, I must look old enough to be a grandmother! The realization came as a shock, and with it the awareness that she hated it. Funny. She'd always thought of herself as young. Even with a grown married daughter she'd never had an image of herself as a matron, much less a grandmother. But to this twentyish salesperson, she was obviously too old to have small children of her own. It was a little thing, but the impact was great. Face it, Lindsay thought. You're the older generation now. And what's so bad about that?

Smiling, she paid for the frame. "Thank you," she said. "It *is* just right for my grandchild's picture. That's what I'll use it for. I'm so glad I saw it in your window."

Still looking amused, she joined her mother on the sidewalk.

"What's the joke?" Pauline asked.

Lindsay told her about the exchange inside the store. "Maybe it's time I had my face lifted. Apparently it ain't what it used to be."

"Do you mind so much, Lindsay? Getting older, I mean. Not that you're old, for heaven's sake! Forty-seven. And you could pass for thirty-five. But it bothers you, doesn't it? The thought of being a grandmother is a shock. I know. I remember how I felt when S.P. was on the way."

Lindsay looked at her incredulously. "Did you, Mama? Did you feel kind of depressed as well as happy? I never knew that."

Pauline smiled. "You don't think I'd have let you know, do you? Any more than you'll let S.P. know. It's an odd reaction, the news of your first grandchild. You're delighted, but there's a gnawing little feeling of self-pity inside. As though somehow the child you love has taken away the last vestige of your youth. For just a few seconds, you almost resent her. As you did in the shop. But that passes, darling. It's like jumping into an ice-cold swimming pool. The first moment is terrible, but after that you're lighter than air."

They walked another block before Lindsay answered. "You're a wise, wise lady, Mrs. Thresher. The second one in my life. I'm damned lucky. You and Gandy always understood me, even when I was at my worst."

"That's no trick, my dear. We always loved you very much."

217

19

*H*oward Thresher was taking his time about leaving this world. All through the summer, he held on to the thread of his life. Thin and feeble as he was, he was also strong-willed and impatient. He demanded Adele take him out of the hospital. He was determined to go home.

"I've slept in the same bed for more than sixty years," he said. "Damned if I won't die in it, like a gentleman. Not in some ugly hospital room, with a bunch of tubes stuck in me! It isn't dignified. I won't have it!"

Despairingly, Adele had turned to Lindsay and Geoff. "I don't know what to do with him," she said in their apartment that evening. "He belongs in the hospital, where he has proper attention. If I bring him home, we'll have to have nurses round the clock. Special equipment. Not that I mind," she added hastily, "but he can't get the same care. I'd never forgive myself if I shortened his life."

"We know how you feel," Geoff said soothingly. "You've been a wonderful, devoted wife, Del. You've given him everything, for more than twenty years. You won't be harming him by bringing him home. It's what he wants. Which means that's what you want, too."

Lindsay felt as though she were going to be violently sick. Never forgive herself, would she? God, what a phony Adele was! Probably couldn't wait for her husband to die. She'd given him nothing but grief. And pretending she didn't mind setting up a small hospital in the apartment! Like hell she didn't! She hated the idea, not because it might deprive Howard of care but because it was messy, inconvenient for her.

Bitch! I'll never forgive you for what you put Papa through, she thought. He had his faults, plenty of them. But he didn't deserve the wounding he got from you.

"There's no question you have to bring him home, Adele," she said coldly. "I don't know why we're even discussing it. It's Papa's last wish. I imagine you can stand having your apartment disrupted for a little while. It can't be very long. Of course, if it's too much trouble for you, we'll bring him here, though it won't be the same. He won't die in his own bed, but at least he'll go surrounded by people who really care for him."

"Lindsay!" Geoff was horrified and angry. "How can you talk to Adele that way? You know she's only thinking of what's best for your father."

Lindsay didn't even try to hide her sarcasm. "Of course she is. She always has, haven't you, Adele darling?"

"I've tried, Lindsay." The other woman looked away as though she didn't want them to see her misery. "It hasn't been easy. Your father is a demanding man, and I'm . . . I'm so much younger. But I've tried to make him happy. Tried every way I knew to please him."

Geoff, seated next to her on the library couch, patted her hand. "We know that," he said again. "No one could have been more loyal or loving. You must forgive Lindsay. She's terribly upset. We'll help all we can, Adele. Whatever you need, at any hour, just pick up the phone and we'll be there."

"Provided Geoff isn't in Outer Mongolia on business."

He glared at his wife. What the hell was the matter with Lindsay? It was one thing not to be fond of her stepmother, but still another to be so cutting, so downright cruel. And to use this moment to snipe at him for his traveling! It's outrageous, Geoff thought.

"I won't be doing that much traveling for the next few weeks," he finally said, calmly. "I'll be here, Del. Don't worry about it."

She looked at him helplessly. "Thank you, Geoff. It's wonderful to know there's someone dependable nearby. I feel so alone, so lost and frightened." Daintily, she put a handkerchief to her eyes. "I'm glad I have you. Both of you. We go back a long time. Lindsay helped me through *my* father's death when we were children. Now she's helping me through the loss of *hers*. You're wonderful, Lindsay. So strong and certain. I wish I had half your discipline."

Lindsay could hardly keep from spitting out a four-letter word. If they gave out Academy Awards for nonprofessional tragediennes, Adele would be a shoo-in. What an actress she was! And Geoff was swallowing it, enjoying the flattery, believing she really was the pathetic, grief-stricken wife. I can't stand it! Lindsay thought. I can't sit here silently and let her do her number, making a fool of my husband, maybe even thinking she's fooling me.

"You're strong in your own way, Adele," she said in an even tone. "You'll be all right. I remember what a quick, admirable recovery you made when James died. It was worthy of applause. I'm sure we'll all feel the same awe for your recuperative powers when Papa passes on."

Geoff couldn't believe his ears. Lindsay was being deliberately heartless. This was her girlhood friend and, like it or not, her father's wife. How could she behave so badly? Poor Adele. She looked as though Lindsay had struck her. It wasn't fair. The woman had a dying husband. No one had a right to talk to her that way, not even someone who hated her. Lindsay does hate her, he realized. Hates her passionately, beyond reason. I never guessed how deep her loathing for Adele goes. But that's no excuse. Whatever the reason, now is not the time to strike out at this woman.

"I'll see you home, Adele," he said. "You must be exhausted. And whenever you're ready to take Howard out of the hospital, let me know. I'll be happy to come and help you. Lindsay will too, of course."

With a deep sigh, Adele got to her feet. "I can't begin to thank you for standing by. You're all the family I have since Mama went." Her voice broke. "You're so fortunate, Lindsay. You still have your husband and your mother to turn to. And a wonderful daughter and son-in-law."

"And don't forget our almost-born grandchild while you're counting our blessings for us, Adele. I wouldn't want you to leave out one of the cast of characters."

"Lind," Geoff said warningly. "That's enough."

"It's all right, Geoffrey." Adele managed to sound forgiving. "I know Lindsay. She's always been able to cover up her sorrow under a kind of flippancy. I know we love each other. And I know she's grieving for her father already, though she refuses to show it. I'm not as disciplined as you, Lindsay. Not as able to go on. I don't know what will happen to me after . . ." She took Geoff's arm. "You're right. I am exhausted. I'd better get some rest." She straightened and gave a picture

220

of false courage. "I'll bring Howard home tomorrow. I will be grateful if you'll help."

"Of course we will, won't we, Lind?"

Lindsay smiled grimly. "I wouldn't miss it," she said.

It was nearly two hours before Geoffrey returned. Lindsay was in a rage. As it grew later, she told herself not to show how angry she was, but when he finally let himself into the apartment she was sitting in a chair waiting for him, her eyes flashing.

"What did you do, take her home by way of El Morocco?"

He ignored the sarcasm. "We walked."

"Six blocks? You must have crawled!"

Geoff lost his temper. "What the hell's the matter with you? I've never seen such behavior as you exhibited tonight! For God's sake, Lindsay, the woman's husband is dying and you did everything but physically beat her up! Can't you see the state she's in? I know you've always held a grudge against her for marrying your father, though I don't know why it's such a vendetta with you. Even so, there's no reason to cut her to ribbons. She's not as bright as you. It's like taking advantage of a child. She doesn't know how to begin to fight back when you unleash that sharp tongue of yours!"

"All of which does not explain where you've been for two hours."

"Christ! You are incredible! You sound as though you're jealous of her."

"Should I be?"

Geoff mixed himself a drink. "I'm not even going to answer that. It isn't worthy of a reply." He sat down and said reasonably, "Look, honey, I know you're upset about your father. Even when our parents are old, we rebel against losing them. But he's seventy-nine. You can't keep him forever. I remember when my dad died. I felt as though the bottom had dropped out of the world. But that's how it is. No good being angry at death. And no good taking out your anger on the survivors." He looked squarely at his wife. "Maybe you are entitled to an explanation for these past two hours, at that. We walked home. I took her to the door. She asked if I'd mind sitting with her for a bit until she calmed down. We had a drink and talked. And then I left. That's it."

"And did you apologize again for my behavior?"

"Dammit, Lindsay, you simply won't give an inch, will you? No, I

221

didn't apologize, though I probably should have. You behaved like a fishwife. As a matter of fact, we didn't talk about you at all. Adele was reminiscing about the days when we were young, when James and I were in the war. She talked mostly about him, if you must know. How cheated she felt that she'd never really been able to show him how she loved him. How close they'd been through their letters, but how much she wished they'd known each other. Intimately, she meant."

Lindsay laughed. "Intimately? That's funny. That really is funny. God, how Papa would laugh if he could hear that one!"

"Now what's that supposed to mean?"

"Geoff, she never let Papa come near her. She's frigid. She was repelled by him."

"What are you talking about? I don't believe that for a minute! You must be crazy, Lind. They were married more than twenty years. You're trying to tell me that there was no sex in that marriage? Maybe not in these last years, of course, but earlier there had to be. Adele's a totally feminine woman. And your father fancied himself a great lover. Whatever put such a stupid idea in your head?"

"Papa told me. Oh, not in so many words, but he made it clear that the marriage was a total failure in that way. It hurt him terribly. It really broke him, I think. He couldn't understand rejection. Couldn't endure it." She shook her head. "I'll never forget that conversation. 'There's nothing worse than a loveless marriage,' he said. Those were his exact words. And he went on to talk about the disappointment some virgins felt. How awful it was for them and their husbands. He never mentioned Adele, but he was talking about her. And himself. I'm as sure of that as I'm sure of my own name."

"I don't believe it," Geoff said again. "Lind, I think you *wanted* to believe she was terrible to your father because you so resented the marriage. I'm sorry, but you'll never convince me Adele's a cold woman. I think she was wrong to marry a man so much older. Maybe she was disappointed he wasn't the lover she suspected James might have been, but she's too good, too decent to take out her disappointment on her husband. Even if she'd hated sex with him—and I doubt that too—she'd have done her duty. She's that kind of conscientious woman."

Lindsay lost control. "Oh, stop it! Stop being such a blind fool! You've always been a sucker for appealing women. You spoiled S.P. rotten. She could get anything she wanted out of you. And as for that creature in England—" Lindsay stopped. The look on Geoff's face told her she'd gone too far. Well, all right, she thought defiantly. Maybe it's just as well the truth comes out. What does it matter now? It's ancient history. I've lived with it all these years. I never meant to tell him I knew, but what difference does it make? Thanks again, Adele, she thought sardonically. If it hadn't been for this discussion about you and Papa I'd never have blurted out my secret.

"How did you know about that?" Geoff's voice was strained.

"How else? Through that woman you admire so much. James told Adele and she told Papa, who felt it his duty to tell me. Wonderful! I could have lived the rest of my life without *that* piece of news! But, oh, no. Darling Adele had to confide all. She knew damned well Papa would run right to me. She's always hated me, Geoff. Always envied me. And not only me. She hates the world. I suppose a shrink would say that's because she hates herself."

He only half listened to that last part. "You've known all these years," he said wonderingly, "and you never mentioned it. Why, Lindsay?"

She sat back, deflated. "Because I decided you were more important to me than my pride. I made up my mind I'd forget it, as long as you came home to me. Besides, by the time I heard, I was pregnant. I was going to have an abortion. I even got as far as a doctor's office, but I couldn't go through with it. And when you came home and we had S.P. and you were so happy with her, I was sure our marriage could survive your little wartime romance."

He looked stunned. "You were going to destroy our child? You nearly murdered our daughter?"

Lindsay let out a little cry of pain. "Don't put it that way, Geoff, for God's sake! She wasn't a person then. Just a thing. A fetus. And I was so confused, so afraid. I didn't know whether you were ever coming back to me. I wasn't sure you hadn't fallen in love over there." Lindsay began to weep. "Damn Adele! If I *had* gotten rid of the baby it would have been her fault. When I think how close I came, I get gooseflesh. She nearly cost us S.P. because she couldn't resist making trouble. She'd lost her man and she couldn't stand my having you." Lindsay dabbed at her eyes. "I'm sorry my brother died, but I'm glad he escaped that icy bitch. I only wish Papa could have been as lucky."

"And you've hated her all these years." It was a statement rather than a question.

"Hate her? Of course I hate her. She's a sneaky, conniving, dirty

223

little troublemaker. And when I watch you falling all over her, being taken in by this act she's putting on, I could kill both of you!"

"I'm sorry you ever had to know about that other thing," Geoff said quietly. "I won't lie. It was important to me, Lindsay. There was a time when I wasn't sure what to do about it. You're right about that. But I hoped you'd never know. It's difficult to explain what one feels during a war. Sort of a what-the-hell attitude takes over, like every day might be your last. Corny, but true. But once I knew it was you I wanted, I hoped you'd never find out. I didn't think you'd forgive me, to be honest about it. Not being the loyal person you are. And also because I knew how affected you were by what Howard did to your mother." He was very subdued. "You've known all these years," Geoff said again. "And blamed it on Adele. That's wrong, Lind. You're wrong about her. I don't think she meant your father to tell you about me. Why should she want to do that? I think she must have confided it in a moment of need to tell someone. He's more to blame for repeating it. No, don't interrupt. Let me finish. As for her rejection of your father, I really can't buy that either. I think Howard was playing on your sympathy. Or maybe trying to explain away his own inadequacy. Who knows? The only thing I do know is that he's far too selfish a man to have spent more than twenty years with a woman who didn't return his affection. And Adele's too decent to have put him through that. I don't like to speak ill of your father when he's dying, but I'd bet money that all the things you blamed Adele for were his doing. Why did he tell you about me? He was the *last* one to cast stones! As for his marriage, maybe Adele was disappointed, but only because she's such a loving, giving person and Howard Thresher has never been an unselfish man. If he couldn't perform as a husband, my hunch is he'd have blamed it on his wife. Sorry, my dear, but that's my opinion."

Lindsay stared at him. "She really has hypnotized you, hasn't she? You're wrong, Geoff. Dead wrong. She's evil, that one. I wouldn't trust her out of my sight. It's going to be very serious if you side with Adele against me."

"What sides?" he said impatiently. "There are no sides. It's over. All of it. Our problems happened more than twenty years ago. As for her marriage to your father, that's been over for years as well. My God, Lindsay, how can a forty-six-year-old woman have any kind of ongoing life with a seventy-nine-year-old man? She should never have married him in the first place, but she did. She must have loved him. At least she's stuck by him all this time. Give her full marks for that!"

"I give her full marks for nothing, except for being a busybody and a fraud. When Papa dies, I never want to see her again. God help her if she starts making noises like a step-grandmother when S.P.'s baby comes! I'll scratch her eyes out!" Lindsay flushed. "I'll try to behave while Papa's alive, for his sake, even though every moment of that performance will make me sick. But after that, Geoff, no more, I never want her in this house again."

In October, Howard died in his own bed. Geoff and Lindsay were called in the middle of the night and told to come quickly. As she hurriedly dressed, Lindsay wondered whether she should call her mother. Almost immediately, she decided against it. A deathbed scene with her father's two wives was unthinkable. Pauline had never set foot in that apartment since the day she left it more than thirty years ago, and to reenter it now in a secondary role would be almost indecent. I won't even call to tell her he's dying, Lindsay thought. What good would it do? Her logical mind could never understand why people were awakened with bad news when there was nothing they could do about it. It could wait until a reasonable hour tomorrow morning. No need to disturb her now.

It seemed strange to go back to the place where she'd grown up. Even though she'd made her peace with Adele years before, at least a surface peace, she'd managed not to visit the old apartment after Howard's remarriage. It hadn't been too bad when he was there alone, after the divorce. Even when he'd redecorated, turned it into a bachelor's lair, she hadn't minded, though she still saw the ghost of Mama everywhere. But now, as she unwillingly entered the living room, she recognized nothing about the place. Adele had turned it into a home for herself, Lindsay realized. It was all pastels: pale peach walls, white carpets, blush-colored furniture, dozens of delicate petit-point pillows and fluffy afghans. The dwelling place of a virgin, she thought angrily. This look had nothing to do with Papa. How had he stood it? It was like living inside an ice-cream cone.

Only his bedroom bore traces of the strong, masculine image Howard worked so hard to project. There were fine hunting prints on the walls, a big mahogany dresser with his monogrammed silver brushes, a deep leather chair, and a table piled high with unread copies of the *Wall Street Journal*. And he lay, eyes closed, in his old four-poster mahogany bed, the one he'd shared with Pauline. He looked so small and frail, so lifeless that Lindsay was unsure they'd gotten there in time. She was trembling as she whispered to the doctor, "Is he . . .?"

"He's still alive, Mrs. Murray. Barely conscious, but I think he'll know you if you want to speak to him."

She was dimly aware of Adele standing in a corner of the room, weeping softly. Quietly, Lindsay approached the bed and took her father's almost lifeless hand.

"Papa," she said softly. "Papa, I'm here."

For a moment he didn't respond. Then he opened his eyes and tried to focus on the face above him. The trace of a smile touched his thin lips.

"Pauline. You've come back. I always knew you would." The words came slowly, with effort, almost inaudible but loud enough, Lindsay knew, for the rest of them to hear. She opened her mouth to say it was she, Lindsay, but before she could speak, Howard pressed her hand with all the strength he had and said, "Hold on to me, dearest. Don't let go. Forgive me. I love you." He sighed deeply. "Pauline . . ."

She felt his fingers go limp. For a few seconds she stayed at his bedside. She forgives you, Papa, Lindsay said silently. She loves you too. She put his hand gently back on top of the covers and rose wearily as the doctor came forward.

"He's gone," Lindsay said.

Adele let out an anguished moan and tried to rush forward but Geoff held her back, soothing her, saying comforting words.

Lindsay looked at them scornfully. Then, without another word, she turned and left the room.

"I should have come to New York for Grandpa's funeral," S.P. said.

Lindsay shook her head. "No, you shouldn't have. The doctor told you that. Seven-month-pregnant ladies don't need to go racing around on airplanes."

Lindsay had decided, on the spur of the moment, to go to Chicago for a visit with her daughter, telling herself she missed S.P. and wanted to see her and be reassured she was all right. The young woman was obviously in good health, but she was gigantic. Lindsay looked at the enormous bulge and said, "Are you sure you're not going to have twins?"

"God forbid! One is more than enough."

There was an odd tone in S.P.'s voice, a disturbing note. "Is everything all right with you?" Lindsay asked. "You don't sound too happy."

"Robin's happy enough for both of us, Mom."

"Meaning you're not?"

"Honestly? No, I'm not. I had no intention of getting pregnant so soon. It was a blasted accident. I was just beginning to enjoy life here. The job was fun and I was doing well. I even hoped to be made the buyer in one of the branch stores. And then this." She looked with disgust at her extended stomach. "I've had to give it all up. I could just spit! I begged Rob to let me abort, but he reacted like I'd suggested dancing naked down Michigan Avenue. I never saw anybody so horrified. I told him he was a bloody hypocrite. All that big song and dance he does about population control whenever our friends get together. But when it's *his* doing, that's something else. It's perfectly okay to bring another hungry mouth into the world as long as it's his!"

Lindsay turned pale. "Darling, I had no idea you felt this way. I thought you were delighted. I imagined, knowing you, that you'd planned it. I'm sorry you don't want a baby, S.P., but you shouldn't even have considered an abortion. It's illegal and dangerous. I'm sure Robin was thinking more of you than anything else when he forbade it."

S.P. wouldn't be mollified. "Forbade it," she repeated. "Right there the unfairness begins. It's my body, Mother. I have a right to decide what to do with it!"

Echoes of the past, Lindsay thought. That's how my mind worked when I was carrying you. Thank God I didn't do it. You have no idea that you very nearly weren't born yourself.

"As for its being illegal," S.P. went on, "that won't be true forever. You wait and see, Mom. One of these days abortion will be legal. Along with a lot of other privileges women are entitled to."

"Maybe," Lindsay said dubiously, "but I'll be terribly surprised the day that law is passed."

"But you'd be for it, wouldn't you?"

"From a practical standpoint, yes. I know it's something women will always do, legal or not. And it breaks my heart, knowing what they have to go through. The humiliation and dirtiness of it, as well as the danger to their lives in the hands of some quack. God, it sickens me to think about it. But I can see the other side too. Life is precious. I wonder at what point it really begins, and whether it's morally acceptable to terminate what rightfully belongs to another."

S.P. looked at her curiously. "You seem to have given it a lot of thought, Mother. Any personal experience involved here?"

"No. Of course not," Lindsay lied. "But I've had good friends who went through it. I even went with one of them to one of those butchers in New Jersey years ago. It was a hideous experience. I still have nightmares about it."

"Did your friend have the abortion?"

"No. She changed her mind, thank God."

She *is* talking about herself, S.P. thought. She felt a chill, remembering how Lindsay had often told her of the months before she was born, when her father was overseas and she was afraid he wouldn't get back in time. My God! She nearly aborted me! She must have suffered the tortures of hell. I wonder why she even considered it? She and Dad have always seemed so happy. Deliberately, S.P. laughed. "I'm really making this sound like a third-rate melodrama, I'm afraid. I'm not as miserable as I sound, Mom. I've almost adjusted to the idea. And of course I'll be dippy about the baby when it arrives, as delighted as Rob is already. Wait till you see him. He's just one enormous grin. You'd think he invented the 'begats,' as they say in the Old Testament."

Lindsay relaxed. For a moment she feared she'd revealed too much. S.P. was quick. It was dangerous to have said as much as she had. She could kick herself for sounding off about New Jersey and that doctor. Maybe even now S.P. wasn't fooled, but at least she was going to pretend to be.

"Going back to Grandpa," S.P. was saying, "I really should have come. He wasn't a bad old thing, and I should have been there out of respect to you and Grandma."

"Your grandmother didn't attend the funeral."

S.P.'s eyes widened. "Grandma didn't go? How come? She isn't sick, is she?"

"No, she's fine, physically. Emotionally, Papa's death hit her hard. I've almost never seen her cry the way she did when I told her. She just couldn't bring herself to be the ex-wife in such a public way. She said that right belonged to Adele and she wasn't going to embarrass everybody by showing up as a second widow." Lindsay smiled sadly. "Quite a woman, your grandma."

"She still loved him, didn't she?"

"Very much. I think leaving him years ago was the hardest thing she ever had to do. I think she felt married to him right up the end."

"That's sad. And kind of beautiful."

"I suppose," Lindsay said. "I said much the same thing to her not so long ago, and she said maybe a psychiatrist would say she was just plain sick, keeping an old torch burning for so long."

"You're kidding! Grandma said that?"

Lindsay nodded. "I know what she means. Sometimes we go on loving a man long after we know we shouldn't." Damn! There I go, Lindsay thought. She'll pick me up on it. She'll know I'm talking about myself again. Why did I make such a stupid remark? Maybe subconsciously I want her to know how things are between Geoff and me. Maybe I came here for that very reason, to unburden my soul.

S.P. was staring at her in that penetrating way, the same look she had when Lindsay spoke so passionately about going to the abortionist with her "friend."

"Mother, are you and Daddy having problems?"

"It's nothing, darling. It will pass."

"You're a rotten liar, Mom. I can read you like a book. What's going on?"

"Darling, this is no time to burden you with my silly troubles. Not in your condition."

"Oh, damn my condition! So I'm going to have a baby next month. That only affects my belly, not my ears!"

Despite herself, Lindsay smiled. What a funny, marvelous person S.P. was. Straight from the shoulder, caring, eager to listen and help. But no one can help, Lindsay thought. I've got to live through this and handle it the best way I can if I don't want to lose Geoff. Still, I long to talk to someone. I can't confide in Mama. Not really. She's too much involved.

"Well," Lindsay said, trying to sound unconcerned, "your father and I don't exactly see eye to eye about Adele. That's the problem."

S.P. looked puzzled. "Adele's the problem? That dim bulb? What's she up to? Making a fuss about Grandpa's will or something?"

"No. His will was perfectly in order, as you'd expect. So much for

Adele, Mama, and me, most of which will eventually go to you. It's . . . it's the way she's acting around your father. She won't move without him. Calls him half a dozen times a day. Consults him on every detail of her life. You should have seen her at the funeral. Geoff was practically holding her up at the grave site." Lindsay smiled mirthlessly. "She's having a wonderful time playing poor-little-widow. What a farce! She never even loved Papa. She made his life a living hell. But now she's using this phony bereavement to get close to your father. God knows what she has in mind. She despises me, and it's mutual. I've told Geoff I won't have her in my house." Lindsay shrugged. "That was my latest dumb decision. Now he goes to hers."

Her daughter was thunderstruck. "What are you saying, Mother? That she's after Dad? I can't believe that! She's a pill, but she's not *that* unscrupulous."

"You don't know how bad she is. I won't go into it now, but she's done wicked things before. This wouldn't be the first time she's tried to hurt me. She's succeeded in the past, but dammit, she won't again!"

"Of course she won't! My God, Mother, you know Daddy isn't really falling for that stuff. He's just softhearted. I'm sure he's only being kind. Once she's on her feet, he'll pay no attention."

"She's never been *off* her feet, honey. Believe me. She's about as grief-stricken and helpless as Lizzie Borden. But she's giving a great imitation. And your father is buying it. He really thinks she needs him. He's a sucker for a clinging vine, and that, unfortunately, is something I've never known how to be."

S.P. felt sick. Trouble between her parents was the last thing she'd ever thought of. She'd always held them up, in conversations about marriage, as a living example of people genuinely happy after twenty-eight years together. She believed that. The idea of her father with another woman was unacceptable, impossible. Mom's imagining it, she told herself. She's jealous for no reason. Daddy's too bright to louse up a good marriage. And never for a ninny like Adele.

"Mother, I'm sure you're overreacting. Do you feel guilty because you have some silly idea you've been neglecting Dad? Spending too much time on your business, perhaps? Honey, I think you're wrong about his being seriously interested in Adele or anyone else. He loves *you*. He always has and he always will."

There was no point in pursuing it, Lindsay realized. S.P. would not tolerate the idea of her father even looking at another woman. No good going into his past. *Their* past. S.P. adored him. He was the model father, the perfect husband. Lindsay had no intention of destroying that illusion. S.P. would only hate her for it if she did. In any case, Lindsay thought, I have no intention of giving him up. I didn't before and I won't now. I won't repeat my mother's mistake. I'll fight for him if I have to, let him hate me if he must, but I'll never, never walk out.

"I'm sure you're right, darling," she said. "I'm just tired, I suppose. The shop, and Papa's death. And I'm anxious for my grandchild to arrive. I'm sure I'm making too much of this Adele business. I'm glad we talked. You're a darling to listen to your old mother's fancied fears." She smiled. "I feel much better. Thanks, baby. You make such damned good sense. Sometimes I feel our roles are reversed and you're the wiser and more experienced one."

"Seems like I did a little crying on your shoulder too. Sorry about that. I'm not all that upset about the baby. Swear to God. Once I got over the shock, I really simmered down. I haven't had an outburst like that since the third month, believe it or not." S.P. grinned. "You brought it on yourself, you know. You're so damned easy to talk to. I know that whatever I say, you'll understand."

Lindsay returned her smile. "Same to you, sweetheart. I guess it did us both good to carry on like a couple of put-upon females. Things seem less dreadful when you can talk them out with a friend. Thanks, friend."

"Geoff, I don't know how I'd have gotten through this past month without you." Adele looked at him gratefully across her dinner table. "You've been an absolute tower of strength."

He brushed aside her thanks. "Think nothing of it. I haven't done that much and you know it. You've had competent lawyers and accountants. They've done all the work."

"There are other kinds of help. Even more important ones. Moral support, for instance. You've given me that, and I'm deeply grateful."

"Forget it," he said again. "After all, you're family."

Adele sighed. "If only I were. If only Lindsay didn't hate me so much. I know it hasn't been easy for you. I'm sure you've come to my rescue over her violent objections."

"Oh, no, it hasn't been like that. Lindsay doesn't mind."

"Adorable liar. I know she minds. You wouldn't be here at my dinner table tonight if Lindsay wasn't in Chicago."

231

Geoff didn't answer.

"She can't forgive me, can she." Adele's question was rhetorical. "I wish she'd try to understand. We were so close once. Like sisters. Better, because we chose each other. And now Lindsay thinks I'm her enemy. Lord knows what she thinks. Maybe she even imagines I'm trying to steal her husband."

Geoffrey laughed uneasily. "Come on, Adele. Don't be silly. Lindsay knows you'd never try a thing like that. Don't even entertain such an idea. You sound as paranoid as she does." He stopped short and cursed himself. That was a terrible thing to say about his wife. But it's not far from the truth, Geoff admitted to himself. Lindsay *was* paranoid about Adele. If he so much as spoke her name, the atmosphere became charged with electricity. He'd taken to seeing Adele in the late afternoon on his way home from the office, rarely mentioning these visits to Lindsay. God knows they were harmless enough, but she got furious.

As he had often before, he wondered how Lindsay could justify this unending rage against her one-time friend. She was too smart, too sensible to hang onto these old grudges, even if she believed Adele had been deliberately spiteful. He did not. She was gentle, kind, and, yes, good. She bolstered a man's ego. In his heart he envied old Howard all those years with this gracious, beautiful woman. She did not compete, the way Lindsay did, with that damned decorating business or whatever it was. She didn't make him feel apologetic because he indulged his daughter or because he was almost more eager than Robin for the arrival of the baby. If Adele thought he had flaws, she gave no indication of it. Sometimes the adoring way she looked at him made him almost uncomfortable. As though he were some superman who could do no wrong. It was unnerving in a way, and yet he had to admit he liked it. It felt good to be admired, even if he hadn't done anything to deserve it.

And she was sensitive, tactful, too, he thought as he walked home after dinner. She gave no hint that she even heard his tasteless reference to Lindsay's paranoia. They'd had coffee and a liqueur and chatted easily about his work until eleven o'clock. Then he'd given her a brotherly peck on the cheek and left. A nice evening, he thought. Relaxed and easy.

The phone was ringing as he opened his front door. He rushed into the library and aswered it. Lindsay was on the other end.

"Geoff? You took so long to answer, I was about to hang up."

232

"I just came in the door. What's wrong? Why are you calling so late? It's after eleven here."

"Nothing's wrong. I tried you earlier but there was no answer. Where were you?"

Without thinking, he said, "At Adele's."

"Oh?" Frostiness came over the wire. "What's today's problem? Did she develop a terminal case of hangnail?"

"Lind, must you always be sarcastic when Adele's involved? There was no problem. She knew you were away and took pity on me and asked me to dinner. Big damned deal!"

"*Very.* How did she know I was away? Did I miss an announcement in Earl Wilson's column?"

Geoff sighed. How much longer was this going to go on? The rest of their lives? Adele knew Lindsay was in Chicago because he'd told her. But he wasn't going to say that and have a long-distance fight.

"I don't know how she knew. What difference does it make? She invited me for a good meal. She was merely showing her appreciation for a few favors I've tried to do since your father died. Good God, don't make a federal case out of it! The woman's grateful, that's all."

"I'll bet. How grateful is she?"

His anger flared. "Don't be vulgar! Lind, this has got to stop. You're absolutely possessed!" He took a deep breath and tried to control himself. "Skip it," he said. "We can talk about it when you come home. When *are* you coming home, by the way?"

"That's what I called for. I'll be in on American at four fifteen tomorrow afternoon. At Kennedy. Is it convenient for you to meet me?"

Damn. It wasn't. She'd probably think he was inventing an excuse, but it was the truth. "Unfortunately, I can't, honey. There's a big client meeting at four. But I'll send a limousine."

"All right. Thanks."

She seemed about to hang up and Geoff shouted, "Hey! Wait a minute. Is S.P. there? May I speak to her?"

"She's gone to bed. She wanted to talk to you, but you weren't home in time."

"What do you mean? It's only a little after ten out there. They never turn in this early."

"Geoffrey, S.P.'s pregnant, remember? She needs her rest. She's about to make you a grandfather, in case you've forgotten in the heady

233

glow of being a hero to your mother-in-law. Good night. See you tomorrow."

He held the dead line a moment before replacing the receiver. Why are you doing this, Lindsay? he thought. Are you deliberately setting out to destroy us?

It never occurred to him that she was reacting, defensively, to his own unreasonably discontented state of mind. He felt himself to be the injured party in this unannounced war between them. But he did not, for one moment, feel that their differences amounted to anything more than a minor skirmish. He only hoped Lindsay would soon come to her senses.

20

*T*iming. We give it many names: Destiny, Fate, Kismet, the will of God. Whatever we call it, lives are changed and molded by it, in small or drastic ways beyond our control. The precise, exquisite influence of timing moves people into new positions as surely as a spring flood rearranges the landscape. It is as unavoidable as life. Or death.

Adele's widowhood was an example of the power of timing. Had Howard Thresher chosen to die two years earlier or, for all anyone knew, two years later, the effect of his demise might not have had such a profound effect on others. Unfortunately, the hand that plots our course selected the exact moment when Lindsay was her most anxious and Geoffrey his most vulnerable. It was also the point when Adele had reached the limit of her endurance.

To her, Howard's death was an overdue blessing. She was ashamed to admit to herself that she wished for it. Yet that was true. From the vantage point of twenty-two years later, she knew the psychiatrist was right. She'd been like a swimmer drowning in the misery of James's death. She'd reached for the nearest thing to him and married his father to hang on desperately to some trace of the future she'd lost. She'd been a fool and she paid for it, much more than her husband had. After a relatively short period of unhappiness, Howard had simply accepted the mistake, not without bitterness, but with realism. If his wife gave him no affection, other women did. It was not the life he'd hoped for, but he made the best of it with as little deprivation to himself as possible.

The enormity of what she'd done almost overwhelmed Adele. It was a sin, she knew, not to be a wife to Howard, but try as she would she could not welcome him as a lover. In her eyes he was more than an old man. He was virile enough, but his slightly aging body against the youthful firmness of her own filled her with horror. Every assault on her was like rape, and she'd been relieved when in rage, disgust, and wounded pride he'd stopped making the overtures which ended so disastrously for both of them.

But Adele's guilt was sincere. In the second year of their marriage, she found courage to suggest they divorce.

"It's not fair to you, Howard," she said. "I'm not what you need. We made a mistake. There's nothing shameful about admitting it."

He'd been furious. "No! Not a chance! Easy enough for you, my girl, to let people think you married a man who couldn't satisfy you. That's what they'd think, you know. That I was too old. I won't be laughed at behind my back as a failure. It was bad enough to be ridiculed for marrying a woman younger than my daughter. I won't have people saying they were right, that I made a fool of myself."

She looked at him wonderingly. "Do you care so much what people say? Enough to ruin the rest of your life, and mine?"

"If that's the way you see it, yes, I care enough. I have my pride. Nobody's going to call Howard Thresher a two-time loser."

"But this is no marriage," she protested. "You can't be happy living this way!"

"I've long since given up the idea of being happy." His tone was patronizing. "Happiness is for fools, mindless fools. There is only lack of total misery, a compromise with the absurdity of life. You'd better learn to make that compromise, Adele. That much, at least, you owe me."

Reluctantly, she accepted her sentence, her powers of reason weaker than the remorse she felt for once encouraging him to believe she loved him. And for the next twenty years she stayed with him, was even faithful to him, such was her idea of marital fidelity for women. At forty-six, she was, in all but the technical sense, still a virgin, unmoved by passion, her sexual urges sublimated almost to the point of nonexistence.

So it was with shame, during the last months of Howard's illness, that she found herself attracted to Geoffrey Murray. In his presence, she felt a stirring of excitement. Appalled by the discovery and unable to resist being near him, she knew nothing could come of it. He was Lindsay's husband, her own stepson-in-law. And yet she dreamed of him, trembled at the feel of his arm around her when he comforted her, longed to turn her mouth to his when he kissed her lightly on the cheek. It was shocking, shameful. Her guilt toward Lindsay was worse than anything she'd felt toward Howard, though in this case her wrongdoing was only in her mind.

And always would be, she told herself firmly. This low she would not stoop, even if she could. Persistent as her desires might be, they must be overcome, forgotten if possible, certainly never revealed. Yet, as though she could not help herself, she invented excuses to see him, still convincing herself that it was only a scrap of comfort that could harm no one.

Adele was not the devil Lindsay believed her to be. She'd never meant to hurt her friend. Burdened with the knowledge of Geoff's wartime affair, she had felt secure in confiding the secret to Howard and had been deeply troubled when his sense of righteousness caused him to betray her. Nor had she truly set out to make her husband miserable with her rejection of him. She married him in misguided innocence, not for spite, as Lindsay seemed to think.

But she was also not the angel Geoffrey thought she was. Even in her guilt, she'd hated Howard. And she did envy Lindsay. She always had. Since childhood, Adele's life had been barren. Deprived of her father, saddled with a rattlebrained mother and a boorish stepfather, James had been her one hope, and she was not allowed even that gift of love. Lindsay, on the other hand, had had it all: devoted parents and a wonderful, generous grandmother; marriage to the man she wanted; a beautiful, happy daughter who'd soon give her a grandchild. Even a career, Adele thought bitterly. One that started late and which, since it was Lindsay's, had prospered overnight, making her not only richer but famous and respected. Lindsay's man had come home safely from the war; Adele's had not. Yes, Lindsay had always had everything she wanted. Still had. It was unfair. Adele went to church and prayed for forgiveness for her sins, but she still coveted everything about Lindsay's life, including her husband.

The evening Geoff dined at her house had been the closest she'd ever come to letting him know how she felt. When he left, she'd undressed and stood in front of a full-length mirror, critically looking at herself, wondering if she'd look beautiful to him. She blushed, alone in her bedroom. What was this madness? There was no hope. He did not care for her except as an old friend. Yet he had indicated, for the first time, that he was less than perfectly happy. "Paranoid," he'd called Lindsay. Perhaps things were not good between them. Maybe there was some slim chance . . . she caught herself. Fool. Traitor. What nonsense was this? Wishful, terrible thinking, it was. And even if it were not, even if by some miracle Geoffrey could care for her, Lindsay would never let that happen.

She'd kill me first, Adele thought in fright. Lindsay would literally get a gun and kill me.

When he got home from the office, Geoff went to find his wife. She was in her bedroom, unpacking her suitcase.

"How is S.P.?"

Lindsay turned from the closet and looked at him. "And welcome home to you too," she said.

Geoff looked embarrassed. "Sorry. That was abrupt. Welcome home, dear. Have a good trip?"

"Yes, fine." Lindsay relented. No need to be so snippy. Naturally, Geoff was worried about their pregnant daughter. "S.P. is okay, if you'll forgive my speaking in initials." She smiled. "Big as a house. Big as two houses. I asked her if she was sure it wasn't twins. She looks as though she's put on a hundred pounds. The doctor's furious with her, but she says she's so frustrated she does nothing but eat."

"Frustrated? About what?"

Lindsay debated whether to tell him this child was unwanted by its mother. What was the point? S.P. had said she was reconciled. Geoff would only fret if he thought she was unhappy. He never wanted his daughter to be unhappy about anything.

"Nothing special. You know how it is when you've been lugging a baby around for eight months." She laughed. "No, you don't know how it is, do you? But you can imagine. She's uncomfortable and bored, waiting for the big moment. Women get that way. It's perfectly natural."

He seemed satisfied with that. "They'll call us the minute she goes into labor, won't they? You did tell Robin I have the airlines alerted? Even if there's a blizzard, they'll get us there. Thank God, we have that account so I can pull strings if necessary. Chicago in December! What a time to have a baby!"

Lindsay started to say that S.P. hadn't planned it that way. Hadn't planned it at all, for that matter. The hell with it, she decided. He was worried enough as it was. Geoff loves her so much, Lindsay thought. I love her too, but not with this fierce protectiveness. It's almost unnatural, though not in a sordid way. She's the light of his life. If anything ever happened to S.P., I wouldn't vouch for Geoff's sanity. Don't even think such things, she told herself. Nothing's going to happen, except that being so much overweight she'll probably have a hard birth. I'll go crazy with him and Robin if she's in labor for hours.

"So you had a pleasant visit," Geoff said easily. "I'm glad. I'm sure it did you good to get away from here for a few days."

"Yes. I was ready for a little vacation. I'm sure you were too. From me, I mean." She fiddled nervously with a velvet-covered hanger. "Geoff, I'm sorry I behaved so badly on the phone last night. I'm sorry I've been behaving so badly these past months. It's childish of me to keep nursing a grudge against Adele. On the way home in the plane, I made up my mind to get over my anger. And my jealousy. I don't like the things she's done to me, or what she did to Papa, but I've decided to call off the feud. As for the idea of her being after you, it's ridiculous. Not that you're not attractive. Not that maybe she wouldn't like to get her hands on you. But I know she can't. I know you better." She looked at him imploringly. "Forgive me? I really have been out of line."

He smiled at her. For Lindsay to apologize was almost unprecedented, and he was genuinely pleased. Thank God she'd finally realized how infantile this whole thing has been! Everything would be infinitely easier for them all. But it was a sudden change of heart. Almost too sudden. She must have talked it out with S.P., he thought. I hope to God she didn't tell her about that old wartime thing. The idea of being less than perfect in his daughter's eyes disturbed him, but he didn't pursue it. Let well enough alone. If she'd make her peace with Adele, that would help. He hated seeing Lindsay's stepmother behind her back. Not that there was anything wrong about it, but it would be less troublesome if he could tell Lindsay where he was going, or if she'd reverse her decision never to have Adele in this house.

"Of course you're forgiven," he said. "There wasn't anything much to forgive, as far as I can see. I never did understand what got you so uptight in the first place."

It was the wrong thing to say. The worst. Lindsay's face hardened.

"You still don't believe any of it, do you? You honestly don't think she ever did anything spiteful or malicious."

"Please, Lind, don't let's start this all over again. You just said

239

you'd decided to forgive and forget whatever harm you imagine Adele did. Let's stay with that, all right?"

"The two of you," Lindsay said grimly. "I'm always fighting the two of you. Why don't you admit it, Geoff? Why don't you come right out and say you're in love with her?"

"Because I'm not, for Christ's sake! Can't you get that through your head? Don't you know it's possible for a man and woman to be friends?"

"No," Lindsay said. "Not when the woman's Adele. And not when the man is you. I have a good memory. I can still remember 1945."

He shook his head. "You're hopeless. Absolutely hopeless. Am I supposed to pay the rest of my life for one transgression?"

"Only one? What about the out-of-town adventures the past couple of years? I may not have proof, but a wife knows about those things without having to be told. I don't seem to satisfy you any more. What is it, Geoff? Familiarity breeds contempt? The same old body is a bore?"

"Lindsay, for God's sake what's the matter with you? Sometimes I think you'd like us to break up."

"No," she said slowly, "I wouldn't like that at all. But maybe you would."

"I don't know where you get these crazy ideas. What is it? Are you having change of life?"

She looked disgusted. "I wondered when you'd use that one. When in doubt, fall back on the old clichés. If an unattached woman is difficult, she's a dried up old thing who needs sex. If she's justifiably angry in middle age, it's menopause. My God! What would men do without those convenient, stupid rationales?"

"And what would women do without their damned jealousy?" He shouted. "You've never forgiven me, have you? You may think you have, but it's always been there, deep inside you, eating away at you. It's not Adele you're angry with, it's me! Me and that girl in England, who might be dead by now for all I know! Lindsay, you've got to stop it! If you don't, I swear I'll—"

"You'll what? Leave me? Run to Adele? What are you looking for, Geoff? Justification?"

He turned and slammed out the door. I didn't mean things to happen that way, Lindsay thought miserably. I wanted to have a happy homecoming. I want things to be all right with us. I want them to be the way they used to be. I hate myself when this venom comes pouring

240

out. Geoff's wrong. I forgave him long ago. It always develops into this when Adele's name is mentioned. One word leads to another, and our fights get more serious.

She threw herself on her bed and lay staring at the ceiling, wondering what was ahead. Maybe when S.P.'s baby comes, things will quiet down, Lindsay consoled herself. Maybe our first grandchild will bring us back together.

That is what I thought when our child was on the way, she realized. Well, it worked, didn't it? For a while, at least.

For the next month, the Murrays barely spoke, except politely, briefly. There was no mention of Adele, no indication on Lindsay's part that she would ever see her again. Geoff continued to visit Howard's widow. More and more, he found himself enjoying his visits. Adele was easy to talk to, relaxed and refreshing. The conversation never became personal. As though by tacit agreement, they kept clear of controversial subjects, including Lindsay. Adele did not ask after her, and Geoff volunteered nothing. Not until Lindsay called him late one morning in December and said Robin had rung up and S.P. was in the hospital. Then he called Adele.

"Lindsay and I are leaving on the noon flight for Chicago," he said. "S.P.'s in labor. I thought you'd like to know."

"Oh, yes! Thanks, Geoff. I'm so glad you told me. Give S.P. my love." She hesitated. "And tell Lindsay I know everything will be fine."

"I'll do that," Geoff lied. "I'll let you know whether I'm a grandpa or a grandma."

Adele laughed lightly. "Whether it's a boy or a girl," she said, "you'll love it enough to be both."

It was too late when they got there. They raced to the hospital and found Robin in S.P.'s private room. One look at his white face and red-rimmed eyes told them there was tragedy. Lindsay frantically grabbed his arms.

"Robin, what is it? The baby? Is anything wrong with the baby?"

He shook his head.

"Not S.P.! Oh, my God, Robin, don't tell me something's happened to her!"

He broke into violent, wrenching sobs. "They . . . they don't know what happened. The labor was terrible, but the baby finally came." He was almost incoherent with grief. "Her heart . . . it just stopped. F—f—failed. They . . . they couldn't save her, Mom. They tried everything." He held onto Lindsay like a drowning man. "Oh, God, it's all my fault! She didn't want this baby. I killed her. I'll never forgive myself! Jesus, I don't want to live either!"

Despite her horror, Lindsay held the sobbing man with all her strength and tried to comfort him. "Don't, Robin, dear. You mustn't. It wasn't your fault. S.P. wouldn't want you to feel this way. She'd want you to be strong for the baby." Lindsay hardly knew what she was saying. She thought Robin was going out of his mind. And Geoff. Why did Geoff just stand there as though frozen? He hadn't moved or said a word. He's in shock, Lindsay realized. In total, terrible shock.

Even as she thought it, Geoff moved. There was a half-crazed look in his eyes as he started toward Robin. "You son of a bitch! You lousy animal! You shouldn't live! You killed my daughter! And I'll kill you. As God is my judge, I'll kill you, you murderer!"

"Geoffrey, stop it!" Lindsay let go of Robin and rushed toward her husband. "Don't say things like that! You don't know what you're saying!" She stopped halfway between him and Robin. "This won't do any good. It won't bring S.P. back. Geoff, please. Can't you see he's out of his mind with grief? My God, don't make it any more terrible than it already is!"

"He's right," Robin said dully. "I wish he would kill me. I wish I could kill myself." He was quieter now, in utter despair. "It isn't possible. Everything seemed so fine. I don't understand. A freak thing," he said bitterly. "That's what they called it. A freak thing. No history of a weak heart. No sign of it. And then . . ." He began to weep again. "What can I say to myself? What can I say to you?"

Lindsay sank into a chair. S.P. dead? It wasn't possible. Just a few weeks ago she'd been so sweet and funny, as she always was. They'd had such a good visit. Confided in each other, like two girls. My baby, she thought. My lovely, beautiful child. At last the tears came. She sat in the stiff leather chair, and the tears poured down her face.

After his outburst, Geoffrey said nothing. He had walked to the window and stood looking out, every line of his body contorted with a sorrow too deep for words. Lindsay looked at his back, remembering that not long ago she'd thought he'd go mad if anything happened to his daughter. She feared for him now. Deep as her anguish was, she knew she could handle it better than he. Suddenly Geoff spoke, not looking at them.

"What do you mean, she didn't want the baby?"

Lindsay answered, "It doesn't matter now, darling."

"It matters. What did you mean, Robin?"

"It . . . it wasn't planned. She wanted to have an abortion. I wouldn't let her." His voice was hollow. "I should have. She'd be here now. I was afraid for her," he said bitterly. "Afraid for her life if she had that operation. And I wanted a child. Selfishly, I wanted a son." His whole body shook. "Well, I have one now, and I'll curse the day he was born."

"No!" Lindsay stood up. "He's your son, Robin. Hers, too. You have something of S.P. Something precious she left you."

"I want *her*," Robin said. "Nothing's any good without her."

Geoffrey made a sound of disgust. It angered Lindsay.

"What would you have done, Geoffrey? Let her have the abortion? How can you diminish Robin's grief this way? Do you think you're the only one who loved her? Why don't you think of her husband and her child, instead of wallowing in your own self-pity?"

He turned on her fiercely. "Damn you, Lindsay, have you no heart? Are you so strong that even your own daughter's death doesn't destroy your ability to take charge? Don't lecture me. Don't tell me how I should feel about him *or* you! He caused this, and I'll never forgive him. Think of him? I wish I could *forget* him!"

"And your grandson too?" Lindsay was gentle. "Are you going to turn your back on S.P.'s baby?"

Geoff looked away. "I don't want to see him. I never want to see him." He began to weep noiselessly, the tears running between the fingers behind which he tried to hide his face.

I've never seen Geoff cry before, Lindsay realized. A man's tears are terrible, all the more so when he's ashamed of them. Women cry often, sometimes for no reason except the blessed relief of it. But a man holds back, reluctant to show emotion, fearful somehow it reflects badly on his masculinity. Why shouldn't Geoff cry? Why shouldn't he beat his breast and wail? We've lost our dearest one, our baby, our lighthearted, loving Sara Pauline. How will we go on? How will we endure the endless days, thinking of her, missing her, asking God over and over what sense this makes? Why *her?* we'll ask. Why her?

243

She went to her husband and put her arms around him, trying to press her face to his, wanting her tears to mingle with those that flowed down his cheeks. There was nothing to say, nothing to give but closeness. Geoff was still, unyielding. Even now, the hideousness of his loss had not penetrated a mind unable to accept it. Later his suffering would be worse, though the murderous rage he felt toward Robin would grow less with the realization of bleak finality. It may destroy him, Lindsay thought again. I don't know if we can survive this, any of us.

Poor Robin. He'd never cease to blame himself. He didn't need Geoff's wild recriminations. He'd be harder on himself than any other human could be. And the baby, the poor little motherless baby. Lindsay's heart went out to the grandchild she'd not yet seen. Geoff doesn't mean it when he says he never wants to see his grandson. Of course he will. He'll love him in time, for the boy's sake as well as for the memory of his mother.

Lindsay took a deep breath. I must keep myself under control, she told herself. The time for mourning is later. There were things to be done, and neither Geoff nor Robin was in a condition to do them. Arrangements must be made to take S.P. back to New York, to the Murrays' burial plot in the cemetery in Queens. Unless Robin wanted something different. It was his right; he was her husband. He'd have to decide.

I can't bear it, Lindsay thought, her arms still around her unresponsive husband. I'm the mother, the bereaved mother. The child who came out of my body is dead, but no one's thinking of me.

Her sense of injustice and self-pity left as quickly as it had come. She could not afford the luxury of collapse. Not yet. In a crisis, she acted first, fell apart later. Geoff thought that was strength. It was not. It was, as always, reality. Reality and the need to go on.

They brought S.P. home to New York and laid her to rest quietly. A married couple, the man a friend of Robin's at the agency in Chicago, took S.P.'s baby to stay with them until his father's return.

Lindsay secretly hoped Robin would ask his wife's parents to take the baby, but he did not. In fact, the evening of S.P.'s death, he came to her and said, "Mom, I want to keep my son. I thought about asking you to take him. That would be easier for me and maybe better for him. But he's all I have. I'll raise him the best I can, find a good nurse to be with him during the day and be with him myself the rest of the time. I'll try to be both mother and father to him. I think . . . I think that's what she would have wanted."

Lindsay hid her disappointment and her doubts. A young man, alone trying to bring up a child? She wasn't sure it was right for either of them, but perhaps it was the only way. At the hospital, Geoff wouldn't even look at the baby. Maybe he'd never be able to. At best, it would be a long, long time before he could accept the child who, in his anguished mind, should have been sacrificed rather than born at the cost of his mother's life. Once she'd thought S.P.'s baby might breathe new life into her own troubled marriage. What folly! He'd caused Geoff to become even more remote. And if he came to live with them, his presence would only increase his grandfather's bitterness. It would be no good for the baby. And, selfishly, she knew it would cause terrible friction between her and Geoff.

Above all, looking at Robin's face, Lindsay saw that he truly wanted to raise his son. Even if she could, she wouldn't deprive him of that. If someone had tried to take S.P. away from her, she'd have killed him. Much as she longed to raise her grandchild, it was better this way.

"Of course," she said. "We'd be glad to take him, but you *should* have him with you, Robin. Your instincts are right. It will be hard for you. You'll have to sacrifice a great deal, but it will be worth it." She paused. "Have you decided what to call him?"

Robin nodded. "John Geoffrey. After my father and hers."

"It's a nice name, Robin."

"We . . . we'd already decided on it. John Geoffrey if it was a boy. Jean Lindsay, after its grandmothers, if it was a girl." Robin's eyes filled with tears. "I've got to ask you something. Geoff hates me. I can't blame him. I hate myself. Feeling the way he does, would it be better if I didn't work for him any more? I could try to find another job. Come back to New York, maybe. What do you think?"

Lindsay hesitated. "I can't speak for him, Robin. He hasn't said a word all day, about anything." She glanced toward the bedroom of the Drake Hotel suite. "He's been in there all afternoon, all evening. He's in terrible pain. Indescribable. But for all his agony, I don't think he hates you. Not really. He's fighting a nightmare now. There's no one to strike out at but you. But time will soften that, Robin. He'll understand it wasn't your fault. My God, who could anticipate such a thing with a healthy girl? I don't think, when he calms down, he'll want you to leave the agency. That would be petty and childish, and Geoff is never that.

Give it time. Don't do anything now. If, later on, it's uncomfortable for both of you, then you should leave. But not now," she repeated. "You have a good job. You'll need one to take care of John."

When Robin left, Lindsay tapped lightly on the bedroom door. There was no answer, and as she opened it she saw the room was dark. For a moment she panicked, seized with a ridiculous fear that Geoff might have taken his life. She could make out his form on the bed, fully dressed, curled, curiously enough, in a fetal position, as though he wanted to hide from the world. But then she heard his heavy breathing.

"Geoff, are you all right? Don't you want something to eat, dear?"

No reply.

Lindsay switched on a low light and was horrified by the sight of his ravaged face. He seemed to have aged ten years in an afternoon. Maybe I look just as devastated, Lindsay thought. I haven't looked in a mirror.

"Robin was here," she said. "He's going to call the boy John Geoffrey, after his father and you. They'd already decided that. And he means to bring up his son in a way that S.P. would approve."

Silence.

"It's very brave of him, dear, don't you think? A man alone with the full responsibility of an infant."

Unexpectedly, Geoffrey sat up. The sadness on his face became an ugly sneer.

"Brave? Don't be a fool, Lindsay! He'll be married again in six months. He has no intention of bringing it up alone, you can bet on that. One wife out of the way and another waiting in the wings, I'll bet. He probably already has her picked out!"

"Geoffrey, that's horrible! How can you be so vicious about your daughter's husband? You know Robin adored her. You know he's almost out of his mind. But he's trying to do the right thing. The thing he believes S.P. would want."

"Sentimental slop! He's just trying to play on your sympathy by saying he's going to raise it alone."

"And stop calling the baby it!" Lindsay screamed. "His name is John Geoffrey!"

"His name is nothing. I don't want him named after me."

"You can't very well stop it." Lindsay calmed down. "Geoff, I know how you feel. Don't you think I feel the same? Do you think your anguish is any greater than Robin's or mine? We're dying too, and you

246

know it. Don't be so hard. Please. You're making everything even more ghastly for all of us. I know how you adored S.P. And she adored you. She'd be very disappointed in you if she saw you acting this way. She'd expect you to be strong and sensible, even now. She'd expect you to have compassion for her husband and her child."

"Go away, Lindsay." Geoff sounded defeated. "I'm tired of your speeches. I'm weary of your long-suffering heroics. Go away and leave me alone. If I want to grieve, I'll grieve. And if I want to hate, I'll hate."

Hurt and resentful, she turned to leave. "I felt sorry for you, Geoff. I feared for your sanity today. Apparently, I was right. You *are* insane. I almost hope you are. I'd hate to think that any reasoning man could be so selfish, so totally self-absorbed. There's not an ounce of compassion in you, for me or for that pathetic young man. You don't give a damn about anybody but yourself. Go ahead. Wallow in your misery. At least the rest of us have enough decency to behave like civilized human beings for S.P.'s sake."

He rose from the bed and came toward her. Imploringly, he held out his hand. "Help me, Lindsay. I don't think I can live through this."

She took his hand and held it tightly. I love him so much, she thought. It seems I can forgive him anything.

"It's all right, darling," she said softly. "I know. We'll make it, Geoff. We'll make it, somehow, if we help each other."

21

*I*t was the saddest Christmas season Lindsay could remember. For her, who'd always taken such pleasure in the outward trappings of the holiday, the sight of New York dressed for the occasion was a mockery. The great lighted tree in Rockefeller Center, the festooned storefronts of Saks and Lord & Taylor and Bonwit Teller; the Santa Claus in front of Tiffany's; the Salvation Army band at the doors of Bloomingdale's; even the briefly friendly faces of strangers on the street seemed a reproach. Where was joy when you'd lost your child? Where, indeed, was God Himself?

Geoffrey's deepening depression alarmed her, for him and for herself. After that one pathetic reaching-out in Chicago, he'd reverted to the silent, brooding man she'd seen on the bed at the Drake, scarcely speaking to her, refusing to go to the office, seldom leaving his room, and then appearing unshaven and bleary-eyed. He drank heavily from morning till night. In the days after S.P.'s funeral he retreated to some private hell from which Lindsay feared he'd never return.

All her pleas went unheeded. Any attempt at reasoning fell on deaf ears. It was as though he too were dead, or wished to be. Desperately, Lindsay threw herself into her work, but even that offered little escape, for all business literally stopped around the holidays. Sometimes she sat in the shop all day, never seeing a customer. She gave her two assistants a vacation. There was nothing for them to do either, and they might as well enjoy the festivities. Pauline was her only source of comfort. Devastated as she was, Lindsay's mother put aside her own grief to try to help her daughter. She came to the apartment every evening to dine with Lindsay. They ate alone. The little food Geoff took was sent to his

248

room and only picked at, most of it still there when the housekeeper took away the tray.

On Christmas Eve, Lindsay could bear it no longer. "Mama, what am I going to do? I think Geoff will die too, if something doesn't give. He can't go on this way. My God, I don't begrudge him his grief—I have mine—but we can't stop living!" She burst into tears. "I can't stand it," she sobbed. "I'd do anything to help him. *Anything.*"

Pauline felt utterly helpless. The other losses they had endured had been terrible, but they could be accepted. Gandy was old. So was Howard. Even James, young as he was, met a death that could be explained. But this—this was beyond comprehension. Lindsay had told her everything, including S.P.'s initial inclination to have an abortion and Robin's terrible remorse that he hadn't allowed it. After all these years, Lindsay had even confessed her own near escape from the same thing.

"Thank God I never told S.P.," she said, "though I think she suspected the 'friend' I talked about was me. It must have hurt her to realize I nearly kept her from being born."

"I don't think so," Pauline said. "I think she probably sensed how much you loved her even *before* she was born. Don't reproach yourself for that, darling. Be happy you gave her twenty-two good years of life."

"Twenty-two years," Lindsay repeated bitterly. "That's all. Such a little time. Why? How can you have faith in anything when God is so cruel? Are we being punished, Geoff and I, for our own sins? Is Robin? And what of that poor helpless baby?"

All the clichés about God's will and some great master plan sprang to Pauline's lips, but she held them back. Words meant nothing. The will to survive was all people had to hold on to at times like these.

"Would it do any good if *I* tried to talk to Geoffrey?" Pauline asked. "I haven't seen him since the day of the funeral. Not that I hold out much hope that I can help. He needs professional counseling, but you say he won't hear of it."

"No, he won't. I tried to talk to him about therapy. For both of us. He just said no. He wouldn't even discuss it. But maybe he'd listen to you, Mama. He's always had such respect for you." Lindsay sighed. "God knows it couldn't hurt. He hasn't been willing to talk to anyone. Not even the men who're his best friends." A sad little smile crossed Lindsay's face. "Sometimes I've even thought of asking Adele to see him. He's so fond of her. Maybe he needs to be comforted by a woman softer and more gentle than I." She looked despairingly at her mother.

249

"That's how desperate I am. So out of my mind I'd even bring in that woman if she could do a better job. Crazy, isn't it? I've been jealous of Adele since Papa's death. I still detest her. But if she could reach Geoff, I'd swallow my pride and ask her to help him."

She's torn to pieces, Pauline thought. Dear Lord, that she could even bring herself to consider such a thing! How eaten with fear she is! And how much she loves that man, even to entertain the idea of begging Adele for help!

"Let me try to talk with him, Lindsay. As you say, there's nothing to lose."

Pauline was nervous as she tapped lightly on Geoff's door. I must get through to him, she thought. He's killing himself and my child with him. I can't let her bring Adele into this. What if Adele succeeded in bringing Geoff back, when Lindsay can't? It would be the end of everything for them. And yet she knew Lindsay would rather risk her marriage than see her husband destroy himself.

"Geoff? Open the door. It's me. Pauline. I want to talk to you, dear. Please let me in."

There was a little silence, and then she heard the key turn and Geoff opened the door. She was shocked by his appearance. He was haggard and unkempt. The room beyond was a mess. Lindsay had told her he wouldn't even let the housekeeper in to clean up. She pretended not to notice the stale air, the messy bed, the ashtray full of cigarette butts. Calmly she walked past him and seated herself in a chair. He was, she saw, more than a little drunk.

"If you've come to give me a pep talk," Geoff said, "don't bother."

Pauline looked at him coldly. "I haven't come to give you a pep talk, Geoffrey. If you want to commit suicide, that's your business. I have to assume you're a grown man and know what you're doing. But I will not permit you to destroy my daughter's life with your selfishness. You've had all the sympathy and pampering anyone could hope for, but your self-indulgence has gone beyond normal grief. You're killing Lindsay, and that I will not tolerate."

He stared at her in surprise. He hadn't expected this angry approach. For the first time, he bristled.

"She can always leave," he said. "Nobody's asking her to hang around."

Good, Pauline thought. At least I've gotten a reaction out of him. That had been her only hope: to make him fighting mad.

"She can, indeed. If she weren't so decent, she would. What self-respecting woman could bear to live under the same roof with a drunken bum?" Pauline took a long chance. "Maybe it's *you* who should leave, Geoffrey. Your behavior is more suitable to the Bowery than to Park Avenue. If the only way you can deal with your self-pity is to drown it in liquor, why not go the whole way? I'm sure your grandson will be very proud, one day, to learn that his mother's father was a disgusting weakling who didn't give a damn for anyone but himself."

Geoffrey opened his mouth to yell at her, but suddenly he pulled back and for the first time in weeks a trace of his old, soft smile appeared. "You know how to get to me, don't you? Tough talk. No pity. No coddling. The tigress fighting for her young." Geoff took a deep breath. "Is that how I seem to you? A weak, selfish, self-pitying drunk? Well, maybe you're right at that. Maybe that's all I am."

Pauline was dismayed. For a few seconds she'd dared hope it was going to work. She'd hoped he'd be angry. Furious enough to prove her wrong. I've failed, she thought. Failed Lindsay and failed him. And then, miraculously, Geoff took her hand.

"Thank you, Mama," he said. "That couldn't have been easy for you." He kissed her gently on the cheek. "Tell Lind I'm getting dressed to join you. It's the least I can do on Christmas Eve."

On the second day of January, 1968, the doorman called Adele from the lobby.

"Mr. Murray wants to know if he can come up, Mrs. Thresher."

"Of course, Frank. Send him right up."

Thank God I have my face on, she thought. Hurriedly she smoothed her hair and sprayed on a little eau de toilette before she opened the door. When Geoff stepped off the elevator she was waiting for him. How thin he is, she thought. How gaunt and tired looking. She hadn't seen him since a few days before he and Lindsay went to Chicago for the birth of S.P.'s baby. Mutual acquaintances had told her what happened, and though she read the obituary in the *Times,* she hadn't gone to the services. I'm the last person Lindsay wants there, she reflected, even though I was always fond of S.P.

Nor had she tried to call Geoff. She sent flowers and a little note to him and Lindsay, expressing her condolences and offering to help in any way she could. But the only acknowledgment had been a formal, engraved card, the kind one sent out by the hundreds to thank strangers for their sympathy. She'd heard, indirectly, that Geoff had become al-

251

most a recluse, but she dared not inquire for his health. She was over-joyed to see him now, pleased he had come out of his shell and even more delighted that he'd unexpectedly decided to visit her.

"Come in," she said warmly. "It's so good to see you, Geoff." They sat down in the living room. "Can I give you a drink?"

He shook his head. "I'm on the wagon. Haven't had a drink in over a week. How are you, Adele?"

"All right." She searched for the right words. "I'm so sorry," she finally said, inadequately. "I wanted to tell you, but—well, you know."

"Yes. Thank you."

There was an awkward silence before Adele asked, "How is Lindsay?"

"Remarkable. She has more guts than I. She was crushed, but she didn't come apart. I haven't been worth a damn for almost a month." Geoff's lips twisted as though he was still in pain. "Yes, Lindsay's remarkable," he said again. "She could weather anything."

"But I'm sure she's suffered horribly too," Adele said. "Such a terrible, tragic thing. How is Robin? And the baby?"

"Managing, I guess. Lindsay went to Chicago this morning to see them. She wanted me to go, but I couldn't. I still can't look at them. Either of them." He put his head in his hands. "Jesus, Adele, I don't know what's been worse, my grief or my anger."

"I know," she said soothingly. "That's only human."

He looked up. "Is it? No one else seems to think so. Lind and her mother don't understand. They're so strong, both of them. I don't mean they haven't been wonderful. They have. Lindsay's been so patient, and Pauline finally gave me such hell about my drinking that I was ashamed enough to get moving again. But I know they despise me."

"Oh, no, they don't! I'm sure they don't, Geoff. They love you. It's just hard for some people to comprehend the grief of others. They're mourning too, but it takes different forms with different people. Even so, it's no less deep and real. Lindsay's sorrow must be as awful as yours, but she's not the kind of woman who lets it show. Remember how she was when Howard died? I know she was sad, but she kept herself under control, even at his bedside. Her anger at me is part of her grief, I know. I've always believed that."

He looked at her wonderingly. "You have such tolerance, Adele. Such forgiveness."

She smiled at the compliment. "Thank you, but I think you give me too much credit. I'm just not as competent as some. I don't know how to fight back. It's easier to make excuses."

"You've been making excuses for Lindsay for years. I wish she could understand that."

Adele shook her head. "She won't, Geoff, but never mind. *We* understand. That's a great comfort to me."

"Adele, these past months I've sometimes wished . . ." He stopped. "Never mind. It's not important. I'm glad you're my friend. I need a friend." He looked at her sadly. "Would it be all right if I came here sometimes? Just to talk, the way we used to. Could you put up with me?"

"Of course. Any time you feel like it. I'm proud to be your friend. I'm proud of you. You're gentle and sensitive and loyal. Don't let anyone convince you otherwise."

He stood up. "I'll come to see you soon."

"Yes," she said. "Please do. Soon and often."

Mercifully, inevitably, the passing of time turned the horror of loss into a kind of dull throb of pain that was ever-present but bearable. Like scar tissue over a deep wound, the day-by-day demands of life helped fill the searing hole left by S.P.'s death. There was never a day, scarcely an hour, that Geoff did not think of his daughter, but he began to function again, without enthusiasm but with some show of normality. In mid-January, he began to go into the office a few hours a day. He dreaded that first day of return. If members of his staff commiserated with him, he was sure he wouldn't be able to stand it. He feared he would break down and start to blubber if anyone so much as spoke a sympathetic word.

He need not have worried. His secretary, Gladys O'Reilly, anticipated this and took it upon herself to instruct the department heads at the agency not to mention his bereavement to the boss.

"Treat him as you always have," she cautioned. "No better, no worse. He'll want it to be business as usual. Mrs. Murray says he's still pretty shaky, but the best thing in the world for him is to be involved and forced to think of other things. Pass the word to your people, will you?"

"Sure," the executives said. "No sweat, Gladys."

Gladys, who'd been with Geoffrey for fifteen years, knew him well. Unmarried at thirty-three, she was more than a little in love with

253

him, not that she ever revealed it to him by word or gesture. She was a good-looking woman, tall and verging on the buxom. Currently she lived with a man she didn't love. It was a healthy, undemanding physical relationship that suited them both. But Gladys's heart was in the office, in more ways than one. Her lover knew this and good-naturedly teased her about it.

"If Geoff Murray ever gave you a tumble, you'd leave me like a shot, wouldn't you? Poor old Glad. Don't you know that wife of his will never let him go? He's one of her prized possessions, younger than her antiques but just as valuable to her."

"Don't be an ass," Gladys snapped. "Mr. Murray doesn't know I'm alive. I'm part of the office equipment, like the water cooler and the Xerox machine."

"Come on. He couldn't get along without you. Maybe you have a chance now, at that. There's nothing so vulnerable as a grieving man. A patient, sympathetic woman around all day, sharing his work, fussing over him like a mother hen—well, that could do it, old girl. This could be your big moment."

She laughed. "If I didn't know better, I'd think you were jealous."

"Maybe I am. I know Murray has the best part of you, the inside part. Not that I'm complaining about my share."

"You're an oversexed idiot," Gladys said. "I'm not crazy, Harry Thaw. In fifteen years, Mr. Murray has been a perfect gentleman. He depends on me, that's true. But as a secretary, nothing more. That's the way he is."

"Or *was*." Harry was jealous and trying to be cool about it. "Men get crazy notions, especially at his time of life. What is he, fifty? A restless age. And having gone through what he has the past couple of months, values may seem different to him. He doesn't have to be the hero father-figure any more, you know. He may decide to kick up his heels now. Death sometimes increases the zest for life, once the shock has passed. Watch it, Glad. He may start chasing you around the desk."

"Oh, for God's sake, shut up! Anyway, Mr. Murray isn't fifty. He's not quite forty-nine. And you can take it from me, he's a family man all the way, daughter or no daughter. You're disgusting, Harry!"

"Okay, okay. Don't get your Irish up! Your boss is a saint, a paragon of virtue, without the curiosity of normal men."

She was impatient with this conversation, primarily because it was uncomfortably close to some wishful thoughts she'd had in recent weeks.

254

Mr. Murray *was* different since his return. Quieter and sadder, which made him all the more appealing. He seemed lonely and in need of comfort. There was talk around the office that he and Mrs. Murray weren't getting on too well. Not that that was news. In the last couple of years, there'd been a strain in that marriage. Gladys didn't need the grapevine to confirm the gossip. She heard, from the secretaries of executives who traveled with him, that Geoffrey had his little flings on the road. One or two women had even called him from places like Detroit and Atlanta, saying it was "personal" when she inquired the nature of their business. And she couldn't help overhearing some of his conversations with his wife. More than once there'd been an argument over the phone, with Mr. Murray finally saying angrily, "We'll discuss this when I get home, Lindsay."

And there were, for months, those odd, frequent calls from his young stepmother-in-law. Since S.P.'s death, Adele hadn't called, but before then she'd been on the phone once, sometimes twice a day.

Still, Gladys hadn't believed there was anything to any of it. Mrs. Murray was beautiful, smart, successful. The childhood sweetheart and perfect wife. They'd been married nearly thirty years. for God's sake! People didn't split up after thirty years unless something dramatic happened, Like one of them meeting someone else and falling in love. Or if they underwent some traumatic event that changed their attitude toward their old routine.

Did S.P.'s untimely death qualify as such an event? Would it make Geoff Murray reach out and grab what he could of life, brought up short as he'd been by the tenuousness of it?

Not likely, Gladys told herself. But if it did, she'd be there. He wouldn't be the first man to fall in love with his "office wife." We're the women closest to them, she thought. We understand them better than their real wives, share more of their waking hours, know how to cater to their needs.

Dummy! She scolded herself. None of that would happen with a gentleman like Mr. Murray. Be a realist. You don't exist for him as a person. Even if he did break out of his marriage, she told herself cynically, it wouldn't be with you. It would be with some twenty-two-year-old brainless child. Someone kittenish and gorgeous who'd make him feel young and sexy. That's what men did when they neared fifty. Harry was right about that. It was a dangerous age. But for other men, not for Geoffrey Murray.

* * *

By March, Geoff was back at work full-time, grateful for the demands of the job that kept him from thinking of personal things. Not only S.P. The drifting away from Lindsay that had started long before became more of a rift. They hadn't made love since long before that last trip to Chicago together. And rarely in the two years before that. He knew Lindsay was hurt by his lack of desire for her. She was a sensuous woman, and the lack of physical release frustrated her. But she waited for him to make the first move, not aware that he could not. Not with her or anyone. He seemed to have lost every vestige of sexual urge since his daughter's death.

He wondered, often, about the reason for his self-imposed celibacy. He'd always been easily aroused, had strong needs for a woman. Except for Pamela, Lindsay had fulfilled those needs until his middle forties, when for some mindless reason he began to seek variety. But now even that didn't interest him. No woman did. He supposed, playing amateur analyst, that somewhere deep in his subconscious he equated sex with S.P.'s death. That was weird, morbid, but it was a definite possibility, absurd as his logical mind told him it was. No sex, no pregnancy. No pregnancy, no death. He knew that made no sense, but what other explanation was there? He even wondered if he actually blamed S.P.'s death on Lindsay. Again, idiotic. By the time S.P. told her mother she'd wanted an abortion, it had been far too late for the girl to have one. Yet as he tossed and turned on his bed at night, he thought wildly that there might have been something Lindsay could have done when she saw their daughter in November. She should have talked with S.P.'s doctor then. Maybe there was some clue to the unexpected heart failure, something S.P. had decided to ignore. He knew this was crazy thinking, but in his bewilderment he sought any kind of explanation that might be related to his problem, tried to make it tangible and therefore, perhaps solvable.

He was acutely uncomfortable in Lindsay's presence these days, feeling her unspoken reproach. He wondered how long it would be before she took a lover. She'd been faithful during the war. He believed that. But she was much older now, more sophisticated about such matters. He couldn't blame her if she found a man. He'd hate it, but he'd understand.

Will I ever be myself again? Geoff wondered. Will I ever rediscover remembered ecstasy? When will all the formless demons go away and leave me in peace?

He thought of his grandson, the child he'd never seen. Do I refuse to see him because he was the cause of *my* child's death? Or is he, too, a living reminder of the passion I no longer feel? Bitterly, he wondered whether Robin already was sleeping with another woman. Probably. Geoff envied him his damned virility, his youth and resiliency. Lindsay was in constant touch with Robin and visited him and little John every few weeks. When she returned, Geoff didn't want to hear about it, but she told him all the same.

"The baby is enchanting, Geoff. He looks like S.P. when she was his age, all smiles and gurgles and big eyes. And Robin is wonderful with him. That man is giving his life to his son. He's with him every free minute. Almost too much, I think. Robin should get out, try to forget his sorrow. He's young. Too young to do nothing but work and be a nursemaid to John every evening and weekend."

Geoff was infuriated by her rational approach to life. How could she? Her own daughter dead not four months, and she actually wanted her son-in-law to forget!

"It's his duty to take care of his child," Geoff said stiffly.

"Oh, don't be such an old fogy! Of course he's going to take care of John, but he doesn't have to be a slave to him! S.P. would kick him if she knew!" Lindsay gentled her voice. "Geoff, we can't bring her back by leading unnatural lives. None of us. Not Robin and not you and I. Isn't it time we picked up the pieces, dear? I don't feel I have a husband any more. It's been such a long time."

He felt like a heel. "Lindsay, it isn't that I don't care for you. It's just that I can't seem to work up an interest in sex. I don't think anything would happen if I tried. There's no explanation for it. It's just left me."

He was almost pathetic, but she couldn't feel sorry for him. This was more self-indulgence, more self-pity. She'd been proud and happy when he stopped drinking, sure that was the first step toward healing this mysterious gap between them. But months had passed and it made no difference. She lived with a courteous stranger, a sober man in every sense of the word. It was depressing, like sharing a house with a monk. The unfairness of it made her lash out angrily.

"And what am I supposed to do while you wait around for your manhood to return? It's been months, Geoff. Many months. You were virile enough when you were taking your little road trips. I'm surprised you managed to squeeze me in between your activities in other towns! God, I'd even settle for that now! It would be better than living with a eunuch!"

He didn't fight back. "I know. I'm sorry."

"Sorry! What good is sorry? I don't know what goes on in your head these days, but you'd better pull yourself together—or else!"

"Or else you'll take a lover?" Geoff spoke mildly. "I wouldn't blame you, Lindsay. You're a healthy, attractive woman. There has to be a limit to your patience. I'm surprised you haven't reached it before now."

She stared at him. "Has it come to this, Geoff? Are we so totally washed up you don't care if I sleep with someone else?"

"I care, but I'd understand."

"You're incredible! I think you actually enjoy your suffering!"

"No. I hate it. I don't want to feel this way. I just can't help it."

His sincerity finally touched her. "Geoff, I don't want anybody but you. I never have, not in my whole life. Please, darling, let's try to get reacquainted. We'll go slowly, as though we're courting. But it was always so good for us. It can be again. I know it can, if only you'll try."

"Not yet, Lindsay!" He shook his head. "Some day, I hope."

She wanted to cry. He was out of her reach, perhaps for good this time. As calmly as she could, she said, "What's to become of us?"

He looked at her searchingly, wishing with all his heart he could reassure them both with even the slightest degree of conviction. But he couldn't. She was part of a time he wanted to forget. He knew that now. The realization hit him like a body blow.

"I don't know," he said. "If you want your freedom, Lind, you can have it. A divorce, if that will make you happy."

"I don't want a divorce. I want you to belong to me!"

"I have nothing left to give," Geoff said. "I don't know if I ever could belong to anyone again."

22

In June, Lindsay made a buying trip to England to find antiques for the insatiable American market. She'd been to Europe for this purpose several times before, but always hurriedly, anxious to get back to her family. This time she planned a lengthier visit, eager to get away and stay away from the problems at home. Everyone could do nicely without her. Pauline was in remarkably good health for her age. Robin was managing admirably, and the baby was already growing into a chubby, contented little thing with a discernibly winning personality. As for Geoff, there was nothing to do for him. They lived in a state of civilized estrangement, seeing little of each other, never having another serious discussion about the future of their marriage. He was working longer hours than ever and making more trips to the out-of-town branches, though now, Lindsay thought ruefully, she had no reason to wonder what he did in his free time in other cities. His impotence caused them both terrible anguish: Geoff because he felt less than a man, Lindsay because she longed to be loved and felt increasingly deprived as each day edged her closer to the time she'd be less desirable to any man.

She thought quite seriously and almost clinically of taking a lover. The question, very simply, was where to find one. Martin Wylie, the young man who worked for her at the shop, would have been all too happy to oblige. He was, quite obviously, infatuated with her, but she resisted this convenient solution, not because Marty was only twenty-seven (she had no hangups about the older-woman-younger-man-affair) but because she considered it bad business to get into any kind of personal entanglement with a co-worker. It could only lead to eventual awkwardness on the part of one or the other, or maybe both.

Most of her clients, attractive decorators, were openly gay. Okay for them, but regrettable for her. The "private customers" referred to her by these interior designers, were mostly female, rich insecure wives, nervous about not having the "right" antiques in their expensive houses. Occasionally they brought their husbands to okay a big purchase. Lindsay saw these wealthy men give her approving looks, and on more than one occasion they managed to speak to her alone, saying they'd be delighted if she'd call them at their offices, perhaps for lunch or a little drink. Lindsay always smiled politely and thanked them, but she did not follow up. It was not a case of high principles, for she was a realist. Was there, anywhere in the world, a husband who did not cheat on his wife? But it wasn't for her, the furtive little transient affair. Not that she sought even an ongoing outside relationship. She truly wanted to stay married to Geoff and hoped, against all odds, they'd rediscover what they once had.

I'm faithful in spite of myself, she sometimes thought wryly. And likely to remain so. There seemed to be no suitable candidates even for the kind of impersonal, therapeutic encounter she might accept. She was in the wrong age group. Forty-eight. Too old to know any bachelors. Too young to desire a widower whose wife predeceased him after forty or fifty years. Men of her own age sometimes got divorced, but they were not really free. She'd seldom known a mature man to divorce his wife unless he already had her successor picked out.

On the flight to London, she looked curiously at her fellow passengers in the first class section. Most of them were businessmen, she assumed. It might be possible to start up a conversation with one of them, perhaps enjoy an evening on the town, ending up with a nightcap in her suite and the inevitable progress from there. The hell with it, she decided wearily. It was all too much trouble. She wondered how Geoff used to find his women when he traveled. Did he pick up stewardesses on airplanes? Traffic with secretaries in the branch offices? Ask the bell captain at the hotel to send up a woman? More likely his own executives found girls for him, discreetly and suitably. Geoff would never be interested in a common whore, any more than she could stand the thought of buying sex for herself, even if she knew where such purchases were made.

Lindsay had to laugh. In her youth, when she wouldn't have dreamed of such a thing, it would have been all too easy to find a young man eager to go to bed with her. Now that she was ready, no one offered. Hard to believe she'd slept with only one man in her whole life. In this liberated day and age it was almost embarrassing to admit. But what she told Geoff was true. She never wanted anyone but him. Still didn't. But now she knew how men felt when there was no one to hold and be held by. It was a basic, urgent human need having nothing to do with love or commitment or even, strangely enough, with faithfulness. It was an ache with no gender.

She'd ordered a car and driver to pick her up at Heathrow Airport, and she spotted the chauffeur as she came through Customs. He wore a neat little label, CORONET TOWN CARS.

"Hello. I'm Mrs. Murray."

He touched his cap respectfully. "Good afternoon, madam. Name's Marks. The car is just outside. I'll see to your luggage."

On the long drive into town, Lindsay could see him sneaking glances at her in the rearview mirror. She also could see his face. Not handsome, but interesting. Rugged. He was about forty-five, she judged. Stocky and broad-shouldered. Probably a very sexy man, she thought idly, and then, My God! what am I doing? Have I begun to look at every man as though he's a prospect? She turned away and stared out of the window. There was an excitement in her, a stirring that both frightened and tantalized. Her reactions appalled her. A hired chauffeur, for God's sake! It was disgusting! She'd heard about love-starved women who made passes at bellboys and hairdressers. She was no snob. A man's occupation did not matter to her. But being drawn to a total stranger was out of character for the fastidious, remarkably moral Mrs. Geoffrey Murray. Besides, what did she know about him? He probably had a wife and six children. He might not even like women. It was impossible to tell these days who was "in the closet." In any case, he might be an opportunist or, worse, a blackmailer who preyed on susceptible, middle-aged American women. Lonely ones like herself, looking for a few hours of forgetfulness for which they'd pay dearly.

Nonetheless, despite all the sensible arguments she marshaled against it, she found herself wondering whether this silent Englishman might answer her needs.

"Marks?"

"Yes, madam?"

"Will you be assigned for me permanently? During my stay, I mean."

"I believe that is the arrangement, madam, if it's satisfactory to

261

you. Most of our clients prefer to have the same chauffeur."

I'll bet they do, Lindsay thought wickedly.

"That will be fine," she said. "I want to do a good bit of traveling through the countryside. I buy antiques. I presume it's possible for you to spend time out of London, a few days at a time?"

"Perfectly possible, madam."

Was there an undercurrent of awareness in those three polite words? She'd tried to sound impersonal, businesslike, but perhaps he sensed her thoughts. The damned man is reading my mind, Lindsay thought with dismay. He must have run into my kind many times before. "My kind"? What a degrading category I've put myself in! But it's true. There are millions like me, hungry for affection, for a man who even pretends to care. Why not? she decided coldly. This was by far the best way. A man thousands of miles from home. An anonymous lover she'd never see again. A couple of weeks of make-believe with a person with whom she had nothing in common except lust. She knew, somehow, they shared that. Marks would be a fabulous partner. Amused, she said, "Do you by any chance have a first name, Marks?"

"It's Reginald, madam. My friends call me Reg."

Significant pause. "May I consider myself a friend?"

Small smile in the rearview mirror. Understanding in the clear, dark eyes. Unmistakable inflection in the brief reply.

"By all means, madam."

The two-week stay she'd planned stretched into three. She was incredibly, mindlessly content. Everything went well as far as the buying part of her trip was concerned. She found wonderful pieces of Edwardian furniture in Petworth and ranged through Sussex discovering lovely old bamboo armoires and papier-mâché tables that would bring a fortune in New York. As a businesswoman, she felt a great sense of accomplishment; as a sensual woman, she was released and fulfilled.

She went to bed with Reg Marks the third night of her visit. Although they easily could have returned to London from Brighton, Lindsay deliberately suggested they stay overnight at a small seaside hotel.

"We can buy toothbrushes at the local drugstore," she said.

"Chemist," Reg corrected gently.

Lindsay laughed like a young girl. "All right. Chemist. You're such a stickler for correctness, Reg. I can't even get you to call me by my name. Come on. We're traveling companions. Can't we drop the formalities? If I hear you say madam once more, I'll scream!"

"What shall I say, then? Mrs. Murray?"

"How about 'Lindsay'?" She knew exactly what she was doing. The simple request would tell him what he wanted to know. If he wanted to know it.

He gave her a slow, comprehending smile, but he was wary.

"I'm not sure that's quite proper. You *are* my employer."

Lindsay pretended to pout. "You also said I could be your friend." She dropped her act and looked straightforwardly at him. "You're a very attractive man. I'm sure I'm not the first of your lady clients who's found you interesting. Isn't that true?"

He didn't answer.

"Oh, I know. I know. I shouldn't have asked that question. A gentleman doesn't kiss and tell, does he? And you are a gentleman. Gallant, beautifully mannered. You know how to treat a woman, as most Englishmen do. American men are much too busy to bother with the amenities. Romance is very low on their list of priorities. Particularly with a woman to whom they've been married for nearly thirty years. Are you married, Reg?"

He listened carefully. He'd been observing her closely for the past three days. She was no promiscuous creature, he was sure of that. He suspected this might even be the first time she'd considered an affair. Her false gaiety was a cover for nervousness, as though she'd decided to be unfaithful to her husband but was half terrified by the idea. She was a lady, no doubt of it. But she was also a healthy woman.

There'd been others before her. In twenty-five years of being a chauffeur, Reginald Marks had met dozens of them, gone to bed with quite a few. But they'd never had the quality of Lindsay Murray. She must be—what, in her late forties? But there was an innocence about her, a vulnerability that kept him from responding too readily to her obvious invitation.

"I've known many women," he said carefully, "but I've married none of them. I think, though, that if I were a husband I'd never forget to be a lover as well." He smiled. "Where I come from, people are poor, uneducated. Not the kind you'd ever meet. But they know more of love than the upper classes. The physical and the emotional parts of it. My mum and dad were sweethearts till the day he died. They had six kids, no money, a hard life. They fought like demons. Terrible rows, they had. But they came first with each other. Even before their children."

263

Across the table in the funny little hotel dining room, Lindsay sipped her wine and paid close attention.

"Where did you get your education, your polish?"

"I've had almost no schooling. If I have any polish, as you call it, it's rubbed off, by being around educated people for twenty-five years. I'm not a gentleman. Not in the way we use the word here. I don't have what you have: social graces." He looked down with amusement. "Sometimes I don't know which fork to use, and I wouldn't dare order the wine. But I've taught myself to speak reasonably well and got rid of most of my Cockney accent, though no one would ever think I went to a public school, like Eton or Harrow. I make a decent living doing interesting work, which is more than I can say for my brothers. They're laborers and lorry drivers. Good men, but without ambition. Since I began driving professionally at eighteen, I've tried to learn manners from people born with them. I've been fortunate in some ways. Maybe not in others. My mum says I put myself above my station; that I don't know my place. Perhaps she's right. I'm sure it's why I could never marry a girl of my own class, even though I know it's not ruddy likely any well-bred woman would look twice at me. Not as a husband, that is."

"A woman would be a fool not to look at you," Lindsay said.

"Would *you?*" he challenged. "If you weren't married, could you imagine marrying a man like me? No. You'd take me as a lover, perhaps. Even like me as a friend. But could you introduce me to *your* friends? Could you present me to your parents and say, Here is my husband, uneducated and very limited, a man who was born within the sound of Bow Bells and never really got very far away?"

Embarrassed, Lindsay did not meet his eyes.

Reg smiled kindly. "I was speaking only—what's the word? Hypothetically. You're a lovely lady. Gracious, charming, and very kind. I know you're unhappy and I'm sorry. A beautiful, full-of-life woman like you deserves something better."

"Yes," Lindsay said simply. "I think I do."

They sat silently for a few minutes. Then she rose from the table and said, almost timidly, "I'll leave my door open, if you like."

He came to her that night and every night thereafter. Lindsay had never known such abandonment. Even in the early days of her marriage, she'd never felt this explosive joy. Without experience, she'd been sure Geoff was the greatest partner in the world. Now, with wonderment and suprisingly little guilt, she realized he was not. This man was tender but forceful, gentle but demanding, virile and insatiable. She reacted to him in ways she'd not dreamed possible, reveling in his admiration and desire, losing herself in the discovery of physical excitement on a scale she did not know existed.

She blossomed, looked years younger, found herself needing little sleep. From dusk to dawn, they made love and then lay quietly, telling each other the details of their lives before Reg quietly left her for a few hours. When she spoke of S.P.'s death, he held her tightly, stroking her hair.

"Poor, lovely Lindsay," he said. "My poor darling."

She'd hidden the surge of remembered agony with an effort at flippancy. "Your poor darling grandmother," she'd said. "What a shocking old lady I am!"

"Yes," he teased. "An oversexed old crone if ever I saw one."

"I'm five years older than you. And I have a grandson."

Reg laughed. "That's mildly interesting. Shall I help you into your rocking chair?"

She laughed too, but the banter reminded her that she'd have to go home to all that very soon. This idyll had to end. It was an experience, nothing more than that. It had been an interlude that restored her confidence and would help her cope with what awaited her in New York. Her duty lay there. For all his indifference, Geoff needed her. And there was Pauline to think of. And Robin and John. So many ties, stronger than the ones who held them ever knew.

Besides, Lindsay reluctantly acknowledged, all she shared with Reg was sex. He was right. He'd never fit into her world, even if she was reckless enough to consider it. Realist that she was, she knew there was no future for them. Not that Reg ever mentioned it. He knew it too.

They lay in her big bed in the Savoy. Lindsay loved the expensive tackiness of her London hotel suite: the 1930s look of the spindly-legged "vanity table" with its impossibly dim, frilly-shaded lamps; the overstuffed chairs and old-fashioned ashtrays in the small adjoining living room; the ridiculous little foyer with its coatrack and umbrella stand. It had style and elegance, nonetheless. A kind of reassuring permanence far removed from American hotels with their ultra-modern conveniences and off-putting lack of charm.

She wondered what Reg's flat was like. She'd asked him to take her there, but he'd refused.

"It wouldn't be the thing to do, Lindsay."

"Why on earth not? I'd like to see where you live." So I can picture you there, she thought, when I've gone.

"I wouldn't let you risk your reputation, for one thing."

"Oh, Reg, for heaven's sake! I've been risking it all over England for the past three weeks!"

"Not the same as going to a bachelor's digs. Improper, luv."

She'd laughed, half exasperated, half amused. "Still so correct." She shook her head. "You really are ridiculous, dear heart. Like insisting I ride in the back seat when we're in the car."

"When we're in the car, I'm your employee, madam."

"And in bed?"

"I am your ardent, devoted, and ever faithful servant. Of a different sort."

She reached over and touched him lightly. "I'm going to miss you dreadfully. Will you write to me?"

"No. Best not."

She didn't ask why. He'd be ashamed of his grammar and spelling, she thought sadly. As though I'd care.

"I'll be back in six months," Lindsay said. "Will you be here?"

He pulled her to him. "You may count on it, madam."

Gladys O'Reilly was troubled. Maybe, she admitted to herself, a little disappointed, too. Her boss's wife had been in Europe for nearly three weeks and she'd permitted herself to hope that Geoffrey might turn to her for company. She wasn't sure why she even thought such a thing, except that in the weeks after his daughter's death he'd seemed so much more approachable than he ever had in all the years she'd worked for him. Sometimes he called her into his office just to talk, almost as though there were no one else to whom he could unburden himself. He talked mostly about S.P.: what a wonderful child she'd been, the fun they'd had together when she was growing up. He even confided, unexpectedly, that her loss had made a difference to him and Mrs. Murray, that they were each shrouded in their own sorrow, almost unable to communicate.

In another man, Gladys would have turned this off as the old "my wife doesn't understand me" ploy. But with Geoffrey, she knew it was an honest confession, not designed to tempt her into comforting him in bed. Not that she wouldn't have been happy to. She was crazy about him, so much so that she permitted herself to think he might ask her out to dinner or to the theater. She'd dared hope he might finally have begun to notice her as a person, and when Lindsay went off on the long trip she almost expected him to seek her out.

On the contrary, the weeks of near-intimacy abruptly stopped. Instead, the daily, sometimes twice-daily calls to and from Adele Thresher resumed. Gladys knew they saw each other every evening. At least, she was almost positive that Adele was the other person for whom she made those restaurant reservations for two, and for whom she called the ticket broker for seats to the current Broadway shows. She knew damned well that flowers went twice a week to Adele, for she was the one who ordered them and dictated cards to the florist. Cards that at first said things like *Thank you for a lovely evening—Geoff,* and later, and more alarmingly, *What would I do without you?* Significantly, these and other familiar sentiments carried no signature. Not even an initial.

He must be having an affair with her, Gladys thought unhappily. In a way, it was almost obscene. She was his stepmother, for God's sake! Well, his ex-stepmother-in-law, which was almost the same.

Still, she had to reluctantly admit that he seemed more relaxed, less tense, than he had for a long while. She wondered what would happen when Mrs. Murray came home. It was well known there was no love lost between Lindsay and the woman her father had married. They said Adele wasn't welcome in the Murrays' house, though how "they" knew, Gladys wasn't sure. Word just got around in New York. For a big city, it was surprisingly small. People knew the most extraordinarily private things about each others' lives, gossip picked up at cocktail parties or through friends of friends.

"I have a feeling there'll be hell to pay when Mrs. Murray gets home," Gladys said to Harry Thaw. "Mr. M. has been seeing his stepmother constantly, and Lindsay's going to blow her stack."

"What makes you think she'll know?" Harry asked practically. "I don't imagine he'll be stupid enough to tell her. And I doubt the other woman will."

"Oh, she'll hear about it. There are no secrets in this town."

He eyed her suspiciously. "I hope *you* don't plan to let anything slip."

She assumed an innocent, injured air. "Me? Don't be crazy. I'm loyal to my boss. Why would I do such a thing?"

Harry laughed. "You're about as convincing as a harlot at a church supper. If you thought you had a chance with the great Geoffrey, you'd do anything you could to cause trouble between him and his wife. Don't deny it, Glad, You're nuts about him. I'll bet you even imagined he might ask you out while he was temporarily a widower. You're probably mad as hell that he didn't."

"No such thing! How dare you say such things?"

"Hey, no hard feelings, babe. We're all entitled to our dreams, even the impossible ones."

Impossible, were they? Nothing's impossible, Gladys told herself angrily. Geoff Murray was a fool. He didn't recognize devotion when it sat nine or ten hours a day practically under his nose. It wasn't fair. She'd be so right for him, so good to him. Better than fancy, spoiled ladies like Adele Thresher. Or bored ones who only played at careers, like Lindsay. There must be some way I can make him see me as something more than a secretary, she thought. I've been dreaming up to now but it's time to give this whole thing some very serious attention.

Adele didn't quite know what to make of the past three weeks. Almost from the day Lindsay left for England, Geoff had been in constant attendance. They'd had a wonderful time and she regretted seeing it come to an end. When Lindsay returned there'd be no more dinners and theatre, no more Sunday drives to East Hampton, no more Saturday lunches and leisurely strolls on the safe perimeters of Central Park. Lindsay was coming home tomorrow. This was Adele's last evening in the open company of her stepson.

She grimaced at the word. Stepson. Ridiculous. Why had that popped into her mind? She never thought of him that way. He was Geoff. Childhood friend of hers and James. A sweet, gentle man. And, dismally, Lindsay's husband.

Theirs was a strange relationship, Lindsay and Geoff's, from what Adele gathered. Seemingly, the passion of the early years had turned into tolerant acceptance. They liked each other, in the way old friends who'd shared good and bad experiences did. Probably they would stay married forever. Having weathered so much for so long, neither contemplated life apart, and yet it was not a good arrangement. They were still too young to settle for a routine existence without the bond of physical attraction to soften the rough edges of indifference.

Geoff never said so, in as many words, but Adele correctly suspected that it had been a long while since he and Lindsay had made love.

He made little jokes about his "virtuous life" these days, comparing it to the long-ago affair with Pamela.

"You really loved that girl in England, didn't you?"

"Yes. Very much. At least, I think so. It was such a long time ago. So much has happened since then. I've changed. Sometimes I can hardly remember young Captain Murray." Geoff shrugged. "Not important. Lindsay was pregnant and I had to come home. Don't misunderstand. I'm not bucking for a halo. I wanted to come back. I knew my place was with her, and I chose to be there." He looked at her affectionately. "You're so easy to talk to, Adele. You seem always to understand. Funny, I have no close friends. Neither has Lindsay. Not really close, I mean. Not the kind you know you could go to if things were really tough. We know a lot of people, but friends? You're the only one I have. And poor Lindsay has none, unless you count Pauline." He looked serious. "Some wise man once said everyone should have nine good friends: three older, three younger, three one's own age. I forget who it was. Thoreau, I think. It makes good sense, but I don't know anyone who has that many. Maybe it was easier at Walden Pond."

Adele smiled. "I define friendship as someone who'd take you in if you had no roof over your head. When you think of it that way, it comes down to nearly nobody, doesn't it? Funny, the three of us. Such loners. A pity. We all need someone dependable, someone who loves us despite our faults and weaknesses." She sounded wistful. "I never had anyone like that. Not ever. Maybe James would have been the person. I'll never know. I thought Lindsay was, once, but I messed that up. Well," she said briskly, "no use regretting the past, is there? We've all made mistakes, but we've lived through them. It could be so much worse, Geoff. Lots of people have had harder lives than we. I try to remember that and be grateful."

Dressing for her last evening with him, Adele could see again the strange, thoughtful look Geoff had given her as she spoke. I'm his friend, she thought flatly. Nothing more. There'd not been a single gesture or word between them to indicate any interest beyond quiet, contented companionship. Yet she'd fallen in love with him. And she suspected there was a similiar stirring in him. It was taboo, verboten. An idea not to be entertained for a single moment. But they were far better suited to each other than he and Lindsay. She'd make no overture, nor would he. Their affection for Lindsay was too strong. For Lindsay, feeling as she did about Adele, it would be the final, crushing blow. Whether she believes it or not, Adele thought, I'm still *her* friend too. I always have been.

From somewhere in the back of her mind she remembered an old Jewish folk tale. Something about a criminal being stoned by a crowd, as was the custom in olden days. He said nothing as heavy rocks struck him, but when a small pebble hit he cried out in pain. Asked why he suffered the hurtful stones and winced at the pebble, he said, "The pebble was thrown by a friend."

I'll never throw that pebble, Adele thought. I've hurt Lindsay enough.

23

*F*lying home, Lindsay thought how ironic it was that twenty-three years later she finally understood a little of what Geoff felt for the girl in England. She did want to go back to her husband. That was her place, her sanctuary; it was her duty to go home to the man who needed her. And yet part of her stayed behind. The weeks with Reg lingered in her mind. Because of him, she could live more peacefully with Geoff. Had her husband felt something similar when he returned? Did the memory of illicit love perversely strengthen his attachment to his legal mate? Perhaps. For so many years after the war, they'd lived in harmony, devoted to each other and their child. Only recently had the estrangement begun, deepening with their individual absorptions in other things. She felt strong enough to change that now, if she could.

I'll be a better wife, Lindsay made herself believe. More patient with him. Less competitive. She felt purged and relaxed, not ashamed. Her affair took nothing away from Geoff. It did not threaten him. It was, she reasoned, actually a favor, for it eased her frustrations and would keep her from making futile, resentful demands on him. She could exist peacefully as a "roommate" in a sexless dwelling, as long as she could escape now and then and return to Reg.

I must go back every couple of months, she decided. Six months was far too long to lie alone. Geoff would not be suspicious, for her buying trip had been so successful it easily justified more frequent ones. She was sorry to deceive him, but she wouldn't dream of confessing her infidelity, as her father had done to Pauline. No, she wouldn't openly insult Geoff that way, even if she felt a selfish need to ease her conscience by transferring her guilt to his shoulders.

He'd come to meet her, and she felt a twinge of remorse at the sight of his familiar face. But her next thought was that he looked much better, more relaxed. And then, almost unhappily she realized, it must have been less of a strain on him, not having me around.

Geoff kissed her briefly and said, "How was the trip?"

"Marvelous. Very successful. How are things here?"

"Not too bad. I've been busy. We got that big account we were pitching for. Superior Foods. Out of Chicago. Ten million dollars."

"Congratulations! That's terrific!" Lindsay hesitated. The Chicago office was Robin's responsibility. He must have brought in this important piece of business. She'd been right about that, at least. No matter how bitterly Geoff felt about his son-in-law, he was too much the businessman to lose such a valuable employee. Marvelous the way men could separate their personal lives and their work, she thought cynically. Geoff might unjustly blame Robin for S.P.'s death, but she supposed he had to admire his ability, even if that admiration was grudgingly given.

"Does Robin get the credit?"

Geoff frowned. "Yes. Of course."

"I don't suppose you've congratulated him." The minute she said it, she was sorry. She hadn't been back five minutes and she was provoking another argument. Damn you, Lindsay, she scolded herself. Can you never control that sharp tongue?

But Geoff didn't seem to take offense. "No," he said slowly, "I haven't. Not directly. I sent an office memo, congratulating the staff, but I haven't spoken to him."

Lindsay took his arm. "Couldn't you?" she asked gently. "It's been seven months, Geoff. Don't carry this hatred forever. You're punishing yourself as much as you are Robin. And there's the baby to think of. Wouldn't you like us to be a family again?"

"That's impossible, Lindsay. I can't forget—"

"Nor can I. But we can accept. We must accept what can't be changed."

He helped her into the car. "We'll talk about it later," he said, settling into the seat beside her.

The driver turned in the direction of Manhattan. They rode silently for a few moments, and then Lindsay said lightly, "Well, what have you been doing for fun? Dating your secretary?"

He gave a little laugh. "Hardly. Gladys isn't my type. And even if

272

I decided to play around in your absence, I'm smart enough to do it with someone outside the office."

"Did you? Outside the office, I mean?" I'm crazy! Lindsay thought. Why am I opening up this area of discussion? Do I have a subconscious wish to confess? Or does my guilt make me almost hope he's guilty too?

Geoff looked pained. "I've been faithful. I'm almost sorry to say that. Ridiculous, isn't it?"

Lindsay didn't answer. He was trying to tell her that his old problem still existed, that he couldn't make love to her. She wished with all her heart he could. Then the other thing would no longer be necessary. Deliberately, she changed the subject and began to chatter about her trip. Marty had done a very good job in her absence, she said. She'd talked to him once a week and things were well in hand. In fact, she went on, she probably could make more frequent buying trips in the future, now that she knew the business wouldn't suffer. There were areas other than England she wanted to explore: France, Italy, Spain. The European market changed constantly.

Geoff listened almost with amusement. "Sounds like *you're* planning to become the traveling member of the family."

"Oh, not really," she said hastily. Then, "But maybe I should. My absence seems to agree with you. I haven't seen you look this well in ages."

He took a deep breath. There had been times in the past few weeks when he felt he might be a man again. With Adele. She was so soothing, so unthreatening, and yet her very coolness produced the first stirring of excitement he'd felt in a long while. He'd suppressed his feelings, not only because of Lindsay but because he couldn't be entirely sure such attentions would be welcomed by Adele, though he felt they would. Most of all, he was terrified of failure. That was the truth of it. What if he approached Adele, was accepted, and then disappointed her and himself? The humiliation was too terrible to contemplate. Yet he felt happy that, for the first time in months, he wanted someone. Why, of all people, did it have to be this woman who reawakened his sensuality? Why did he sense she was physically drawn to him too? There'd been no overt moves on either side, but it was the kind of thing two adults knew without discussion.

He put aside the idea of an affair with Adele. No good. If passion returned, it must be with Lindsay. She'd been faithful and patient. Anything else would be grossly unfair. Still, he did not tell her he'd been seeing Adele, platonic as it was. Lindsay would never believe that. Sexually cold as she believed Adele to be, she'd be sure the other woman would seduce him if she could, if only in spite. She's as unreasonable about Adele, he thought ruefully, as I probably am about Robin. Maybe she's right. Maybe neither of us should carry our hatred forever.

Last night he'd told Adele that Lindsay was coming home.

"I won't be able to see as much of you," he said. "I'll miss your company, but—well, you know how it is."

If Adele was unhappy, she hid it. "Of course, Geoff. I'm sorry too, but I understand. Maybe you can pop in for a drink now and then, on your way home from the office."

"I wish it were different," he said. "I wish we could all be friends."

Adele smiled wistfully. "Yes, that would be nice, wouldn't it?"

Without thinking, he made one bold final remark. "No, it wouldn't. I'm lying. I'd like to keep on seeing you alone as I have been. What I'd really like is to . . . to know you better."

She hadn't been shocked or angry. She simply smiled again and shook her head without answering.

Thinking of that brief episode, Geoff said unexpectedly, "About Robin. I suppose you're right, Lindsay. I've let my grief consume me. In my heart, I know S.P. . . . S.P.'s death wasn't his fault, but I had to blame someone, something. He was the only one I could blame. It's terrible to know you're being unfair and that you're incapable of changing the way you feel. I . . . I can try to make it up with him, if you think he's willing. It's never easy for me to admit I'm wrong, you know that. But I have been wrong and I'm sorry."

Lindsay looked at him with astonishment which quickly changed to delight. "Darling, of course he's willing! He's been so unhappy about the way you feel. He worships you, you know." She leaned over and kissed him on the cheek. "You're doing the right thing, Geoff. It takes a big man. But I know you'll be glad." She settled back, eyes shining. "You couldn't give me a better welcome-home gift!"

Even as she spoke, she realized how that sounded. The same thought struck both of them: wanting her again would be an even better gift. Lindsay actually blushed. Never mind. His physical incapacity was certainly caused by his emotional state. If he got control of the latter, the rest would follow. She reached for his hand.

"I'm proud of you," she said.

"Damned little to be proud of. I can't promise to hug and kiss him, you know. I'm just going to try to be civilized."

Lindsay nodded. Then she said quietly, "Geoff, wouldn't you like to see the baby?"

He hesitated. "Yes," he said. "Yes, one day I would."

She crossed her fingers. "Why don't we go to Chicago next week?"

"So soon? I don't know, Lindsay. I'm not sure I'm ready for that. The pain. He'll remind me so much—"

"You're wrong. He'll make you feel happy. S.P. would want you to know your grandchild. You can give him so much, Geoff. And you'll get so much back. You were always such a wonderful father. She'd want you to give that same kind of love to John."

He hesitated. It was too fast. Maybe too soon. But who knew for sure?

"All right," he said. "Let's give it a try."

"Guess who's coming to see you, Johnny?" Robin lifted his seven-month-old son high in the air. "Your grandfather, that's who! Your mama's papa. How about that, sport? Isn't that great news?"

The baby laughed, waving his little arms in delight as Robin swooped him up and down exuberantly.

"We'll show him what a big, tough fellow you are, won't we?" Robin looked at his son, his heart almost bursting with love as it always did when they were together. Thank God I decided to keep him with me, he thought. At first I didn't think I could bear it, seeing him every day, being reminded of S.P. But he's given me a reason to live, even to be happy when I thought I'd never know anything but despair.

He'd been fortunate to find Jane Graham, too. A cheerful woman of sixty-five, she came every morning before Robin left for the office, taking brisk charge of John until his father returned. She was as kind as a grandmother and efficient as a nanny, and she genuinely loved the baby. He was more to her than a child she was hired to care for. She treated him as though he were one of her own.

"Poor little motherless tyke," she said the first time she saw him. "There, there, Johnny darlin'. Don't you worry. Auntie Jane will take good care of you." She'd turned a sweet, wrinkled face to Robin. "And don't you worry either, Mr. Darnevale. I raised six of my own, God bless 'em, and I have ten grandchildren scattered every which way

275

around the country. I don't see them often. It'll be nice to have a baby to fuss over again."

"I'll be enormously grateful to you, Mrs. Graham. He's so damned little. I wasn't sure how I was going to handle it until you appeared."

"Well, don't you fret. I'll be here every day, rain or shine."

"Only five days a week," Robin said. "I'll take care of him nights and weekends."

"All right, but I can always come extra time if you want to go somewhere of an evening or a Saturday or Sunday. I'm glad to have something to fill my time. I'm a widow, and television's terrible on the weekends. No game shows or soap operas." She smiled. "I miss my husband. Gone eight years and I still look for him around the house, automatic-like."

"My wife . . . my wife died six weeks ago, Mrs. Graham. I've had a trained nurse looking after John since then, but now he just needs good motherly care."

"And he'll surely get it from me, I promise you that." She looked troubled. "I'm sorry about your wife. She must have been very young. Was it an accident, if you don't mind my asking?"

"No," Robin said painfully. "She died in childbirth."

"God save us! What a terrible thing! And so rare. You hardly hear of that these days."

He swallowed hard. "They did everything they could."

"I'm sure of that, sir. And you mustn't blame yourself. People do. A man especially, I guess, in a case like that. But you have to believe it was the will of the Lord, Mr. Darnevale. There's no other way to explain it."

He thought of the abortion S.P. had wanted. Was that the will of the Lord too, that he deny her the thing that might have saved her life? He tried to believe so. He tried to believe there was some divine purpose in all this misery, that John was meant for great things, or that S.P. was spared some terrible thing later in her life. It was all he had to hang onto: blind faith. Without it, he'd have tumbled into a pit of suffocating sorrow, never to surface again.

Remarkable the recuperative powers of humans, he thought now. Not that his sadness had disappeared. Far from it. He thought of S.P. every day of his life, longed for her, wept at night because she wasn't beside him. But he was young and healthy and he had John. Thank you, he said to her memory. Thank you for the precious gift you left me.

Their friends, his and S.P.'s, cautiously suggested he start getting back into the world. They all had attractive, unmarried women friends he'd enjoy dating, they said. It was no good his doing nothing but working and staying home with John.

Robin appreciated their concern and politely put them off. He wasn't ready to see another woman, not even in a casual way. One day he would be, but not yet. It was too soon. The memory of his wife was too fresh, the horror of her unexpected death still too vivid. He needed to heal. For now, the demands of the office and the fascination of the baby were enough. He was lonely, but even that was preferable to the role of "eligible man," for he was too full of sorrow to make the small talk and go through the amenities expected of him if he resumed any kind of social life. And too full of remorse, as well. Much as he adored his son, John was unwitting proof of his father's selfishness. If I hadn't insisted the boy be born, he thought over and over again, I'd still have her, and God help me, if I had it to do over again, I'd sacrifice John. He was not a religious man, but he prayed S.P. knew and forgave him, since he found it impossible to forgive himself.

When Lindsay telephoned and said she and Geoff would like to come and see him and the baby, Robin greeted the news half joyously and half anxiously. He'd had no conversation with his father-in-law all these months. Now they were arriving for a family visit! He wondered why Geoff had agreed to it. He hoped everything would go well. It was bound to be awkward. Robin recalled all too vividly that terrible scene in the hospital when Geoff called him a murderer and would have physically attacked him if Lindsay had not managed to calm him down. She'll probably be the buffer again, Robin thought. Thank God for her level-headedness.

Deliberately, he did not book them into the Drake, where they'd spent those terrible few days last December. He got them a suite at a small elegant hotel on Lakeshore Drive, not too far from his apartment, sent flowers to arrive a few hours before they did, arranged a car and driver to meet them at O'Hare Airport. He would go out with the car, to welcome them. He thought of taking John with him, and then realized that was crazy. You didn't drag a seven-month-old infant to an airport, not even with Mrs. Graham to look after him. Anyway, it would look hokey, as though he'd set up a public meeting between Geoff and his grandson to avoid an emotional private confrontation.

He was there, alone, when they came off the plane. Lindsay looked marvelous. She seemed ten years younger. She hugged Robin and kissed him warmly on both cheeks. Geoff hung back a moment and then shook his son-in-law's hand almost formally.

"I'm happy to see you, sir," Robin said.

"Good to see you." Geoff's voice was almost gruff.

Lindsay linked arms with both of them as they walked toward the luggage area. "You're looking well, Robin. Congratulations on the new account! Geoff says you did a marvelous job of bringing that into the agency. He says there were tough competition from four other shops. You must have worked your head off!"

"Thanks. It was a team effort. Everybody helped."

"Well, of course! I mean, these things are never accomplished by one person, are they? It's like the Academy Awards. Boring as those tributes to the 'little people' are, I'm always glad when the star has enough humility to admit he owes a lot to others."

She knew how inane this nonstop chatter sounded, but she couldn't seem to help it. I'm nervous, she thought, nervous as a cat. How would Geoff react when he saw little John? Would he and Robin ever feel easy with each other again? What would Geoff say and do when he saw their daughter's child? It will be all right, she reassured herself. He wanted to come. I didn't drag him here.

Geoff and Robin were equally aware that she was babbling on in an effort to cover the strain between them, and they were both grateful. But each, in his own way, felt slightly annoyed.

Why does she always try to run interference in every difficult situation? Geoff thought almost angrily. It's as though she's afraid I'll get out of line, as though she has no confidence in my control. No, that wasn't fair. She had every reason to be jittery after the way I behaved last time I was here. I'm edgy too. Maybe it was a mistake to come.

When are they going to ask for John? Robin wondered. She's deliberately not talking about him, as if she's afraid to bring up the subject. And Geoffrey's so silent, almost sullen. Why the hell did he come if he still hates me so much?

In the limousine, things weren't much better. Lindsay stared at the driver's back, thinking of Reg. She thought of him every time she was in a chauffeur-driven car, missing him, wishing those broad shoulders she

278

knew so well were behind the wheel. She fell silent, and so did the men with her. The drive into town seemed endless, and with each mile her apprehension increased. Geoff wasn't as ready for this as she'd hoped. And Robin was tongue-tied, whether with anxiety or resentment, she couldn't tell. None of them had so much as mentioned the baby. He was the reason they were together at last, but it was as though he didn't exist. To hell with this, Lindsay thought. Somebody has to put an end to this ridiculous charade.

As they glided up Michigan Boulevard toward the hotel, she said calmly, "When are we going to see John, Robin dear?"

"As soon as you want to. I'm sure Mrs. Graham has him all spruced up for the occasion."

"Let's go there now, before we check into the hotel." Lindsay turned to Geoff. "All right with you, darling? I can't wait to see him." She looked expectantly at her husband, willing him to agree.

"Sure," Goeff said. "Why not?"

The meeting between Geoff and his grandson was a disaster. Mrs. Graham had, indeed, dressed him in his best romper suit, one Lindsay had sent from New York. The baby looked adorable in the little yellow outfit with a picture of Snoopy embroidered on the collar, and he was smiling and cooing as his nurse brought him into the living room. Knowing this was John's first visit with his grandfather, she went directly to Geoff, offering the baby to him.

"Here you are, Mr. Murray. Here's your beautiful boy."

Involuntarily, Geoff took a step backward.

"You can hold him, sir," Mrs. Graham said. "He's heavy, but you don't have to be afraid of dropping him. Look how he smiles at his granddaddy, Mr. Darnevale! He's a smart one, our little John. He knows who loves him."

Dear God, he isn't going to take him! Lindsay thought with dismay. Geoff seemed frozen, as though he were being offered some evil thing. His face contorted with anguish, but she saw a mist come into his eyes and then, robotlike, he stretched out his arms and let Mrs. Graham put John into them. Suddenly, his face crumbled as he looked down at the laughing child. Tears ran down his cheeks.

"He . . . he's beautiful," Geoff said brokenly. "My grandson. My baby's child." He held John so tightly that the baby began to squirm and the laughter changed to howls of protest.

"Darling, you're squeezing the life out of him," Lindsay said mildly.

"What? Oh, I'm sorry." He loosened his grip. "I didn't think. I saw . . . I saw his mother. It was like holding her again." Geoff looked stricken.

"Here, Mrs. Graham, you'd better take him. I'm out of practice."

"Let me." Lindsay took John from him, cradling the infant in her arms, making reassuring little noises until he stopped crying and presented them, once again, with his sunny smile. "There, sweetheart," she said, "your grandaddy didn't mean to frighten you. He's just very, very glad to see you, darling. That was a bear hug, Johnny." Over his head she smiled at Geoff, as though to say thank you for responding as I hoped. But it was a fleeting moment of relief.

Geoff looked anything but happy. He didn't return her gaze and he didn't look at the child again. Aimlessly, he began to wander around the living room, picking up small objects, once looking briefly at a photograph of S.P. in her wedding gown and hurriedly putting it down as though he couldn't bear the sight. He allowed no pictures of their daughter in the apartment in New York. He wants no reminders, Lindsay realized sadly. He doesn't even want to see her child.

Robin said nothing, but he knew, as well as Lindsay did, that while Geoff had seemed to soften for one moment, he was unable to accept John. In his mind, the baby, like its father, had taken from him the most precious thing in the world. He couldn't tolerate the sight of Robin. He couldn't even be near this innocent child. I hoped so much, Robin thought. I wanted them to love each other. It's no use. He can't handle it.

"I think we should be getting on to the hotel, Lindsay. We haven't even checked in. They may not hold our rooms."

"All right, Geoff." She handed John back to his nurse. "Thank you for taking such good care of him, Mrs. Graham. I can see how you love him."

"I do, indeed, Mrs. Murray. He's such a good baby. And Mr. Darnevale's a wonderful father. It's not often you find a man as patient and devoted as your son-in-law. He gives his life to this child. You should see Johnny when Mr. D comes home in the evening. His little face lights up like a Christmas tree!"

Robin tried to laugh. "You're biased, Mrs. Graham. He loves you more than he does me."

"Don't you believe that for a second, Mrs. Murray. John waits for his daddy. That might sound crazy, him being so young, but he does. I can see it."

"I'm sure he does," Lindsay said. "Mr. Darnevale is just being modest."

"Lindsay!" Geoff's voice was sharp. "We really have to go."

She nodded. "Join us for dinner tonight, Robin?"

He hesitated. "Well, if you're not too tired—"

"What kind of talk is that?" Mrs. Graham said. "You know you planned to have dinner with your family. I've made all arrangements to stay."

"She bosses me a lot," Robin said, smiling. "All right. Pick you up about eight? I thought we might go to Maxime's." He turned to Geoff. "That suit you, sir?"

"Fine. Good-bye, Mrs. Graham. Nice to have met you."

"I'm sure I'll see you again, Mr. Murray. You'll be back tomorrow, won't you?"

Geoff was already halfway out the door. He pretended not to hear.

They left Chicago the next afternoon. Lindsay went to the apartment to try to explain to Robin, but he wouldn't let her.

"You don't have to tell me," he said. "I saw it all yesterday. He can't accept John. It hurt too much to see S.P.'s baby. I understand."

"I'm sorry," Lindsay said helplessly. "He was like a deaf-mute at dinner last night. It must have been agony for you too. I do apologize. He can't help it. He's really a sensitive man, you know. Maybe one day he'll be strong enough to accept what happened. I thought he was ready to. He seemed to be when we discussed it in New York. Even for a few minutes yesterday, I hoped—"

Robin cut her short. "I know. We all wanted it to turn out differently. Even *he* did, I'm sure. But he couldn't make it happen." He looked sympathetic. "It must be hard for you, living with that kind of grief. I know you've suffered just as much, but you face facts, even when they're hideous. I do too, as best as I can. We'll be all right. But what about him?"

Lindsay shook her head. "I don't know, Robin. I just don't know."

On the plane back to New York, Geoff halfheartedly tried to

281

apologize. "I know you're disappointed, Lind. So am I. I wanted to be able to take that child to my heart. But I couldn't." His voice was barely audible. "Yesterday, when you said I was squeezing the life out of him, God forgive me, I almost wanted to. I know he's innocent, but when I looked at him I hated him. For the first moment I was overcome. I thought I'd been wrong, that I could love him. But then I saw . . . her. And it all came back, all the anger of remembering that if it weren't for that baby she'd be alive. I know I'm a beast to feel as I do. But it will never will be any different."

He expected Lindsay to lash out at him, to tell him he was selfish and cruel and virtually insane. He'd expected it last night when he told her he wanted to go home right away. But she hadn't been angry. She still wasn't. Only sad. Regretful. And incredibly understanding.

"You can't help how you feel, Geoff. I'm sorry for you; you're missing something wonderful. But you can't order your mind to accept what your heart will not."

Her gentleness surprised him. In the ten days since her return from England, she seemed a different person. The old, angry, rebellious Lindsay had not reappeared. The woman who came back was almost serene, like a devoted sister. What happened over there? he wondered. What caused this complete change of attitude? Last night he'd told her to stay on in Chicago, even though he couldn't, but Lindsay refused.

"No, I'll go back with you. I can come again whenever I feel like it. I think you need me more than Robin and John do. I don't want you to go back alone to that empty apartment."

Had three weeks away from him produced such an alteration in personality? It was hard to believe. Harder still to think it was a permanent thing. He was both glad and sorry. It made life more pleasant at home. But it made him more guilty about the fact that he no longer loved her.

And it made the thought of Adele utterly impossible.

24

*I*n mid-August, Lindsay decided to return to Europe. She'd been home only six weeks, but they'd been restless ones. Her relationship with Geoff was placid. There were no arguments, no scenes, but there was also no fire. Our marriage has become totally colorless, she thought with regret. Washed out. Washed up. How is it possible to love in a two-dimensional way? That's what I'm doing. He's there, my husband, and I still love him, but life with him is a study in pastels. A pale, boring, gently tinted picture.

The image reminded her of Adele and Adele's apartment, all subdued and sickly sweet. Lindsay had not been in that apartment since the night of her father's death. Geoff had. He liked the woman. She wondered whether he still dropped in to see her on his way home from the office. He never mentioned her as he did in the days after Howard died, when Adele wouldn't write a check for the phone bill without asking Geoff's opinion. Maybe she still asked Geoff's advice. Lindsay didn't know. She'd put Adele out of her life, rarely thought of her. For some reason, she imagined Geoff had too. He clearly was interested in no woman, not even his wife.

A month after the unhappy visit to Chicago, Lindsay had, once again, suggested he seek professional help. She'd mentioned it before and Geoff had angrily rejected the idea that his impotence could be cured by therapy. This time he'd merely shaken his head in resignation, not even answering. She'd been stirred to the first feeling of anger she'd expressed since her return.

"Dammit, Geoff, don't you want to get well? Aren't you even curious to find out what's caused your condition?

He hadn't risen to the bait. "I know what caused it. So do you."

"No. If you're blaming it on S.P.'s death, you're wrong. You were disinterested in me long before. But even if I accepted our loss as the reason for your total abstinence, I'd still have to say there's something unnatural about that too. It's been eight months. People never entirely get over the death of a child, but they don't stop living like normal wives and husbands. If anything, they're drawn closer together, for comfort, if nothing else."

"I'm sorry, Lind. It hasn't worked that way for me. I know it's hard on you. You're a physical person. Sooner or later, you'll find a lover. I know that. I'll have driven you to it."

Stop being such a damned martyr! she wanted to say. Be a man, the way you used to be! But she held back the impatient words. "And that wouldn't upset you?"

"I told you before. It would, but I'd have to accept it."

She was tempted to tell him she already had found someone. But why do that? She didn't believe he'd take such news calmly. No one would unless he really didn't give a damn, and Lindsay didn't believe that was true. She felt he still loved her. She didn't want to make him unhappier than he already was.

When she announced she was going back to Europe, he'd merely said, "So soon?"

"I left a lot of things undone. Since I've been home, I've heard of other places I didn't get to, in the north of England. And I should do France as well, even though it's the tourist season and probably will be crowded as hell." She felt a little ashamed, he was so unsuspecting. "You don't mind, do you?"

"No. You're free to do what you want."

She longed to say she really wanted to be with him, intimately. She looked forward to seeing Reg for the pure sexuality of it, but she'd gladly have foregone that forever if only Geoff would love her. She was using Reg, she knew. Just as Howard used women other than his wife, as Geoff had once used Pamela. Reg filled a need. He was a convenience, having nothing to do with her heart. Did that make her a "loose woman," she wondered? No, she thought, it makes me a modern one, free of the old strictures and taboos. Like a man, I can take sex for its own sake, without emotional involvement.

But she could not sincerely believe, as some freethinkers did, that an extramarital affair helped hold a marriage together. A corner of her conscience bothered her. True, this release made it possible for her to stay married to Geoff. But not the way she'd have preferred to be married. Not at all.

All right, she told herself sternly, that's enough of that! Go to Reg and get these longings out of your system. You have no alternative.

She cabled Coronet Town Cars, giving them her flight number and arrival time. She also added REQUEST DRIVER REGINALD MARKS DURING MY STAY. HE IS MOST COMPETENT AND ACCOMMODATING.

Well, that was true enough. She hoped they'd show Reg the cable. He'd get a kick out of it. It was more amusing to "engage his services" this way. It would give them something to talk about, at least.

For two weeks after Lindsay left, Geoff didn't call Adele. He made up his mind he wouldn't. What was the point? He was afraid he'd really get involved this time. He'd not even spoken to her since Lindsay's return at the end of June, except to tell her they were going to Chicago. He'd not called since, almost ashamed to admit how he felt toward his own grandchild. More than that, he wouldn't risk seeing Adele alone any more. It was unfair to Lindsay, who'd been so kind and patient.

But he was terribly lonely. Politely estranged as they were, he missed his wife. Missed the awareness of another living soul in the empty apartment, the charming face across the dinner table, the stimulation of her enthusiastic chatter about the remarkable progress of her antiques business.

He had trouble sleeping, and late one night he suddenly realized, to his joy and astonishment, that he wanted her. The discovery filled him with elation. He remembered their lovemaking, every detail of it, and felt the old, welcome hunger. Dammit, he thought, half amused, wouldn't it be just my luck that the urge returns when she's thousands of miles away! But if it had come back once, it would again. He'd have to tell her. Maybe she'd cut short her trip and come home for a reunion.

He fished out the itinerary she had left in case of an emergency. She was in the south of France, in Beaulieu, at a hotel called La Reserve. Geoff glanced at his watch. Midnight. Six in the morning there. Early to call, but this was a special occasion. He couldn't wait to share the happy news with her.

Jubilant with relief, he placed a person-to-person call. After a slight pause, he heard the overseas operator in conversation with the night clerk at La Reserve.

"New York calling Mrs. Geoffrey Murray, person-to-person."

The heavily accented voice of a man was faint but clear. "*Attendez, s'il vous plaît.* Ah, yes. Suite Sixteen. You wish to speak with Madame Murray or Monsieur Murray?"

The New York operator spoke to Geoff as though he couldn't hear the conversation. "Did you want Mrs. Murray or Mr. Murray, sir?"

Idiots! "There *is* no Monsieur Murray there, operator. They're confused." He forgot for a second that the desk clerk could also hear him. "Damned dumb Frenchman. Tell him he's wrong. Lord, they can't even get a message straight over there!"

Before the operator could repeat the call, the clerk responded coldly. "Beg pardon, madame. I have made no mistake. Your party is the one who is not correct. Madame Murray and Monsieur Murray occupy Suite Sixteen. Which one does the gentleman desire?"

"Sir?" the New York voice inquired. "Is it still *Mrs.* Murray you want?"

Geoff's hand felt leaden on the receiver. "Never mind," he said. "Cancel the call, please, operator."

He hung up, feeling numb. Lindsay had a man with her. Some bastard who was even using *his* name. How dare she! he thought furiously. Why not? a little voice inside answered. You've expected it for a long time. You've almost encouraged it. Why are you so outraged now that it's happened? Because of the way she handled it, he decided, trying to be rational. My God, if she had to have an affair, what kind of man has she chosen? She must have bought him, must be paying his way. Any man with two nickels to rub together would have his own room and be registered under his own name. What self-respecting man would masquerade as someone else?

He felt a terrible sense of desolation, picturing Lindsay in bed with another man. Nothing had prepared him for this actuality. He'd been free enough with his high-flown theories about her needs, but when the chips were down he hated the idea of Lindsay belonging, even temporarily, to someone else. She was his wife, dammit! And you've been some lousy husband to her, he thought in the next breath. You've caused this. If you'd given Lindsay what she needs, this never would have happened.

All right. She'd forgiven him his infidelities. He'd forgive hers. He wouldn't even tell her he knew. When she came home, he'd be waiting

286

for her, ready to make love in a way that would make her forget whoever it was she'd picked up in Europe.

God, he prayed, let that happen, please. Don't let my imagination come between us. I don't want these mental pictures of Lindsay with another man. Let me be whole again, for both our sakes.

Unaware of the phone call, Lindsay was happy. The south of France was so beautiful, so romantic; it was everything she'd ever heard about. The Côte d'Azur, playground of the beautiful people. She and Reg toured the countryside, exploring out-of-the-way villages. This time she sat up front beside him in the Mercedes she'd had shipped over from England.

"I won't drive through France looking like some overstuffed dowager in the back of a big black car," she told him when he met her in London. "I'll make arrangements with Coronet for something less regal, for God's sake! And I'll tell them they're to let you come to the Continent with me. They'll do that, won't they?"

Reg smiled. "It's quite usual, madam. We're frequently engaged for services outside the country." He looked at her with desire. "I've missed you, luv. You can't imagine how happy I am that you came back so soon."

"I was afraid you'd find some young thing if I didn't," Lindsay teased. "A big, gorgeous man like you. You must have to fight off the ladies with baseball bats. Or is it cricket bats?"

"Neither. I haven't found anyone like you. Would you believe I've been with no one since June?"

Lindsay felt a slight twinge of alarm. He mustn't read more into this than she intended. Of course he wouldn't, she told herself. He'd been the one, early on, who'd said he only fitted into her life as a lover. But he mustn't misunderstand her early return. She didn't love him; she simply needed him. And she wasn't going to tell him she'd had no one either. It might sound as though she'd been pining for him.

"I think you're a lovely liar," she said lightly. "You're dear to spare my feelings, but you don't have to. I don't expect fidelity, for heaven's sake, except when I'm on the premises! And then, by golly, I demand it! And the same, dear heart, goes for you."

"You're beautiful, Lindsay."

"Of course," she said flippantly. "Everybody knows that."

But there was a change in him this time. He didn't protest any of the arrangements she made, not even when they checked into hotels under the name of Mr. and Mrs. Geoffrey Murray. It hadn't been easy to do. It was necessary to present both passports, but Reg, with a twenty- or fifty-dollar bill supplied by Lindsay, always managed to get the concierge aside and make a deal.

"You can sign me in under Marks," he'd say quietly, "but the lady doesn't wish to have anyone in the hotel know about our . . . arrangement. She'd like the suite registered as Monsieur and Madame Murray." He'd smile conspiratorially. "You know how Americans are. So bloody concerned about appearances."

The French were adept at looking the other way when it came to matters of the heart. Besides, they knew all Americans were peculiar, particularly rich females touring with their lovers. It seemed stupid to Reg. It would have been just as easy for him to take a room and still spend his nights in Lindsay's, but she had an odd, stubborn way of looking at it.

"I want to wake up next to you. I know room service waiters don't give a damn," she said, "but I'll just be more relaxed if the staff and anybody we meet thinks we're married." She smiled. "That's naïve, isn't it? But it makes me more comfortable."

All right, Reg thought. If it makes her happy, what difference?

"You're a little daft, you know. All this trouble and money for nothing. Why don't we register as Mr. and Mrs. Reginald Marks? We could explain that your passport is in your professional name or some such thing. Why must we be Murrays? I don't mind, actually, though if you call me Geoffrey in public I probably shan't answer."

"Darling, I have to be available under my own name in case there's an emergency at home. My mother is seventy-eight years old. One never knows. And I have a little grandson. Also there's my business. They might try to reach me."

"And your husband?"

Did he sound just a shade jealous?

"He won't call. We don't have that much to say to each other even face to face."

It worked out beautifully. They lingered on into September, finally driving slowly back through the beautiful French countryside to Paris, stopping at a charming *auberge* every night, eating exquisite food and drinking fine wine and making passionate love. Lindsay managed to make enough purchases to justify the trip as a business expense. She didn't need anything. She'd bought enough in England in June to carry her into the fall selling season, but she stumbled on some lovely old French furniture and was delighted with her treasures.

In Paris, she decided it was too risky to do the "Mr. and Mrs. Murray" thing. There was too much chance of running into someone she knew from New York. Besides, the Plaza Athénée would not be so understanding about the unorthodox passport arrangements. She and Reg took separate accommodations, spending their nights together in her suite but making sure, as they had at the Savoy, that she was alone in her room at breakfast time.

She decided to fly home from Paris, letting Reg take the car back to London. They'd been together nearly six weeks. It was early October, and Paris was soft and even more romantic, somehow, than the hot, sun-filled Côte d'Azur.

"I hate to leave you, darling," she said on their last night.

"Must you?"

"You know I must. Nothing's changed, Reg dear. I still have a family. I have to go home."

"I know. It's been wonderful, Lindsay."

"Perfect."

He didn't ask her when she'd return. By tacit agreement, they behaved as though they knew there'd be another time and there was no need to ask when. Sometimes Lindsay felt rather unfair about the arrangement. All well and good for her to have two worlds, but what of Reg? She asked him once whether he might not marry one day.

"Would you be heartbroken?" He was obviously teasing.

"Only a little. I'm disgustingly selfish, but only up to a point. You *should* marry, Reg. You'd be a marvelous husband."

"Lindsay, I told you the first time we met that the kind of woman I want, I can't have." With uncharacteristic openness he added, "And now I know that's true. I've met the only woman I want and I can't have her, except now and again."

"Don't say a thing like that! You don't mean it. You know it isn't possible. Don't make me feel worse than I already do."

He'd held her close. "I'm not expecting anything, luv. You know that. We understand each other perfectly." He laughed easily. "My word, old girl, all my friends know I'm a ruddy confirmed bachelor. It wouldn't be cricket to disappoint them."

She smiled at his parody of upper-class English speech, but her heart was heavy. If only Geoff loved me this way, she thought. Or if only I loved Reg enough to dare try to make a life with him. Both, regrettably, were impossible.

He'd been determined not to do it, but the day after the phone call to France, Geoffrey sought out Adele. He argued with himself before he did. It was dangerous. Unfair to her. He was a despicable fool, but he was lonely and, despite the sophisticated attitude he tried to assume, hurt and disappointed by Lindsay's unfaithfulness. Not to be ignored, either, was the return of his sexual drive. No explanation for it. Perhaps, as Lindsay had said, he was finally coming to grips with his bereavement, and with his emotional recovery his physical well-being was restored.

Almost nine months, he thought sadly, since they'd lost S.P. Nine months for gestation, nine months for grieving. Like a woman carrying a child, perhaps he too had come full term.

Strange. He might have held firm to his resolve to wait for Lindsay had it not been for Gladys O'Reilly. The morning after he learned about "Mr. Murray," he appeared early at the office, haggard and red-eyed. He'd not slept a wink all night and knew he looked as terrible as he felt.

"Are you all right?" his secretary asked solicitously. "You don't look well, Mr. Murray. Anything I can do?"

"No thanks. I'm just a little off my feet. Probably something I ate."

"Or *didn't* eat. I don't think you take care of yourself when Mrs. Murray's away. Isn't that housekeeper feeding you properly?"

She sounded so like a concerned mother that Geoff smiled. "Don't fuss over me, Gladys. The meals are fine. It's just that I don't have much appetite. Eating alone is a good way to lose weight. Maybe I'll write a book about it. Diet books are sure-fire best-sellers. I could call it 'Slimness Through Solitude.' Or maybe 'Desserts for the Deserted.' What do you think?"

"I don't think it's very funny."

"Sorry. I guess you're right. This doesn't seem to be my morning for one-liners. The fact is, I couldn't sleep last night. I'll make up for it tonight. To bed by eight, lights out by nine, and tomorrow I'll be as good as any other creaky old middle-aged man. Not to worry, Gladys."

"Not to worry." That was Pam's favorite phrase. He rarely

thought of her any more, could hardly remember her face. But he could still remember the touch of her, the laughter and the loving. Geoff's face softened with the memory, making him look young and vulnerable.

Impulsively, Gladys stepped out of character for the first time in fifteen years. "Mr. Murray, would you have dinner with me tonight?"

He was startled. "What?"

"Why don't you come to my place for dinner? I may not be as good a cook as the one you have at home, but I'm better company. I'll get a couple of steaks and make a salad. You can bring some wine, if you like. You need company." She hesitated and then said pointedly, *"Female* company, I imagine." There was no mistaking the look in her eyes.

Geoff stared at her. My God, Gladys is giving me an open invitation! After all these years. I can't believe it. She's sorry for me. Jesus, I really must look like a basket case to warrant such pity! He tried to turn her unmistakable overture into a joke.

"What is this? Be-Kind-to-the-Boss Week?" He smiled. "It's sweet of you, but it's enough that you have me on your hands all day. Putting up with me for the evening is above and beyond the call of duty. Thanks anyway, Gladys. Maybe you and Harry could go out to dinner with me one evening soon."

"I didn't plan to include Harry. I thought it would be just you and me. A nice quiet evening at home. Harry's upstate visiting his mother for a few days, so you see I'm as lonely as you are."

Her meaning was obvious, but Geoff still tried to pretend he didn't understand. "We won't die of our temporary loneliness, either of us. I really appreciate your kindness, but I'll take a rain check. You don't have to worry about me, though it's typical of you. I do appreciate it. You're a good friend."

She looked as though she wanted to hit him. "Friend? Is that the only way you've ever thought of me, as a friend? Are you really so blind? Can't you see I've always loved—"

He interrupted her. "Don't say things we'll both regret. I'm flattered. And grateful. You're an understanding woman. My God, we've worked together so closely for fifteen years that you seem part of me. I couldn't bear to lose you. Don't spoil it. Don't make it impossible for us to go on working together."

Don't humiliate yourself, he added silently. And don't say things that will make me feel like a bastard because I don't want you as you

291

seem to want me. I'm flattered, that's true. I do want someone. But not like this. Not a shabby little affair that would be messy the morning after.

Gladys drew herself up proudly. "I apologize, Mr. Murray. Please forgive me for forgetting my place."

"Gladys, don't. You know I didn't mean it that way. It's just that I—"

"Never mind. I made a mistake. Let's both forget it, okay?" She busied herself straightening papers on his desk. "I think you'd better return these phone calls first. And Ben Barker wants to meet with you about the Mammoth Radio campaign. Will there be anything else?"

He felt foolish and helpless. "No. Not right now." He tried again to explain. "Please don't be angry. You're very desirable. It's only that I know you—that is, *we*—would regret getting involved. They never work out, these office romances. Besides, you have Harry."

"And you? What do you have? A bored wife who's so in love with you she runs off to Europe every chance she gets? Or maybe that vapid fool who wishes she could have married you instead of your father-in-law? What makes *you* so damned pure, Mr. Geoffrey Murray? Is it beneath you to be loved by a secretary? Do you only go to bed with women in the Social Register?"

He felt sick. Why had he let this get so far? Why hadn't he just let her leave the office with dignity when she tried to? No, he had to try to explain, to soften the rejection, and now she'd blown it. After that insulting outburst, she couldn't stay. Damn women! Damn his own big mouth! He took a deep breath.

"Gladys, if you think that way, I don't know how we can go on working together."

"You won't have to worry about it. You have my resignation as of now."

He wanted to stop her, to tell her it was silly, that this was only a stupid misunderstanding. Maybe he was wrong. Maybe he should have accepted her invitation. She was a sensible woman. Perhaps she could have handled it. But could I? Geoff wondered. No. No way. He couldn't imagine himself as the stereotype boss who crawled into bed with his secretary and then was all business in the office.

"Very well," he said. "I'm sorry, Gladys. Terribly, terribly sorry."

"I'm not," she said evenly. "I'm glad I see you for the snob you really are."

After she left, he sat for a long time staring at the closed door of his office. He supposed he should feel some kind of ridiculous male pride that he was the object of such blatant desire. Most men would be pleased to know they were still attractive enough to be invited to bed without having to ask for it. He felt only empty and inadequate. Was Gladys right? Did he have some kind of class-conscious hang-up that made him able to relate only to women of his own kind? It seemed to be true. Lindsay was of his world. Pamela came from a good background. He didn't count those faceless females he used to go through the motions with out of town. They didn't expect an ongoing affair; they were one-night entertainment, no more meaningful than attending a burlesque show.

He was aware that he was aroused. Why? Was it memories of past lovemaking or the excitement of having Gladys offer herself to him? He'd heard that many men were more passionate after an argument. It had never happened to him that way, but now he was almost frantic. Before he could change his mind, he dialed Adele's number.

"I'd like to see you this evening, if you're free."

She sounded as though she expected his call. "I'd like that too. Can you come for dinner?"

"Fine. Seven-ish?"

"I'll be looking forward to it, Geoff."

He hung up and sat back in his big chair, wondering why he'd done what he'd vowed not to do. Lust, he thought bitterly. You're a lecherous old seducer. He knew he'd go to bed with Adele that night if she'd let him, and he had little doubt that she would.

Why not? he thought angrily. Lindsay's getting what she wants. Am I not entitled to the same? And Adele. He seriously doubted that she'd ever known what it was like to be with a virile man. He suspected that beneath that demure exterior lay a passionate woman, a responsive one never fully awakened by the father figure she'd married.

For a fleeting moment, the old fear that he couldn't perform came back to haunt him, but it was only a momentary anxiety. He'd had more than one indication that all was well again with him. His pulse raced. God! he thought, if Adele doesn't want me, I'll go crazy.

He need not have worried. It was as though she'd read his mind over the phone, even though the words between them had been as casual as ever. She greeted him at the door in a caftan that was almost, but not quite, see-through, and her greeting told him what he needed to know.

293

"I sent Cook home for the night," she said. "She left us a cold supper. We can eat it whenever we're ready."

He looked at her, marveling at her coolness. Adele smiled.

"We've known each other too long to be coy, haven't we, Geoff? Your voice gave you away. You didn't know that, did you? It was the most seductive voice I've ever heard." She put her arms around him. "I've been waiting years to hear that voice. If you didn't mean it, I'll try to convince you."

He held her tightly, feeling the firm body beneath the sheer robe.

"Are you sure, Adele? I can't offer you marriage. We know that."

She understood. "I'm not looking for marriage. Only love." She threw her head back and laughed. "Not even love, perhaps."

Geoff kissed the slender white throat and then, more passionately, the open, willing mouth. How hungry he was. How starved for this.

"I'm glad dinner can wait," he whispered. "I'm not sure when I'll be ready for food."

Adele ran her hands down his back. "Carry me," she said softly.

He picked her up, surprised to feel how light she was. Her eyes were closed, a smile on her lips. For all her years, she was like a sensuous child.

It's going to be wonderful, Geoff thought as they moved to her bedroom. How fabulous to feel this way again. And to know, with certainty, how it was going to be. . . .

"James must have known," he said later. "He must have intuitively been sure you were the most exciting woman in the world. Good God, Adele, why did you waste your youth on that old man?"

She put a finger lightly on his mouth. "Hush. We won't speak of the past. Or the future."

He bit back the words he wanted to say. Caution, Geoff. Be sure before you speak. Be certain you want this for more than a night. It's been so long for you. Maybe you're carried away by the triumph of the moment. Don't be rash. There's too much to consider. Wait. Go slowly.

But by the time his wife returned, he knew he was totally, willingly captivated. It only remained now to tell Lindsay.

25

*L*indsay came home determined to repair her shaky marriage. She was a little disappointed that Geoff had sent a car to the airport for her. She'd rather hoped he'd be there himself. I really missed him, she thought. Reg is wonderful, but I missed Geoff and the life he represents. We're *right* together, always have been. There've been some bad years lately, but if I try harder I know I can set things straight because that's the way I want it to be. I haven't been soft enough, giving enough. From now on, I'm going to devote myself to him, to us.

She went as far as half deciding to give up the antiques business. In a way, she supposed, it threatened Geoff. Men didn't like successful, independent women. Not unless they were so secure within themselves that they felt no competition. The hell with the business, Lindsay thought. I proved I can do it. That's enough for me. I don't need to go on with it.

And she wouldn't go on with Reg either. He was sweet, devoted, but she didn't love him. It had been almost a relief to leave him. Their affair was too intense, too demanding. I'm forty-eight years old, Lindsay told herself. It's too much to keep acting like an oversexed twenty-one. I love to be loved, but I'll have that again with Geoff, and it will be familiar and satisfying. She was convinced that with a change in her attitude, the old excitement could be revived. Not the breathless passion of their teens but a warmer, surer, more contented desire built on the solid foundation of shared years.

It was three o'clock in the afternoon when she let herself into the apartment. She said hello to the housekeeper, dropped her coat and bag on the bed, and called Geoff's office to announce she'd arrived safely. An unfamiliar voice answered his private wire.

"Gladys? Is that you? You sound different."

"Miss O'Reilly isn't here any more. This is Mrs. Pawling, Mr. Murray's secretary. Who's calling?"

Gladys not there after fifteen years? Lindsay couldn't believe it. "This is Mrs. Murray," she said. "Is my husband in?"

"Oh. Mrs. Murray. Mr. Murray left a message for you. He said he'd be a little late getting home this evening, but he'd be there in time for dinner."

"I see. Thank you, Mrs.—"

"Pawling."

"Yes, of course. Mrs. Pawling." Curiosity overcame her. "What happened to Gladys O'Reilly?"

"I couldn't say. She left very suddenly. I've been here six weeks."

"Well. Fine. I do hope you're enjoying it."

"Very much, thank you. Mr. Murray is lovely to work for."

How very strange, Lindsay thought as she hung up. She couldn't imagine Geoff without Gladys. What on earth could have happened? She was sure Geoff hadn't fired her, not after all this time. He depended on her to run his office life. He'd never let her go. Men don't like change of any sort, Lindsay reflected. They even hate it when you move furniture. They don't like getting used to a new secretary. And they stay with wives they no longer love because it's too upsetting to think about moving out. No, Gladys must have left for some reason of her own. Maybe she married that man she was living with, though from what Lindsay gathered, Gladys wouldn't have given up her job even if she legalized her living arrangements. And she wouldn't have taken another job, even if she'd been offered a better one. She was devoted to Geoff. Sometimes Lindsay thought the woman was in love with him. She hoped Gladys wasn't sick. She was a good sort, despite her sometimes irritating, overly proprietary air. It was a mystery. She'd ask Geoff as soon as he got home.

She also wondered, idly, what was so important that he'd be late her first night back. Maybe he simply wasn't all that eager to see her. After all, the idea of a new life was strictly hers. She hoped he'd feel the same, but she didn't know. She'd written to him from Europe but never had a reply. It hadn't worried her at the time. She was moving around so fast it was almost impossible for mail to catch up. Now she felt vaguely apprehensive. What if Geoff didn't want to start over? Nonsense. Of course he would. If she was prepared to make all the concessions, why shouldn't he?

She thought of unpacking and decided to call her mother first. Pauline's still youthful-sounding voice made her feel better.

"Welcome home, darling! When did you get in? How was the trip?"

"Just came in ten minutes ago. Everything was fine. How are you?"

"Spry for a relic." Pauline sounded amused. "Not ready for the old folks' home just yet."

"And you never will be. You're going to die with your Gucci boots on, right in the middle of raising hell at some committee meeting."

"Lindsay, you are a disrespectful child and I love you to pieces."

"I love you, too, Mama. Can you come for dinner tomorrow night?"

"I'll work it out. How's Geoff?"

"Okay, I guess. He couldn't meet the plane and he's not home yet. Haven't you seen him while I've been gone?"

Pauline hesitated. "No. Not really."

"What do you mean, 'Not really'? You have or you haven't."

"I just mean he's called several times but we haven't been able to get together."

"Really? I didn't know he was so busy. I imagined him sitting alone, pining away for me. Or at least crying on your shoulder." She was only half teasing. Geoff adored Pauline. Last time Lindsay was away he'd taken her to lunch several times and to dinner once or twice. Why had he made himself so scarce this trip? For a moment she felt nervous. Could it possibly have something to do with Gladys O'Reilly? That could account for her leaving. If she and Geoff were having an affair he'd never let her stay on in the office. That wasn't his style, any more than it was Lindsay's. She remembered his saying once, about a business associate, "The guy's stupid. If he has to fool around with his secretary, why the hell doesn't he get her a job someplace else?" Lindsay felt anxious.

"Mama? Do you think Geoff's all right?"

"What do you mean, 'all right'? You'd have heard if he wasn't."

Lindsay sighed with relief. Of course. She was being foolish. She said good-bye to her mother and hung up. Just because *you've* behaved badly, Lindsay Murray, she scolded herself, don't think Geoff has too. She took a long tub filled with bubble bath and sprayed herself with the perfume he always liked. She put on a clinging jersey housecoat that showed her figure to advantage and took special pains with her hair and makeup. She grinned at herself in the mirror when she finished. You wicked witch, she said to the image. Damned if you're not out to seduce your own husband!

Pauline frowned when she hung up the phone. Obviously, Lindsay didn't know what the rest of New York did: that Geoff was seen everywhere with Adele. She'd been disbelieving when she first heard the gossip from an old friend who took fiendish glee in relaying it.

"I think you should know, Pauline, that your son-in-law is running around with your late husband's widow. Far be it from me to spread ugly tales, but I couldn't bear for you to hear it from some heartless stranger."

Pauline had stared at her, openmouthed. Then she quickly recovered. "Rubbish! I don't believe a word of it. Geoff and Adele have always been friends."

"From what I hear, they're much more than that." The woman looked sorrowful. "Oh, dear, why must I be the one to tell you? I can imagine what this does to you. Your daughter's husband, and with that terrible woman who took Howard away from you."

"No one took Howard away from me," Pauline said coldly. "I divorced him when Adele and Lindsay were children. As for Geoffrey's being unfaithful, I'm sure that's simply vicious speculation among a bunch of tiresome old women who have nothing better to do than invent sensational rumors."

"Well! If you mean me, I resent that! That's the thanks I get for forty years of friendship! I was only trying to warn you so you could warn Lindsay. My heavens, it certainly doesn't pay to try to be kind!"

"No good deed goes unpunished."

The woman was shocked. "How can you be flippant at a time like this, Pauline Thresher? All your friends are so upset at your humiliation!"

"I'll bet they are. They're probably crying their eyes out and tracking down every dirty little rumor they can pick up."

Her friend had left in a huff, no doubt to report back immediately to the others that Pauline was devastated. Well, that at least would be no lie, Pauline thought. I *am* devastated, though I made up my mind that old biddy wouldn't see it. It can't be true. Geoffrey couldn't. Not with *her*. Not with that dreadful Adele who's already caused so much pain.

But in her heart she knew it was true. And she knew Lindsay would be wounded beyond repair. She could only pray it was a passing thing and Lindsay would never find out. God knows *I* won't tell her, Pauline thought. I don't see my "duty" as Howard once saw his.

"I'm going to tell her. Tonight."

Adele looked miserable. "Oh, Geoff, I hate for you to do this. Are you sure you don't want me to be there?"

"I'm quite sure. I know you mean well, but it would only make things worse. This has to be between Lindsay and me."

"I know. It was a ridiculous suggestion. It's just that I dread the idea of your facing this alone. God knows how she'll take it. One thing is certain: she could handle it better if it were any other woman but me."

"But it *is* you," Geoff said. He got to his feet. "I'd better be going. It's nearly seven. I'll call you later, darling."

"Yes. Please do. I'll be so anxious."

He kissed her gently. "Don't be. Lindsay constantly surprises me. She may take this a helluva lot better than we imagine. She might even be relieved. It hasn't been much fun for her, these past few years, being married to me. For all I know, she may want out as much as I do." He tried to smile. "She certainly gave a good imitation of an unhappy wife on this last trip. Try not to worry, Del. I'll phone you as soon as I can."

"I won't worry. I love you, Geoff."

"And I you, sweetheart."

Not worry? Adele almost had to laugh as she closed the door behind him. She was more than worried. She was tiptoeing on a tightrope of panic. She feared Lindsay's cleverness more than she did her wrath. She was far less sure than Geoff that Lindsay would be pleased to be free. Even if she no longer loved her husband—a fact Adele doubted— Lindsay was too smart to give him up without a struggle. What forty-eight-year-old wife married nearly thirty years wanted to be alone? It was a dismal prospect for a middle-aged woman, no matter how attractive she was. Suitable men were few and far between in these middle years, a fact to which Adele could all too well attest.

I'll be a bundle of nerves until I hear from him, she thought. What if Lindsay turns on her charm and Geoff is seduced by her all over again? She closed her eyes and shuddered, imagining him in bed with his wife, momentarily forgetting about his new love and later calling to say, apologetically, that it had been a mistake, that he and Lindsay had patched things up. It was all too possible. Lindsay was glamorous and skilled at lovemaking. More skilled than she, Adele was sure. Geoff told her she was wonderful, but she knew she was inexperienced and still cold, though she found Geoff less distasteful as a lover than her husband had been. She wondered again how she could have stood Howard even as rarely as she had in the first days of their marriage. If only sex wasn't so important to men! And Lindsay liked it as much as she hated it.

Stop these terrified thoughts! she commanded herself. Geoff really loves you. No matter what Lindsay does, she can't take him away from you. For once, things are going the way *you* want them to. This time *you'll* be the one who has everything. This was victory, she supposed, and she tried to enjoy it. But it had overtones of ugliness as well. She knew what Lindsay would call her: homewrecker, tramp, scheming bitch. I don't care, Adele thought. For the first time in my life I have a chance to be married to a suitable man. It's my need. And my right.

He dreaded this discussion, but there was no way to postpone it. He couldn't play-act for days, pretending he was the same Geoff she'd left behind. He was not admirable, but at least he'd be honest.

Lindsay heard the door open and flew to him, smiling with pleasure. She threw her arms around him and hugged him, the familiar body pressed close to his, the familiar perfume enveloping him.

"Geoff, darling, I'm so glad to be home! I missed you so much!" She turned up her face for his kiss. He touched her lips lightly and drew away from her. Lindsay pretended not to notice his lack of response.

She led the way into the library and busied herself at the bar, chattering nonstop. "You don't mind if I have a martini, do you? I'd like to break out a bottle of champagne to celebrate my return, but since you're not drinking, I'd sure as hell finish it off by myself and get absolutely blotto." She looked lovingly at him. "And I don't want to be smashed tonight. We have so much to talk about, darling. I've been doing a lot of thinking about us. It's going to be different from now on. *I'm* going to be different. I think I'll sell the business. It's begun to bore me anyhow. And we should take a long trip together, if you can get away. Hawaii, maybe. We could have a second honeymoon. We never really had the first one, did we? So—"

"Lindsay, I have to talk to you. Sit down and listen to me carefully, please. This is important."

She felt a chill, but she hid her alarm. It was going to be something unbearable. Still smiling, she settled herself in a chair and looked at him innocently, as though she expected good news. "Yes, dear?"

The words came out baldly, as though they were torn out of him.

"Lindsay, I want a divorce."

Her expression was blank, unreadable. There was a long pause before she said, "Why?"

He took a deep breath. "I've fallen in love with someone else. I want to marry her." Nervously he plunged on. "Lind, it hasn't been any good between us for a long time. I don't know exactly why, but we both know we haven't had a real marriage for years. Neither of us is happy together. At least, apart, we'll have a chance."

She didn't move. "Who is she?"

"Is that important?"

For the first time she showed a flash of anger. "It's Gladys, isn't it? It's that damned, trashy little secretary. I knew it when I heard she'd left. How could you, Geoff? How could you get tangled up with that common woman? My God, you must be crazy! An affair; all right, I could accept that. But divorce me to marry that ordinary creature? No. Not on your life! I won't let you make such a stupid mistake."

He stared at her, taken by surprise. "It isn't Gladys, Lindsay. She did imagine herself in love with me, but when I told her I wasn't interested she left. You know I'd never have anything to do with an employee."

To hell with Gladys, he thought. Why are you even wasting time explaining that? You're stalling, Geoff, you damned coward. You're afraid to tell her who it really is. Go on. Get it over.

"It's Adele," he said. "We love each other."

Lindsay looked as though he'd thrown cold water in her face: startled, incredulous. Then she began to laugh. Not a pretty laugh. Brittle, harsh, verging on the maniacal.

"Adele!" Lindsay laughed uncontrollably. "Sweet, innocent little goody-two-shoes Adele?" Her body shook with terrible mirth. "Oh, that's funny! That's really, really funny! You and Adele? It's hilarious! It's too ridiculous for discussion! My God, Geoff, why don't you kidnap a Mother Superior and marry her? It would make just about as much sense!"

"Stop it!" he commanded. "Get hold of yourself, Lindsay! This is no joke. Stop that insane laughter or I'll have to slap you out of your hysteria! Listen to me! I'm dead serious about this. I know what you think of Adele. You're wrong, of course, but that doesn't matter now. What does matter is that we be free, which is what we both want."

Lindsay controlled herself. "Speak for yourself. It's not what *I* want. I love you, Geoff. I've never wanted anyone but you."

He hadn't meant to say it. It just came out. "Is that so? What about the mysterious 'Mr. Murray' who so obligingly shared your room at La Reserve? Don't tell me you didn't want him. And God knows how many others."

At last, Lindsay's eyes filled with tears. "So that's it. You found out about Reg. That's why you're doing this. I don't know how you found out, but I swear to you it meant nothing to me. Nothing at all. I was just lonely. You didn't want me. I needed someone. And he was the only one. There were no others." She went to him and knelt in front of his chair, looking up at him beseechingly. "Geoff, don't destroy us because of one mistake. I was wrong. I humbly beg your pardon and I swear I'll never see him again. I'd already decided that before I came home. I had such plans for us. I was going to be different, more thoughtful, less selfish. I still can be. We can be happy again, Geoff, if you'll forgive me." She was weeping uncontrollably now, her hands clutching the sides of his legs. "I can see why you ran to Adele. You were hurt and angry with me. I don't blame you. But I'm back now, and it will all be good again."

He felt wrenchingly sorry for her. "Lindsay, don't," he said gently. "It wasn't because of the man. You've forgiven me in the past; I'd not do less for you. This has nothing to do with fidelity, dear. It's incompatibility we're talking about. I've found peace with Adele. I feel needed and admired."

"*I* need you. *I* admire you. Geoff, I can give you peace, if that's what you want. God knows I can give you more excitement than that cold, calculating, sexless bitch!"

His pity gave way to anger. "What do you know about Adele?

Nothing! You've painted her the way you wanted to see her: as the woman who stole your father and threatened your marriage. You were wrong, Lindsay. She didn't do either of those things. She tried to be a friend to you. She's always admired you, but you're not big enough to believe that."

Lindsay stopped crying and looked at him coldly. "She's exactly what I think she is: a devious, underhanded, lying monster. She's always wanted everything I had. She feeds on envy and deceit. I'd rather see you dead than married to her! Adele!" She spat out the name. "Mooning over James. Telling tales about you and that English girl. Seducing a man old enough to be her father. And then denying him the rights of a husband because she's frigid. Do you really think I'll let you go to a creature like that?"

His expression was as cold as her own. He wouldn't insult Adele by defending her against Lindsay's irrational bitterness involving James and Howard, but he couldn't resist denying the last accusation.

"You're wrong, Lindsay. Adele is far from frigid. She's fabulous in bed. Much better, I'm sorry to say, than you."

She let out a little cry. "You bastard! You stupid, ignorant fool! You can't see what an actress she is, can you? You're as blind as my father was. But you'll find out the truth once she's hooked you. Just as he did." Then abruptly, without warning, she gave in. "All right," she said tonelessly. "There's no hope for us. I didn't know you could be so cruel. My God, how that woman has brainwashed you! You can have your divorce, Geoff. Go ahead and marry Adele. And God help you."

He'd won. Why didn't he feel happier about it? In his anger, he'd said a terrible thing to Lindsay. It wasn't even true. Adele wasn't a better lover, but she offered things Lindsay could not: a soothing presence, utter concentration on him, and, yes, blind adoration. In Adele's eyes he could do no wrong. For more than twenty-nine years he'd felt manipulated, right from the night of their elopement. I'm being unfair to Lindsay, he thought. She can't help taking charge. But it's been such a fight with her. With Adele, there'd be no battles. He wanted to tell her that it wasn't true about Adele being more sensuous than she. That, in his own way, he still loved her, even if he couldn't live with her. But what good would it do? He and Lindsay could never be happy again. Apart, they could hope for some kind of better life, just as he'd told her. He believed that. He also regretted it.

"I'll pack a few things and leave tonight," he said quietly. "I'm sure you'd prefer that." He got out of the chair and looked down at her sadly.

"Yes." She seemed almost indifferent.

"I'll be at the club if you want to reach me."

Lindsay didn't answer. She remained a limp little heap on the floor, crumpled, he thought with shame, like a piece of tissue paper he'd thrown away. A wave of nausea hit him. Twenty-nine years. A child born and dead. A grandson. And memories—so many memories. For a moment he wavered, not sure he could do it. He'd never been a heartless man, and Lindsay's despair was almost unbearable to see. Adele had survived alone. She was better prepared for it. But what would happen to Lindsay? She was not as strong and self-sufficient as she wanted the world to believe.

I can't do it, Geoff decided reluctantly. I can't walk out on her. I want to go, but I can't. I'll stay and try to make it work, the way she planned. He leaned over her. "Lindsay—"

She looked up, eyes blazing. "Get the hell out of here!" she said furiously. "I hate you! I never want to see your rotten, lying face again!"

"What are your plans, dear?" Pauline asked.

It was January 1969. Geoff had gotten a Mexican divorce in December, and he and Adele planned to marry in February. Except in her lawyer's office, Lindsay had not spoken to him since those last violent words in their apartment. She was more bitter than she'd ever been in her whole life. For the first time she retreated from the world, nursed her injured pride, and thought constantly about revenge.

"Plans?" she said now. "I don't know, Mama. I'm not sure."

"Darling, I know how hurt you are. How angry. But it's not like you to be so lifeless. You've gone through worse, Lindsay, and never faltered. I can't bear seeing you like this."

"Worse? What's worse than being deserted by your husband? God, Mama, the humiliation of it! He's made me look like a fool. *Both* of them have!"

"Is that all that bothers you, Lindsay? How you look to the world? Or how you imagine you look? Let me tell you something, my dear. People have very short memories. One doesn't remain the topic of conversation very long, thank heavens. I found that out. Your problem seems all-consuming to you, but I assure you most of your friends give it very little thought. They gossip for a few days, and then a newer, juicier tidbit comes along and they barely remember your situation, much less spend time discussing it. I think you're being supersensitive. You've lived a remarkably long time before encountering your first rejection. That makes it harder, I suppose, but it's fortunate, too."

"I've been rejected before!" Lindsay snapped. "You seem to forget that girl in England. And the others he took up with."

"But he always came home to you, didn't he?" Pauline asked kindly. "He's not coming home this time, darling. You must accept that and make a new life for yourself without him. You've neglected your business since October. You haven't been to see Robin and John, not even when that child had his first birthday. All you've done is sit and brood and build up more hatred inside you. There comes a time when such bitterness is self-destructive, physically as well as emotionally. You're all I have Lindsay. Selfishly, I can't stand seeing you make yourself sick."

Lindsay shook her head stubbornly. "I'm not going to get *sick*, Mama." She smiled a grim little smile. "To quote a Kennedy, I'm going to get *even*."

26

In mid-January, Reg received a cable from Lindsay, announcing her arrival in two days. He was surprised and pleased and not a little baffled. PLEASE MEET ME PRIVATELY, the message read. VERY IMPORTANT. He took this to mean, correctly, that he was to come for her in his own car, though he wasn't sure why. He also wondered what was so important. There'd not been a word from her since October, when he last saw her. He'd decided that she might never be in touch with him again. After their last, long, intimate trip, she might well have felt they were getting too involved. Philosophically, he accepted that, as he accepted most things in his life. He knew what to aspire to, and the lasting love of a woman like Lindsay Murray was not one of them. Geographically they were thousands of miles apart. Socially, intellectually, they lived on different planets. In some ways, he wished he'd never met her. If he'd come from a different world, he might have hoped to make her fall in love with him. But knowing this was impossible only made the out-of-reach dreams harder to bear and the options available to him less attractive than ever.

He dressed neatly in his "civilian" clothes and stood waiting for her, as he had before, outside of Customs. She saw him instantly, and her familiar smile warmed him. But only for a second. There was a smile on her lips but her eyes, as she came closer, looked expressionless, almost vacant. He'd never seen that look before. Lindsay was always the epitome of cheerfulness, even in those first dark days when her eyes were sometimes clouded with grief for her daughter. This time she looked wounded. Half hurt, half angry.

To his further astonishment, she ran to him, threw her arms around him, and gave him a passionate kiss, oblivious of the amused stares of other passengers. She'd never before displayed such public affection. But then, Reg realized, he'd never before met her at the airport except in his role as chauffeur.

"Darling," she said, holding on to him. "I can't believe I'm here! You don't know how happy I am to see you!"

The effusive embrace made him slightly uncomfortable, but he hugged her hard and said, "Well, luv, this *is* a surprise!"

For an instant, the old impish Lindsay returned. "My arrival or my greeting?"

He smiled. "Both, I suppose. Let's get out of here. My car is nearby. A good deal less posh than you're used to, but I assumed that's what you meant by meeting you privately."

Lindsay beckoned to the porter to follow with her bags. She linked her arm through his and said, "Yes. This is a different kind of trip. I'm not here on business."

They said nothing more until they were well on the road to London. Reg drove in silence, waiting for her to explain. She was quiet for a long while. She must be composing what it is she wants to tell me, Reg thought. She must be deciding how to say what it is that's so important.

In this, he was wrong. For most of the hours of the flight, Lindsay had rehearsed what she intended to do. She'd wait until they were in the Savoy. Then, over a cozy drink, she'd spring her surprise. She'd even decided what words she'd use.

But in the car, she changed her mind. Why wait for the proper atmosphere? The answer would either be yes or no.

She turned to look at the strong profile.

"Reg, will you marry me?"

If he'd not been such an expert chauffeur, he probably would have driven the car off the road. As it was, he took only a quick look at her, as though to see whether she was making a joke. She seemed deadly serious.

"I don't understand, Lindsay."

"Don't understand a proposal? Come, come, darling, you must have had them before. I'm asking you to make an honest woman of me." She smiled wistfully. "This is the second time I've had to do that.

307

I proposed to my husband, too." She corrected herself. "My ex-husband, I should say."

He was almost as surprised by this as he'd been before. "Your ex-husband? Are you talking about Geoffrey?"

"That's the only husband I've had. So far, at least. We were divorced last month. By mutual agreement, of course. All very friendly and highly civilized. It just wasn't working. My behavior here certainly proved that."

"But I thought . . . that is, you always said—"

"I know. I was afraid to admit I'd fallen in love with you. I almost couldn't bear to leave you in Paris. I really tried, when I got home, to put you out of my mind. I didn't write, did I? But it was no use, Reg. I knew you were the only man I wanted."

He was thoroughly confused.

"But we both know . . . I mean, I'm not right for you, Lindsay. We've talked about the difference in our backgrounds. How impossible it would be. This abrupt change—I can't quite grasp it. It's the last thing I expected."

She touched his arm gently. "Don't you love me, Reg?"

"You know I do."

"Then will you please marry me right away?"

"Right away?"

"Why not? We certainly don't need a courtship. To borrow a phrase from a friend of mine, 'We did that already.' We know each other. We've talked and traveled together and made love. If we care for each other and we're both free, why wait? We're not young things who need to be engaged. Every minute is precious." She stopped, frowning. "Is that what bothers you, Reg? That I'm five years older?"

"For God's sake, Lindsay, that's the *least* of my worries! Does it bother you that I'm five years *younger?*"

"Of course not. Don't be silly."

"I don't want to be silly," he said. "And I don't want you to be. That's my big worry. I don't know if you'd be happy with me. I'm not sure I could live up the role of husband of a rich American lady. I might bore you when the whole physical thing between us simmers down. We have so little in common, really. It's rather frightening."

"Not to me. I always know what I want. All my life I've known what's right for me. And I'm never wrong."

He turned into the big driveway of the Savoy. "You were wrong about your marriage," he said softly. *"That* wasn't right for you."

Lindsay shook her head impatiently. "Nobody's perfect," she said.

A week later, Pauline received a cable from her daughter: REGINALD MARKS AND I MARRIED TODAY. VERY HAPPY. WILL TELEPHONE DETAILS LATER.

Pauline felt faint. Who on earth was Reginald Marks? Lindsay had never so much as mentioned knowing anyone by that name. Married? It was incredible! Lindsay had told her she was going to London on business. Never a word about a man there. Who was this stranger? What wild, impulsive thing had she done? Pauline reached for the phone and called the Savoy. No, they said, sorry, madam, there's no Mrs. Murray registered. No Mr. and Mrs. Marks, either. Wait. Mrs. Murray had been there a week before, but she'd left the hotel. No, sorry, there was no forwarding address.

Pauline was half crazy with anxiety. There was no one to talk to, no one to ask about the mysterious Reginald Marks. Unless, perhaps, Geoff. She hesitated. It seemed insane to call her former son-in-law to inquire whether he knew the man his ex-wife had married. But at this point, Pauline was so frantic she'd grasp at any source of information. She reached Geoff at his office. He sounded very pleased when he came on the wire.

"Pauline! What a nice surprise! How are you, dear?"

"I . . . I'm not very well at this moment, Geoffrey. I called because . . . well, Lindsay's in England and—"

She heard alarm in his voice. "What's wrong? Are you sick? Do you want me to come right over?"

"No. No, I'm all right."

"Is it Lindsay? Has something happened to Lindsay?"

"No. That is, not exactly." Unable to help herself, Pauline began to cry. "Geoff, she's married somebody. A man named Reginald Marks. I don't know who he is. I never even heard of him."

"Lindsay's married?" He sounded stunned.

Pauline tried to compose herself. "Yes. In London, yesterday. Have you ever heard of him, Geoff? I'm so worried. It's not like her to be so secretive. I had no idea. I thought perhaps you . . . that maybe she said something to you when she returned from the last trip. I just don't know what to do. I can't even find out where she is."

"Get hold of yourself, dear. Calm down. Wherever she is, I'm sure she's all right. Did she say anything else?"

"Just that she's happy and she'll call later with details. Geoff, how could she? Where would she meet someone and marry him in a week?"

It wasn't a week, Geoff thought. It's been months. Reginald Marks must be the mysterious "Mr. Murray" who was registered with her at the hotel in the south of France.

But he couldn't tell Lindsay's mother what he suspected. He couldn't even be certain of it himself. Yet it was highly probable. Lindsay wouldn't marry a man she'd known only a week, not even to prove a point.

He repeated the phrase to himself. Was it possible that Lindsay was only making a nose-thumbing gesture toward him? Was this her way of saving face? Did she imagine it was revenge? Ridiculous! Yet the suspicion remained. He could almost imagine her saying to herself, "I'll show them. I'll make everybody believe *I* was the one who wanted the divorce to marry someone else. I did the rejecting and Geoff, on the rebound, was caught by Adele." He shook his head. If that was true, it was pitiful. Poor Lindsay.

"Geoffrey? Are you still there?"

Pauline's voice interrupted his thoughts. "Yes, dear, I was just trying to think what to do. About finding her, I mean. Sit tight for the moment, Pauline, and let me make a call. And try not to worry. We know she's all right."

It was a long shot, but he got the manager of his London office on the phone and asked him to call every Reginald Marks in the area and ask whether there was a Mrs. Lindsay Marks there.

The man on the other end of the wire clearly thought he was crazy. "Good heavens, Geoffrey, old man, do you have any idea how long that will take? I daresay there are dozens of Reginald Markses round and about London. It would be like calling all the John Smiths in New York State. Can't you give us any more information? An address, perhaps? Or a business affiliation?"

"If I could give you that, Desmond, I wouldn't be asking you to do it the hard way, would I?" Geoff was unmistakably annoyed. "For God's sake, man, you must have some secretary you can put to work on this. Try sparing your own for a day or two, if you can tear her away from making your social engagements!"

The sarcasm surprised Desmond. Geoff must have some madly important reason for this odd, time-consuming wild goose chase. It was the first time he'd ever sounded so rude.

"Very well. We'll get right on it. I can't say how long it will take, but we'll give it our best."

Geoff was ashamed of his boorishness. "Sorry, Des. I didn't mean to snap that way. It's a personal thing. You understand."

Desmond didn't understand at all, but an order was an order. As he gave the instructions to his surprised secretary, he wondered what it was all about.

The young woman wondered, too, but she didn't question the assignment. She did say, "If I locate the lady, sir, what shall I do then?"

Good question. "For now, we just want to locate her, Miss Yardley. New York will take it from there."

Whatever that means, he thought. Who in blazes was Lindsay Marks? Geoff Murray's wife was called Lindsay. Not a usual name. But it couldn't be she. Or could it? None of my affair, Desmond thought. What the boss wants, the boss gets. Perhaps.

It was not until the following afternoon that Miss Yardley appeared, triumphant, in his office. "I think I've found her, sir."

"Really?"

"Yes, sir. There's a Reginald Marks in Hampstead, Christchurch Hill." She gave him the street number and telephone. "The lady who answered said she was Mrs. Marks and that her name was Lindsay. She sounded American."

"I see. Did you find out anything else?"

Miss Yardley looked offended. "You didn't tell me what to ask. Anyway, the lady sounded rather suspicious. She wanted to know why I was calling. I told her it was a survey for the telly. I hope that was all right."

"It was just fine, Miss Yardley. Thank you. You did a marvelous job."

Now what? Geoff wondered when Desmond called with the information. Unquestionably, it was Lindsay, but what to do now that they'd found her? Damn her. Why didn't she call her mother? What was this stupid secrecy all about? He rang up Pauline.

"My London people tracked her down, dear. We have an address and telephone number."

"I can't understand it, Geoffrey. Why hasn't she called me? She's

311

always been so considerate. There must be something terribly wrong. Lindsay wouldn't worry me like this unless she was unable to speak to me, or afraid."

For the first time, Pauline sounded like a frail old lady. Her voice trembled and she was obviously distraught.

"Do you want to call her?" Geoff asked. "Or would you rather I did?"

Pauline did not hide her relief at the suggestion. "Would you, Geoff? I'd be so grateful. I should do it myself, but I'm too upset. I'd probably just cry and make no sense."

"I don't mind doing it. Maybe it's better. I'll make sure she telephones you."

He did mind. Terribly. What did one say to an ex-wife who had to be hunted down like a criminal because she was so damned thoughtless she hadn't let her mother know where she was? Was she ashamed of something? Was it possible she was having some kind of nervous breakdown? Maybe she wasn't married at all. The hell with it. He placed the overseas call to the number Desmond had given him. In a few minutes, he heard her voice.

Without preamble, he said, "Lindsay, what the hell are you up to? Your mother's worried sick! It's been two days since she got your cable."

Lindsay seemed infuriatingly relaxed. "Hello, Geoffrey," she said. "How are you? How's the bride-to-be?"

He could have strangled her. "I didn't go to all the trouble of finding you to discuss my health or Adele's. For God's sake, Lindsay, what's going on?"

"Mother knows. I cabled her that I was married. What's everybody so up in arms about? I was going to call her tomorrow."

Geoff gritted his teeth. "Has it occurred to you that she's a very old lady and that this bombshell practically killed her? You might have had the decency to warn her. To explain. Who is this Reginald Marks? What does he do? What made you marry him on the spur of the moment? God Almighty, Lindsay, you're behaving like an irresponsible child!"

Lindsay sounded amused. "My, my, aren't we getting ourselves in a tizzy! You sound more like my *father* than a man I used to be married to." Then she became angry. "What gives you the right to intrude in

312

my life? We're nothing to each other any more. I didn't tell *you* who to marry, so don't meddle in *my* affairs!"

"I don't give a damn who you marry!" He was totally exasperated. "Don't flatter yourself that I'd go to all this trouble if it wasn't for your mother! She was too upset to call you herself. That's why I did it. Now, for God's sake, give me some details I can give her, and that will be the end of this nonsense between us!"

"All right. I married an Englishman named Reginald Marks. He's free, white, and forty-three. I've known him nearly a year. He's been my chauffeur whenever I came to Europe on business. We're living in his flat until I can find a more suitable one. He's clean, decent, and sexy. Anything else you want to know?"

Geoff was aghast. "Your chauffeur? Lindsay, are you serious?"

"Why shouldn't I be? What's wrong with that? He isn't a drug dealer or a pimp. You needn't be such a snob."

Irrelevantly, he thought of Gladys O'Reilly's parting shot. "I don't think I'm a snob, Lindsay. I'm simply amazed that a working-class man would fit your qualificatons for a husband. How well do you know him? Have you met his family, his friends? Will you live in London? What made you rush into this?"

"Well, at my age it certainly wasn't a shotgun wedding, old boy," she said flippantly. "I've been having an affair with him practically since the day we met. You should understand that. You've had your own. Besides, you know very well I was a wife in name only."

"All right. Never mind that. I knew there was someone. But why *marry* him, Lindsay?"

"Why are you marrying Adele? I fell in love. Did you think that was your prerogative only? You certainly haven't wasted much time setting your own wedding date."

He felt totally frustrated. No good trying to explain the differences between the two marriages. Lindsay *had* done it to prove a point. He was now dismally sure of that. He tried to speak reasonably.

"I hope you know what you're doing. I wish you well, you know that."

"Thank you. Same to you."

"You will call Pauline right away?"

"I'll call her. I promised I would. Tell her not to worry, Geoff. I'm blissfully happy. I should have done this a year ago."

Lindsay replaced the receiver and tried not to burst into tears. Her sarcastic responses were an effort to camouflage the unhappiness she felt. When she proposed to Reg, she'd had only one thing in mind: to save her pride and prove to Geoff and the world that she could marry before he did. But even before the ceremony, she knew she was making a dreadful mistake. She was sure Reg knew it too. In the preceding week, he did everything to show her what she was getting into, giving her a chance to change her mind. Stubbornly, Lindsay pretended not to be dismayed by the ugly little flat he lived in, by his blowsy Cockney mother and his lorry-driving, almost illiterate brothers, by the other chauffeurs and their crude wives who were his friends from the garage. It was almost as though he was trying to disgust her. But she refused to appear even mildly distressed.

She'd been gracious and unpretentious, friendly to these people whom she found vulgar and boring. She went out of her to way to try to make them like her. It wasn't easy. They had nothing in common except Reg, but Lindsay struggled to make small talk with these men and women who almost literally did not speak her language. She could barely understand their accents, totally missed the point of their rhyming slang, found herself desperate for any topic she could share with her soon-to-be in-laws and her new "social set." Somehow she remained cool and smiling, aware of their smirks and whispers, knowing full well they thought Reg had been clever to find himself a crazy, rich American divorcee who'd be his insurance policy for life.

When they returned to the Savoy after the first awful meal at his mother's dreary, overcrowded flat, Reg had looked at her sadly.

"See, luv? It isn't going to work. You can't relate to my friends."

"Don't be silly. They're genuine down-to-earth people. The kind we call 'the salt of the earth.' I like them. I only hope they like me."

"Ah, Lindsay, don't pretend. They're ignorant and clumsy. You were like an orchid in a vegetable patch."

"Vegetables nourish. Orchids are fancy but useless." She smiled. "Don't upset yourself, darling. All right, I admit they're different. I expected them to be. But we'll get on. I'm not marrying *them,* Reg; I'm going to live with *you*."

"But they're part of me, don't you see? They're all I know. The other side of me, the one you've seen before, isn't what I'm really all about. I like to be around rich people with good manners and fine educations, but they're not real to me because I'll never be one of them."

"You will be, dearest. You'll fit into my world better than I do yours. You have innate style. I told you that the first time we met. You have the polish and manners of a gentleman."

He shook his head. "It's crazy, Lindsay. I can't imagine why you even want to try it. I can't picture myself in New York, visiting your mother on Park Avenue, meeting your son-in-law's big-shot friends in Chicago. The whole idea of America scares me to death, start to finish." He shook his head. "No, it won't work. I love you, but I'm no husband for you."

He just assumed that they would go to New York. Lindsay had assumed so too, but now she reconsidered. She was more intelligent than Reg and she'd adjust better to a new environment. Why shouldn't they live in London? She adored the city. There was nothing to take her back to New York. She'd sell the business to Marty, let him pay for it gradually. If Pauline wished, Lindsay would move her to London too. She could go back once or twice a year to see Robin and John. Later, the boy could come to visit her. Yes, that was the answer. That was perfect. And she'd never have to worry about accidentally running into Geoffrey and Adele.

Full circle, she thought without amusement. Nearly twenty-five years ago she feared it was Geoff who might desert her for another spouse and home in England. Now it was she who'd do the very same thing. It wouldn't be an easy transition, but it was a hell of a lot better than the role of rejected, divorced woman on her own in New York.

In the next breath she thought, Stop kidding yourself, Lindsay. You're getting into something you can't handle. What will you do with yourself in London? Who'll be your friends? How will you and Reg live? Money was no problem. She had plenty. But contentment was something she couldn't buy. Dammit, I'll make it work, she decided. We'll have a lovely flat. I'll make new friends. We'll travel a lot. Of course, Reg would have to give up his job. She could hardly imagine herself a chauffeur's wife. Well, okay. Hs didn't need to work, thanks to Gandy and Papa and her own business ability these past years. They'd be lovers and playmates and to hell with everything else.

27

To her credit, let it be recorded that Lindsay tried hard to adjust to her new life in the first months of her marriage to Reg. Almost meekly, she gave in to him on certain things and compromised on others, using, for her, unusually gentle persuasion to overcome his resistance about changes that were necessary to her life. She found herself in a position of constantly trading favors, so to speak.

There was, for example, the matter of where they would live. Reg felt they should stay on in his flat, where he could afford the rent. Lindsay was stunned by the idea. Live in this dreary little three-room place? Impossible! Not even if she were to renovate and redecorate, from the dark little foyer to the equally dim W.C.

"Darling, please don't be stubborn," she said. "I want to make a lovely new home for us." Her eyes sparkled. "I've been investigating. There's a lovely flat in Albany that I think, with a little finagling, I can get."

"Albany! Don't be daft, Lindsay! That's the poshest place in London. Why don't you suggest we move into Buckingham Palace with the Queen? I hear Prince Philip's going to ask Parliament to increase her allowance. Maybe they're hard up enough to let us a few rooms."

Lindsay laughed. "I'm not thinking of anything grand, sweetheart, even in Albany. Nothing like an American woman I know who's thrown seven flats together there. Just something comfortable. The one I've seen has three bedrooms and servant's quarters, but it's really quite modest."

"Modest! You could put my whole bloody family in half a place like that!"

316

God forbid, Lindsay thought. The evenings with his family were only slightly worse than those with his friends at Reg's favorite crowded, noisy pub. She felt so alien in his sphere. What did she know or care about Henry Cooper, Johnny Pritchett, and Howard Winstone? When their names came up in Reg's group one evening, she'd innocently inquired whether they were friends she hadn't met. The table exploded in laughter, the men slapping their thighs and the women giggling at her question.

"Not bloody likely," one of the drivers from the garage said, "unless you have a punching bag in your living room."

This baffling response must also have been very funny, for it sent the group, including Reg, into a new wave of hysterics. Lindsay sat quietly, wondering what the joke was.

"They're British boxing champions, luv," Reg finally explained.

She was annoyed. "Well, how am I expected to know that? Would you be any more intelligent if I mentioned Lee Trevino and Jack Nicklaus?"

"No," Reg said. "Who are they?"

"Trevino defeated Nicklaus and won the U.S. Open golf championship last year."

The group looked at her silently for a moment.

"Golf?" one of the men finally said. "That's a game for toffs. Old gents wandering around banging at little balls with sticks. Golf's a rich man's game. Now if you want to talk cricket or wrestling, that's something else."

Lindsay didn't answer. I don't want to talk anything with any of you, she thought. I don't even want to be in your company. But she simply smiled and pretended not to notice their condescension. Remembering that and other boring evenings she'd endured, Lindsay was determined not to go along with Reg on the matter of their living quarters. She'd had enough. They *would* move to Albany, no matter what he said.

"Dear, I've really tried to please you, these past months. I know what a proud man you are, and I love you for wanting to support us. But I can't be happy in this place. Truly, I can't. Do let me have my way in this."

He felt like a heel. He knew she couldn't live here. He'd kept insisting on it just to hold onto to some feeling of independence. Just as he flatly refused to give up his job with Coronet, even though he knew Lindsay wanted him to. He'd have enjoyed a rich man's life, the one she painted: traveling and lallygagging around, buying clothes in Bond Street and imported cigars at Dunhill. But he was afraid of being her lapdog, her possession. He'd married her because he truly loved her. It wasn't the money. The money could only destroy him if he let her take over.

"Albany," he muttered now. "Some address for a chauffeur and his wife! I'll feel like a fish out of water in that fancy place."

Not as much as you'd feel like one on the upper East Side of New York, Lindsay wanted to say. She'd kept the apartment there, the one she and Geoff had bought. It was part of the divorce settlement, and when she decided to live in London something still made her hang onto it. Like a hedge against disaster, she realized. A haven to run to if this doesn't work out for us. Terrible thought. It *was* going to work. Still, she couldn't sever all ties with the place she really thought of as home. One day they might want to live there. Who could tell?

To her relief, Reg had given in on the London flat. Just as she'd given in when she recognized his need to continue working. It didn't matter, at the moment. She had no friends here who might raise eyebrows at her husband's profession. Later, she thought, when we're settled, we'll talk about that part of our life. Once ensconced in a civilized home with all the amenities, his ideas about a lot of things will change.

"Well, all right," he finally said. "I know you want it. I'm not in favor of a man living beyond his means, but it would be stupid of me to expect you to go one hundred percent my way. The apartment and the fixing up will be your share, Lindsay. But I'm still paying the food and the monthly expenses. Agreed?"

"Yes, darling, of course." It was a lie. He couldn't begin to afford the monthly expenses. Not the entertaining she planned when they started to make friends suitable to invite to Albany. Never mind. What was one more little fib? She'd not told the truth since the day she returned. She made him believe she was the one who wanted the divorce from Geoff. That she'd come back to Reg because she was desperately in love and couldn't live without him. Even when she heard from Pauline that Geoff and Adele were married, she pretended to be unconcerned, even pleased.

"My ex has married a friend of mine," she told Reg.

"Oh? He didn't wait long, did he?"

"Longer than I did," Lindsay snapped. Then, realizing how she sounded, she laughed. "Of course, I knew what *I* wanted when we were divorced. Poor old Geoff had to start from scratch."

Reg suspected she was shaving the truth, but he simply said, "Who is she?"

"Nobody special. We were children together. She's a widow."

Why can't I tell him the real story? Lindsay wondered. He'll probably find out one day and never believe anything I say again. I just can't go through it, all that sordidness of Adele marrying my father and then my husband. Reg would know the truth about my divorce, as well. Better to keep my mouth shut. I must warn Mama, if she ever comes here, not to let the truth slip out.

In September, Pauline decided to pay a visit to Lindsay. She'd not seen her in eight months, had never met her new husband or had a look at the apartment Lindsay described in such glowing terms. It struck Pauline that Lindsay's letters said a great deal about Albany and very little about Reginald Marks. In the beginning, Pauline had urged her daughter to come home at least for a visit, since she'd regrettably decided to make her home in London.

I want very much to meet Reg. It's strange having a son-in-law you can't even picture. If you love him, Lindsay dear, I'm prepared to do the same, but it will make me feel infinitely easier in my mind if he and I can sit and talk and get to know one another.

She did not say that she was seventy-nine years old and who knew how much time was left to her? True, she was in good health, and once she recovered from the shock of Lindsay's unexpected marriage, she'd regained almost all her old energy and interest. But she missed her child and wanted to make sure that this stranger she'd chosen was a good, kind man.

Not that I could do anything about it, she thought, if he were not. Lindsay hadn't consulted her mother beforehand. It was unlikely she'd listen now, even if the man turned out to be someone Pauline could not trust. She had no reason to think she wouldn't like Reg. In her first letters, Lindsay had raved about him: his gentleness, his sense of honor, his reluctance to touch any of her money:

Reg is so proud. I had to beg and plead to be allowed to take the apartment. He only agreed because he knew I wanted it so much. And he won't hear

319

of giving up his job, though I hate his uncertain hours even more than I dislike the idea of his being subservient to a bunch of demanding tourists. Well, we'll work all these things out in time. Right now, I'm concentrating on whipping the new place into shape. It's going to be glorious, Mama. And when I'm settled, you must come to visit. I miss you so much, darling, and hope you're taking care of yourself. If I get you here, I may even talk you into staying! Wouldn't that be wonderful? You'll love London. Obviously, it's changed since you and Papa were here, but certain things never change, including the courtesy and kindness of the English themselves.

Pauline noticed that Lindsay did not even refer to the possibility of visiting New York. The omission troubled her. For some reason, Lindsay did not want to bring her new husband to her country. Between the lines of enthusiasm about Reg's good qualities, Pauline read a hint of something like embarrassment. "Subservient," she'd said. Was Lindsay ashamed of being married to a blue-collar man? She'd never felt that her daughter was class conscious. Pauline had no such bias, though heaven knows Howard had been a terrible bigot about such things. He'd turn over in his grave, she thought, half amused, if he knew his daughter had married a workingman. He'd probably be angrier about that than about his second wife and his former son-in-law.

Mercy, how her mind wandered these days! Why did she drift off to thoughts of Howard when it was Lindsay she was concerned about? Well, it was a natural progression. Adele's marriage made her think of Geoff, who'd sounded shocked when he reported Lindsay's marriage to her former chauffeur. He's a bit down-the-nose too, Pauline decided. In his own way, Geoff is as stuffy as Howard. No wonder he and Howard found Adele appealing. They both liked wishy-washy women. Probably because they'd both married such definite ones the first time around.

She went back to musing about Lindsay. As their correspondence continued over the spring and summer, Pauline increasingly sensed her daughter's uneasiness. There were constant references to Reg's friends, who "had a language all their own," and to Reg's favorite pub, described as "something right out of a middle-class English film." There were no outright complaints, but there was a sense of plaintiveness, a lonely ring to words intended to be brittle and amusing. It was Lindsay's latest letter, however, that made Pauline decide to take the trip.

The apartment is beautiful, just about finished, and, if I do say so myself, it's exquisite. Now all I need are people to show it off to. Reg's friends would

320

come, I suppose, but I don't see much of them any more. I'm afraid they don't like me very well, Mama, and I can't honestly say I care. Reg meets his buddies on his own, which is fine with me. Better to let them get together over a pint and talk sports or shop without my having to sit there and be bored to death. Don't think I'm complaining. Reg is marvelous to me and we're very happy together in most things. I'm planning to introduce him to some amusing people I've come to know, decorators and press people, mostly. He'll be as uneasy in that crowd as I am in his, but we understand each other's needs.

Do you indeed? Pauline thought. A marriage with two separate sets of friends as different as chalk and cheese? Not good. Her worry increased. She wrote and asked Lindsay if it would be convenient for her to have a houseguest for a couple of weeks in September, and Lindsay replied enthusiastically that nothing would please her more.

Pauline saw no need to mention her trip to Geoff. They spoke rarely these days, for though they were still fond of each other, Adele's role as Mrs. Geoffrey Murray made social intercourse quite out of the question. Instead, Pauline rang up Robin and told him her plans.

"That's wonderful!" he said. "I know how much you miss her, and I'm sure she misses you just as much. When were you last in London?"

"Oh, my lord, almost sixty years ago! Can you believe such a thing? Mr. Thresher and I toured England on our honeymoon. I daresay I'll see fewer horses and carriages this time. And fewer bedrooms," she added naughtily.

Robin laughed. She was a wonder, this nearly eighty-year-old lady. Always a light touch. He adored her. So did John. In June, Robin had brought the baby to New York to see his great-grandmother. Eighteen-month-old John had had a lovely time with Pauline, hanging on to her as though he knew who she was. Pauline had been like a child herself, holding him, playing peek-a-boo, making John gurgle with delight.

"How's my little darling?" she asked now.

"Terrific. Growing like a weed. Mrs. Graham says he's going to be a football player. I think more likely basketball."

At the other end of the phone, Pauline frowned. Mrs. Graham took wonderful care of John, but the child needed a mother. It was going on two years now. Time Robin got interested in someone. Neither he nor his son should be alone any more.

"Robin," she said hesitantly, "do you ever think about . . . about a mother for John? I don't mean to meddle, but you're still a young man, and if there were some nice girl—"

321

"You're spooky," he said kindly. "What do you do, read my mind? I've kind of hesitated to tell you. I mean, I didn't know how you and Lindsay would feel. But there is someone I'm interested in. Her name's Constance Bellman. I met her a couple of months ago. I don't know if anything will come of it, but it's the first time I've found anyone who might . . ." His voice trailed off.

Might replace S.P., Pauline silently finished for him. She was glad.

"Is it serious, Robin?"

"It's getting that way. She's the advertising manager for one of our clients. Bright lady. Nice. Twenty-six and never married."

Pauline felt a slight twinge of dismay. A career woman? Why not someone who'd devote herself to John, a girl who'd want other children too? But things were different these days. All intelligent girls worked, and many of them managed careers *and* homes and families.

Now it was as though Robin was reading *her* mind. "She loves John. She'd like to have three more just like him, she says."

"Good. That makes me happy, Robin, for all of you. Will you bring her to see me when I return?"

"Of course. And if you want to, tell Lindsay, will you?"

He'd obviously made up his mind to marry Constance. "Yes," Pauline said, "I'll tell her. It will make her happy, I'm sure."

He never mentions Geoff, she thought as she hung up. Nor does Geoff mention him and John. It was sad, really. Pauline knew about the one trip Geoff and Lindsay made to Chicago to see their grandson and the disastrous result of that visit. She wondered if Geoff sent Christmas and birthday gifts to the child, as Lindsay did. She supposed Adele would see to that as a matter of course. She's always had good manners, Pauline reluctantly conceded. At least I can give her that.

She went on with her plans for the trip, thinking how much she and Lindsay had to catch up on, including this latest development. Lindsay would be delighted for Robin and the baby, she knew. Geoff, when he heard, would probably consider it only one more evidence of his son-in-law's bestial nature. Poor man, he'd never forgive Robin for the natural desire that conceived his grandson and which he never stopped seeing as the death warrant for his daughter.

I can't worry about Geoffrey's obsession, Pauline decided. I'm much too concerned about Lindsay.

* * *

Lindsay met her flight and supervised the stowing of her luggage in a shiny brown Bentley which she expertly drove herself.

"Lovely car," Pauline said, sniffing. "Nothing like the smell of real leather. Or money."

Lindsay laughed. "It was my extravagant forty-ninth birthday present to myself. I love it. A car gives you such a feeling of freedom."

"You drive well, though I don't know how you ever got used to being on the wrong side of the road."

"It wasn't easy, but it was that or no wheels at all. There seemed to be something wrong with the idea of a chauffeur's wife hiring a chauffeur."

There was that same sliver of disdain Pauline could almost hear in Lindsay's letters. She decided not to pursue it. "I bring you love from Robin," she said.

Lindsay brightened. "How is he? How's John?"

"Fine, both of them." Pauline hesitated. "I think Robin's going to be married. Nothing definite, but he sounded as though he'd made up his mind. He wanted me to tell you he thought he'd met someone who'd be a good wife and a good mother to John."

"Oh?" Lindsay's lips tightened almost imperceptibly. "Well, I suppose I shouldn't be surprised. But I wonder why he doesn't just live with her, instead of getting married. I thought that was the fashionable thing these days."

"Lindsay, really! They might want other children. And would you want your grandson to grow up in that kind of atmosphere?"

"Why not? It wouldn't make *him* illegitimate. Besides, Mama, I don't think marriage is such a red-hot idea. People seem to get along better when they're not legally tied. It might make for a more loving household for John, as well as for them." She shrugged. "But Robin's much too conventional for that, I suppose. Or too young to know better. Who is she?"

"In charge of advertising for one of his clients, he said. She's in her mid-twenties. Never been married. Her name is Carolyn. No, that's not right. Constance, that's it. And for the life of me I can't remember her last name." Pauline shook her head. "Lately, I have the old-folks syndrome. I can vividly remember things that happened forty or fifty years ago, but I don't know what I had for lunch yesterday. It's a bore. I wish next year would hurry up so I could be eighty."

Lindsay glanced at her curiously. "For heaven's sake, why?"

"Eighty's a landmark and people treat you differently than they do when you're seventy-nine. At seventy-nine, if you drop something it just lies there. At eighty, people pick it up for you. You get to be special, I think, like a fragile antique that has to be taken care of because it might fall apart if you don't."

Lindsay laughed. "Mama, there's nobody like you. Every day you remind me more of Gandy. Do you know I still pick up shiny pennies when I see them? Even if they're called pence over here. I have a whole jar of them, hundreds of reminders of her, just like she said." Lindsay sobered. "She was terrific, wasn't she? Siding with you, that way, when you divorced Papa. And making life comfortable and independent for both of us. What a great lady! I wish I were more like her. She made the best of everything and never howled about her own troubles. I guess she didn't have a very happy life, did she? Grandpa must have been a terror, just like Papa. Of course, in those days, women didn't do anything about a bad marriage. They were stuck with it. You and I live in better times."

Pauline didn't answer for a moment. "I don't know, Lindsay," she finally said. "Maybe we were better off when we didn't have such freedom of choice. Oh, I know that's heresy, these days, but sometimes I think it was all for the best when society frowned on divorce. Maybe those women tried harder to make marriage work, knowing there was no escape. Maybe they were happier in a less-than-perfect union than we've been in our state of free choice." She was deliberately baiting her daughter, hoping to find out more about Lindsay's marriage. She was arguing a cause she didn't believe. Of course women should be free to leave men who were physically cruel or flagrantly unfaithful. Or with whom they had nothing in common. Or men they'd married in a rush of hurt pride or even a spirit of revenge. She waited, but Lindsay chose to let the subject drop.

"I can't wait for you to see the flat," she said abruptly.

"I'm even more anxious to meet your Reg," Pauline replied.

Lindsay gripped the wheel more tightly. "He's . . . he's different, Mama. I mean he's nothing like Geoff, so don't expect that. They say people marry the same kind of person over and over again, but I didn't. Reg is faithful, for one thing." She looked straight ahead. "He's a gentleman, in his own way. That is, he's polite. But he's also kind of a . . ." She groped for words.

"A diamond in the rough?" Pauline suggested. She smiled. "I wish

324

I could think of a more original phrase, but that's what you mean, isn't it?"

Lindsay nodded. "He's kind and gentle. He tries to understand me, but it's hard for him, He hates my friends, the ones I've made since I've been here. And he drinks a lot. Too much. I've been drinking too much myself, I'm afraid." She pretended to laugh. "I've got to cut it out. I've put on five pounds this year, did you notice?"

"No, darling. You look beautiful to me."

"You're just prejudiced."

"That's true," Pauline said. "And I always will be."

The thought of his new mother-in-law's arrival sent Reg into a panic. What would she think of him? Would she overlook his strange speech, his lack of education, even the table manners that Lindsay sometimes tactfully corrected? How did she feel about a son-in-law who was trained to say "Yes, madam" and tip his cap to ladies like her?

He poured himself another stiff whisky and water, the fourth he'd had since Lindsay left for the airport. He knew he was getting a little drunk. So what? He needed courage to face this meeting. Lindsay had wanted him to go to the airport with her, but he'd refused, saying he was sure she'd like some time alone with her mother.

"To prepare her for me," he'd added.

Lindsay looked worried but she said, "Don't be silly. What's to prepare? She's dying to meet you, dear. She's going to love you."

"Tolerate me, is more like it."

"Oh, stop it!" Lindsay sounded annoyed. "Why do you always get snappish when you're about to meet someone connected with me? It's the same way with my friends. You get all uptight when I ask anyone here. Uptight and drunk," she said coldly. "For God's sake, Reg, please be sober when Mama arrives."

"Yes, madam," he mocked, making a low bow. "Certainly, madam. Anything you like, madam."

She felt sorry for him. He really was afraid of meeting Pauline. Lindsay put her arms around him and kissed him. "It's going to be fine, darling. Truly it is. You're going to be good friends."

Bloody unlikely, Reg thought now, as he downed another whisky, neat. Lindsay was right about one thing, though: he did get nervous around her friends. Some friends! A bunch of fops from the antique business. He didn't know what to say to them, was sure they were making fun of him behind his back, them and their elegant la-di-da manners. At least my friends are men, he thought angrily. They may not be college graduates, but they know a hell of a lot more about real life than these freaks Lindsay's taken up with.

Why should he worry about them? Or Mrs. Thresher, either, for that matter? They could take him or leave him. Lindsay knew what she was getting when she married him. Who cared about the rest?

Satisfied he was in the right, he helped himself from the bottle. By the time Lindsay and Pauline entered the flat he was standing in front of the drawing room fireplace, swaying slightly, a foolish, drunken grin on his face.

Lindsay's heart sank. She'd been afraid of this. Reg was so nervous about meeting his mother-in-law, she wasn't really surprised that he'd overindulged. False courage. Poor Reg, it had become a way of life with him. She smiled brightly, pretending not to notice his condition.

"Darling, here's Mama."

He weaved across the room and bowed unsteadily over her hand.

"Delighted to meet you, Mrs. Thresher. Welcome to London." The words were slurred and the elaborate gesture almost comical, but Pauline hid her dismay.

"I'm so happy to meet you too, Reg. And please call me Pauline. It will make me ever so much more comfortable."

Reg grinned. "Right-o. Pauline. Nice name. Nice lady."

Lindsay nervously stepped in. "You must be tired after your flight, Mama. Wouldn't you like to rest awhile? I'll show you to your room." She couldn't wait to get her mother away from Reg. "We have so many plans for you while you're here! The theater, of course. Doesn't every American make a beeline for the theater in London? So much of it! So good! And so cheap compared to New York! And the shops, of course, are a wonder. I'm mad for Fortnum and Mason. Can you imagine a food store where the clerks wear frock coats and striped trousers while they're doing up parcels for gentlemen in bowler hats?"

Pauline laughed. "That, at least, I can remember. It was the same fifty years ago. What about Knightsbridge? Still as busy as Times Square?"

"Nearly, but ever so much more attractive and polite. Harrods is wonderful. We have nothing remotely like it at home. Nothing like it anywhere in the world, I suspect. Do you know customers can have letters sent to them in care of the store? And there's a kennel for patrons' pets and a place for chauffeurs to stay while their employers are shopping—" She stopped, seeing the look on Reg's face. "I mean . . . that is . . ."

He seemed to have sobered up remarkably since her return. "Don't be upset, luv," he said. "Pauline knows what I do for a living."

"Of course," Pauline said. "And I see nothing remarkable about it. In fact, Reg, I hope you'll take me sightseeing if you have the time. You certainly must know more about this city than most. Certainly more than my scatterbrained child, who probably doesn't know one public building from another."

"I'd be honored to take you. I not only know every inch of it as a driver, I was also born here, you know, in a part of London most tourists never see. You tell me when you want the guided tour, Pauline, and I'll give you one fit for the Queen herself, bless her soul."

Lindsay smiled with relief. It was going to be all right. She could tell that Reg was captivated by Pauline. And Pauline would go out of her way to make him feel at ease.

"All right, you two. Plans later. Right now, Mama's going to rest!"

She led the way down the corridor to a beautifully appointed guest room. Pauline was full of admiration.

"It's beautiful, Lindsay! Such lovely things! Gandy was right. She knew you were the one in the family who really appreciated the fine things she loved so much. Where did you find all these treasures?"

"I've had plenty of time to shop. I'm antiquing so often at Camden Passage and Portobello Road the shopkeepers think I'm still a dealer." She grinned. "I let them. Makes things cheaper."

"Do you miss working, Lindsay?"

She nodded. "Yes, I do. But I won't go back to it full time ever again. It's important for me to be around when Reg needs me. He's . . . he's not very secure, you know. Not since we've been married, at any rate. I'm afraid I've made him too dependent as it is. Adding a full-time career would be the last straw."

Pauline hesitated. "I worry about this marriage of yours, darling."

"I know you do. I won't lie, Mama. I worry about it too. Reg is a different man. Or maybe he's not different. I don't suppose I really knew him that well when I married him. It's hard for him. Hell, it's hard for both of us! But we'll muddle through. I'm determined we will. I think he's determined too, but he's not really as tough as I. Isn't that odd? A man from such a rough background, and he's more sensitive than I, who was practically swaddled in Porthault sheets." Lindsay seemed far away. "It should have all been so different. Everything went so crazy after S.P.'s death. Is Geoff happy, do you think?"

"I don't know. I don't hear much from him, though we're still friends. I hope you don't mind that."

"No, I don't mind. People shouldn't have to take sides in a divorce, not even mothers. Anyway, you're being lovely to Reg and I'm grateful. I'm sorry about his condition. I'm sure he is too. He'll try to make it up to you, I know."

"And I fully intend to let him," Pauline said. "I was quite serious about sightseeing. I know it bores you to death, but I really love the historic sights, and no one, as I said, could know them better than Reg, who's been wheeling tourists around London for years. You can do Bond Street while I see more important things."

"I suspect you'd also like to spend some time alone with him, wouldn't you?"

"Well, yes. I'm not meddling, Lindsay, but maybe he'll open up a little to me if we're alone. If you'd rather not, I won't, of course."

"Go right ahead, Mama. You might find out some things I need to know too."

Such was not the case. Reg was eager to please Pauline, proud of his city, and delighted to show it to her, but he kept the conversation deliberately impersonal, like a tourist guide. She remarked how much cleaner and shinier the buildings looked than she remembered, and he informed her, in a rehearsed voice, of the Clean Air Act passed in the mid-fifties. Tons of coal dust were removed, he said, making London shine as it did before years of soot and smog covered it. He showed her the statue of George Washington in Trafalgar Square and took her to watch the gorgeously uniformed Queen's Cavalry ride through traffic on their way to Whitehall and the Horse Guards building.

They wandered, amused, through Carnaby Street where the last of the "mod" generation was holding forth. And Reg, trying hard to be amusing, explained that the Hyde Park bridle path, called Rotten Row, had come by its name because Londoners never mastered its French title, Route du Roi.

"That means road of the king, you know," he said.

Pauline, whose French was impeccable, smiled and said, "Indeed? I rather think I prefer Rotten Row. It's less pretentious."

Reg also took great pleasure in telling her that London really was a collection of small towns, each having its own name, such as Chelsea and Primrose Hill and Lambeth, all within the confines of London.

"And then there's Dockworkers' London," he said quietly. "Not the same as the others. It's Cockney. Working people. My family's still there."

Pauline finally saw her chance. "Oh? I'd like to meet them, Reg. Couldn't we visit? After all, we're all related now."

"No, I think not. I'm sure you'd be charming, but they wouldn't know how to act around a lady like you. They're mighty uneasy around Lindsay, for that matter, though they try not to show it."

Pauline was silent for a moment. Then she said, "Reg, you're not happy, are you?"

Eyes on the road, he simply smiled a crooked smile. "Happy? Well, now, I don't know many who are. Cheerful is what we try to be, though not always that either." He looked sad. "It's not my happiness I care about. You know that. *She's* the one who matters."

He meant Lindsay, of course. Pauline didn't answer.

"I'm all wrong for her, you know," Reg said. "It's plain enough to see. But I love her, Pauline. Whatever else you think, remember that. I've loved her since the first day I saw her. That's enough to keep us going."

"She knows you love her, Reg. Try to be good to her, will you?" Pauline sighed. "Lindsay's not always easy. She's used to having her own way. But then, I suppose, so are you. And I daresay that's where the trouble lies."

"Trouble?" He pretended innocence. "No more than any man and wife, I imagine. We'll work through this, Pauline."

"Yes," Pauline lied. "I'm certain you will."

28

*W*hen she wearily reentered her apartment two weeks later, Pauline found the usual stack of mail waiting. She ran through the bills, the ads, the charity pleas and set them aside, opening only those envelopes which looked personal, among them a note from Robin, written only three days before.

I think our conversation just before you left for England must have given me the slight push I needed, dear. I asked Connie to marry me, and she said yes. Hallelujah! I was all for a quick, quiet ceremony, but her parents want some kind of a do, hopefully modest. So the date's been set for November 10 and I'm counting on your being here. I'm writing to Lindsay, too, and hope she and her husband will come. I'll also see that Geoff gets an invitation, but between us, I don't expect him to show. Just as well, probably, particularly if Lindsay arrives.

He went on for a paragraph about Connie and how happy he was.

John adores her as much as she loves him, so everything is just about perfect. Even Mrs. Graham is pleased. I was afraid she'd throw a fit, she'd had the house to herself so long, but Connie charmed her to pieces and endeared herself entirely by asking Mrs. G. to stay on as John's nurse. So everybody's on a small pink cloud!

Pauline smiled wanly. Everybody in Chicago, she thought. Not here or in London.

The trip had been as distressing as she feared. From that first embarrassing, drunken introduction until the day she left, it was as though they were all playing parts. Lindsay was the smiling, devoted wife, pretending not to notice Reg's ridiculous behavior. Reg was almost obsequious. He practically tugged at his forelock, Pauline thought, as though I were not his mother-in-law but some rich American client he had to please.

And I? I was the worst of all, Pauline reflected. I went along with the game, pretending to ignore the misery in my daughter's household. We didn't talk about the problem again until just before I left. When Lindsay said, "This is my chosen bed I'm lying in, Mama. Things will straighten out."

Straighten out? How, for God's sake? She has an alcoholic husband and the world's strangest collection of young men hanging around. She's ensconced in one of the most beautiful apartments I've ever seen, and she might as well be living in a museum filled with visitors who care no more for her than tourists care for the curator of the Victoria and Albert. She has no real life. Alone, or with those people when Reg is out on one of his infrequent jobs, or when he's socializing with his old friends. Tense and nervous when Reg is home, humiliated by his Uriah Heep manner toward me and his resentful attitude toward the hangers-on she's acquired in desperation.

Only once did Pauline feel she might be getting through. At the last minute, going back to Heathrow in the car, she said, "Reg loves you, Lindsay, but do you love him?"

"I married him, Mama."

"That's no answer."

"It's the only one I have."

"My God, Lindsay, can't you admit you made a mistake? What are you, Oriental? Is saving face the most important thing in your life?"

That was when Lindsay said things would straighten out.

"Come home, darling," Pauline pleaded. "This is no life for you. If you don't want to leave Reg, why don't both of you come back? It will be better in New York. I'll be there, and all your old friends. You'll be happier there."

"No. I can't do that, Mama. The only thing Reg has is his job. You don't really want him to start over as a chauffeur in New York, do you? What if he was assigned to drive some of your friends? Can't you see him parked outside Caravel while you were inside dining with them? Or having my acquaintances add a tip for him to their limousine bills?" She shook her head. "He belongs here, Mama. This is where he lives."

331

And where he'll die of drink, Pauline thought. She felt sorry for the man. He knew his marriage was wrong too, but like Lindsay he'd stick it out to the end, however bitter that might be.

And there was nothing she or anyone could do.

In mid-October, Adele handed Geoff an envelope which had been opened. "This came today, dear," she said. "It was addressed to both of us."

He took it without interest. Another invitation, he supposed. Hopefully not to one of those two-hundred-dollar-a-plate testimonial dinners he was always being tapped for. Or one of Adele's damned pet charities which were forever holding galas and auctions and exhibits for the benefit of the vanishing mongoose or the endangered cuttlefish. It was neither. With a slight twinge of surprise, he read:

Mr. and Mrs. Crawford Bellman
request the honour of your presence
at the marriage of their daughter
Constance

to

Mr. Robin Matthew Darnevale
on Saturday the Fifteenth of November
Nineteen hundred and sixty-nine
Church of St. Chrysostom,
Chicago, Illinois

There was also an RSVP card for the reception and a stamped return envelope to Mr. and Mrs. Bellman at the same address. He wondered fleetingly whether it was a small reception in a modest house or a big one in a mansion. So Robin was remarrying. Geoff was dismayed to feel a sinking sensation in the pit of his stomach. What the hell did he care what Robin did? But I do care, he thought unreasonably. I care that he's replacing my child. I'm angry that anyone should step into S.P.'s shoes. That's crazy. All right. So it's crazy. It's still the way I feel.

"Shall we go to the wedding?"

Geoff started. "Are you out of your mind, Adele? Go to the wedding? I've hardly spoken to the man in nearly two years. Why would I want to go to his wedding?"

"He *is* your son-in-law."

"*Was.* My daughter is dead, remember?" He was instantly sorry.

Poor Adele. Why did he have to bite her head off? She couldn't guess the insane reaction he felt. "No," he said more calmly, "we won't go. I'm sure the invitation is only a matter of politeness. Robin doesn't expect us."

"Well, I think we should go," Adele said primly. "He's the father of your grandchild. It's bad enough, Geoffrey, that you choose to ignore John. Your own flesh and blood. It would be a snub not to go to his father's wedding."

"A snub?" Geoff laughed. "You'd think I was insulting my dearest friend! I told you, Adele, we don't even speak, Robin and I. The only reason I keep him at the agency is because he's a valuable man in Chicago. Let's don't worry the subject to death, okay? I don't intend to go, so please write a nice, proper note of regret and send them something from Tiffany if that will ease your conscience."

Adele looked at him slyly. "I think you're afraid to go."

"Afraid?" Jesus, he was beginning to sound like a parrot! "Why would I be afraid?"

She shrugged. "Maybe you're worried that Lindsay will be there."

Adele looked back at him blandly. "I think you're scared to death of running into her. *And* her husband. I think that's the real reason you won't go."

"Don't be idiotic! Lindsay means nothing to me. She could marry six times, run through the whole damned United Nations, and it wouldn't bother me! Hell, if I had the least desire to go to that wedding, Lindsay wouldn't stop me. You know that, Adele."

"Even if *I* believe you, nobody else will. They'll all think you stayed away because you were afraid of seeing her and that Marks person."

"And who, may I ask are 'they'?"

"Robin. Pauline. Probably the whole staff of the agency in New York and Chicago. Not to mention Lindsay, who'll probably enjoy the speculation."

"That's rubbish. You just want to go and preen yourself in front of Lindsay as the new Mrs. Murray. That's what this is all about, isn't it?"

Adele looked indignant. "You know it's not, Geoff. How can you be so horrid? I just know what's good manners. Like it or not, Robin's still part of your family. Your grandson's father. I hate to see you look like a spiteful man. Or, worse still, a cowardly one. I think it would be a mistake for you not to attend. It will make you look so petty."

He frowned. Damn her, maybe she was right. There would be more talk if he stayed away than if he went. Besides, Lindsay probably wouldn't even be there. He doubted she'd come all the way from England for this.

And there was something else. In the past few months, he'd admitted only to himself that he'd behaved badly toward his son-in-law. It wasn't as though Robin killed S.P. God knows he loved her. It was the kind of thing that could happen to any man, but Geoff's grief had blinded him to that. He seemed to lose his balance where anything concerning S.P. was concerned: her death, her child, now her widower's remarriage. It wasn't logical. It was time he got over this one-sided feud. I'd like to see John again, he thought suddenly. I could handle it now. Enough time has passed. I'll never have another grandchild. Or another child. Adele is long past childbearing age, even if she were to sleep with me often enough to conceive one. He put that unhappy thought aside.

"Maybe you're right," he said slowly. "I never thought how I looked to other people. Odd, I suppose. A man who never sees his grandson or has any contact with his daughter's husband. Not that I care what people think," he added hastily, "but I suppose it would be a slap in the face if we didn't show up. Okay, write and accept. I'll have the office make hotel reservations."

Adele smiled. She hoped Lindsay would be there. She'd like to get a look at the Englishman. More than that, she'd like to watch Lindsay's face when they met again and it was now Adele who was Mrs. Geoffrey Murray.

Guiltily, because it was addressed to Mr. and Mrs. Reginald Marks, Lindsay did not mention the invitation to Robin's wedding. Instead, she invented an excuse to go to New York, making up something about her share of the business she'd sold to Marty.

"He wants to expand," she told Reg, "and since I'm still a limited partner he'd like me to look at the new location."

Reg was unsuspicious. He didn't seem to care that much, these days, what she did. How fast this whole marriage has come unglued, Lindsay thought sadly. But then, it never was very solid to begin with. It was a union based on sex, and sex was still the only thing that held them together. In bed they made each other happy, but that was such a small part of life. An important one, to be sure, but it left most of the hours empty and incomplete. Yet we need each other, she told herself. I need him because I can't bear the thought of being alone, the way I was during the war. And he needs me because, I suppose, I represent something or someone he never dreamed he could have.

It also was not pleasant to realize that she'd come to mean something else to Reg: his meal ticket. His drinking was now undeniably a problem. Often when the garage phoned he was too drunk to accept an assignment. Lindsay took the calls, lying that he was ill or out of town. Soon, she knew, they'd take him completely off the list. They'd long since put him on an "additional driver" basis. This meant he drew no regular salary and worked only when all the regular men were busy. He earned next to nothing, and the worst part was he no longer seemed to care. He'd begun to take his comfort, his luxury, for granted. There was plenty of liquor, a soft bed, and a willing woman. He was never abusive or even unkind, but he had gradually become an almost silent, utterly dependent, seemingly resigned presence. Lindsay was dreadfully sorry for him, and for herself as well. This wasn't what she'd bargained for. Not this subdued, helpless person. I've changed him completely from the attractive, vital man I first met, she thought unhappily. I've alienated him from his friends and his family and thrown him into a life he hates but has finally accepted because of me. He's miserable, so he drinks to forget what he's become. And the more he drinks, the more hopelessly he's trapped. The more hopelessly we're both trapped.

She knew she'd never leave him, but there were moments when she had to get away, and the invitation to Robin's wedding was irresistible. She was ashamed she didn't want Reg to go with her, but it would spoil everything. He might get drunk and embarrass her, as he had with Mama. She'd die if that happened in front of strangers. Die a thousand times if Geoff and Adele happened to be there. Not that they would be, of course. Geoff hated Robin. He'd hardly go to his wedding. The truth was, she didn't want anyone to know what a miserable failure her marriage was, and if Reg were with her, it would be all too obvious. She hadn't fooled Pauline. How could she expect to? But Pauline wouldn't laugh at her, or gossip. The others would be only too happy to spread the word that the high and mighty Lindsay Thresher Murray had married a low-class, besotted clown.

She hated herself for this cruel appraisal of him, but sometimes she hated him too, for his lethargy and his pathetic begging to be loved. He seemed almost unaware of her activities, yet he clung more tightly than ever. He seldom left the house, and now, when she urged him to look up his old chums and spend an evening at the pub, he just shook his head.

"Why not, Reg? You always enjoyed that."

"I don't belong with them any more. All they talk about is the garage."

"Well, darling, if you'd start working again, you could talk about it too." She sounded, she realized, more like an indulgent parent than a wife.

"You hated it when I spent so much time working. Now that I'm not, you hate that too."

Lindsay sighed. Both things were true. Dammit, she wanted to say, there's a happy medium, you know. If you're not going to work, then be sober and amusing. Presentable, at least, so we could entertain people. She didn't do that any more, either. It was too risky to invite anyone. The last time she had a party it was awful. Reg got monstrously drunk, fell over a Chippendale chair, and smashed a Sèvres figurine to pieces. She'd had to help him out of the room and into bed, trying to laugh it off, saying that the host was just a touch too "enthusiastic."

"I'll be gone a couple of weeks," she said as she prepared to leave. "Will you be all right? Promise me you'll eat. Mrs. Withers is going to make nice meals for you, Reg. She'll be so upset if you don't enjoy them."

He was sober but hung over that morning. "I'll be all right. Don't worry. Say hello to Pauline. Enjoy yourself. And come back soon. You *are* coming back, aren't you?"

"Darling, what a cockeyed thing to say! Of course I'm coming back! Whatever put such an idea in your head?"

"Wouldn't blame you if you didn't. Not much here for you, is there, old girl?"

Her heart hurt. "*You*'re here for me," Lindsay said. She kissed him tenderly. "Take care of yourself, darling. Maybe . . . maybe ease up on the booze a little? Surprise me when I get back?"

"Right. I'll do that."

"And have some fun too. Why don't you look up the old gang? Have a few laughs with them. I don't want you to be lonely." God, she was clucking like a mother hen! Guilt, she thought. You're up to your armpits in it. "I'll call you," she said. "And if you need me, call Mama's." She bid the housekeeper good-bye. "Take good care of Mr. Marks, Mrs. Withers."

"I will, madam. You enjoy yourself."

"It's business, you know. I don't think there'll be much time for enjoyment." Fool! Why was she making explanations to the housekeeper?

"Yes, madam, I know. But try to relax a bit anyway." Mrs. Withers flicked a knowing glance at Reg. "It will do you good, this bit of holiday."

Yes, Lindsay thought, settling into her seat on the plane, it will do me good. It's almost a year since I've been free. Uncomfortably, she wondered why she'd chosen that word. She'd meant: almost a year since I've been *home*. Same thing, maybe. America, the home of the brave and the land of the free. She couldn't wait to see it again. She'd been a fool ever to leave.

The wedding was so beautiful she couldn't bear it, Lindsay sat next to Pauline in the lovely old flower-filled church, watching Constance come slowly down the aisle on the arm of her father. She was an exquisite bride, and Robin, waiting at the altar, looked gentle and protective, even more handsome than he had on a similar day a little more than four years ago.

Four years. Was it only four years since she'd adjusted S.P.'s veil and scolded her to stop wriggling? It seemed much longer, so different had the world become. Lindsay's eyes filled with tears, thinking of her daughter. Why? she asked herself, as she so often had. Why did it happen to her?

She dared not turn around, but she could almost feel Geoff's eyes. He and Adele were seated in the row behind her. She saw them when she and Pauline entered the church, but so far they'd not exchanged a word, barely even a glance. Tactful of Constance, not to put all "the family" in the same pew. Bad enough that they couldn't possibly avoid each other at the reception later.

She was amazed to see Geoff there at all. She'd had only a quick glimpse of him, but he looked older, more tired. I suppose I do too, she thought, though we're not old. Geoff's only fifty. God, how young we were when we married! Stupid, sex-starved kids, too properly reared to have an affair and too immature to take on the responsibilities of marriage. And yet we did well for a long, long time. I wish it had been forever.

It was good to realize, sitting there in that tranquil atmosphere, that her bitterness toward her ex-husband was gone. I don't hate him any more, Lindsay thought. I suppose I never really did. I was hurt and angry, but I've always loved him.

Pauline stirred slightly. I'm just like Mama, Lindsay mused. There was only one man for her too. Even if she couldn't live with him.

"Hello, Lindsay."

The familiar voice behind her startled her so that she nearly spilled her champagne. She turned and managed a bright smile.

"Hello, Geoff. How are you?"

"Fine, thanks. And you?"

"Just great."

There was an awkward little silence, and then they said, simultaneously, "Wasn't it a lovely wedding?" and burst out laughing.

"I always told you to stop stealing my lines," Geoff said.

She grinned up at him. "And I always told you to get a new script writer."

The smile left his face. "It's awfully good to see you, Lindsay. I think about you a lot."

She looked down at her glass, avoiding his eyes, not answering.

"Your husband didn't come?"

Lindsay fought to regain her poise. "No. He was terribly sorry, but he's up to his eyebrows in business. He just couldn't get away."

"That's too bad. He still in the same line of work?"

She looked at him defensively. "Yes. He's still a chauffeur." There was defiance in her voice. "And a damned good one."

"I'm sure of that. You bring out the best in any man."

The words, spoken pleasantly enough, angered her. "You didn't seem to think so, as I recall. I seemed to bring out the worst in you."

He didn't fight back. "No, I brought out the worst in myself. I was terribly mixed up during our last years."

Lindsay felt nervous. This conversation had taken much too intimate a turn. It also was going on too long. Across the room she saw Adele watching them appraisingly, a smug little smile on her face. Damn her, Lindsay thought, she looks as though she's enjoying this.

How sure of herself she must be. How sure of Geoff. I won't let her see how this upsets me. She smiled, a bright, social smile.

"Adele looks well. Her new life must agree with her."

His expression gave away nothing. "She seems happy enough."

And you, my darling? Lindsay wanted to say. Are you happy? Or are you regretful, too? Do you wish we could take it all back, all the misunderstanding and alienation, all the pain and the injured pride?

"I'm rather surprised to see you here, Geoff. I didn't think you'd come."

"And I hoped to God *you* wouldn't."

She looked at him, startled. There was no mistaking his meaning.

"When are you leaving Chicago?" he asked.

"Late tomorrow. I want to spend some time with John. We only arrived last night, and I haven't even seen him. Mama and I thought we'd visit him tomorrow morning." She hesitated. "And you?"

"Do you mean when am I leaving or when am I visiting John?" Geoff looked at her intently. "I'm staying on an extra day as long as I'm here. I have some business meetings on Monday." He paused. "Funny. I planned to visit John tomorrow morning too, but I suppose that would be awkward."

She felt Adele's eyes boring into her. To hell with her. "Why should it be? We're his grandparents, and civilized enough to be pleasant though estranged. I don't see anything wrong with our seeing him together. Adele and Mama should be chaperones enough for us."

"I hadn't planned to take Adele."

"Oh, well, Mama will be a respectable duenna, I imagine."

Geoff smiled. "Maybe you'd lunch with me afterward? The two of you, I mean."

Lindsay looked at him evenly. "Would Adele approve of that?"

"I don't see why she wouldn't. But does it matter?"

"No," Lindsay said, "it really doesn't."

"Where are you staying?"

"Watergate Tower."

"Fine. I'll pick you and Pauline up about ten. Will that be all right?"

Lindsay couldn't resist. "You're sure Adele won't mind being left alone on Sunday? The stores are closed. Whatever will she do to amuse herself?"

"Don't, Lindsay," he said gently. "Sarcasm never became you."

339

"I see you managed not to speak to Adele," Pauline said drily as they took a taxi back to the hotel, "but you certainly had a nice long chat with Geoffrey."

Lindsay smiled. "I noticed you arranged to park yourself on the other side of the room from her too. We did a pretty damned good job of pretending she was invisible, didn't we?"

Pauline breathed a little sigh. "You know, I don't really care about her one way or the other any more. I don't hate her, I don't resent her, I'm supremely indifferent to her." She squeezed Lindsay's hand. "And you? Did it bother you to see her again?"

"Not as much as I would have thought. I was aware of her, particularly when Geoff and I were talking, but it didn't seem to matter to me, either. She's a nothing. I can't even be bitter about her any more." Lindsay frowned. "I wonder why that is? I thought I'd despise her until I died."

"Maybe it's because you know she's never been happy a day in her life. And never will be, I suspect. You can't hate someone like that. You can only pity them. Or feel nothing at all."

Lindsay sat thoughtfully for a moment before she said, "Geoff's going to visit John tomorrow."

"Really? Well, I'm delighted. I'm glad he's had a change of heart. His presence at the wedding certainly would indicate that. I'm very pleased for his sake, as well as Robin's and John's. Poor Geoff. He just needed time, I suppose. His grief was so intense. No more so than yours, my dear, but he didn't have as much self-discipline. He gave in to it, Lindsay. Men do, sometimes, even more than women. And it's terrible to see."

"And harder to live with. I wish I'd had more patience, Mama."

"I know, darling."

They were nearing the hotel. "Geoff wants to pick us up in the morning and take us to Robin's. Then he'd like us to have lunch with him." She paused. "Adele won't be with him."

"I see."

Lindsay turned to her, half amused. "Now what does that mean? When you say, 'I see,' it has more significance than a whole oration from anybody else."

Pauline pretended innocence. "Whatever are you talking about?"

340

"Come on, Mama, don't play those games with me. You think there's something special in this invitation? Don't be silly."

"I won't if you won't."

Lindsay laughed. "You don't think I'm dotty enough to try to start something with Geoff again? Forget it, Mother dearest. A burned child dreads the fire, to gild an old coin. No, I'm married. So is he. We're a couple of old grandfolks going to see the kid and having a social bite later to discuss him. That's it. All of it."

"Naturally. Then you won't mind if I don't join you for lunch? I promised to call an old friend. One of the last remaining relics, along with me. I said I'd lunch with her."

"Old friend? I didn't know you had any old friends here."

"Oh, yes, my dear. We date back to the Ice Age. I rang her up this morning, before the wedding, while you were dressing."

Lindsay looked at her suspiciously. "What's her name?"

"Sophie. We went to school together."

"Sophie," Lindsay repeated. "Mama, you wouldn't be inventing Sophie, would you? You don't have some crazy idea about throwing Geoff and me together, I hope. Because it won't work, you know. Life isn't a romantic novel, with everything turning out right in the end."

"Who, me? Lindsay, how could you think such a thing?"

Lindsay looked at her fondly. "I can't possibly imagine," she said. "Forgive me. It must be all that champagne. Be sure to remember me to Sophie. Promise?"

Pauline kept a straight face. "Of course I will, dear."

Geoff made a careful knot in his tie. "You don't mind my going to see John alone, do you? I know it would only bore you."

Adele rustled through the Sunday papers. Why were out-of-town papers always so foreign? Who cared about Mayor Daley anyhow? "What did you say, Geoffrey?"

"I said I hoped you could amuse yourself for a few hours while I visit John."

"Oh, *that*. It's perfectly all right, darling. I had enough of your family at the wedding. Besides, I'm not sure I could bear to witness your mea culpa scene with your long lost grandson."

Geoff gritted his teeth. How had he gotten so hopelessly entangled with this impossible woman? Because she's a damned good actress, he thought. So sweet and soft and understanding when Lindsay and I were at each other's throats. So sexy, when I needed that. And now so sharp-tongued and cold. My God, she's the coldest woman I've ever known. Lindsay was right. She's frigid. What a fool I was to think it was Howard's fault. This one couldn't be moved by Cary Grant. She's a beautiful, selfish iceberg. And just as immovable. Nine months of this loveless marriage. What torture it must have been for her to pretend passion with me the few months before!

Adele riffled through the ads. There was a little dress at Marshall Field that didn't look too bad. Maybe she'd hop over there on Monday and have a look. Thank God she was still a size eight.

"Lindsay looked a bit heavy, didn't you think Geoffrey? She seems to have put on *pounds*. All that dreadful English food, I suppose. She probably wallows in heavy cream. Or perhaps she's drinking. She has the look of a drinker, if you ask me. Well, why not, poor old thing. If I were married to a chauffeur I'm sure I'd drink too, though I'd have too much pride to show up in front of my old friends looking all bloated and puffy."

Geoff scooped the contents of the dresser top into his pockets, not answering.

"I suppose you thought she looked beautiful," Adele said.

"As a matter of fact, I did."

"Oh, really, Geoff! You're such a romantic! You still see her as she was at nineteen. Well, she's forty-nine now, and her looks are shot." She kicked off a mule and looked down at her well-pedicured feet. "Thank God I've taken care of myself. I think it's a woman's duty."

"Lindsay was more interested in other kinds of 'duty,'" Geoff muttered.

"What? What did you say, dear?"

"Nothing, Adele. I'll see you later."

"Give my love to Lindsay."

Halfway out the door he turned and stared at her. Adele smiled.

"Darling, I know you're going to see her. Such a charming picture you'll make! The loving grandparents cooing over the baby. I'm touched."

"How the hell did you know—"

Adele's face changed. "So you *are* going to see her. I suspected it. Geoff, you're so naïve. You fell right into that little trap, didn't you? I watched you last night. You were mesmerized. I knew you'd figure a way to see her again. Well, go ahead. It won't do you any good, you know. Maybe you can lure her to a hotel room this afternoon, but you'll never be free to remarry her. I promise you that."

He was white with rage. "You . . . you unspeakable—"

"Naughty, naughty. A gentleman doesn't call his loving wife names like that."

29

Over lunch, Lindsay was euphoric. "Wasn't he wonderful, Geoff? Have you ever seen a handsomer, better-natured little boy?"

"Nor one harder to catch. That little devil can toddle around faster than I can run after him."

"He looks like S.P., don't you think? Same eyes. Same smile. It's a joy to see him. A comfort. Like there's something of his mother still alive."

"Lindsay, how can you? How can you be so matter-of-fact about it? It damned near killed me, just looking at him."

Unthinkingly, she placed her fingers over his. "I know," she said. "Me too. But she'd want us to love him and be glad she left him to Robin. And to us."

He dropped his head and quickly kissed the small, familiar hand. Lindsay drew back as though he'd burned her.

"Don't do that, Geoff."

"Sorry." He looked straight into her eyes. "I love you, Lindsay, I've never stopped. I think I was temporarily insane for a while. Letting you go was the worst mistake of my life. I never wanted to be married to anybody but you."

A hundred responses rose to her lips. Then why did you walk away? she wanted to scream. Why did you stop making love to me? Why did you drive me to this man I never wanted to marry? And why did you allow yourself to be taken in by Adele? How could you, Geoff? How could you have ruined both our lives this way?

After a moment she said quietly, "I never wanted anyone but you, either. It just happened. It's done and it can't be undone."

"Can't it? Other people remarry."

"Not people like us. Not in our circumstances." She sat up straighter. "All right, apparently we both made a mistake. I admit I did. I never loved Reg. I married him to show you somebody wanted me, even if you didn't. Insane, isn't it? But that's what rejection can do to a presumably rational human being."

He nodded slowly. "I suspected as much. And I was just as crazy, thinking Adele was the kind of hero worshiper you never could be. Thinking I wanted a wife without spirit, without challenge. I must have been mad." He reached for her hand. "But it isn't too late, Lindsay. Adele will make me pay through the nose, but I don't care. I'll get a divorce. So can you."

She shook her head. "I can't, Geoff. You don't understand about Reg. What I've done to him. He was happy enough before. He didn't want to marry me. He knew it was an impossible match. But I was so damned determined. And now I've cut him off from his family and his friends, made him so miserable he's drunk most of the time. He can't even keep a job any more. I've put him into a world he doesn't understand, and made it impossible for him to return to the one he does. No," Lindsay said, "I can't abandon him now. He'll never get on his feet again. I have to take care of him."

Geoff abruptly released her hand. "That's absurd. You don't turn a man into something he doesn't wish to be. It's not your fault. Don't go through the rest of your life a martyr, Lindsay! He'll survive. He did before. He will again."

"He won't. He can't. How could I live with myself if I just walked out, saying 'Ta, ta, old thing, it's been nice knowing you'? Do you know he actually asked me if I was coming back from this trip? He was pathetic. 'There's not much here for you,' he said. He almost broke my heart."

"But he's right, Lind. There isn't anything there for you. It's all here. Your home, your family. Even me, if you'll have me again." He looked at her beseechingly. "Please, darling. We were wrong, but must we pay for it forever? Give Reg money. Set him up for life. I don't care. But for God's sake think of your own future too! Even if you don't come back to me, I can't bear to see you saddled with someone you only pity. You have nothing in common with him. You'd be doing him a favor to let him go back where he's happy and at ease."

She thought she would die, sitting right there in that restaurant.

The temptation was almost irresistible. It could be the way it used to be. A life together. A love together. God give me strength.

"I'm sorry," she said. "I can't. You don't understand how I feel. He needs me, Geoff."

"So do I."

Where were you when *I* needed *you*? Lindsay thought. "I must go," she said. "Mama will be waiting. We have a plane to catch."

"Lindsay, please...."

She gathered her coat around her. "Don't say any more. I can't bear it."

"Will I see you again?"

The tightness of her throat almost strangled her answer. "I don't know," she said. "Don't be in touch with me, Geoff. Be kind. Care enough for me not to make it harder than it is."

Where was he? Lindsay looked around the airport. There was no sign of Reg. Strange. She'd cabled him her flight number and arrival time. She rang up the flat and spoke to the housekeeper.

"I'm at the airport, Mrs. Withers. Is Mr. Marks on the way?"

"No, madam. He's here."

"There? What's wrong? Is he ill?"

"Not exactly, madam."

Of course not. He was more likely too drunk to drive. Or he'd forgotten she was returning. Or he just damned well didn't care.

"I see," Lindsay said. "Thank you. I'll get a cab."

An hour later she let herself into the apartment. It was so quiet. Where was Reg? In a drunken stupor on his bed? Passed out in the drawing room? Lindsay braced herself and walked into the main salon. He was asleep on a sofa near the fireplace. For a long moment she stood looking at him, at the room. It was wrong, all of it. He didn't belong here, this hulk of a man scrunched up on the small Georgian sofa. He was out of scale with the delicately wrought furniture, the pale walls, the silk hangings at the windows. He belonged in a place where the furniture was overstuffed and bought on the installment plan, and there was always a smell of cooking cabbage. Not here in a roomful of antiques, not where the fragile aroma of crushed roses in potpourri jars pervaded the air. He doesn't fit in my house, Lindsay thought. God help us, he doesn't fit anywhere any longer.

And yet, sleeping, he looked so peaceful, so vulnerable, she felt ashamed. It's not his fault. He can't help being what he is. Or what I've tried to make him be. She walked over and shook him gently.

"Reg. Reg, I'm home."

He opened his eyes slowly and tried to focus. Then, abruptly realizing who it was, he sat up and shook his head as though to clear it.

"Lindsay! How? What? What time is it?"

"Nearly midnight."

"But . . ." He rubbed his hands across his face. "Oh, no! I must have fallen asleep, waiting till it was time to go get you. Ah, I'm that sorry, luv! How did you get home? Took a cab, I expect." He stood up, falteringly, and kissed her. "Forgive me. I was so damned tired, I just dropped off. Withers should have called me. Damn that woman!"

The smell of stale liquor on his breath revolted her. Tired, was he? From what? Lifting a bottle? 'Dropped off,' indeed! Blotto from booze was more like it. And blaming Mrs. Withers for not waking him! Didn't he have even that much sense of responsibility, to stay sober and awake to meet his wife without having to be prodded into it? Her thoughts registered on her face and Reg, bleary-eyed, recognized them.

"You're angry. I don't blame you."

Not answering, Lindsay turned wearily away. He came after her, trying to touch her, clasping her from behind, his hands on her body.

"I've missed you so, luv. It's been terrible without you." He held her close against him, his voice low and intimate. "You're all I have, sweetheart. Let me tuck you into bed and hold you."

She turned on him. "In your condition, I'm sure that's all you're able to do."

He stepped back as though she'd struck him.

"You're drunk, Reg. As usual. Is this your idea of a homecoming? That I take a taxi from the airport and arrive to find you passed out? Do you think you can make it all right by going to bed with me? My God, is this your idea of marriage: liquor and sex?" Once started, she couldn't stop. "I suppose you've been in this condition since the day I left. God knows you've been in it for months, even while I was here. Lying around all day, too lazy to work, not even leaving the house! It was better when you were at least mobile. It was more endurable when you spent time in that filthy garage trading dirty jokes with the other chauffeurs! It was even a relief when you went out with your stupid

347

friends and sat guzzling beer in that tacky pub! I suppose they don't want you any more, is that it? I know the garage doesn't. It wouldn't surprise me if your friends were fed up with—" She stopped, horrified. How could she be so cruel, so vicious? At the sight of his stricken face, she burst into tears. "Oh, darling, I'm so sorry," she said. "I didn't mean it. I'm just exhausted and disappointed you weren't there waiting for me. I don't know what got into me. Can you forgive me?"

He seemed quite sober now. Not even angry.

"It's all right," he said. "Everything you say is true. I'm not much good to anybody. I can't get work, and my friends don't feel close to me any more. To them, I'm a rich woman's husband. One of the toffs. They don't act the same with me, and I don't feel I belong with them either. I notice things now I never did before. The way they dress and eat and talk. How crude they are." He laughed bitterly. "As though I'm not. But before, I didn't know any different."

"Reg, I'm sorry. I really shouldn't have said—"

"No. It's all right. I knew it before you said it. You want to hear something, Lindsay? While you were away I was so bloody lonesome I used to go out in the kitchen and try to visit with Withers. Offered her a drink, hoping she'd talk awhile. And do you know what she said? 'I'm sorry, sir, but it isn't fitting for me to socialize with the master.' Funny, huh? I don't belong with your friends or mine. I don't even belong with the domestics. What do you call that, Lindsay? Limbo? That's the word, isn't it? I'm just hanging there, halfway between everything."

Lindsay was frozen. She'd not realized how analytical he was. No wonder he drinks. He knows he's lost. We've got to get out of here, she thought. England is still too class-conscious. At least, the generation we come from is. We'll go home. We'll start over. We'll just be Mr. and Mrs. Reginald Marks there. Not Reggie Marks who married the rich American woman. Not Lindsay Marks who married her sexy chauffeur. New York is a melting pot. Everyone fits in. Who your parents are, where you went to school, those things don't matter as much in America. In that wild moment, she truly believed that was the answer. Yes, it would be good for them there. A fresh start away from the disaster that drew closer every day.

"Darling," she said. "I've been thinking. . . ."

Martin Wylie propped himself up in his king-sized bed and looked at the sleepy girl beside him. She was a new employee, very young and very willing. She'd been hired a week ago, and two days later she and her boss were lovers. Pretty little thing, Marty thought. Not heavy in the brains department, but otherwise . . .

"Hey," he said, "I had a letter this morning. Lindsay's coming home. She wants us to get her apartment in shape for her."

She didn't open her eyes. "Who's Lindsay?"

"My partner."

Joyce lifted heavy lids. "I didn't know you had a partner. I thought you were the head honcho."

"Well, I am. That is, I bought the business from Lindsay when she moved to England. But she still owns part." Marty lit a cigarette and stared at the ceiling. "Weird. I didn't think she was ever coming back."

"Why did she go to England in the first place?"

"Her husband walked out on her. She couldn't take it. Ran off and married the guy who used to drive her when she went over there on buying trips."

Joyce became wide-awake and interested. "No kidding? She married her chauffeur? Far out!"

"Yeah. And she's bringing him back with her. I wonder how that's going to sit with her mother and all her tony friends."

"What happened to her ex?"

"Oh, he married the dame he dumped her for. That's a kick too. She'd been married to Lindsay's father."

Joyce frowned. "I'm not sure I follow that. He married his— what? His stepmother-in-law?"

"Bingo."

"Isn't that incest or something?"

Marty laughed. "Next best thing to it, I guess. Especially since his new wife was Lindsay's best friend when they were kids."

"You're putting me on. You made up the whole thing."

"Could I make up a thing like that? What do you think I am, some spaced-out writer? It's true. Every word of it. I just wonder what she'll do now, with a husband who doesn't know how to do anything but drive a car. I hope to hell she doesn't have some crazy idea about giving him a job in the shop. That's all I need: a dumb limey with no experience."

"What's Lindsay like?"

"Pretty. And smart. Sexy, too. And don't call her Lindsay. To you she's Mrs. Marks."

"She's old, though, isn't she?"

"Yeah. Kind of. She must be damned near fifty."

When Pauline got word of Lindsay's return, she was delighted. But not as delighted as she'd have been a few weeks before. She was happy that Lindsay had come to her senses, that she was returning to the place she belonged, even though Pauline had qualms about her remaining married to that pathetic, alcoholic man. But if she can't leave him, her mother thought, at least they'll be here where people love her.

People love her. In a strange way that was the problem. In the back of her mind was the nagging, troublesome idea that Lindsay's meeting with Geoff in Chicago might have had something to do with her sudden decision to return. If so, that was bad news, sorry as she was to admit it. Nothing would have pleased her more than to see Lindsay and Geoff together again, but it was quite impossible. Lindsay had told her, on the plane to New York, about their luncheon. Hearing it, Pauline wished she hadn't invented "Sophie." Things would not have gotten so sticky if she'd been there.

"Geoff still loves me, Mama," Lindsay said tonelessly. "He wants us to get divorces and remarry."

Pauline wasn't surprised. In fact, at that moment she was even hopeful. "What did you tell him?"

"That it was impossible, of course. I couldn't desert Reg. I'm rotten, but not that rotten."

"But you love Geoff, Lindsay."

"Love isn't always the most important thing. Yes, I love him. I wish to God I hadn't been so impetuous. If I'd just ridden it out, I'd be free now, when he realizes the mistake he's made with Adele. But that's not the way it is. I owe too much to Reg. Little things like duty and loyalty. The kind of things you and Gandy taught me to believe in."

Pauline fell silent.

"You know I'm doing the only decent thing, Mama. Admit it. I know you wish Geoff and I were still together. So do I. But you wouldn't like me very much if I just walked out on a man I've driven to drink, would you? Tell the truth. Would you honestly approve of that kind of careless, irresponsible behavior?"

350

"Darling, I'd approve of anything you do. I'd like you, no matter what."

"Maybe. But I wouldn't like myself." Lindsay shook her head. "No. I'm going back and see it through. I've made Reg build his life around mine. I bought him and paid for him and I can't throw him away like a worn-out shoe."

Remembering the conversation, Pauline felt troubled. It had been easy enough earlier to urge Lindsay to relocate herself and her husband, but now she had doubts. What would he do here? As Lindsay said, he couldn't be a chauffeur. People wouldn't understand, no use pretending they would. But most of all, Pauline worried that Lindsay's troubled state of mind might delude her into thinking she could have both Geoff and Reg. She might be rationalizing that she could stay married to Marks and still see Geoff, perhaps have an affair with her ex-husband. It wasn't on moral grounds that Pauline cringed from such an idea. She was far too sophisticated a woman to be as shocked by extramarital affairs now as she had been almost thirty-five years ago. She simply knew that there'd be tragedy, somehow, if Geoff and Lindsay played with this rekindled fire. Who'd precipitate the tragedy, she didn't know. Reg, perhaps, in a drunken moment. Or Adele in a fury. She shuddered, praying Lindsay had no idea of inviting such danger, that she and Geoff had too much sense to even consider it.

But who knew about those two troubled souls? Who could predict what would happen when there was no longer an ocean between them?

Dammit, Pauline thought, I'm almost sorry she's coming home.

Once she made up her mind, Lindsay moved quickly. After the terrible homecoming scene with Reg, she was more loving than ever, remorseful and bound to make up to him for the things she'd deprived him of.

Somewhat to her surprise, Reg began to behave better too. He still drank, but less heavily, and he made an effort to be attractive and pleasant to the few friends she had. Probably, Lindsay thought, the air is finally cleared between us. We both said what we felt, all the evil spirits are exorcised, and we can start over with a better understanding of each other.

And not only had Reg not put up an argument about moving to New York, he actually seemed pleased by the prospect. He worried only about a job.

"I can't be a driver there," he said. "It would be awkward for you."

"Why don't you start your own limousine service? Nothing wrong with that. One of the biggest jet-setters in New York owns a fleet of taxis. Why don't we think about setting you up in your own business?"

"On your money."

"Why not? I can't think of a better investment. You can repay the loan when you're in the black. I'll even charge you interest."

"It would be mighty expensive, luv. Limousines cost the earth."

"So start modestly, with a couple of them, and work up."

"You really think I could?"

"I know you could. I know you can." Lindsay laughed. "Oh, Reg, it will be wonderful for both of us! Thank heavens I kept the apartment. All I have to do is write to Marty to get it spruced up."

"The apartment you shared with Geoff?"

"Well, yes. Do you mind?" She looked troubled. "If you do, we can always look for another place. Of course, this one is all furnished and comfortable. It must still be in pretty good shape, though I haven't lived in it for a year. But if it bothers you—"

"No. It doesn't bother me. Word of honor." He smiled. "Reggie Marks on Park Avenue. My old mum won't believe it. Course, she never believed we lived in Albany either. She was never here."

Lindsay was defensive. "Well, that's not our fault. We asked her often enough."

"I know. Mum's of the old school. Says she has no business in a place like this. She knows where we live, all right. I didn't mean that. But she always thought I overstepped myself." His face clouded. "Maybe I did, at that. I've never felt much at home here, Lindsay, to tell you the blinkin' truth."

Lindsay kissed him tenderly. "It will be different in New York. Wait and see. Everything will be different."

Back in her old home, she felt happily that things would be right now. She excitedly dragged Reg through the apartment, showing him Gandy's wonderful old possessions, pointing out the treasures she'd lived with most of her life. There was only one bad moment, when they came to Geoff's bedroom.

"This is where he slept, eh? You had separate rooms?"

"In the last few years, yes."

352

"Don't approve of it. No wonder you got divorced."

She tried to make light of it. "Darling, separate bedrooms didn't cause our divorce. Actually, it's quite a good idea. Much more romantic, like a lovers' tryst."

"I'm not sleeping in his room."

"Sweetie, it isn't his. It's yours."

"You don't want me in your bed?"

She hid her exasperation. "Reg, stop behaving like a child. After all, separate bedrooms are very much a European custom."

"A Continental custom," he corrected her. "Not English. Didn't know it was American, either."

She burst out laughing. "Oh, for the love of Pete, if it's such a big deal, forget it. I just thought you'd be more comfortable." She pressed close to him. "You know I love sleeping with you. I always have."

He seemed mollified, but Lindsay secretly was a little put out. One thing she'd missed in the last year was her privacy. Reg was around day and night, always sharing her bed in Albany. She'd rather hoped to have a room to herself here. Not that she didn't want him to visit it often, at any hour. She remembered how unhappy she was toward the end when Geoff kept to his own quarters. Still, it was civilized for people their age. A shared double bed was for the newly married.

What an odd thought! We're newly married, Lindsay realized. Only a little more than a year. Why did it seem forever? Because it's been like a prison sentence, she answered herself. Resolutely, she put such disloyal thoughts from her mind. It had been bad, but it was going to be good now.

Hand in hand, they wandered through the big, spacious rooms.

"Marty did a marvelous job," Lindsay said, "He thought of everything." She touched the petals of long-stemmed white roses. "Even my favorite flowers." Her eyes wandered down to a bit of cardboard tucked under the vase. She hadn't noticed it before. Reg was looking at the view from the window. Quickly, Lindsay picked up the card.

Welcome home, it said. And it was signed simply, *G.*

Reg turned as she was reading the card. "Somebody else send the flowers?"

Lindsay casually tore the message to bits. "No. They're from Marty, just as I thought. Sweet of him, wasn't it?"

He nodded, pleased. "Yes. Very kind of him. He must be fond of you, Lindsay."

"He is. Very fond."

She wondered if Reg could see how hard her heart was beating. She felt as though it were going to jump right through her dress. Geoff, leave me alone! I didn't even want you to know I was here. Mama, she thought. Mama must have told him. Well, why not? New York was big, but you couldn't hide forever. And there was no need to. Geoff was part of her past. And there, by God, he would remain.

30

*I*t was February when they returned to New York, the bleakest, grayest, most depressing month. Like most people, Lindsay hated February, the middle of winter, offering still more cold and gloom, without March's promise of spring. "It's one of the more sensible things God did," she used to grumble to Geoff, "making it the shortest month of the year."

Geoff had looked amused. "God didn't make February. Men did."

"Well, then *they* used their heads, for once."

Walking to her lawyer's office near Grand Central, Lindsay smiled, remembering. She didn't hate February 1970. Even the biting wind and bleak sky didn't depress her. She was home. She felt strong and useful.

"You're looking very chipper," the lawyer said. "Nice to have you back, Lindsay. How's Pauline?"

Daniel Fields had been their attorney forever. An old friend of Howard's, he'd handled Gandy's estate and her father's, and kept a careful eye on "the Thresher ladies," as he continued to call them.

"Mama's fine. Eighty next August, you know. We're going to have a bash. She wants to celebrate." She told him Pauline's comments about reaching such a formidable age.

"Never lost her sense of humor," Fields said. "Only mistake I ever knew her to make was when she stopped tolerating Howard's childish escapades. She should have just kept laughing them off."

"Easier said than done, Dan."

"Yes, I'm sure. The ego is a fragile thing." He put on his glasses. "Well, now, what have we here?" He sorted through the pages of her file folder. "Everything seems in good order. Your investments are solid enough. No tax problems. Thank the Lord you weren't silly enough to give up your citizenship when you remarried. How is your husband, by the way? I'm hoping to meet him."

"You will. Actually, he's the reason I'm here. We want to set up a corporation. He's going to open a limousine service. I'll finance it. But it's to be in his name: Reginald Marks."

"Oh?" Dan peered over his bifocals. "Will that be the name of the company?"

"Yes. We wanted something British and snobby. The best thing we could come up with was Reginald Marks Ltd."

As she said it, a disloyal thought came to mind. "Limited" was appropriate for Reg. Stop that! Jokes at your husband's expense aren't funny. It was a perfectly good name for his business. Light-years better than the things he'd suggested. His favorite choice was "Reglind." He'd thought it very clever, combining their names that way. She'd laughed it out of existence.

"Reglind?" Lindsay repeated. "That's terrible! It sounds like something people name their sailboats. Honestly, Reg! If we ever buy a beach house you'll probably want to call it 'Lay Me Dune.'"

He hadn't been amused. "All right, Lindsay, what do you suggest?"

"Why not your name? As simple as that."

"But it's really your business, not mine."

She'd become impatient. "Oh, for heaven's sake, don't be so literal! It's only my money. *Our* money, I prefer to think. It's *your* business. You're the one who's going to make a success of it."

"I do hope so," he'd said.

Dan was making notes. "How do you want this drawn up? As a partnership?"

"Yes. No. I mean, shouldn't it be his corporation? In his name?"

"There are all sorts of complications, Lindsay. Things we have to put in to protect you. Insurance. Indemnities against legal actions. The limit of your responsibility—"

"Dan, you know I don't know about things like that. Just do it, will you? A loan, I thought. Something simple. And as soon as possible. I'm anxious for Reg to get started."

He took off his glasses and leaned back in his chair. "May I talk to you as a friend? Kind of an uncle?"

"Sure. Shoot."

"Are you positive you want to do this? A limousine service is highly competitive. You're up against Fugazy and London Town Car and a lot of other very successful, established firms. It's a risk, Lindsay. You could lose a lot of money. There's a big investment in the cars and garage. There's a payroll to be set up, withholding taxes, unemployment. . . ." He hesitated. "You'll need an office staff as well as drivers. I know Mr. Marks is an experienced chauffeur, but is he a business man as well? That is, are you sure he can handle it?"

Lindsay flushed. "Mama's been talking to you, hasn't she?"

Dan Fields didn't answer.

"Okay. I understand the lawyer-client privilege thing. You probably already know Reg has had a drinking problem. But he's over it now. He's not educated but he's smart, Dan. And I want to give him an incentive to be the man he was. He needs something to take pride in. It's bad for him, being supported by me."

"He still will be."

"At the beginning. But he's bound to pay back the investment money, with interest." She fiddled nervously with the clasp of her handbag. Then she said, "Dammit, what else can I do? He must work at something and he doesn't know anything but cars."

No use arguing, Fields thought. She's a desperate woman, if ever I saw one. Pauline had confided her worries to him and he had grave doubts, not only about the business venture.

"Very well, Lindsay. I'll get the proper papers drawn up, and you and Mr. Marks can sign some kind of agreement that will protect his pride and your money. Let me handle it."

She smiled gratefully. "Thanks, Dan. I knew you'd come through."

He showed her to the door and kissed her on the cheek. "By the way," he said, "have you seen anything of Geoff since your return?"

"No. Why?"

"Nothing. I just wondered. He's my client too, you know. The only thing I didn't handle for him was your divorce."

Outside, the wind seemed angrier, the clouds more threatening. Shivering, Lindsay hailed a cab, wondering why she suddenly felt so upset. Nothing Dan said about the risk of this business venture was news to her. She too had doubts, but she was willing to gamble. It was that last, offhand reference to Geoff. Had he been consulting Dan also?

Or did she merely imagine the lawyer slightly emphasized "your" when he mentioned divorce?

"No," Adele said coldly. "Absolutely, positively, unequivocally no, Geoffrey. I will not agree to a divorce."

"Del, it's a mistake. You know it as well as I do. I'll provide generously for you, but we're not suited, my dear. The blame can't be laid on either side. Let's just agree to disagree. We were both wrong."

She'd calmly gone on wrapping Christmas gifts. "I don't even care to discuss it," she said. "It's out of the question."

"Why, for God's sake? This is a farce! You won't sleep with me. We have nothing to talk about, no interests in common. Why should we stay married?"

"Why not?" she asked reasonably. "What's the point of *not* staying married? I certainly don't intend to marry again. I've had two dismal experiences with the sacred institution." She looked up. "This wouldn't have anything to do with the fact that Lindsay's coming home, would it? Everybody's talking about it. What gall! Coming back here brazenly with that servant she married!"

"He's not a servant, Adele. The man is a professional driver."

"Of what? Racing cars?" She laughed. "You make him sound like a playboy instead of a chauffeur. You never stop defending her, do you? You've never really gotten over her. Well, my dear Geoffrey, if you have some wild idea that you and she are going to get divorces and walk off hand in hand into the sunset, you can forget it. I'm not stepping aside for Lindsay."

He was furious. "You're crazy! I haven't heard from her since the day of Robin's wedding."

"Correction. The day *after* as far as I know. Did you find a little Chicago motel that afternoon? How was it? As exciting as you remember?"

"Shut up! You're disgusting!" He took a deep breath. Anger wasn't going to help. "Del, I swear to you this has nothing to do with Lindsay. All right, I admit I talked to her about the possibility of our getting married again, but she wouldn't hear of it. She feels she has a duty to this Marks. She's going to stick with him come hell or high water."

"How saintly. She must look lovely in her martyr's robes. Probably has them made to order at Hardy Amies." She held an elaborately

358

packaged box at arm's length. "How do you think John will like this? Isn't the paper adorable with all those pictures of Snoopy on it?"

He looked at her in amazement. Could anyone be this cool, this unconcerned, when her husband told her he'd proposed to his ex-wife? My God, she was incredible! He gave a hollow laugh.

"John is two years old, Adele. I hardly think he'll notice your fancy wrapping job."

"I know that. But Constance will. She appreciates my taste." Adele began humming under her breath. "I do love Christmas," she said. "I've found the perfect thing for you, dear. You're difficult to buy for. I never know what to give you."

Give me tenderness, Geoff said silently. Give me love. Or if not, at least, in the name of mercy, give me a divorce.

The next day he went to see Dan Fields.

"She'll ruin you," Dan said. "She'll take every nickel you have."

"I don't care."

"Yes you do, Geoff. You've worked hard for what you have. Why throw it away?" The lawyer looked at him speculatively. "What brought this on anyway? You've been married less than a year. Is there, by chance, someone else?"

"No one. At least no one who'll have me. I just want out, Dan. She's distant. Cold. Incapable of love."

"She's also faithful and injured. Or so any judge will see her if she contests a divorce. Which she will."

"Dan, what am I going to do? I can't live with her."

"We can try for a legal separation. See how that works. Maybe she'll meet someone and want to finalize it. That will go easier on your wallet."

Geoff snorted. "Fat chance. She'll never marry again." He considered the option for a moment. "Well, it's better than nothing, I suppose. I don't plan to remarry either. I just want to breathe."

"Breathe carefully," Dan said. "And don't let her catch you panting with passion."

"Maybe I should," Geoff said. "At least she'd divorce me."

"And you'd pay through the nose the rest of your life."

Geoff tried once again. "Dammit, it's only money! I'd give anything to be rid of her. Jesus, when I think how well Lindsay behaved. . . ."

"Don't compare the star with the stand-in, my boy. You're dealing with the replacement for the leading lady. Quite another thing. Lindsay loved you enough to let you go. And she had too much pride to keep you against your will. Not this one, in either case. She has an ice cube where her heart ought to be."

When he left the office, Geoff felt a little better. At least he'd be semi-free. Certainly emotionally more peaceful, even if still legally bound. Dan Fields was extraordinary. He must be damned near Pauline's age, but he was as sharp as ever.

He knows Lindsay is in the back of my mind, Geoff thought. I'm not fooling him. Maybe the only one I'm fooling is myself.

The parting from Adele was absurdly low-key.

"I'm getting a legal separation," he said, "since you won't agree to a divorce."

"Are you?" She sounded as uncurious as though he'd said he was buying a new suit. "Well, I can't force you to live with me, I suppose. Who's handling it for you? Lindsay's lawyer?"

"*My* lawyer."

Adele smiled. "Same thing. Whatever, tell him to be prepared. My expenses run very high."

"So I've noticed."

"Geoff, you really are very stupid."

"I know. I've known that for a year."

He took a furnished sublet on East 63rd Street and waited for Lindsay to come home. He kept checking with Pauline, pretending to be casual about Lindsay's return and not deceiving her for an instant.

"Geoff," she finally said, "you're not holding out any false hopes, are you? Lindsay will stick to that man, you know. She feels she must."

"I'm aware of that, dear. I didn't leave Adele for that reason."

"I devoutly hope not, for your sake. And Lindsay's. Don't make things hard for her, Geoff. She still loves you."

"I won't. But you *will* let me know when they return?"

"Why?"

"I always want to know where she is, that's all. I swear I won't approach her."

Pauline looked at him sympathetically. It was terrible not to be able to get someone out of your system. She knew that firsthand. So, unfortunately, did Lindsay. She wanted to tell Geoff that she wouldn't let him know when Lindsay arrived, but he looked so pathetic, she reluctantly agreed.

"Give her a chance, Geoffrey," she said. "Don't get her life all stirred up again."

"I won't. I promise. She asked me the same thing in Chicago."

He'd kept his promise. Beyond the roses (he hadn't sworn not to send flowers, only not to approach her), he did not intrude. She didn't acknowledge the gift. He didn't expect her to. He kept track of her through Pauline and through the few mutual friends Lindsay had gotten in touch with since her return. Ashamed to listen to their gossip, he nonetheless craved every word of it and was guiltily glad that they didn't understand how she could have married someone like Reg Marks.

"He's so . . . so lower-middle-class," they said. "No small talk at all. Really can't think what Lindsay sees in him."

His dinner partner one evening was less subtle. "The man positively exudes sex," she said. "I don't know why everybody's so astonished. I'd take him on myself if he were on the loose. Who cares if he can't talk?"

Geoff wanted to hit her. "I'm sure there's more to Marks than that," he said stiffly.

The woman looked at him in amusement. "Why? That's quite a head start. You can overlook a lot of things when the lights are low."

"He's starting a limousine service," the woman across the table chimed in. "Lindsay's backing it, of course, so we'll all have to give him our business."

"I hear he has a drinking problem," the man next to her said. "Not sure I want to hire a chauffeur who's smashed all the time."

"He won't be doing the driving, silly! Besides, they say he's licked that."

"Probably interfered with his sex life," Geoff's dinner partner said.

"Excuse me." Geoff rose from the table. "Just remembered I have to make a phone call. I'll be right back."

"You dare not say anything against Lindsay when Geoff's around," the second woman cautioned when he was out of earshot.

"Who said anything against Lindsay? I envy her. She had enough guts to buy what she wanted. Wish *I* had!"

"Norma, you're terrible! What makes you think she didn't fall in love?"

Norma shrugged. "Have it your way," she said.

For the first four months of their return, things went swimmingly. Reg and Lindsay were deeply involved in getting Reginald Marks Ltd. off the ground. They bought two cars, hired drivers, found a garage with office space, and engaged a girl to answer the phones. Lindsay composed and inserted ads in *The New Yorker* and *Cue,* and these, plus word of mouth, began to attract business. During May and June, they could hardly keep up with the reservations. Lindsay was jubilant. Even Reg had to admit that it looked as though they had a good thing.

"I don't know how you got it all together so quickly, luv. Must have cost a packet to make things move so fast."

Lindsay didn't tell him how much it had cost. With generous "donations" anything could be speeded up, from car deliveries to office supplies, and she hadn't hesitated to bribe and wheedle her way so that they were in business by April 1.

"That's the good old U.S. of A.," she said. "We move faster over here." She smiled. "You've heard of Yankee ingenuity, haven't you?"

"I've also heard of Yankee dollars. It worries me, Lindsay. I'll be years paying you back."

"So what? We have years."

She felt happy for the first time in a long while. Reg was sober and working hard. So much for you, Dan Fields! Even Pauline seemed to have more confidence in Reg than she did in the beginning.

"I must say, he's surprised me, Lindsay. He's a different man from the one I met in London."

"I told you not to worry, Mama."

"Well, I'm delighted to be proven wrong. He obviously knows what he's doing in his line of work. Are you managing to have any fun, as well?"

Lindsay made a little face. "Well, if you mean is Reg a social lion, I'm afraid the answer is no. He's terribly awkward around my friends. Practically says nothing. But he'll get over that too. It's just a matter of confidence and getting used to our ways. When the business is a big success, he'll stop being so shy."

362

Shy? Lindsay's being very generous, her mother thought. Reg is not so much shy as conscious of his limitations. He doesn't know what to talk about to her friends. Didn't in London. Doesn't here. It troubled Pauline that people were being downright nasty about this "boor" Lindsay married. Word traveled fast. She knew what they were saying about Lindsay's "dumb but sexy" new husband. She only hoped the ridicule didn't reach her daughter's ears.

At least he's not drinking, Pauline thought gratefully. Bad enough to have an inarticulate man. A mumbling, besotted one was unthinkable. And Lindsay did seem reasonably content. She was so happy to be back in New York, to see Reg's business working out, and to have him on the wagon. Pauline had thought she might want to go back into the antiques business she still had a share in, but Lindsay said no, she was busy enough helping Reg at the moment.

"Besides, Marty's doing fine," she said. "I don't approve his taste in romance. Sleeping with that girl in the shop is a dumb idea, but it's his affair." She twinkled. "In every sense of the word."

It delighted her mother to see her bouncy and enthusiastic again. Thank God, Geoff had apparently kept his word. He hadn't called or tried to see her. In fact, he avoided her.

"I'm such a Boy Scout," he told Pauline, "that I even check when I'm invited anywhere, to be sure Lindsay isn't invited too. How's that for nobility?"

"You get a gold star," she said. "Thank you, Geoff. How are things with you?"

"Not too bad. Peaceful, at least. Of course, I'm a non-person: non-husband, non-bachelor. It's kind of an odd spot, but it has its points."

"Do you see Adele?"

"No. We communicate through lawyers. She demands and I write checks."

"I'm sorry."

"Don't be. I think it's called paying the piper." He smiled. "I'm a reformed citizen, you know. I've been to Chicago once a month since Robin and Connie were married. They're very happy and it makes me feel good to see them. And that young John! What a kid! Two and a half going on twenty. Bright as a button. Well-mannered and well-adjusted." He cocked his head at her. "Do I by any chance sound like a doting grandpa?"

"Yes."

"Right. And I like it. I'm crazy for that boy. How could I have ever rejected him? It seems impossible now."

"You never really did, Geoff. It was part of your grief. Nothing against that little fellow. Or Robin either."

He showed a flicker of sadness. "I behaved like a bastard, and I paid for that, too. It was the final straw for Lindsay and me." He hesitated. "She's really doing all right, isn't she?"

"Yes," Pauline reassured him. "Better, frankly, than I expected."

"Good news for some, bad for others. I wish I could say I was glad, but I gave up lying for Lent. "I don't suppose you'd give Lindsay my love when you see her?"

"No."

Geoff grinned. "I thought not," he said.

July oozed in, hot, sticky, and ominous. The limousine business, like everything else in New York, went into a decline and Reg grew nervous and testy.

"What happened?" he asked Lindsay. "We were doing so well in May and June."

"Darling, this is a deserted village in the summer. Not like London, full of tourists. Everybody goes away. It will be slow until after Labor Day in September. You mustn't let it worry you. Things will pick up again in the fall. We'll probably need more cars and drivers by October."

He didn't believe her. "Plenty of rich people visit New York in the summer. They're just not using us."

"Reg, that's not so. Nobody who hires limousines comes to New York in July and August. And I told you: the natives run for the hills. Or the beaches. There's not a single one of our friends in town."

"*Your* friends."

Lindsay looked at him suspiciously. The same old aggrieved tone, half hostile, half pathetic. And she realized, slightly drunk.

"Oh, Reg, you haven't started again!"

"Started what?"

"You know what: drinking."

"Hell, just a few drinks this afternoon in the office. With the boys. Nothing else to do. Bloody phone never rang."

"Reg, you can't! They're your employees! You mustn't set a bad example. Drinking on the job! Oh, no, darling. Don't do that. In fact, please don't start again for your own sake. You were doing so well. I was so pleased."

"Don't tell me how to treat chauffeurs. I know more about them than you do."

Lindsay looked grim. "Do you? What do you know about being a *boss* of chauffeurs?"

"Nothing. You're the boss of *everything*." He turned away. "Leave me alone, Lindsay. If a man wants to drink, he'll drink. God, don't be such a nag! Maybe with a little whisky I can stand things better: this crazy country and this rotten business! Maybe I can even put up with your hoity-toity friends. I might even be able to tolerate being your damned trained monkey on a stick!"

She stared at him, speechless.

He turned red. "I'm sorry. I didn't mean any of that. You're wonderful. I'm just so scared. So bloody scared. I love you so much it frightens me. I know you're right about everything. I shouldn't drink. I shouldn't be chums with my drivers. But can't you understand? I'm lonesome. There's nobody within thousands of miles who gives a rap what happens to me. Only you, sweetheart. Don't be mad at me. I'm sorry. So help me, I'll never do it again."

She put her arms around him and said soothingly that it was all right. She understood. It was the terrible heat. He wasn't used to that. And it was scary starting a business, moving to a new country, making friends. She murmured all the right words, as one might to a terrified child. And she believed none of them. It was never going to work. He'd never rise to her expectations, never come near her hopes. He was a great, blubbering baby and she felt terribly sorry for him.

She also, in that moment of disappointment, came close to hating him.

31

"*W*hat kind of bash would you like for your birthday, Mama?"

Pauline was glad Lindsay couldn't see her face. God forbid they ever perfected those television phones they kept talking about. A nightmare of an idea, people being able to see you when they rang up! Right now, for instance. It was fortunate Lindsay couldn't see how she dreaded that question.

"I'm far too old for birthday parties, darling. It's sweet of you, but I really don't want a bash, as you call it. Why don't you and Reg and I just have dinner if you're free?"

"Not a chance, This is the one you said you looked forward to, remember? The big eight-oh. What happened to all that wonderful catering-to you were so crazy for? It might as well begin with a bang on the twenty-second of next month. I'm ready to spring for the celebration of your choice."

Pauline was evasive. "I honestly don't want anything special. I'd prefer something quiet. I'm just not up to a lot of fuss."

Lindsay was alarmed. "What's the matter? You're not sick, are you? Is there something you're not telling me?"

"No, of course not. I'm perfectly fine. Disgustingly healthy."

"Well, then, you're not going to get out of a party. If *you* won't decide what kind, *I* will. Just give me a list of people to invite."

"Truly, Lindsay, there isn't anybody. When you get to be my age, all your friends have either died or moved to Florida. Don't be difficult about this, dear, please."

"Don't *you* be difficult, Mama! No one you want to invite? I never heard such nonsense! You have scads of friends!"

Did have, Pauline thought. The fact was these days she saw only one or two of her once vast circle of acquaintances. Gossipy old biddies! Forever making snide remarks about Lindsay's new husband. Or subtly probing to find out whether Pauline felt vindicated that Adele couldn't hold Geoff. As though she gave a damn about Adele! Geoff, yes. In her mind, he was the only son-in-law she'd ever have. But she wasn't going to discuss Lindsay's past or present marriages with any of her "good friends." She resented their curiosity and gradually dropped out of contact with them. These nosy old ladies were not the people she cared to celebrate with. But Lindsay wouldn't be dissuaded from some kind of party. Pauline sighed.

"All right, dear, let's compromise. Something small and suitable."

"I wasn't planning to rent Madison Square Garden." Lindsay sounded relieved. "Okay. Reel off the names."

"Well, Dan Fields, of course."

"Our eminent attorney. Right. And . . . ?"

"And Rae Walters, and Lucille and Tom Grove."

Lindsay made a note. "Yes. I have them. Go on, Mama."

"That's it, dear."

"That's *it?* Darling, you've named four people. With Reg and me, that's seven. That's no party; that's the contents of a telephone booth!"

Without thinking, Pauline said, "Or a limousine."

On the other end of the line, Lindsay was quiet. Then she said, "I see. That's it, isn't it? It's Reg. You're afraid he'll embarrass us in front of your friends."

"Oh, no, Lindsay! I didn't mean that! Not for a moment! I don't even know why I said limousine, except they hold seven passengers. It was just a slip of the tongue."

"A Freudian one." Lindsay sounded sad rather than angry. "You're right, of course. Stupid of me to ignore the obvious. I understand why you don't want a big party, Mama: for the same reason I haven't given one since our return. I'm terrified Reg will get drunk and make a spectacle of himself. Or even," she said bitterly, "stay cold stone sober and be a fish out of water. I just wasn't thinking. It seemed like such a good idea to have a lot of people who love you. But it's impossible. I've made it impossible, haven't I?"

"Lindsay, don't talk rubbish! Stop making a melodrama out of this.

You have it all wrong. I told you the truth! I just don't feel close to a lot of people any more. It has nothing to do with Reg. Or you. Or anything except my age."

"Mama, you always were a lousy liar. You've probably dropped your old friends because they talk about Reg and me. It must be hard for you. I'm sorry."

"Lindsay, if I could reach you, I'd smack you! You're twisting my words, and I won't have it! Have I ever given you a hint of such a thing? It's all in your mind. Now stop this, for heaven's sake!" Pauline was shaken by the correctness of her daughter's analysis, but she tried to sound amused. "All right, you stubborn girl. If you insist upon dragging me center stage as living proof that one can survive eight decades and not be dotty, I'll go along. I'll make a list and send it to you today. How many? Twenty? Fifty? Five hundred? Pity the circus isn't in town. You could rent three rings and we'd perform in all of them."

Lindsay managed to laugh. "You're incorrigible!"

"Not at all," Pauline said with mock hauteur. "I'm just practicing how difficult I'm going to be when I really *do* reach eighty." Her voice softened. "It's sweet of you to want to give me a party. And I'll love it. You'll have the list tomorrow. Day after, at the latest. And I'll get myself something smashing to wear. One of those slinky sequin sheaths by Norell, maybe. And in bright red, of course. What's the good of being ancient if you can't be outrageous?"

They hung up on this high note, but for a long while after Lindsay sat staring thoughtfully at the telephone. Pauline was right in the apprehension she tried to hide. Reg was an embarrassment. Worse than ever these days. Once again, as Mama knew, his drinking was totally out of control. She'd had to put a manager in the garage to handle what little business there was these days. Dan advised her to liquidate it and take a tax loss, but she stubbornly hung on, insisting that things would pick up in the fall. She didn't say it to the lawyer, but she also hoped that Reg would pull himself together when he got busy and interested again. Faint hope it was. He was even unhappier than she. They had nothing any more. Even his maudlin attempts at love-making were a humiliation to them both. The heavy drinking took its toll on him physically. And even when he tried to come near her she was repelled by the odor of liquor that seemed to spread from every pore of his body. It was terrible to see, this disintegration of a man. She felt helpless to change it, and he rejected all her suggestions of therapy or Alcoholics Anonymous.

"You're all I need, Lindsay," he said. "You're my life."

Sometimes she wanted to scream that she couldn't take responsibility for anybody's life. That he should divorce her and go back where he belonged. I'd provide for him, she thought, if only I didn't have to watch him dying by inches and know it was my fault.

She often thought that God was punishing her for being unfaithful to Geoff. Or for using Reg to save her foolish pride. Or both. She was not a religious person, but she feared the Almighty was making her pay for her sins. And she was paying. Not a patient or tolerant soul by nature, it took every ounce of her strength to stay with this man she didn't love, never had loved, except in a blindly physical way.

But, she reasoned, God must also want her to suffer, for she couldn't, for the life of her, tell this sad, broken man that the farce of their marriage must end. Horrified by her own thoughts, sometimes she wished he would die. It was the only peace he'd ever know. Lord forgive me! she prayed. But what good was he, even to himself? What was worse, she was afraid Reg knew it too.

There also were those black moments when she was so depressed she thought of taking her own life, but she was too cowardly. Life, any kind of life, was precious. And there were things to live for. Pauline would not survive such a shock. And there was little Johnny. She cared about him passionately, even more deeply, she supposed, than she might have if S.P. had lived. He was going on three, a happy and enchanting child. Her only truly joyous moments these days were when she flew to Chicago to see him and Robin and Connie, that totally happy family. As happy, she often thought, as Geoff and I were when S.P. was growing up.

She did not allow herself to think often about Geoff. He was not divorced, but what difference would it make if he were? She had a commitment to Reg, a bargain to keep. If Geoff were free tomorrow she'd stay married to the one whom she'd made dependent. It was not heroics or martyrdom that made her determined to do so. Turning Reg out would destroy the last shred of self-respect she had. It was masochistic, she supposed, but in another way it was selfish. She had to be true to something, even if only to herself.

*　　*　　*

"Lindsay's giving a party for Pauline's eightieth birthday," Connie said. "She wants us to come to New York for it. And stay with her and her husband. And, of course, bring Johnny."

Robin took the letter addressed to both of them. "She's taking over the St. Regis roof, I see." He whistled. "A hundred and sixty people for dinner and dancing! Wow!"

"We'll go, won't we?"

"Sure, Pauline and Lindsay are two of my favorite people." He glanced at his wife. "And we'll get to meet the mysterious Mr. Marks, I presume."

"Yes, I wonder what he's like. Lindsay hardly mentions him in her letters or even when she comes to visit. Sometimes I almost forget he exists."

"Sometimes I get the feeling Lindsay would like to."

"Robin, what an awful thing to say! You don't know that. He's probably a perfectly nice man."

"Could be. But if you had a perfectly nice husband, wouldn't you bring him with you to Chicago? Or at least talk about him? Lindsay acts as though she's ashamed of him."

"Do you really think so?"

"I don't know. There've been rumors. People from New York say his limo business is a flop. And that's he's one, too. The word from back East is he's a loser, and definitely lower-class."

Connie looked angry. "New Yorkers are such snobs!"

Robin laughed. "Don't go all middle America on me, honey. *I* didn't say it."

"Well, I don't believe it! Lindsay wouldn't marry anybody like that. She's the classiest lady I know."

"Even classy ladies make mistakes, and the classiest ones have too much dignity to admit it." Robin frowned. "I've always believed she never loved anybody but Geoff. My hunch is this was an impulsive thing because she was hurt and angry when he walked out. I'd bet she regrets it, but she'd never let anyone know."

"If that's true, it's very sad," Connie said.

"Damned right it is. Because Geoff still worships her."

"Do you think he'll be at the party?"

Robin shook his head. "No way. I know he hasn't seen her since our wedding. He told me so. Not his choice. Hers."

"How can people screw up their lives so thoroughly?"

"Easy, my love. Vanity, wounded pride, rejection, self-delusion. I could recite a litany of little pinpricks that finally produce a gaping wound. That's how marriages and friendships come apart. Sad but true."

Connie kissed him gently. "We'll never let it happen to us. If I feel pinpricks coming on I'll get a Voodoo doll."

Robin smiled. "Good idea. If that time ever comes, pick up two. His and Hers. Like bath towels."

For the next couple of weeks, Lindsay busied herself with preparations for the party. She hand-addressed all the envelopes, realizing that there were people on the list she hadn't heard of or thought about for years. Many of them, she remembered, went back to her childhood, when Mama and Papa were together and James was alive and Adele was her dearest and most trusted friend. *I knew some of these people even before I knew Geoff,* she thought, *and I feel as though I've known* him *all my life.*

Don't think about that. You deliberately didn't even thank him for the roses he sent last February. You're afraid, Lindsay. Dreadfully afraid, remembering the last lunch in Chicago. The best thing is to pretend there is no Geoffrey Murray. And no Adele, either.

The thought of that cruel, selfish woman made her cheeks burn. Even with the limited contacts she still had, Lindsay couldn't help hearing the vicious things Adele said about her. And the awful things she also said about Geoff: that he was sadistic, self-involved, conscienceless. Just as she'd painted herself the long-suffering wife of Howard Thresher, so Adele now gave the impression of a loving woman who'd tried hard to live with a conceited, overbearing man. *Bitch!* Lindsay thought. *Someone should silence that evil tongue.* But no one did. People preferred to believe the worst, and Adele was good at pretending to be what she was not.

Angrily, Lindsay stamped the final envelope. She wished she could invite Geoff to Pauline's party, but it was impossible. He and her mother had great affection for one another. Pauline would love to have him there, and he'd love to come and wish her many happy returns. *They'd* handle it, Lindsay thought, *but I couldn't. I'd be a wreck, knowing he was in the room. Bad enough to worry how Reg would behave. I don't* need the whispers about my ex-husband and me.

She put rubber bands around the packets of envelopes, deciding to mail them on her way to the St. Regis. She perked up at the thought of how pretty the party would be. The roof, though enclosed, had a magnificent view of the New York skyline, the perfect backdrop for a lady who'd lived all her long life in the heart of the city. Inside, the decor was elegant and romantic with pink tablecloths and glittering gilt and crystal chandeliers. It cost the earth to hire it for the evening, but it was worth it. MacDonald Forbes would do delicate, fanciful floral centerpieces for the twenty tables. She engaged the orchestra and ordered the dinner: mousse of lobster, beef Wellington, salad with cheese. Pauline's favorite food. They'd serve only French champagne. To hell with courses of white and red wine. This was a champagne night all the way.

She was on her way now to consult with the maitre d' about the dessert. It was a problem. The world was on a diet. And anyway, Pauline would kill her if there was some corny birthday cake afire with eighty candles. She'd be embarrassed enough when they played "Happy Birthday to You," but dammit, she'd just have to suffer one tradition. Lovely fresh fruit and sherbet, Lindsay decided, walking down Madison Avenue. And on each table a platter of petit fours, each one bearing an initial "P" in icing. Okay, a little tacky, but there had to be *something*.

Absorbed in her planning, eyes down, a little smile on her lips, Lindsay heedlessly bumped into a tall man as she crossed 70th Street.

"I'm so sorry," she said automatically before she even looked up.

"Never be sorry, Lindsay. Leave that to me."

"Geoff! Well, imagine bumping into you!"

"Literally." He grinned at her. "How are you?"

"Fine. And you?"

"Good for the moment, though I expect we'll both be dead momentarily if we don't get out of the middle of the street." He took her arm and escorted her to the sidewalk. "You seem very preoccupied, or are you just trying not to break an ankle in our wonderful New York potholes?"

She paused on the corner, smiling up at him. "Both. Walking in London is infinitely less hazardous to the health, but living in New York is better all the same. By the way, thank you for the roses. I'm a few months late, but . . ." She felt suddenly shy.

"I know. I didn't expect to hear. It pleased me to send them." Hurrying pedestrians kept brushing past them. "We seem to be blocking traffic. Can I buy you a drink somewhere around here, out of the crowd?"

"At eleven in the morning?"

"Ah. Right. Coffee, then? Eggs Benedict? Squab on toast? Anything à la carte, out of season, and under glass?"

Lindsay couldn't help laughing. "All right, coffee. The Polo Bar of the Westbury is just there, if they'll give us a cup before the lunch crowd arrives."

The cool dimness of the restaurant was soothing after the scorching street, and Lindsay sank gratefully onto a banquette. "I can only stay a minute," she said. "I'm dashing to the St. Regis. I'm giving Mama a party there on the twenty-second. It's her eightieth."

"I remember."

"Robin and Connie and John are coming from Chicago. I'm sure you'll see them while they're here. I wish I could . . . that is—"

"I'd like to be at the party, but that might be awkward for you. Don't worry about it, dear."

Lindsay looked at him curiously. "Wouldn't *you* find it awkward? People whispering about us and wondering?"

"My darling Lindsay, I doubt very much that most people remember anything about us. We're yesterday's news."

"That's what Mama once said, more or less."

"She's right. Oh, they may speculate now and then when our names happen to come up, but I assure you they'd hardly notice my presence at a big gala. Not that you're going to ask me, nor should you." He took a sip of his coffee. "You know, if you'll forgive my saying so, I don't think it's people you're worried about. I think, for some reason, you don't want me to meet your husband. Or you don't want him to meet me. I doubt you give a damn about the others."

For a moment, Lindsay didn't answer. "I find all this modern mixing of ex-spouses a little too sophisticated for my taste."

"Nonsense. I don't believe you. You could carry off losing your panties at an audience with the Queen." He smiled at her. "You haven't by chance done that, have you?"

She wouldn't be diverted. "Geoff, I'm sorry. Mama would love to have you there, but I just can't."

"Fair enough. Let's press on to other things. How's the shop?"

"I gave it up. Finally sold my interest to Marty."

"Oh? No fun any more?"

She avoided his eyes. "Not exactly that. I've been too busy with . . . with my husband's limousine service. He's not well, and I've had to get a manager and keep an eye on things myself."

"I see. I'm sorry. That he's not well, I mean."

Abruptly, she shoved her cup and saucer aside. "Dammit, why are we playing this cat-and-mouse game? Reg drinks. I'm sure you know that."

"I've heard," Geoff said quietly. "I did once too, if you remember."

"Yes. And in a way I drove you both to it."

"Don't be ridiculous, Lindsay. Self-flagellation doesn't become you."

"But it's true. I'm impossible. Spoiled. Selfish. My God, I never stop thinking of myself!"

"I know better, my dear. I know how hard you tried with me, and I wouldn't accept your help. For anything wrong you've done, don't blame yourself. Blame me."

She fished for a handkerchief and wiped her eyes. "Now, on top of everything else, I'm blubbering like a baby."

Geoff looked at her lovingly. "You know, that's quite nice to see. You probably need to cry, Lind. I do. A lot."

She looked straight at him. "Geoff, come to Mama's party, will you? It would mean so much to her."

"You're sure, Lind? I feel as though I've pushed you into it. I don't want to spoil the evening for you."

"You won't. I've been silly about it."

"What about your husband? He won't mind?"

Lindsay smiled mirthlessly. "Unfortunately, he probably won't even know you're there."

32

$\mathcal{R}$eginald Marks was not a stupid man. For all his limitations, his early environment and lack of formal education, he was an instinctive, if not intellectual, human being, well aware of his own motivations and those of others.

Since that day, more than a year and a half earlier, when Lindsay had arrived with her sudden proposal of marriage, he'd recognized the fact that overwhelming love for him had not been the driving force behind her actions. He'd pretended to believe everything she told him, wanting to believe because he truly loved her deeply. But he'd known from the start that she was behaving with the irrationality of the injured party striking back. His conscience had forced him to try to dissuade her. Hadn't he pointed out the differences between them and the dissimilarity of their interests in every area except the bedroom? He'd known, all too well, what small chance they had for a happy marriage.

Yet Lindsay was so stubbornly set on it that he'd agreed. And in all honesty, despite his reservations, he'd been stunned by his good fortune. As he told her more than once, she was everything he aspired to and dared not hope for. She was beautiful and sexy and rich. And above all, she was a lady, something men of Reg's class were used to admiring only at a distance. He tried hard to convince himself that with compromise on both sides the unlikely union could work.

It was only a matter of weeks before he knew it could not. He was as uncomfortable in her atmosphere as she was in his. Living in the luxurious flat in London did not suit him. He never got over the feeling of being a servant entering some rich man's house. As foreign as his friends were to Lindsay, so hers were to him. He liked her mother. Pauline was a kind woman, unfailingly gracious to him even when he was at his worst. But behind the gentle voice and smiling eyes, he sensed her distress. He couldn't blame her. Her only child married to a man who barely spoke her language, could not adjust to her ways, had nothing to offer socially or economically. Pauline knew what lay behind Lindsay's reckless move. Knew and was saddened by it.

There were times, many of them, in those early days when Reg decided to have it out, calmly and clinically, with his wife. They would agree, in a sensible, mature conversation, that it was an impulsive, emotional marriage and the sooner ended the better. But he could never bring himself to attempt such a talk. Not only because he loved her and, against all odds, wanted to be with her, but also because he correctly guessed that Lindsay's pride would be destroyed by a second failure. Foolish as that pride was, it was important to her. Important to pretend to the world that she didn't care for Geoffrey Murray. That she loved Reg Marks. That she'd created a whole new, wonderful life. It was a terrible game she was playing, one that brought her no real happiness. But it was her game and Reg would go along as best he could.

But it was a role not even an accomplished actor could indefinitely sustain. Too much in love to leave her, too concerned to let her suffer a second humiliation, he did the only thing he could: he sought forgetfulness in drink, trying to mask his feelings of inadequacy under the swaggering, false confidence of a drunk.

It was no answer. He knew that. But he could not explain to Lindsay that, sober, he couldn't face the unequipped, miscast man her well-intentioned actions had forced him to become. Drunk, his own failings did not pain him so. And perhaps, subconsciously, he hoped that she would grow to despise him enough to leave him, putting her own feelings above the pity she felt.

What a god-awful muddle they'd made of things! They did not belong together, and yet they got deeper and deeper into a situation that seemed to have no solution. In a crazy way, they cared so much for each other that they could not part: he, held by love and concern for her self-respect; she, bound by a sense of guilt for taking him out of his world into hers.

On that early August morning when Lindsay and Geoff accidentally met, Reg, desperately hung over, paced the Park Avenue apartment and tried to focus on their future. Where would they be ten years from now? Twenty? He'd be a hopeless drunk and Lindsay his caretaker. He'd blown the one chance he'd had to become a businessman on his own. He was thousands of miles from anyone he could talk to. He had no friends in this foreign land and was not likely to make any Lindsay could accept. God knows hers would not accept him. They'd made that condescendingly clear. And yet, even knowing that in the long run she'd be happier for it, he could not make up his mind to leave her alone, once more rejected, her humiliation worse this time because she'd been abandoned by a nobody. That would be even more degrading than the defection of that first man, the one who'd been considered right for her.

Angry, troubled, helpless, Reg poured himself a stiff drink. This was the first thing he should stop, of course. He damned well knew it. But he couldn't. Without the false courage of whisky he'd come apart. A vicious circle, he thought. The more I drink, the more unhappy Lindsay becomes. And the more unhappy Lindsay becomes, the more I drink. She thinks I need her. I do, in my heart. But she needs me more. Because I'm the only man who adores her.

For once, Pauline lost her composure. Over the luncheon table at Le Côte Basque, she nearly choked on her cold lobster.

"You did *what*?"

"I invited Geoff to your birthday party," Lindsay said calmly. "We ran into each other on Madison Avenue this morning and had a cup of coffee. I decided to stop being so silly. He's my ex-husband, but there's no reason we can't be friends. People pay no attention to that kind of thing these days. I know couples who get along better after they're divorced than they did when they were living together." She took a deliberate bite of her veal piccata. "Besides, Mama, he adores you. And you him. Why shouldn't he be part of the celebration?"

"I'm amazed he accepted."

Lindsay looked surprised. "Why, for heaven's sake? There'll be loads of people there he knows."

"That's exactly why. My dear, you know it will be the topic of conversation, Geoff turning up at a party you and Reg are giving! Do you really need more gossip around you?"

"Darling, you've done a hundred-and-eighty-degree turn. You were the one who said people didn't pay any attention to yesterday's news. Geoff said the same thing. That's really why I decided I was being supersensitive. Now you're telling me just the opposite." Lindsay grinned. "If I didn't know you better, I'd almost think you were afraid we'll steal the spotlight from the star of the show."

"Lindsay, don't make jokes. You know that's not what's worrying me."

The younger woman stopped teasing. "I know. You're worried that Reg will get drunk and make some kind of ridiculous scene. And that, of all people, I don't want Geoff to see what a sad excuse for a man Reg has become. I thought about that. And then I said to myself, So what? This is my husband. If I can take him as he is, so can everybody else. Including Geoff. All right, Reg has a drinking problem. Millions of people do. Geoff reminded me this morning that he once had the same trouble. He should be the last to cast stones."

"But Geoff conquered his problem," Pauline said.

"And Reg will get over his." Lindsay set her jaw firmly. "He was doing fine until business got bad. He doesn't know how to cope with things in this country, but he'll learn. We have to give him time. After all, he's been here only six months. I didn't find it easy to get used to England, either."

Pauline sighed. "Who is it you're trying to convince, darling, me or yourself? He'll never be what you want him to be. I feel sorry for him, Lindsay. It's all too much for him to handle. And I don't know how long you can go on pretending it will all change."

"Forever, if necessary. I'm not going to fail again, Mama. And Reg loves me. I won't let him down."

"Sometimes you remind me of your father. Howard had that same kind of bulldog tenacity. He never got over the fact that I left him. And you'll never get over the fact that Geoff left you. Tell the truth, Lindsay, you're still hell-bent on proving you can find someone to worship you, aren't you? Don't let your vanity ruin your life, my dear. You saw what Howard's did to him. Poor Howard. So flattered that he could marry a woman young enough to be his daughter. And so miserable for years with her, but too stiff-necked to admit it."

Lindsay flushed. "I don't see that the comparison is germane, Mama. I didn't marry someone Robin's age."

"No, but you also married out of your frame of reference, and you're going to stay with it even though you know it's wrong."

"Well, I don't happen to agree with you," Lindsay said angrily. "And I honestly don't need a lecture. I'm fifty years old. Old enough to know exactly what I'm doing, without needing my mother to point out the error of my ways. At least *I* got a second husband!"

"So you did," Pauline agreed quietly.

Lindsay was instantly ashamed. "Oh, hell, Mama, I didn't mean to sound so horrible! Please forgive me. You know I love you more than anything in the world. It just hurts when you . . . when you criticize me."

Or when I come so painfully close to the truth, Pauline thought. "It's nothing," she said. "The heat's probably got both of us. I don't know how we got so far off the subject, anyway. Let's talk about my party. Tell me what you're planning."

"No chance. The party's no surprise, but at least the details will be. I do want it to be nice for you, darling. I'm sorry about asking Geoff. I hope that won't spoil anything for you. I thought you'd be pleased."

"Of course I'm pleased. I love Geoff in spite of everything."

Lindsay didn't answer for a moment. Then she looked directly into Pauline's eyes. "So do I, Mama," she said.

Robin, Constance, and Johnny arrived two days before the party, bringing with them, as agreed, a beaming Mrs. Graham. Over the telephone, when Connie proposed it, Lindsay enthusiastically seconded the idea of John's baby-sitter making the trip.

"I'll feel much better knowing she's with him when we're out," Lindsay said. "And I'm delighted not to have to scout around for some stranger. You and Robin can have Geoff's—I mean the second bedroom, and we'll put Mrs. Graham and Johnny in the other one. It's a bit cramped for two, but I'm sure they'll manage."

"Manage?" Connie laughed. "Mrs. G. is off the wall with excitement. She's never been in New York and she can't wait. I think she'd sleep on the kitchen floor if that was the only way she could come."

Jane Graham was, indeed, bubbling with excitement. She was impressed with Park Avenue, extravagant in her praise of the apartment, impatient to see the sights.

"I'm just dying to go to the top of the Empire State Building and the Statue of Liberty," she said when they were settled. "And I hear you have to ride the Staten Island ferry and visit Grant's Tomb and take the sightseeing boat that goes all around Manhattan Island! I suppose you've done all those things a thousand times, Mrs. Marks."

Lindsay smiled. "I'm ashamed to admit I've never done one of them, Mrs. Graham. New Yorkers are terrible. They don't pay any attention to the points of interest in their own town. I'm sure that's true of the natives of any city. Like everything else, we too often take the familiar for granted. But you'll have plenty of time to explore. I want to be with my grandson every minute of the day, so if Mrs. Darnevale agrees, you can be free to roam."

"Mrs. Darnevale may be doing a little roaming of her own," Connie said. "Henri Bendel, here I come!"

"Bankruptcy, there I go!" Robin said. He turned, genially, to a silent Reg. "These women! They were born with charge plates in their hands. They can spend it faster than we can make it, can't they?"

"I wouldn't know. I don't pay the bills," Reg said.

There was an awkward pause, during which Robin mentally kicked himself for his stupidity and Lindsay wanted to slap Reg for his lack of tact. Connie quickly broke the tension.

"Don't look for sympathy, Robin, you fraud," she said. "I'm a working woman, remember? My clothes mania is my own problem."

The difficult moment passed and they relaxed, chatting about other things. Only Reg took no part in the conversation. He took Johnny off to a far corner and began showing the child a big book with photographs of vintage automobiles, explaining each one to the fascinated but uncomprehending little boy. Mrs. Graham, satisfied her charge was in good hands, went out to the kitchen to make friends with the housekeeper.

From time to time, Lindsay glanced toward her husband and her grandchild, both absorbed in the pictures. Connie followed her glance.

"He's awfully good with children, isn't he?"

"Apparently," Lindsay said. "This is the first time I've ever seen him with one. They seem to be getting along famously."

"He's a nice man, Lindsay," Robin said quietly. "Shy, but he has dignity."

"Yes," Lindsay answered, almost surprised to find she believed it. It had been so long since Reg was calm and sober. She'd nearly forgotten what a contained, peaceful person he could be. If only he'd be this way all the time, she thought. She heard him laughing with Johnny. What a long time it had been since she'd heard Reg laugh! "It's hard for him," Lindsay said in a low voice. "A strange country, unfamiliar people, even a new way of doing business. It's nice to see him happy."

The young couple said nothing. They weren't sure what they'd been prepared for. A loud, overbearing boor, they supposed. Not this reticent man with the gentle hands and the sad eyes.

Later, in their room, they discussed it.

"He sure isn't Geoff," Robin said.

"No, but I like him. I don't know exactly why, but I feel sorry for him. He seems so lost. You can tell he worships Lindsay. Just the way he looks at her. But it's as though he's scared of something. Maybe of loving her too much."

Robin nodded. "It's funny. I expected someone totally different, from the things people said. Some kind of drunken lout, I suppose. He may not have breeding, but he's a gentleman."

"And a sober one," Connie said. "I told you you can't believe people. Especially New Yorkers."

Robin did a Jack Benny imitation. "Now cut that out!"

Connie laughed. "Okay. I'm sorry. But I'm on Reg's side."

"Honey, there are no sides. He's Lindsay's husband and what she loves, we'll love."

His wife kissed him. "Good boy," she said. But privately she was uneasy about Reg. He looked bewildered, frightened, like a child trying hard to be on his best behavior. Except for that one bitter remark about not paying the bills, he'd shown no antagonism. Yet Connie knew he was a disappointed, even an angry man. He has a right to be, she thought sadly. I'm sure Lindsay can't help it, but she doesn't love him.

As Geoff dressed for lunch with the arrivals from Chicago, he felt ridiculously happy for the first time in years. Perhaps it was wishful thinking, but it was as though everything was coming together again. It all started with that chance meeting with Lindsay. Proper as it was, it seemed a milestone. She'd been glad to see him. She'd even invited him to Pauline's party. True, he'd almost shamed her into doing that, but she had done it, and he took that as a good sign. If ever we can communicate, he thought, we can work things out again. She forgave me for Pam. Certainly she can understand how unstable I was when I got involved with Adele. In a way, Lindsay pushed me into it. If she hadn't been with Marks in France, I'd never . . . no, that wasn't fair. Lindsay had every right to look for someone else. I drove her to it with my childish behavior. I even drove her into this marriage, I suppose. Silly, lovely woman, needing to pretend she didn't care.

She did care. Geoff was certain of it. He refused to believe it was too late for them. Other people remarried. Somehow I'll make Adele divorce me, he thought fiercely. I should never have listened to Dan Fields in the first place. What difference if it costs everything I have? I can make more. Except in the first couple of years of our marriage, money's never been a problem with Lindsay and me. Maybe it would have been better if we'd had less of it. Or if Lindsay had had less of it. Then she wouldn't have been able to buy that Englishman.

What a rotten thing to think! Who says she bought him? Geoff felt suddenly deflated. Maybe I'm only seeing what I want to see. Maybe she really is in love with him and wouldn't have me again even if I were free. That's what she told me in Chicago. It could still be true. She might not leave him even if I made it possible for her to come back to me.

Nevertheless, I will get a divorce. Adele can't care whether she's married or not as long as she has plenty of money. I can't believe she's that stupid. Or that vindictive. To all intents and purposes she has no husband any more. We're legally separated. Her social standing won't be decreased by a final decree. I'll see her next week and beg, if I must. And I'll be smart enough, for once in my life, to lie about Lindsay.

He allowed his thoughts to return to his ex-wife, wondering if there was any chance of her changing her mind about today. On the phone last night, Robin had, with good reason, sounded surprised when the conversation got to that point. His son-in-law had rung up to announce that he and Connie were in town and would like to take him to lunch today.

"Lunch is fine," Geoff said, "but you're my guests. I won't have it any other way."

Robin laughed. "Okay, we'll fight over the check later. The important thing is, we want to see you while we're here."

"You'll see me at Pauline's party. Not that I don't also want to do lunch."

"Oh? I didn't know you were going to the party. That is, I guess Lindsay forgot to mention it. Anyway, that's fine. Two visits are better than one, and I doubt we'll have much of a chance to talk with the festivities going full blast."

Geoff felt vaguely disappointed that Lindsay hadn't said he was invited. Well, why should she, you old fool? It probably wasn't nearly as important to her. And, realistically, it wasn't a subject one deliberately brought up in front of one's second husband. Geoff wondered whether she'd told Reg Marks at all.

"Right," he said heartily. "I'm sure half of New York will be at the St. Regis. Where would you like to have lunch?"

"You name it."

"How about the Waldorf? Peacock Alley? It's quiet there and a good place for kids. You *are* going to bring John, I hope."

"If we can pry him away from Lindsay," Robin said. "She's planning to send Mrs. Graham on a day-long tour of New York so she can have Dennis the Menace all to herself."

"Well, if she won't be separated from him, maybe she'll join us for lunch." Geoff hoped he sounded casual, but his heart was racing.

That's when Robin sounded startled. "Join us? Well, I don't know about that, Geoff. That is . . . I mean, I'll ask her, but I wouldn't count on it. Better make the reservation for four."

"Sure. No problem. Twelve thirty okay? But you promise you'll bring John?"

"I promise, He's yours, too."

Lovely words, Geoff thought as he hung up. Thank God that finally worked out, despite my hysterical behavior. He shuddered, remembering how close his grief had brought him to irreconcilable alienation from his grandson. He'd been a raving maniac in those first months after S.P.'s death. He understood now how nearly unbearable sorrow could warp the mind. How it could present itself as murderous rage, unjustly but perhaps understandably. His loss was no greater than Lindsay's or Robin's. He simply hadn't had their control, their admirable discipline.

As he slipped a handkerchief into his breast pocket, he hoped Lindsay would be at lunch. It seemed to him there'd be something symbolic about it if she showed up. As though it meant she also wanted them to be a family again.

Earlier that day, Connie watched for a chance to speak privately to Lindsay. In midmorning, while Mrs. Graham was dressing John, and Robin and Reg were both taking showers, she cornered Lindsay coming out of the kitchen.

383

"Talk to you a minute?"

"Sure. What's up?"

"Geoff's invited us to lunch today."

"Us? You mean you and Robin? That's nice, dear."

Connie hesitated. "Well, he'd like John to come, too."

"Oh." Lindsay looked disappointed. "Reg and I were going to take him to the children's zoo in Central Park."

"I know. Robin told him you wanted to spend the day with John, but of course—"

"But Geoff has as much right to him as I, you mean. Well, I suppose I can't argue with that. I have the three of you for two days. I guess Geoff's entitled to two hours."

"He said he hoped you'd join us, Lindsay."

Her face went white. "No. No, I couldn't do that, Connie. I mean I couldn't disappoint Reg. He's planning on being with me today. He'll be disappointed enough not to be with John. He's developed an instant passion for that boy. It was all he talked about when we went to bed last night: how wonderful Johnny is." Lindsay sighed. "It's too bad Reg never had children of his own. He really loves them. I was surprised to see how good he was with the baby. He . . . he hasn't even had a drink since you arrived."

Connie didn't answer.

"I'm sorry," Lindsay said. "I didn't mean to get off on that, but I suppose it isn't news to you that Reg has a drinking problem."

"We've heard rumors, but I didn't believe them."

"They're true enough, unfortunately. He is an alcoholic. He has his reasons, God knows. I suppose everyone with that disease has his reasons. I only wish he'd get some help, Connie. He's basically a good man, a kind one. I'm . . . I'm very fond of him." Lindsay took a deep breath. "Well, enough of that. Thank Geoff for me and tell him I'm sorry I can't make it."

"Lindsay . . ."

"Yes, dear?"

"Why did you invite Geoff to the party tomorrow night?"

"Why shouldn't I? He and Mama have always been devoted. I'm rather surprised you even ask. Your generation is so much more sensible about ex-husbands and wives than mine was. Do you think there's something wrong with my including Geoff? After all, he's only one of a hundred and sixty people, for heaven's sake!"

384

"Is he?" Connie asked. "Just another guest?"

Lindsay didn't flinch. "Of course. What else would he be?"

"I don't know. Would you like to tell me? I don't mean to overstep, but I'm not sure you have another woman to talk to. There's Pauline, of course, but that's different. I just have a feeling there's a lot on your mind, and I only want you to know that if you want to lay it on me, it'll be strictly between us girls."

Lindsay smiled affectionately. "You're dear, Connie, and I appreciate it. There are problems, I don't deny that. But everyone has them. Mine are no worse than most and not as bad as many." The smile faded. "There's one thing I would like to say, though. I don't know if I've ever told you how happy I am that Robin and John found you. You're as near as anyone could ever be to my own daughter. The love you've brought that man and that child is something special. I guess I'm especially grateful for Johnny's sake. I'm afraid I'm thoroughly dotty about him. So is Geoff, I gather. That's good, and I know you're part of the reason." She brightened again. "There. End of speech. Have a good lunch, darling."

"Sure you won't join us?"

Lindsay shook her head. "Positive. Once in a while I'm overcome with the need to be a good wife. This is one of those times."

385

33

$\mathcal{A}$t ten o'clock, as she was finishing the last of her spartan breakfast from the tray in front of her, the telephone next to Adele's bed rang. It was Janice Carlton, one of the few women she was friendly with.

"Hi," Janice said, "what's new?"

"Nothing. I'm still in bed. What's made you surface so early?"

"Paul and his damned golf game. He was crashing around before eight. I couldn't get back to sleep. Says if they don't tee off early he'll have heatstroke on the ninth green. Sometimes I think it is a catastrophe to be devoutly hoped for."

Adele smiled smugly. "There are advantages to being alone. Geoff always drove me crazy in the morning. He'd keep barging into my room with all kinds of annoying instructions for the day. I never could convince him that women hate conversation at the crack of dawn."

"Not all women, apparently." There was a little barb in Janice's voice. "His ex-wife obviously doesn't. Peggy Rodgers saw Geoff and Lindsay going into the Polo Bar of the Westbury the other morning. She said they were laughing and looking very wide-awake."

Adele set her cup carefully in the saucer. Geoff and Lindsay? She kept her tone offhand when she answered.

"Oh, *that.* Yes. I know. Something about their grandson," she lied. "Geoff said they were meeting to discuss a trust fund."

"Oh? Really? I didn't know you and Geoff were on speaking terms."

"Of course we are. It's a very friendly separation." Once launched on the fabrication, Adele couldn't resist embellishing it. "I don't want this spread around, Jan, but Geoff and I are on the verge of a reconcili-

386

ation. He's promised to reform and—well, it's probably foolish of me but I've half agreed to give him another chance."

"No kidding! That's wonderful, Adele! In that case, I suppose you'll be going with him to Pauline Thresher's birthday party tomorrow night. We are. And Geoff told Paul at the club that Lindsay had invited him."

Adele gritted her teeth, but she still managed to sound cool. "No, I passed on that one. He asked me, of course, but it seemed inappropriate. Pauline and I were both married to the same man, in case you've forgotten."

"Of course. I *had* forgotten. It was a hundred years ago, wasn't it?"

"Not quite, darling. Still, I wouldn't want to embarrass the old lady. I told Geoff to go without me."

Janice smiled. Adele was lying like a cheap rug. She had no idea Geoff was seeing Lindsay. And all that bull about a reconciliation! Adele must be livid. Served her right. She really was a nasty piece of work.

"I wish I had your sense of security," Janice said sweetly. "I'd have a fit if Paul was hobnobbing with his ex, even if we were legally separated. It's marvelous that you and Geoff have such a perfect understanding. When do you think you'll get back together?"

"We haven't set a date, but I daresay it'll be quite soon. Of course, you'll be the first to know, Jan dear. That is, if you haven't heard it already from one of our concerned friends."

"Well, it's wonderful news," Janice said again. "I'm so happy for you, Adele. We were all terribly worried when we heard he might go back to Lindsay. That would be so humiliating for you, dear. I'm delighted there's no truth to that rumor."

"Not a shred. And you can tell the girls I said so."

Adele hung up, fuming. So he was seeing her again! Probably had been ever since she came back from England. And now they were getting positively brazen about it. How dare he go to Pauline Thresher's party! Liar! Pretending Lindsay's return had nothing to do with his wanting a divorce. Well, he could whistle for it. If she'd ever entertained the idea of giving him his freedom, he'd bloody well changed her mind now. Geoffrey Murray would stay married to her the rest of his worthless life. Let Lindsay live with *that* one.

*   *   *

387

"You look positively ravishing, Mama." Lindsay reached out her hand as the doorman helped Pauline into the limousine.

"Thank you. I like being one of Bill Blass's 'ladies,' even though I'm sure he doesn't normally design for eighty-year-olds." She glanced at the others. "You all look pretty grand yourselves. Constance, that's a lovely gown. And Reg and Robin, dinner jackets make you both look even handsomer. I think you should always wear them."

Robin laughed. "I'd sure stop traffic on Michigan Avenue at eight in the morning."

Reg, sitting in front with the driver, said nothing, but he did turn and grin at his mother-in-law.

"How's my great-grandson?" Pauline asked as the car pulled away.

"Pooped," Connie said. "It'll take him a week to get over this trip. And a year to recover from the spoiling by grandparents. He's already in bed and threatened with unspeakable punishment if he dare set one foot outside it."

"Why on earth would he?"

"He's incredible, Mama," Lindsay said. "You put him down and in two hours a little face comes poking around the corner and he's wide awake and wanting to play. Mrs. Graham's going crazy with him since they've been here. He's so charged up he won't sleep. And she's so exhausted from sightseeing she can hardly stay awake to watch him."

"I think he's going to be a rock star or a night watchman," Robin said.

"The kid's at his best after dark."

"I think he's going to be a race car driver," Connie said, reaching forward from the jump seat to pat Reg's shoulder. "His step-grandpa's taught him the name of everything with wheels."

Reg spoke for the first time. "He's a smart little bloke. Knows exactly what shelf the auto books are on, and he's made me go through every one with him."

"And you hate it," Lindsay teased. "Honestly, talk about spoiling! If any damage has been done, Connie, you can blame that English fellow. He's Johnny's slave."

"It's kind of you, Reg," Pauline said.

"I like it. It makes me feel important. Like I have a hand in the little blighter's education."

Pauline glanced at Lindsay.

"He's been great," Lindsay mouthed.

Pauline nodded in satisfaction.

"I still think it's wonderful of you to spend so much time with him, Reg," Connie said. "And it *is* educational. All Robin knows about a car is that if you don't put gas in it, it won't go. I expect we'll have to buy John some automobile picture books of his own when we get home. And a fleet of model cars, upon which I probably shall step and break a leg."

"You probably will, at that," Robin agreed. "But I agree, Reg. You've been a hero. Making conversation with the little people takes patience. I keep forgetting how limited their grasp is."

"Maybe that's why it's easier for me," Reg said. "I'm just a kid myself. Pretty childish, I suppose."

Pauline felt Lindsay stiffen in the seat beside her.

"Being child*like* is quite different from being child*ish*," Pauline said gently. "Actually, it's a wonderful quality, and too few people have it. John is fortunate that you're one of them."

"Amen," Connie added. "You've saved our sanity with those books, Reg. We owe you one."

Reg turned around and bowed his head. "My pleasure, madam."

Lindsay's heart gave a leap. He sounded exactly as he had when they first met: that amused, half-mocking voice. He'd been so different these past two days. Totally sober, quite relaxed, apparently at peace with himself. Please, God, let it continue, she prayed. When they leave, don't let him go back to what he's been for months.

They were the first arrivals at the St. Regis, and when Pauline went in to look at the big room, she gasped with pleasure.

"Lindsay, it's simply beautiful! The tables are a triumph! Will you look at those centerpieces? I've never seen such original arrangements." She gave her daughter a quick little kiss. "You make me feel like a debutante."

Lindsay was pleased. It did look like fairyland, inside and out, where even the skyscrapers seemed to have cooperated by twinkling with thousands of lighted windows. It would be even more beautiful when it was filled with expensively dressed women and dinner-jacketed men. The air would be delicious with perfume and sparkling with the sound of light conversation against a background of lively music. She'd gone to great pains to make everything perfect, even arranging place cards for a hundred and sixty people. When they came in, they'd receive their table numbers, go through the receiving line to greet Pauline and the family, then gather in the cocktail area before going in to dinner. It should go smoothly and happily, and Pauline would know how much people loved her.

For a fleeting moment Lindsay's mind went to one who surely did: Geoff. She half regretted asking him, still troubled by the speculation his appearance probably would arouse; even more disturbed, she admitted to herself, by this nearness to him. No doubt he'd ask her to dance. What a fool I am, Lindsay thought. After all these years I can still be nervous about being in his arms, even impersonally on the dance floor.

She'd put Geoff two tables away from the one she and Reg would share with Mama, deliberately seating him so that his back would be toward them. I don't want to look up all through dinner and see him watching me in that special way of his. And I don't want him looking at Reg, probably noticing that my husband doesn't have the easy grace of men like himself.

She'd waited until the last minute, almost before they were ready to leave, to tell Reg that her ex-husband was coming. "Oh, by the way, dear, I don't know whether I remembered to tell you that Geoff's invited tonight. You'll finally meet."

Reg's eyes met hers. "That should be interesting," he said.

Lindsay gave a forced little laugh. "Not particularly, I'd think. I wouldn't have asked him except that he's so fond of Mama. You don't mind, do you?"

"Mind? Why should I? He belongs to your past, doesn't he?"

"Of course! He's in the same category as high school yearbooks and World War Two, part of my misspent youth."

Suddenly Reg became angry. "Lindsay, don't insult me by trying to make me believe you feel nothing for a man you lived with for thirty years. I may be stupid but I'm not blind. I see your face whenever somebody mentions his name. I know who sent your favorite flowers the day we arrived. And I'm sure it wasn't Pauline's idea to invite him this evening." He calmed down. "It's all right. About his being there, I mean. Don't worry. I won't embarrass you in front of him. I'll be a perfect gentleman. I'll even try to use the right fork, in case he's watching."

She went white. "That's not fair! I haven't seen him since the day I went to England and I never intended to, except that we met accidentally on the street and . . ." She faltered. "Reg," she said earnestly, "it's long over between Geoff and me. Didn't I prove that when I came running to you? Have I done anything to make you think I regret it?"

"No, Lindsay, you haven't. You're too much of a lady for that." He tilted her chin up and kissed her lightly. "I'm the one who regrets what I've done to you. If it wasn't for me, you might be back with the man who suits you better in every way."

"He doesn't! Oh, damn, how did we get into this? We're making a whole thing over nothing!"

"So we are," Reg said calmly. "Come along, darling. It's time to go."

She thought of that brief, revealing conversation as she and Reg, Robin, and Connie flanked Pauline in a welcoming line near the elevator. Reg would be charming and well-mannered to all these people. He was aware of her nervousness and she knew that tonight, at least, he'd be sober and on his best behavior. She felt a little ache of pity for him. He knew he was out of his element. He probably dreaded this immersion into a critical society, his first since they came to New York. But his inherent British politeness would carry him through. She gave a sigh of relief. Even Geoff would see that she'd married a charming man.

She stationed herself at the head of the line, introducing the guests to her husband before they passed along to greet Pauline, who handed them along to Robin, who, in turn, presented them to his wife. It all went smoothly. She shook hands and gave the prescribed little midair kisses and said warmly, "I don't think you've met my husband, Reginald Marks." She was beginning to relax when Geoff finally appeared. She'd forgotten how handsome he was in evening clothes, how easily he wore them and how distinguished he looked. She smiled and took his outstretched hand, praying hers did not feel clammy.

"Geoff. So happy you could come." She turned to Reg. "Dear, this is Geoffrey Murray. Geoff, my husband, Reginald Marks."

The two men shook hands, smiling at each other.

"Glad to meet you," Geoff said. "Belated congratulations."

Reg was equally composed. "Thanks. I know my gain is your loss."

Geoff glanced briefly at Lindsay. "Yes. You're a lucky man." He nodded and moved on to kiss Pauline.

Lindsay gave Reg's arm a quick little squeeze. Solemnly, he winked at her. "Okay?" he whispered.

"Perfect," she said under her breath.

Mrs. Graham woke with a start, not sure what had pulled her out of her exhausted sleep. Was it a car crash she'd heard? Park Avenue was so noisy sometimes. She checked the bedside clock. Quarter past eleven. Instinctively, she looked over at John's bed. It was empty. Wide awake, she got up and put on her bathrobe. Where could that little devil be? She poked her head in the bathroom. Nothing. He must be wandering around the apartment. She never spanked him, but she'd give him a good scolding and put him back to bed. That child! He was a study in perpetual motion.

Annoyed, she made her way through the hall. There was a light in the living room. She hurried toward it. Heaven help him if he was playing with some of Mrs. Marks's precious ornaments! He knew he wasn't supposed to touch things on the table, but she wouldn't be surprised if—

In the doorway, she froze and then let out a scream. Near the bookcase, Johnny lay face up on the rug, blood trickling from his scalp. Around him were half a dozen big books and a heavy brass bookend shaped like an elephant.

She ran to the child. He was unconscious but breathing, and there was a huge gash in his forehead. For a second or two, she was paralyzed with fright. There was no one in the house. Even the housekeeper had the night off. Her mind raced. She'd ring for the elevator. No. Better to call that 911 emergency number and get an ambulance. Or should she call his parents first? She had the number of the St. Regis written down in case, as they'd said, "she needed anything." She tried to stop the bleeding with the hem of her nightgown, but the cut was too deep. He was deathly white. She was afraid he was dying.

Get help, she thought. Call 911. Oh, my God, I can't remember this address! Almost hysterical, she ran to the elevator and leaned on the button. It seemed hours before the operator came to their floor.

"The little boy," she shouted at the startled man. "He's hurt. Please call an ambulance! Quickly!"

"I'll get the super," the man said.

"No, no! Police. Hospital. Call someone!"

"All right. Be right back."

Leaving the front door open, she rushed back to Johnny. He was so pale, so still. Sweet Jesus, don't let him die! she prayed. She knelt beside him, futilely trying to stop the bleeding, talking to him as though he could hear. Why didn't someone come? She dared not move him, even though it was so frightening to see him lying there on the floor.

In less than five minutes the superintendent appeared. He was a calm, almost courtly man, composed despite his disheveled appearance. He spoke gently to Mrs. Graham.

"It's going to be all right," he said. "The ambulance is on the way and Lenox Hill Hospital is only a few blocks from here. Just calm down now. They'll take care of him."

"His parents. I must call his father."

"Where's the number? I'll do it."

"It's there. On the table. They're at a party for . . . oh, God, they'll never forgive me. I'll never forgive myself." She stayed close to John, rocking back and forth, weeping. She heard the super get through to the St. Regis Roof and then, after what seemed an eternity, he apparently had Mr. Darnevale on the line.

"No sir, I'm not sure what happened. The ambulance from Lenox Hill is on the way. I'm afraid I can't tell. Yes, it's his head. Looks like he struck it on something. Yes, sir, I'll tell her."

He hung up. "The boy's parents are leaving for the hospital. They'll be there almost as soon as you are." He helped Mrs. Graham to her feet. "Come along now. Get a coat to throw over yourself. You'll want to go in the ambulance with him."

Connie looked terrified as Robin came back to the table. "What is it? What was that call?"

"Don't make a fuss. You'll panic everybody. It's Johnny. Some kind of accident. They're taking him to the hospital."

"An accident? What happened? Is he all right?"

"I don't know, darling, I pray to God he is. The super called. Apparently Mrs. Graham is going in the ambulance with him."

"Ambulance! Oh, my God, Robin!"

"Try to be calm, sweetheart. Hopefully it isn't serious, but we have to leave instantly." He looked around. She was alone at the table. "Where's everybody?"

"Pauline is dancing. So's Lindsay, with Geoff. I . . . I don't know where the rest are. I think Reg went to the men's room."

"I have to tell them where we're going. You speak to Pauline. I'll get Lindsay."

At that moment, Reg returned. He took one look at their agitated faces and asked, "What's wrong?"

Briefly, Robin told him.

"Oh, no!" Reg said. "Oh, God, no!" He sank into a chair and then immediately got up. "What do you want me to do?"

"I'm not sure," Robin said. "Stay put for a minute, will you, while we get the others?"

Connie went out on the floor and, managing to be calm, asked Pauline if she'd mind coming back to the table. Robin found Lindsay and Geoffrey. Even in that nightmare moment it flashed across his mind how right they looked together, how absorbed in each other. He tapped Geoff on the shoulder.

Geoff pretended to be annoyed. "Go away, boy. No cutting-in allowed."

"Geoff, it's important. I need you and Lindsay at the table for a minute, please. Right now."

His voice told them it was serious. Quickly they followed him off the floor.

"It's John," Robin said when they were seated. "He's been hurt somehow. They're taking him to Lenox Hill. I don't know how serious it is, but Connie and I are going straight there. We'll call you as soon as we know something."

Pauline clutched her heart, and Reg instinctively put his arm around her. Lindsay, too, was speechless with fright. Only Geoff reacted quickly, authoritatively.

"Lindsay and I are going with you. Marks, you take Pauline home. Make any excuse you have to, but get her out of here. Tell Janice Carlton, she's the one in the pink dress over there, to tell people it's just a little problem, and that they should stay and have a good time. Jan's cool. She'll handle it." He turned to Lindsay. "Come on, darling. Don't worry. I'm sure he's fine. Kids are tough. Whatever it is, he'll be all right."

Lindsay clung to him. "Geoff, the baby! What will we do if anything happens to *him* too?" She tried not to weep. "Robin, please let's hurry. I know you're even more frantic than we are. Oh, God, our precious Johnny! Geoff, he *will* be all right, won't he? Say he'll be all right!"

"He will be, sweetheart. I promise you."

Pauline only half listened to the conversation, but Reg, supporting her, heard everything, heartsick not only for the child but for himself. In this terrible moment, Lindsay had not turned to her husband. It was as though Reg Marks didn't exist.

"Go along, Geoff," he said. "Take Lindsay. I'll speak to Mrs. Carlton and see Pauline home. Call us at her apartment as soon as you can."

Geoff nodded absently. He was already helping Lindsay out of her chair. Suddenly, Lindsay stopped.

"Mama. You'll be all right?"

Pauline nodded. "Yes, dear. Reg will take care of me. You four had better hurry."

34

*H*ot and humid as the August night was, Lindsay shivered as they raced up Park Avenue toward the hospital. Terrible memories of a Chicago hospital haunted her, mingling with her fear for Johnny. Not again, Lord, she prayed silently. Not S.P.'s child, too.

They'd hailed the first cab outside the St. Regis, leaving the car for Pauline, and Geoff leaned forward anxiously, urging the driver to make it as fast as possible to the emergency entrance. Aside from that, on the short ride no one spoke. Lindsay knew she was not alone in her terror. Geoff and Robin also must be remembering another time. And poor Connie was deathly pale and tense. She loves John as though he were her own, Lindsay thought. They all adored the little boy. Including Reg. In the past two days Lindsay had seen a new side of her husband, the tender, patient, gentle side of a man good with children.

I barely spoke to him when we left, Lindsay realized. It was Geoff I turned to automatically, instinctively. But that was natural, wasn't it? Geoff is John's grandfather. Reg was, *is* an outsider. He'd been calm, steady when Geoff was issuing orders. He'd taken charge of Pauline, doing as he was told, stepping into the background as though he, too, knew that was his place.

The cab had barely stopped before Robin was out of it, racing like a madman into the hospital. Geoff threw a bill at the driver as they hurried after him. Mrs. Graham was distractedly pacing the corridor and Robin grabbed her roughly.

"How is he?"

The woman burst into tears. "I don't know. He's inside. They haven't told me anything. Oh, Mr. Darnevale, I'll never forgive myself! If anything happens to that child—"

Connie put her arms around the stricken woman. "It'll be all right," she said soothingly. "Whatever happened wasn't your fault, I'm sure."

"It was! I didn't hear him get out of bed. I didn't know he was going to climb up on a chair and try to reach one of those automobile books." Mrs. Graham was sobbing uncontrollably. "He must have pulled at one and it fell on him. So did some others. And the big book-end . . . it hit his poor little head. He was all bloody and terrible when I got there. Oh, dear God, why couldn't I have stopped him?"

Frantic as she was, Lindsay could feel nothing but pity for the woman. Jane Graham loved John too. For the first part of his life, she was as close as anyone except Robin could be. God knows Geoff and I weren't much help, Lindsay thought. This woman took my daughter's baby and gave him the love and care that's made him the happy little fellow he is. She closed her eyes, trying not to picture the boy clambering up to reach the high bookshelf. Damn Reg! Why did he have to get Johnny all excited about those stupid pictures! No. That wasn't fair. The baby's happiest hours had been with the big man who'd shared his enjoyment. Reg had talked to Johnny on his own level, understanding the lively curiosity of a small person.

Robin had disappeared. Lindsay saw him talking earnestly to a nurse who kept shaking her head and gesturing at some distant room. After a while, Robin came slowly back.

"He's in X-ray," he said. "The nurse can't tell us anything. We have to wait for the doctor."

"Is he conscious?" Geoff asked.

Robin shrugged. "I don't know. God, I feel so helpless!"

Lindsay went to him, trying to comfort him as she had on another day in another hospital.

"Robin, dear, he'll be all right. I know he will. He's a strong little boy."

He looked at her with haunted eyes. "We've been here before, haven't we, Lindsay?"

"No." She made her voice firm. "It won't be like that other time." She took his hand and said softly, "Please speak to Mrs. Graham. Poor woman. Can you imagine the guilt she's feeling?"

Robin looked angry. "Why shouldn't she feel guilty? We left him in her care. She didn't watch him. Too busy enjoying a good night's rest to do what she's paid for!"

"Robin, that's unjust! She can't stay awake twenty-four hours a day. And you know what an active child John is."

"Or *was*."

Lindsay wanted to scream. "Don't say that! He's not going to die! God wouldn't permit it!"

"I'm sorry," Robin said. "You're right. It was nobody's fault. I'm just half out of my mind. You must be, too. All of you." He took a deep breath. "Let's sit down over there and wait for the doctor."

Geoff, who'd been so organized and capable earlier, now seemed more helpless than any of them. He'd not said a word since they arrived at the hospital. Lindsay drew him aside.

"Are you all right? You look ill, Geoff."

"Do you believe in retribution, Lindsay? Is this my punishment for refusing to accept John in the beginning? When I remember how I felt ... what I said to Robin that day ... how I couldn't even look at the boy ... "

Everything comes back to *you*, doesn't it? Lindsay suddenly realized. You're not thinking about the child or his father. Not thinking about me. All you're concerned with is yourself: whether it's *you* God's striking at. But she did not say these things. This was Geoff as he always had been: self-absorbed, introverted in spite of the assured facade he presented to the world. I've loved him so much I never wanted to admit his selfishness, she thought. And I love him still, even as I deplore it.

"Darling, you mustn't think that way. You've more than made up for that early anger. It wasn't even anger, Geoff. It was grief and refusal to accept. No one can be punished for those very human feelings."

"I don't know," he said. She saw tears in his eyes. "I've been so damned arrogant. So self-righteous."

"Hush," Lindsay said. "Come and sit with the rest of us. There's nothing we can do now but wait and hope."

It seemed an eternity before a tired-looking white-coated man approached them.

"Mr. Darnevale?"

Robin leaped to his feet.

"Your son is going to be all right. He had a nasty whack, and

398

there's a slight concussion, but no internal damage. Lucky kid. Another half inch and it would have been big trouble. He might have a scar just above the left eye, but I'm sure he can live with that." The doctor smiled. "Might make him look pretty rakish, like he's been in a duel."

The five of them breathed an almost simultaneous sigh of relief. Geoff and Lindsay rose to their feet, hand in hand, while Connie stood beside her husband, smiling, tears of joy in her eyes. Only Mrs. Graham remained seated, motionless, head bowed, silently thanking the Lord.

"Can we take him home?" Robin asked.

"I think it would be wise to let us keep him here overnight. I don't expect any complications, but it's better to watch him for another twelve hours or so."

Connie frowned. "But he's so little, doctor. He'll be frightened, all alone. Can't I stay with him?"

"I wouldn't worry, Mrs. Darnevale. He'll sleep through the night. And tomorrow morning you can come and fetch him."

Robin nodded. "Whatever you say. Can we see him now?"

"Sure. Say hello and then we'll tuck him into pediatrics for the night."

Lindsay, still holding Geoff's hand, stepped forward. "May we all go? We're his grandparents. And Mrs. Graham is his nurse. We've all been so worried."

The doctor nodded. "Okay. But just for a minute. He's still pretty woozy."

Robin put out his hand. "I don't know how to thank you, doctor."

The kind young man brushed aside the thanks. "Nothing to it, Mr. Darnevale. He's a refreshing change. Most of our nights are spent treating drunks or attempted suicides. Car accident victims. That kind of thing. It's something of a relief to treat a simple bump on the head. Particularly one that wasn't caused by a mugging. An emergency ward isn't usually such a routine place. I'm glad, for his sake and yours, that this was only a minor crisis in the middle of the night."

The suffering he must see! Lindsay thought. Shootings and stabbings and life-and-death situations like heart attacks. We're so fortunate. When I think what might have happened . . .

"The nurse will show you where your boy is," the doctor said. "Remember, he's half out of it, so don't be alarmed."

But when they got to Johnny, they couldn't help being frightened.

He looked so tiny on the big rolling table that would take him upstairs. His head was swathed in bandages, and he lay very still. Robin and Connie spoke to him softly, but he simply looked at them, bewildered, like a little old man who couldn't imagine what had happened to him.

Even though the doctor had reassured them, Lindsay fought hard to convince herself that the child really was all right. Geoff turned away, unable to look at the helpless baby. Mrs. Graham had refused even to come with them.

"I'll wait here," she said. "I can't bear to see what I've done."

Lindsay wanted again to comfort her, but she was more anxious to see John. Later, she thought. Connie and I will be able to get Mrs. Graham over this unreasonable self-accusation. I'm sure they'll all have to stay in New York for a while. John can recuperate at my apartment. We'll get our own doctor in the morning, just to make doubly certain everything's okay.

They stayed with him only a few minutes before a nurse and an orderly came to take him away. Connie broke down as they started to wheel him off.

"Robin, we can't leave him! At least, let's spend the night here in the waiting room!"

"Honey, it's all right. You heard the doctor. We'll be back first thing in the morning. Come on, darling, let's go home and try to get a little rest. We've all had a terrible scare. Thank God it wasn't worse."

Lindsay agreed. "Yes, Connie, dear, let's go home."

They walked back down the corridor to where Mrs. Graham was still waiting. Robin, once he'd calmed down, was his old, considerate self.

"He's going to be fine, Mrs. Graham. No more serious than falling off a seesaw. Come on. We're going home. You'll come with us to get him tomorrow and you'll have your hands full with him for a while after that." He helped her to her feet. "You musn't blame yourself for what happened. It wouldn't have been any different if we'd all been home."

They found a checker cab big enough for the five of them, and Geoff dropped them off at Lindsay's door.

"Do you want to come up?" she asked.

"No, thanks. I'll speak to you first thing tomorrow." He was still ashen. "I'm sorry I wasn't more help."

"You were wonderful," Lindsay said. "You took charge, the way you always have."

He shook his head. "Automatic reflex. I fell apart when we got there."

Robin was helping the ladies out of the cab. "Don't be silly," he said. "Did you hear me? You were great, Geoff. Thanks."

It was not until they were back in the apartment that Lindsay realized Pauline and Reg must be frantic, waiting to hear something. For all they knew, Johnny could be dead. She was appalled by her thoughtlessness. I forgot about them, she thought. It seemed to me, in the past few hours, that I was with the only family I have.

When the other four rushed frantically out of the St. Regis, Reg had felt not only alarm but a terrible sense of desolation. Terrible visions of what might have happened to Johnny came into his head, yet even while he worried he was aware that in time of crisis it was Geoffrey to whom Lindsay turned. She still loves him, Reg thought. She still thinks of him as her husband. I'm only a substitute for what she wants, and a poor one at that.

No time now to think of himself or even of Lindsay. He left Pauline, sitting stunned in her chair, and went to find Janice Carlton, as he'd been ordered to do. He took her aside and said, calmly, "Mrs. Carlton, there's been an accident. Something's happened to Robin's boy. We don't know any details yet but the others have gone to the hospital and I'm going to take Mrs. Thresher home. Geoff asked if you'd be kind enough to explain to anyone who asks. Tell them it's nothing, but the family had to leave. Say they're to go right on with the party, will you?"

She looked at him wide-eyed. "What is it? What's happened?"

"We don't know," he repeated. "Probably a very minor thing."

"But nobody will believe . . . I mean, how can people stay on when Lindsay and Geoff and the others have left? Why don't we just make some kind of announcement and let everybody leave?"

Reg sighed. "I don't know. I agree with you that it's the end of the party, but Murray wanted it this way. I'm just relaying his instructions. Sorry, Mrs. Carlton. Do the best you can, will you? And thanks awfully for your help."

He left her and went back to Pauline, helping her out of the room.

Curious stares followed them, but they kept on going, explaining to no one. Pauline leaned on him heavily and it was not until they were in the limousine that she began to cry.

"Oh, Reg, if anything's happened to that baby it will kill Lindsay and Geoff. First their own daughter. Now this."

He patted her hand. "There, there. I'm sure it's nothing serious. I'll stay with you until we hear from them. They should call soon after we get to your apartment. They said they would."

She was silent on the drive up Park Avenue and equally so when they got to the apartment. When Reg suggested she lie down, she simply shook her head and took a chair in the living room, waiting for the phone to ring. Reg sat opposite her, as still as she. The waiting was hell and went on for hours. At one point, Pauline roused herself to ask Reg to get her a little brandy. He quickly complied and then resumed his seat.

"Don't you want something, too?" Pauline asked.

He shook his head. "Nothing, thanks."

Funny, Reg thought, I really don't want a drink for the first time in a long, long while. I want my head clear. I want to think. He let his mind go back to those few terrible moments after the phone call. Lindsay had scarcely been aware of him. She'd reached out for Geoffrey Murray as though it was the most natural thing in the world for her to turn to the man closest to her in every way.

I've always known she didn't really love me, Reg told himself. I've always felt she married me to prove something to him. But I thought I could change that because I love her so much. I pretended to myself that I could make her happy, but I never have. Not in all the ways that count. And knowing I was failing made me try less and less. She hasn't been able to depend on me for anything. Me with my drinking and resentment of her help. Me with my childish refusal to even try to adjust to a different life. It's as though I've had my finger on the self-destruct button all the time. And I've been destroying her and any chance we might once have had.

He closed his eyes wearily. I must let her go. She's too loyal, too sorry for me to make the move. It's up to me. I'll go back to England. She can divorce me and marry Geoffrey. It's what she wants. It's the least I can do for her. I was right never to aspire to a woman like this. But I wanted her so much.

He looked at Pauline, at the patrician profile and the slim, ladylike

402

hand slowly raising the brandy to her lips. They're disciplined, Reg thought. She and Lindsay. Honorable women. Bound to their obligations in the way well-bred people are. I have no place in their lives. I never saw it quite as clearly as I did tonight.

What is Pauline Thresher thinking? he wondered. About her great-grandchild, of course. But is she, too, thinking of Lindsay and what she's made of her life? Pauline loves Geoffrey. That's why he was at her birthday party. She's always been kind to me. Well-mannered. Considerate, as she was in the car earlier this evening. But she must hate me for spoiling Lindsay's life when she knows her daughter should be with one of her own kind.

The telephone interrupted his thoughts. He glanced at his watch. Nearly two o'clock! In a moment they'd know.

"Answer it, will you please, Reg? I . . . I'm afraid to."

Lindsay was on the wire. "It's all right," she said quickly. "Tell Mama."

He turned to Pauline. "Lindsay says it's all right."

Pauline took a deep breath. "Thank God. What happened?"

He turned back to the phone. "What was it?"

As Lindsay explained, his face turned white and beads of perspiration broke out on his forehead. "Oh, no! Oh, God, it's my fault! If I hadn't gotten him interested in those books! I never dreamed . . . it never occurred to me . . . Lindsay, are you sure he's going to be all right?" He listened for another moment or two and then said, "Yes. I'll ask her. Anything she wants. Hang on a mo." Once again he spoke to Pauline. "Lindsay wants to speak to you."

She took the receiver, and once again Lindsay recounted the accident. Pauline nodded, frowning, and then said, "Of course Mrs. Graham mustn't blame herself. She won't when she sees it in the rational light of day. What? No, of course he mustn't either. It was no one's fault. We can only thank the Lord that it wasn't serious. No, I don't need anyone to stay with me now that I know John is in no danger. No, dear, you have no room for me. In any case, I'm perfectly all right here. I'll be able to sleep. You do the same. Reg will be home directly." She hung up. "We're blessed, Reg. And you mustn't feel guilty. That's nonsense. Lindsay and Robin wouldn't dream of blaming you. Nor would anyone else. Nor, certainly, should you blame yourself. You made that child so happy, showing him those cars. He loved learning from you."

"If he hadn't wanted to learn more, this never would have happened." Reg's voice was bitter. "I spoil everything I touch. I've ruined Lindsay's life. You know that, Pauline."

"I know no such thing. You're upset. We all are. It's been a terrible few hours, and we're all exhausted. Go home now, Reg. Lindsay's waiting for you. And thank you, my dear, for being so understanding of us all." She looked at him levelly. "You can change things, you know. It's up to you."

"No," he said sadly. "I can't. I'd give anything if I could, but it's too late." He kissed Pauline's cheek. "But thank you for trying to make me believe it. I wish I could. No use. You saw it tonight. You know who Lindsay wants."

"I saw nothing except a frantic, distracted woman," Pauline said. "One who was thinking of no one except a little boy. Don't read meanings into what people do in panic, Reg. At times like those, reactions aren't rational, or necessarily significant."

"I'd give my soul to believe that. But it's time to stop fooling myself. Good night, Pauline. I'm sorry your birthday ended on such a sad note. Lindsay wanted so much to make it a day you'd always remember."

"It's not one I'm likely to forget. And it did have a happy ending. Our precious baby is all right. That's the best birthday present I could hope for."

She leaned for a moment against the door after she closed it behind him. Poor man. He'd come to grips with reality in that instant when Lindsay turned to Geoff. She wondered whether Reg believed it when she said people often reacted emotionally in ways they did not truly mean.

For that matter, she wondered whether she believed it herself.

35

The Darnevales and Mrs. Graham had already gone to bed when Reg returned to the apartment, but Lindsay was still up, waiting for him. She looked exhausted, yet she smiled wearily and said, "It was quite a night, wasn't it?"

Reg nodded. "You must be half dead. Why don't you turn in?"

"I will soon. I thought we might have a nightcap together."

"I'll fix you one," Reg said.

"Not going to join me?"

His eyes went to the corner of the room where the overturned chair and the scattered books and bookend remained in disarray. "No. After tonight I don't know that I'll ever want another drink."

Lindsay looked puzzled. "I don't understand. Your drinking had nothing to do with Johnny's accident. Not that I wouldn't be pleased to see you taper off, but I don't get the connection."

He handed her a light Scotch and water. "Maybe we'd better talk about it tomorrow, Lindsay. You've had quite a night. We all have."

She recognized a strange, serious new note in his voice. "No," she said. "Let's talk now. I'm too keyed up to sleep."

Reg sat down. "All right, we'll talk." There was a little silence as though he was trying to think how to begin. Finally he took a deep breath, clenched his hands in front of him, leaned forward in his chair, and said, "Lindsay, I'm going to leave you. Don't feel it's your fault in any way. It was just a terrible mistake for both of us."

She stared at him, momentarily speechless. Then she said, "I don't understand. I know you haven't been happy in New York, but I thought you loved me and . . . and needed me."

405

"I do love you. I'll always love you. But needing you has been the worst thing for me. And for you too. It's turned me from a man into a child: someone you had to take care of and protect and apologize for. Like a child. I've added nothing to your life, Lindsay, and I never will. I've only been a headache and a heartache for you. And for the first time in my life I've felt useless and unwanted. An intruder. A stranger you took up with in a moment of depression. I don't belong here, trying to be what you expect. I'll never be anything but what I am. I can't be suave and witty and successful the way you'd like me to be. I can't be Geoffrey Murray."

She raised her hand in protest. "I never expected you to be him. Have I ever . . . ?"

"No. You've been too much a lady to say so. But I know it's what you wish. Your mother told me not to judge people when they're emotional, but it hit me tonight, when they called about John's accident. It wasn't me you reached for. It was him. I didn't even enter your mind. Admit it, Lindsay. Murray was the strong person you knew you could turn to." He clasped and unclasped his hands. "That's why I'm going to leave you. There's no other answer. We both need to be free."

"Reg, you don't know what you're saying! I think somehow you do feel responsible for what happened to John, and that ridiculous guilt has mixed you up about us."

He shook his head. "You're wrong. Of course I feel some guilt about the boy's accident. I was the one who got him into those books. But don't you see, Lindsay? He's been the only human being who's looked up to me since the day we married. A two-and-a-half-year-old. A baby. The only one I could really communicate with. Doesn't that tell you something about our lives?"

"No. That's absurd. Equating your mentality with his! If anything, when I saw your gentleness with John I realized what a mature, loving man you are. What a good man. I felt sad that you had no children of your own. That I was too old to give them to you. You'd have been a wonderful father, Reg."

He smiled. "Perhaps. But I'd have had to marry the kind of woman I didn't want. I told you many times I couldn't do that." He grew solemn again. "But all that's not important. What matters is that we come from different pasts and want different things, and that we'll never find peace together. I haven't behaved well, Lindsay. I've been a drunk and a whining boor, angry at you and the world, but mostly angry at myself for failing you. Well, that's over. I had a dream that didn't work. Maybe we both had a dream. But it's morning, Lindsay, and the dream that turned into a nightmare is over."

It was the longest speech he'd ever made in his life, and the most thoughtful. He felt unbearably sad and yet relieved. No more pretending. No more play-acting. And no more self-pity. He'd want her always, but the kindest thing for both of them was to let go.

Lindsay had begun to cry softly. He wanted to take her in his arms and comfort her, assure her she hadn't failed, that she'd done what she thought right for both of them. But he resisted. He knew what that would mean. He'd hold her and she'd cling to him and they'd make love and it would start all over again. All the problems and misunderstanding and humiliation.

"Let's call it a night, my dear," he said. "Try to get some sleep."

She looked up at him. "When . . . when will you go?"

"I don't know. Soon. But not until John is well enough to go back to Chicago. I may be able to help amuse him while he's here."

"Reg, can't we . . . I mean, we must talk more. It's too sudden, too serious."

"We'll talk as much as you like, but it won't do any good, Lindsay." His voice was heavy with regret. "It's a terrible thing to face, but it's never been any good."

When the alarm rang at seven, Lindsay couldn't believe she'd been asleep. It seemed to her she'd cried the rest of the night, that she hadn't closed her eyes for a minute. But she must have dropped into an exhausted slumber somewhere in the early hours. Now, in those first moments of waking, she thought perhaps she had dreamed the whole of the night before: that Johnny was not in the hospital and Reg had not told her he was leaving. But no, it was no dream. Both things were true and she had to deal with them as best she could.

Reg, Robin, and Connie were already at the breakfast table when she appeared. They all looked tired but quite normal and anxious to get to the hospital. She tried to smile, avoiding Reg's eyes as she slipped into her place.

"Did you get some sleep, dear?" Reg asked.

She didn't look at him. "Yes. Some. What about the rest of you?"

"Damned little," Robin said. "When we bring John home I think I'll go back to bed for hours."

"It was a ghastly night," Connie said, "but we have so much to be grateful for. How was Pauline, Reg? I hope she's all right. Do you think it's too early to call her, Lindsay?"

"Let's wait a bit. It's not quite eight. I hope she's still sleeping."

"She was fine when I left her," Reg said. "She's a strong woman." He glanced affectionately at Lindsay. "Like her daughter."

"Amen," Robin said. "Lindsay's seen us all through some bad times."

There was a little pause and then Connie said artlessly, "Is Geoff going to the hospital with us this morning, Lindsay?"

Lindsay felt her color rise. "I have no idea. He did say he'd be in touch, but I think there's no need for us to invade the place like an army. The four of us and Mrs. Graham seem more than adequate to bail out one small boy."

"I agree," Reg said. "In fact, I see no need for me to tag along. Even Mrs. Graham could stay home, couldn't she?"

"Oh, no!" Connie protested. "She's so full of remorse, the least we can do is let her be there when he's released. As for you, Reg, I guarantee you're the one Johnny will be happiest to see. He's absolutely mad about you. I hate to think how he's going to carry on when he has to go back to Chicago and leave his friend 'Wedge,' as he calls you." Connie smiled. "Maybe you and Lindsay should move to Chicago. It might be the only way to keep peace in the family!"

Lindsay stood up hurriedly. "I'd better finish dressing. What time do you think we should go? I'll call for a limousine."

"I think we could safely get there about ten," Robin said. "I spoke to the hospital earlier and they said he could leave around that time."

"I'll phone for the car, Lindsay," Reg said. "Know a very good service. It's called Reginald Marks Ltd., and I hear they can use the business."

Robin and Connie laughed, but Lindsay simply nodded. "Sounds like a good choice," she said. "I've heard rumors they're dissolving the firm."

The young pair looked at Reg when Lindsay left the room.

"Is that true?" Robin asked. "Are you really thinking of closing down?"

"Afraid so. The company hasn't been a spectacular success, you might say."

Robin frowned. "I'm sorry, Reg. Damned shame. It seemed like one hell of a good idea at the time."

Reg got up from the table. "Yes, it did. So did a lot of things. At the time."

When he'd excused himself, Connie turned to Robin. "What was *that* all about? They're acting very funny."

"I don't know." Robin looked worried. "Something's gone sour, and I've got an awful feeling it's more than the limousine business. I haven't been getting good vibes these past couple of days. Geoff's too much in evidence, and you saw how he and Lindsay treated Reg last night: like a servant. I'd bet there's big trouble here, honey, and I'm damned sorry to see it. Reg may be a rough diamond and no intellectual, but he's one good Joe. They don't come any better. I hope to God Lindsay isn't going to do something crazy."

That afternoon, Lindsay went to visit her mother.

"John is fine," she reported. "Lord, the resilience of kids! If one of us had gotten a knock in the head the way he did, we'd be in the hospital for a month! As it is, we can hardly keep him in bed! He has to stay there, of course, but it's practically by brute force! Thank goodness for Reg and his bloody auto books. He's the only one of us who can keep Johnny quiet."

"Reg has a great deal of patience," Pauline said. "There's a sweetness about him that I hadn't quite realized. We talked about a number of things last night, Lindsay. I'm afraid I quite underrated your husband as a human being. He's dreadfully disturbed by what he considers his failures, particularly toward you and your marriage. There's an admirable native sensitivity there. Something the world, including myself, hasn't seen."

Lindsay looked pained. "I know. We haven't been fair to him, any of us. Least of all me." She paused. "Mama, Reg and I talked last night too. Or, rather, he did most of the talking. He's going to leave me. He says we can never find peace together. He believes I want Geoff and I'll never be happy until I have him again."

"I see. And is that true, Lindsay?"

"I don't know. For a long while I thought so. I know I've been comparing Reg to Geoff, feeling disappointed that I couldn't have a second husband as smart and sophisticated and successful as the first. But I never thought of leaving Reg. You know that, Mama. I wouldn't have walked out on him ever, no matter how unhappy I was. I really forced him into this marriage, and I meant to stick by it."

"And now he's letting you out," Pauline said. "Doesn't that make you happy? You and Geoff can get back together. There'll be no more pity, for Reg or for yourself. No more apologies to people you think matter. Reg is doing you a favor, and doing himself one as well. It can't have been much fun for him, trying to live up to someone else's ideals. Small wonder he's been a drinker, antisocial and actually hostile at times. It would take a saint to stay cheerful and smiling when you know the world, including your wife, only tolerates you."

Lindsay didn't fight back. "That is the way it's been, hasn't it? I've felt so put upon, so injured. But it's Reg who's suffered more. Everything had to be my way: where we lived, what he did for a living, even the people we saw and did not see. I uprooted him, making myself believe I was 'bettering' him. And all the while I only wanted the things that pleased me." She gave a great sigh. "What am I going to do, Mama?"

"What is it you *want* to do?"

Lindsay thought for a moment. "I suppose I know more what I *don't* want to do. I don't want Geoff again. I don't think I fully realized that until last night. I saw how really selfish he is, how self-absorbed. All he could think about was whether God was punishing *him*. It was more important than whether his grandchild was dying. Oh, I know he didn't think of it that way. He was beside himself with fear for Johnny, but he kept coming back to his own feelings. I've accused Geoff of many things in the past. Unfaithfulness. Cruelty. But I've never allowed myself to see how weak he is. Do you know, he couldn't even look at John last night? He turned inward, the way he did when S.P. died. He didn't think how the rest of us felt. Not really. It's as though any tragedy is a personal affront to him. He either gets angry or runs. Or both."

"And realizing all this, you still love him?"

Lindsay leaned back and closed her eyes. "I suppose in a way I'll always love him. Or perhaps I love the idea of him. But this morning I knew I could never live with him again. He isn't the supportive man I invented and have perpetuated in my mind all these years. Last night I automatically turned to Geoff when that call came. You saw how efficient and organized he was, ordering everybody around. But that's because at the moment it was almost impersonal and unreal. Later, he

410

came apart over his fears that it was he who was being punished." She smiled wryly. "Ironic, isn't it? The events that were a revelation to me were the same ones that finally convinced Reg I wanted to belong to Geoff. My old habit of looking to Geoff for help seemed a clear sign to Reg that he and I don't belong together."

"Do you, Lindsay? Do you think you and Reg belong together? Don't let these traumatic hours cloud your thinking. Nothing about Reg has changed because you've finally seen Geoff so clearly. There are still all the differences between you. The adjustments you've never made. You must be realistic, my dear."

"I am, Mama. Maybe for the first time ever. I know we both have to change, I more than Reg. I have to give him a chance to stand on his own feet, to get back the self-confidence he had when we met. I have to show him I respect him for what he is, and stop trying to remake him into what I thought a man should be. He's more of a man than anyone I've ever known. I've been wrong about him. I used him for revenge in the beginning and I never gave myself a chance to really love him. I do now. When he told me he was leaving, I thought I was going to die. Not because it meant I'd failed at another marriage. Because I care so much for him. Because he's decent and forbearing and manly in the right sense of the word."

Pauline sighed. "I know you mean every word, Lindsay, but it's not easy for mature people to change. It may not even be possible for you to readjust your values. And Reg may not even be willing to try again."

"I know. But there must be a way to convince him. It can't be too late, Mama. It just can't be!"

"I'm an old lady, darling," Pauline said, "and not much given to hoping for happy endings. But I'm with you, Lindsay, because I do believe you're thinking straight. I don't know how you're going to make Reg change his mind, but dammit, you try! And remember this. You have two things going for you, love and loyalty. Reg has always had them for you. Now show him you mean to return them. You have a faithful, adoring man. I always loved Geoff, but he was neither of those things. Nothing in this world counts for more, my dear. I know. Sometimes I think they're the qualities you've been searching for all your life, the very things your father was never capable of. Reg lacks polish, lacks glamour, but by God he has heart! You've kicked that heart around. We all have, snobs that we are. But you can atone for all of us. And if you

411

try, you can make him and yourself happy by being the kind of wife he deserves. Make him understand that, Lindsay. Do whatever it takes not to lose the only kind of closeness that really counts."

Lindsay nodded solemnly. "I am going to try, Mama. With every ounce of humility in me, I'm going to try."

She didn't go straight home from Pauline's. Instead, she headed for Geoff's address and announced herself to the doorman, who called and then told her to go right up to 15A. Geoff was waiting at the door of his apartment, surprised to see her.

"I haven't been able to reach you all day," he said. "I know you brought John home, but Connie said you went out right after. She told me everything is fine, thank God." He smiled, that warm, charming smile. "Good Lord, where are my manners, keeping you standing in the hall? Come in, darling. Tell me what you think of my bachelor pad."

Lindsay stepped into the hall and glanced at the modern living room. "Very nice," she said.

"Let me show you the rest, what there is of it."

"No. Thanks, Geoff, but this isn't exactly a social call. I just stopped by to tell you something important."

"Well, at least sit down. Fix you a drink?"

She shook her head. "I'm on my way home. I've been visiting Mama. I just came by on an impulse."

He seemed very relaxed. "And a nice one, I must say. I hope you have it more often."

"As a matter of fact, that's what I came to say, Geoff. I'm never going to see you again. I don't want to hear from you. I never should have even had coffee with you or invited you to the party. It was stupid of me. And it caused terrible trouble."

She saw him stiffen. "What are you talking about? I thought things would be different. After last night—"

"Last night was a horror because of John. And because it made Reg think I was still in love with you."

"And you're not?"

"No, Geoff, I'm not. I thought I was. But when Reg told me last night that he was going to leave me so that I could come back to you, I knew I didn't want to. We had our time, you and I, the good and bad of it. And it's all in the past. It can never be repeated."

"You're wrong, Lindsay. We do love each other." He reached for her. "Neither of us has ever loved anyone else."

She drew back. "That's not true. For years I believed it was, but it's not. I love Reg Marks. And you, Geoff, love only yourself."

His face darkened. "That bloody English bastard! What has he been saying to you? What's his rotten little scheme?"

"He has no scheme," Lindsay said. "He plans to get out of my life. And I'm going to do everything in my power to stop him."

"Lindsay, you're crazy! He's all wrong for you! He's a clown. A joke. You can't want a man like that!"

"I can and I do." She turned to the door. "You were Daddy, Geoff. Selfish and challenging and exciting. But I've grown up. I don't need my father any more. I need someone faithful and endlessly loving."

Geoff gave an unpleasant little laugh. "You might as well be describing a sheepdog: faithful, loving, and dumb. Someone who'll sit up, and beg, and heel on command."

She looked at him pityingly. "You'll never understand. I wish you could. I wish, just once, you could give of yourself."

Suddenly he was furious. "Give of myself? God, that's funny! I catered to your every whim, from the day you played on my honor and got me to marry you! I even gave up the woman I wanted because I had to come home to my pregnant wife! I put up with your unfaithfulness with that oaf you finally married! Give of myself? You have a hell of a nerve, Lindsay! What have you given of yourself?"

"Not enough," she said calmly. "That's been my trouble, too. But my sin is worse. I've cheated a man who didn't deserve it." She opened the front door. "Good-bye, Geoff. Good luck. Maybe Adele is the right one for you after all. In many ways you're two of a kind."

She walked for an hour after she left his apartment, desperately searching for the solution. How? Lindsay asked herself over and over. How can I convince Reg that I love him and no one else? How can I make him believe that I want to stay married to him? That my stupid, shallow values are behind me?

If only we could start over, she thought. Somewhere new and fresh. Not England again. There was too much of the old Lindsay there, left over from the days when she tried to move Reg mentally and socially, as well as physically, from the part of London he knew. And not here, in her world, among her friends, in an apartment haunted by the ghost of Geoffrey and another way of life. Not here where she'd tried and failed

413

to make a tycoon of an uncomplicated man who was content not to be a boss. Some people might call it lack of ambition. Geoff certainly would. But there were those who could be happy without status and power, and Reg was one of them.

As for me, Lindsay mused, I don't need all the superficial trappings either. I'm not stupid enough to think I could live in poverty. It's too late for me to be a dowdy woman in cheap dresses and shoes with run-over heels. But if Reg could earn enough of a living to pay our rent and buy our food, to supply the necessities of life, then he'd be generous enough to let me use my money for the little luxuries I've always enjoyed. I know he would. He could be a chauffeur again. They earn a decent living and I don't care any more what my so-called friends think. Besides, if we go away we'll make new friends. Even if I lapse into petty embarrassment, God forbid, it will be among strangers.

If I tell Reg all these things, will he believe me? He must. Because I believe them myself. I've learned my lesson, the hard way. Hell. What am I saying? I made it hard on myself.

She walked slowly toward home. Where could we go? she wondered. Any big city, I suppose. And not too far away from Mama. I must always be able to get back quickly if she needs me.

Suddenly she stopped, struck by a thought. What had Connie kiddingly said to Reg at breakfast this morning? "Maybe you and Lindsay should move to Chicago. It might be the only way to keep peace in the family." Well, why not? They'd be close to Johnny. He'd be almost like the child Reg never had. It would be different but not foreign.

She quickened her step. It was a good idea. Please, God, let Reg agree. Let him see how sincere I am. How much I've put the old ideas behind me. Please make him believe the strongest and truest argument of all: that I've learned to love.

She felt optimistic and almost wildly happy, like a girl with the wisdom of a woman. There's always time to start fresh, she thought. I'm fifty years old. So what? No more yearning for the past while there's still a future to be grasped.

At the corner of 68th and Park she stopped, waiting for the red light to change so she could cross the street. It seemed to be taking its time. Lindsay fumed, eager to get home. And then she looked down and saw something in the gutter. Tears came to her eyes even as a smile of remembrance lit up her face. I am loved, Lindsay thought.

Slowly, almost reverently, she stooped and picked up a shiny penny.

414